Parson Harding's Daughter

When the door had closed, Caroline slipped
from her bed and went to the window. The
greyness of dawn was growing rosy now, and
across the still pale water of the river she could
see a low bank and the outlines of groups of
alien-looking trees. Smoke was curling blue
from some clumps, the smoke perhaps of early
breakfasts, Indian breakfasts. Despite her
wretched night, a leap of excitement warmed
her as she stood there and looked at this foreign
waking world. She, Caroline Harding, of the
parish of Stoke Abbas in the county of Dorset,
England, was about to set foot in India.

Also in Arrow Books by Joanna Trollope
ELIZA STANHOPE

JOANNA TROLLOPE

Parson Harding's Daughter

ARROW BOOKS

Arrow Books Limited
3 Fitzroy Square, London W 1 P 6JD

An imprint of the Hutchinson Publishing Group

London Melbourne Sydney Auckland
Wellington Johannesburg and agencies
throughout the world

First published by Hutchinson 1979
Arrow edition 1980
Reprinted 1981
© Joanna Trollope 1979

Made and printed in Great Britain
by The Anchor Press Ltd
Tiptree, Essex

ISBN 0 09 922290 6

For my mother and father

Author's Note

In the 1770s, the East India Company's Council in Calcutta was headed by Warren Hastings, and consisted of four men selected by Parliament under the premiership of Lord North. Thus the addition of Sir Edward Ashton, bringing that number to five, is purely fictitious.

I

The Reverend Henry Harding surveyed his congregation from the pulpit with a mixture of affection and exasperation. The affection flowed from his handsome and upright person, becomingly clad in Valenciennes-trimmed lawn over decent black, in a benign flood which spread over the whole gathering – save one pew. For that pew, the front pew across the aisle from his pulpit, he reserved his exasperation. He allowed something approaching a smile to lighten his face as his gaze swept over the well-filled silk and serge, the muslin and occasional smock frock of his village flock. It was early June 1775, and the silvery oak door of the church had been left open to allow the light and scent of a summer morning to remind the congregation of all that they had to thank their Maker for. With sunshine and butterflies at the western end of the church and that look of gracious kindliness from their pastor at the eastern end, the people of Stoke Abbas might be forgiven for thinking themselves in paradise already.

All the people, that is, except the luckless five in the front pew across the aisle. The Harding children were profoundly conscious of the exasperation they caused their parent, and of the affront he seemed to suffer anew every Sunday to see them sitting there, as alike as peas in a pod, beneath his well-chiselled nose. The eldest, Eleanor, did not suffer too keenly from her father's scrutiny since she was all too conscious of her own value in the world, and thus impervious, more or less, to the opinion of anyone else.

'There is no need', she would say to her brother Robert, the only one she regarded as having any practicality or sensitivity, both of which qualities she reckoned on possessing herself to the full, 'for such a quality of port, such a needless extravagance of claret. Nor does Papa appreciate what

9

sacrifices I must make to allow for the keep of his horses.'

Robert, for whom life at the Parsonage was only made tolerable by wine and horses, would nod and mumble that his father still needed compensation for the death of his wife. Eleanor would snort.

The late Mrs Harding had been very pretty. She had possessed that kind of soft vivacious prettiness that Josephine Buonaparte was to make so fashionable: on the occasion of her marriage to the undeniably handsome Henry Harding with the excellent living of Stoke Abbas, in the gracious gift of Lady Lennox, already in his pocket, the pair were pronounced a triumph. In a sense, the marriage had indeed been a triumph. They were both kindly, vain and self-indulgent. They were disposed to laugh and make others laugh and they liked life to be pleasant. It was pleasant, too, in the grey-stone Parsonage at the top of a street of model cottages, with the church and the river at the bottom and the green Dorset hills beyond. The only part of this life that was not pleasant for Mrs Harding was the bearing of children which tired her, spoilt her figure and made her, despite several servants, less able to please herself. But what truly distressed both her and her husband, and what really accounted for the irritation in his eyes as he frowned down on them that June Sunday, was that every one of the surviving five was as undeniably plain as their parents were handsome. They were like a row of changelings, a witch's prank played on an innocent pair to punish them for their good looks. It was a malevolent, envious trick of fate, Mrs Harding decided, and not one she cared to endure. She took a chill when the youngest, Harry, was six and made no effort to resist it. She lay in her half-tester bed while a small fire tried to combat the draughts and chills of February, and watched the grey countryside with disinterest until the infection spread to her lungs and killed her. That was ten years ago and the children endured an uneasy illusion that her fading was in some way their fault.

'Your mother's death,' Parson Harding said once to the elder three, 'has left me without a companion in the world. A companion, that is, who is to me as I am to myself.'

A sensation of guilty inadequacy planted itself in the breasts of the two younger listeners which was to blight their confidence for years to come. Eleanor, at nineteen, had felt that her father was being melodramatic and that he took no account of her, Eleanor's, feelings at the loss of her mother. Eleanor might not seem to care what her father thought, but she longed for him to acknowledge her superiority to her brothers and sister.

In the sense that Parson Harding appreciated how well she ran the family, he did acknowledge it. As his lips moved comfortably and sonorously through the familiar sermon on hellfire – ' . . . therefore every tree that bringeth not forth good fruit shall be hewn down and cast into the fire . . . ' he glanced every so often at his family. Eleanor sat closest to him, her narrow bony face set in an expression of severe sanctity under her straw hat. She wore a gown of dark green silk, a little too long to be fashionable, and her fichu had been draped too tightly to be at all softening or becoming to her narrow neck. Next to her sat Parson Harding's three sons: Robert, his eldest, and Charles and Harry, the two youngest members of the family. They too had narrow, long-featured faces, and reddish indeterminate-textured hair, but in them Eleanor's look of uncompromising certainty in herself and life was replaced by an air of doubtfulness. Robert was his father's curate until such a time as a living might be procured for him. At twenty-seven he had not married, since he seemed doomed to become enamoured of women who never noticed him, and as his father ceaselessly reminded him, he could not afford to marry for love alone. Charles and Harry, at eighteen and sixteen respectively, were in the Navy in the tradition of their uncles, and were enjoying a brief respite at home before embarking again on the high seas. Lady Lennox often remarked that she could not imagine whose notion of a sailor they were, for they certainly were not hers. Indeed there was no hearty openness about Charles and Harry Harding, no gallantry, no evident patriotism or sea fever; however, sailors they were and Harry was to distinguish himself under Nelson bearing just the self-mistrusting expression that he wore this present Sunday.

Finally, at the end of the pew, compressing herself into as small a space as possible under her father's scrutiny, sat Caroline. Lady Lennox had once said of Caroline that she was the least offensively plain of the Harding children but Caroline knew, as all plain people keenly know, that that was saying nothing at all. Her face was as narrow as her sister's, her nose as long, but her mouth was wider and softer and her grey eyes had a capacity for absorbing or reflecting light that made them gleam like moonlight. She did not raise them very often to give anyone the chance to observe this silver phenomenon. Conscious of her nose, and her straight colourless pale hair, and her unfashionably tawny skin, she was not prepared to give her eyes, or her sweet and diffident expression, any chance in winning her friends and admirers. By the old maidish age of twenty-six, Caroline had only ever had one admirer, when she was eighteen, and he had gone to India and forgotten her. She did not blame him. She considered herself forget-table.

She looked down at her blue silk lap – a most frivolous shade of blue Eleanor had deemed it – and sighed, and wished she could be outside and not on this narrow over-carved Jacobean pew whose ornamentation dug into her spine. She always seemed to be shut in somewhere, shut in the house under Eleanor's tyranny, shut in church for most of every Sunday, shut in the monotony of her position as Parson Harding's second unmarried and unmarriageable daughter. She had plenty of inner resources, but she never seemed to be allowed to pursue them. She sighed again, audibly this time, and her father's frown deepened.

She was instantly sorry. She loved her father, and was the only one to understand his widowed loneliness. She loved her brothers, too, although she sometimes wished they had more enterprise, that the Parsonage might sometimes have that air of vigour and energy that impressed her so about the atmosphere at Stoke Park when she went on occasional and terrifying visits. As for Eleanor, Caroline supposed that in a dutiful sense she loved her, but Eleanor seemed to do every-thing in her power to make herself unlovable. She was didactic, undemonstrative and quick to take offence – and she had initiated the family habit of calling Caroline 'Carrie'.

The congregation rose in a flurry of creaks and rustles for the Old Hundredth. Caroline could hear Sam Wells, the tenant farmer from across the river, bellowing behind her with the joyousness of one who knows release is near. She smiled to herself and sympathized with him privately. He was such an amiable, clumsy man and his children were like a basketful of tumbling puppies. He would make a great success of the rich land beyond the river, for he worked it with an enthusiasm and dedication Caroline thought wholly admirable. She would go to buy bantam eggs from Mrs Wells occasionally, and would seize any pretext to linger in the dough-and-onion-scented kitchen, or out in the yard among the hens and pigs, and let Mrs Wells tell her of their achievements. Eleanor would scold her for unladylike behaviour and a taste for low associations, but Caroline took no notice. She liked the villagers and was interested in their lives, and was unaware that the age of Lady Bountiful had not yet officially come. She wanted to help where she could, and the cottage people, reassured by her appearance and shy manner, welcomed her help.

The last 'Amen' rang out with fervour. Two hours of a June Sunday morning with the sky as blue as cornflowers can easily appear as two and twenty hours if confined to the dimness of a Norman nave, however beautiful. Caroline rose, and shook out her skirts and gave a smile of appreciation at the Wells children behind her, suffocating in their Sunday cloth and unaccustomed shoes. Eleanor saw the smile, caught her sister's eye and gave the smallest and most unmistakable of frowns. When her upright dark green back was turned for a stately exit of precedence among her father's people – a privilege she could enjoy only if the Lennox family were absent from church – Caroline smiled again at the children. All but the youngest stared stolidly back at her. The youngest beamed widely, displaying two missing teeth.

'Fine children, Sam.'

'We'm blessed wi' healthy 'uns, Miss Car'line.'

She nodded and moved out of the pew behind Harry, still half a head shorter than she was. He and Charles walked closely down the aisle together as if seeking comfort from each other's company. Caroline noticed with affectionate despair how their stockings gave the effect of being made for much larger calves than theirs, drooping sadly as they did from the knee-bands of their breeches. Still, she thought ruefully, apart from Papa we are a shabby and shambling lot; we have no notion how to look. Perhaps St Peter will not refuse a man to paradise simply because his hose are wrinkled. She contemplated, briefly, a heaven full of bent haloes and crooked wings and smiled unconsciously to herself. The Stoke Abbas apothecary, poised in his pew for his proper moment to leave church, saw the smile and was fooled for a moment into thinking Miss Caroline Harding quite handsome.

Outside church, Parson Harding stood gravely and benignly among his flock, his silver locks gleaming in the sunshine, his elegant patrician hands folded in the lawn sleeves of his surplice. Eleanor stood at a little distance, her brothers in dejected attendance, and listened graciously to the garrulity of Miss Spears who captured her ear for no other reason than that she was an impoverished second cousin of Lady Lennox.

'My dear Miss Eleanor, you would never guess, never suppose – or would you? Yes, being a person of such amazing discernment and one who is the trusted repository of so many confidences, I feel sure, quite sure, that Lady Lennox. . . . But, no – I must say no more, indeed I must not. It must be for Lady Lennox to – but I feel sure that already she has . . .'

'Caroline,' Eleanor interrupted imperiously, 'when did we last hear from Stoke Park?'

Caroline, far more absorbed in old Mother Crittall's ferocious complaints about arthritis, which seemed an unjust suffering for June, looked about her vaguely.

'Stoke Park?'

'Yes, yes,' Eleanor said impatiently. 'What news from Stoke Park?'

'I feel sure', Miss Spears began again, edging her absurdly frilled and flounced person nearer, 'that nothing of consequence that Lady Lennox has to impart could she possibly have imparted to my humble self before passing it first to a person of such consequence and absolute trustworthiness as . . .'

Caroline came out of her reverie.

'Is your cat quite well, Miss Spears?'

Miss Spears's social smile of false eagerness was replaced by one of genuine pleasure.

'Tabby? Oh, Miss Caroline, dear Tabby! So good of you to ask! Dear Tabby. After the little accident with the rat trap! Quite recovered, quite. So considerate of you to ask after her. . . .'

'I am very glad,' Caroline said.

'When did we last hear from Stoke Park?' Eleanor said with alarming directness.

Caroline raised her eyes from Miss Spears and the inward vision of Miss Spears' Tabby.

'I have no idea, Eleanor.'

Eleanor's frown was awful.

'My sister, Miss Spears, is never aware of summer or winter, Christmas or Michaelmas. Time is of no consequence to Caroline. If a message from Stoke Park had reached her but two minutes ago, it would be to her as of two months since. There is no doubt a message from Lady Lennox awaiting our return. We will bid you good day, Miss Spears.'

Miss Spears smirked and opened her mouth for another flood of verbiage but something in Eleanor's severity and Caroline's kind but abstracted air gave her pause.

'Good day, Miss Harding, Miss Caroline.'

Eleanor nodded and swept on. Caroline paused and looked back at Miss Spears.

'I do not know what this business about Stoke Park signifies. There is very little communication between the Park and the Parsonage, Miss Spears. There is no need for it, you know. I hope Tabby continues well.'

She smiled, and turned to follow her sister, then stopped again.

'We have a cat at the Parsonage, you know, but she is not sociable like Tabby.'

Miss Spears, melted entirely, watched her walk away with affection. She saw her stopped half a dozen times before the lych-gate, stopped by village people, and saw her smile as she paused, and watched her down-bent head as she listened. Poor Miss Caroline, doomed by lack of looks and money, just as she, Jane Spears, had been doomed thirty years before. Miss Caroline had had a chance once but she had not known what to do with it and she would certainly never have a chance again. One chance was, after all, more than many people ever got. Miss Spears looked up the slope of Stoke Abbas' village street and saw Caroline Harding moving slowly up it and wished for a moment with all the sincerity her trivial nature was capable of that something might glitter a little, just once more, for Caroline.

For her part, Caroline was not thinking of glitter at that moment, nor of Stoke Park, nor its inmates, nor even of Miss Spears' remarkable Tabby. She was walking, with her slightly stooping gait, up the cobbles of the steep street between these pairs of 'model' cottages: cottages no more than fifteen years old and still much admired for the aesthetic and liberal views that designed and built them. They were built of local stone, thatched and gabled, charming to the delighted eye of visitors bowling down the street to the comfortable elegance of Stoke Park in its great green dish of land below.

Caroline knew better. June might well be an unseasonable month for old Mother Crittall to feel her arthritis so acutely, but complaints of the circulation and joints do not stand much chance against walls of literally running damp and floors of beaten earth. Caroline knew too that the thick thatch, so satisfactory to the eye of an eighteenth-century gentleman at the height of fashion for elegant landscape and civilized nature, held the long winter rains with the eagerness of a sponge. The upper chambers of the cottages, where the thatch was unplastered and formed a rustling ceiling to the bedroom itself, always had a moist and marshy air about them and the makeshift beds beneath this dank canopy must always have been as clammy themselves. Caroline knew that interior walls seldom felt dry as she often had need to touch them clambering up rickety stairs to some sickbed above. She thought of Lord Lennox, so kindly, so affable, generally regarded as a most benevolent employer and landlord, and wondered it never occurred to him why a huge number of his tenants were so swollen and crippled and old before their time. Perhaps cushioned before a fire in the library at Stoke Park, such things as damp beds and dripping thatch and coughing children were as irrelevant as the thought of naked savages in the East dancing round in some awful revelry. Such things happened, indeed, but not at Stoke Park.

'Carric, Eleanor says you are to hasten, if you please.'

Caroline jumped. She had fallen into her reverie over the cottages, and had unconsciously ceased walking as she mused. Robert was standing before her with a smile of affectionate amusement.

'Day-dreaming again, Carrie.'

'Yes – no, no, not day-dreaming. I was worrying about these cottages, Robert, they are so damp inside, even in June. The walls are so thick and the windows so small that sunlight never seems to have a chance inside them. Did you see old Mrs Crittall outside church? So bent, Robert, in such pain. . . .'

A spasm crossed Robert's face. He had all Caroline's sympathy of heart, and no strength of mind to put it into practice. He agreed, always, with all her altruism, but always wished she had not mentioned it. It embarrassed him because he knew it would be upon his conscience and he would be unable to act to shift it.

'They do not complain of Lord Lennox, Carrie, you know.'

'Of course not. He gives them a goose at Christmas, and buries their children handsomely when they die of diseased lungs.'

The indignation in her tone made Robert uncomfortable. He looked about nervously lest anyone should have overheard this slight upon the patron of Stoke Abbas.

'I was sent to bring you on quickly, Carrie. Eleanor . . .'

'Of course,' Caroline said hastily, 'I did not mean to delay you, dear Robert. I always seem to come out of church feeling not only reflective, which I should welcome, but melancholy, which I deplore. Why do I?'

Robert swallowed nervously. His own calling, which

should have filled him with profound joy, often made him deeply melancholy too.

'Spirituality is a very solemn thing,' he began hesitantly.

Caroline made a small impatient noise, and flung out her hands.

'I am not aiming at spirituality, dear Robert, I would not be so presumptuous. It was merely an idle speculation as to why Papa's services, for I know no others, tend to depress rather than elevate me.'

Robert looked unhappy.

'I – I do not know,' he said.

Caroline smiled at him fondly.

'No, nor do I.'

They reached the Parsonage gate, and turned instinctively for one last look down that perfection of grey-gold thatch falling away symmetrically to the emerald sweep of the Park slashed across by the Stoke River. Beyond the green rose the hills, which in their turn matured into the great cliffs and bluffs of the Dorset coast. The air was as clear as crystal, every flower in the cottage gardens, every branch of the newly planted beeches in the Park was clearly, minutely visible.

'We are most fortunate,' Robert said, thinking how much of a solace the view was to him.

Caroline, her thoughts upon the comparison between her sparsely furnished but dry and comfortable bedroom and those in the cottages below, nodded and said fervently, 'Indeed we are.'

They opened the gate, and passed between the shrubs, planted by Mrs Harding as a bride, that bordered the apron of land on the south side of the house. Stoke Abbas Parsonage was low and grey, but Mrs Harding had used her charm to persuade Lord Lennox to replace the small Jacobean windows with large and fashionable ones. The new spaces of glass gave the Parsonage a slightly surprised air, but the rooms inside benefited greatly. Caroline and Robert walked silently over the smoothly mown turf and entered a small side parlour papered in a tiny flower-pattern and littered, though tidily littered, with the paraphernalia of family living. Through the doorway into the hall, they could hear their sister.

'My absence from the house for two hours must and shall not be taken as an excuse for unforgivable slovenliness. It is essential that Sundays are run to a strict timetable to enable Mr Harding to fulfil all his most exacting duties. One more lapse and you may seek another position.'

There was a pause, then the sound of footsteps hurrying in the direction of the kitchen. Caroline and Robert stayed where they were, despite a strong urge in the former to run after the footsteps. Eleanor appeared in the doorway, removing her hat as she did so.

'It is impossible to run this house as Papa would wish with such servants. I am quite exhausted. They seem to feel no loyalty to me after all I do for them, and to take a malicious delight in testing my patience. Patsy is well aware that we must dine early on a Sunday in order to allow Papa sufficient repose before the evening service. It is too bad, indeed it is, too bad!'

She sat down heavily and put her hands over her face. Caroline sought frantically in her mind for some distraction from this aggravation.

'Was Miss Spears right, Eleanor? Did a message from Stoke Park await you?'

Eleanor raised an entirely recovered face from her hands.

'Stoke Park? Indeed I do not know, Carrie. How am I to do everything in this house if you dawdle in the sunshine instead of assisting me in even the smallest way to bear my burden? Robert, pray go into the hall and see if any message has come from Lady Lennox this morning.'

Caroline, knowing that as usual there would be no message, stood silently by her sister while Robert left the room. Eleanor said nothing more, but sat upright and alert, her gaze fixed upon the door until her brother reappeared. He held a letter in his hand.

'To me,' Eleanor said imperiously and took the letter. It bore the Lennox crest upon the back. Eleanor tore it open and read it with maddening thoroughness, while Caroline and Robert exchanged glances of thankfulness above her head.

'We are bidden to dine at Stoke Park on Tuesday,' Eleanor said at length. 'Georgiana is engaged to be married, and we are to meet her future husband. The invitation does not specify Charles and Harry.'

'Might they not like to go?' Caroline suggested.

'Certainly not. Papa will be delighted. Georgiana has always been a great favourite of his.'

'I should not mind if Charles or Harry were to go in my place,' Caroline said, recalling the terrible shyness and awkwardness that afflicted her at Stoke Park.

Eleanor rose and tucked the letter into her fichu, patting it with satisfaction.

'Charles and Harry are not invited. You are, therefore you will go.'

2

On the Tuesday morning following Parson Harding's sermon on hellfire, Lady Lennox was in her boudoir, on the first floor of Stoke Park, contemplating in the intervals of her correspondence what would be, in sixty years' time, a most splendid prospect of oaks and beeches. As the trees had only been planted a maximum of twenty-five years, they only gave some idea of the splendour that was to come. Lady Lennox did not regard them from that point of view, however, but only scrutinized them keenly for any sign of blight or damage by sheep or deer. On the walls beside her bureau hung miniatures of her six children: Sophia – naughty, wilful Sophia, now being just as naughty and wilful a married woman as she had been a girl; then Henry, John, George; Jane – who would clearly remain always and invaluably at her side – and finally little Georgiana. It was Georgiana who was the subject of all the correspondence upon cream paper embossed with the Lennox arms. Georgiana was now officially to become Lady Lovell, and the world in general must be informed of the matter. Lady Lennox was a great believer in the dissemination of information. It led to far fewer mishaps if everyone knew everything and had no excuse for pleading ignorance as a reason for incompetence of any kind. Lady Lennox despised incompetence. She had by now told the entire neighbourhood of Georgiana's betrothal so that everyone might be prepared to perform any function required of them at the ensuing marriage. She had, of course, told Parson Harding first, as an old and valued confidant, and as a mark of special favour, subjected her lively family to the uninviting prospect of the three elder Hardings and their father at dinner that day. There had been an uproar at breakfast over the matter.

'As the centre of attention,' Georgiana claimed, 'I refuse to be afflicted by any Harding at all if I cannot have **Parson** Harding himself by me. I will not endure Robert another meal, I declare I will not.'

Lady Lennox regarded Georgiana levelly.

'There is no question of Parson Harding sitting anywhere but by me.'

'I will not have Robert. . . . '

'It is unlikely that you will ever have to sit by Robert again. You will behave to him tonight.'

'Mamma!' Georgiana wailed.

Her father patted her shoulder as he moved towards the sideboard.

'Think of me, my dear. I am doomed to Miss Eleanor Harding. I doubt I shall survive the ordeal.'

Lady Lennox said severely, 'Eleanor Harding is an eminently capable and practical woman.'

'Those are not qualities I seek in a dinner companion, my dear.'

The two Lennox sons at home applauded loudly.

'You should not encourage them, Harry.'

'Why did you ask them to dine at all, Mamma? Why could not you and Georgie simply have called upon them?'

'Because, my dear John, Parson Harding took up the incumbency of Stoke Abbas two years after your father and I were married, and thus is a person to be considered in all Lennox family matters.'

'You should have asked him to dine alone.'

'Unthinkable,' his mother said briskly.

'To whose lot falls the unlovely Caroline?' George wondered to the moulded ceiling.

'To Frank's,' Lady Lennox said, turning with a smile to her future son-in-law, until then fully occupied with his breakfast.

'Oh – oh, I say – I beg you, ma'am – I do not know the lady, may I not be excused? . . .'

The Lennox brothers exploded again.

'It is a real chance for you, Frank,' Georgiana said with mock solemnity.

Frank Lovell looked pleadingly at his betrothed.

'Shall I be very wretched by her, Georgie?'

'Indeed no,' Georgiana cried. 'You will be quite fascinated, will he not, George? For beauty, wit and conversation, there is no one to surpass – '

'Georgiana!' her mother said.

'Oh, Mamma, even you, with your heart of gold, must admit that Caroline Harding is surely the most insignificant person in the county of Dorset. . . .' She stopped.

Lady Lennox had signalled to her husband, and he, rousing himself reluctantly from his lazy and good-humoured abstraction, said with unusual firmness, 'No more, Georgiana, not another word. If you cannot speak charitably, it is better you do not speak at all.'

Georgiana looked a little shamefaced, but brightened immediately at the sight of Frank Lovell's face full of the admiration he always felt at her daring.

'Come riding with me, Frank, and I will instruct you in the art of conversation to a Harding.'

'It is very simple,' George Lennox said. 'In the case of father and elder daughter one listens and never has the chance to speak, and in the case of the son and younger daughter one speaks and longs for a chance to listen which never comes.'

'I should prefer the former,' Frank Lovell said anxiously.

'We know that!' cried John delightedly. 'Why else are you marrying Georgie? You will not have to speak again for the rest of your life!'

Above the uproar, Lady Lennox said clearly that she did not wish to see any of them again until the dinner hour. When they had trooped noisily out, she turned to her husband, idly reading last week's newspaper and humming beneath his breath.

'I am anxious, Harry, that Frank Lovell will not be firm enough with Georgiana.'

Lord Lennox yawned.

'Nobody is firm enough with Georgiana, my love, not even yourself.'

'She makes the boys behave so wildly.'

'Boys?'

'George and John.'

'Ah yes. George and John.' Lord Lennox's thoughts had

run briefly upon his elder daughter Sophia and her effect upon young men. He rose slowly from his chair. 'They will be better when the hunting begins again, my love. The summer is a deuced idle time for a young man.'

'Endeavour not to yawn too frequently before Miss Harding, Harry.'

'We shall all, save yourself, my love, be yawning. It is infernal luck that Henry Harding should have produced such a family as his.'

'They have done quite well, Harry, indeed they have. The only one with no prospects of any kind is poor Caroline, but I do not think she ever hoped for any. Humility must be a great comfort.'

Lord Lennox laughed, and kissed his wife and strolled out into the sunlight to his horses. Lady Lennox, after a moment's regret over the excessive high spirits of her children, an indulgence she dismissed quickly as unconstructive, went in search of the excellent Jane, who always breakfasted early and would be about her household duties. Jane, Lady Lennox reflected, took after herself, and there was solace to be had from that thought.

At the Parsonage, Caroline spent the morning encouraging a small throbbing in her temples to materialize into a headache sufficient to prevent her dining at Stoke Park. She went out, at Eleanor's request, to pick strawberries, and did so in full sunlight deliberately without her hat. The throbbing obstinately refused to intensify. Having brought the strawberries into the kitchen, she avoided Eleanor and escaped to her own room where she proceeded to paint on ivory, without her spectacles. Caroline was a talented miniaturist. She often felt it was attributable to her short sight for only at close quarters was she able to see anything in all its detail. She was engaged upon an oval painting of field flowers commissioned by old Mrs Whitecross of Sturminster Newton, and delicate attention to an ear of corn took all her concentration for a full hour. When she looked up, dazzled at the largeness of objects in the room after the tiny intricacy she had been absorbed in, she was dismayed to find the throbbing quite gone, and her head lamentably clear.

Eleanor swept in, as usual without knocking. Caroline wondered if all families were as insensitive to each other's need or wish for privacy.

'Carrie – there you are! I have been searching for you this good half-hour! I have had a thousand things to do and instead I have been compelled to look for you.'

Her tone was accusing and offended. For a fleeting second, Caroline thought of pointing out that anyone with a pressing list of things needing to be done is better occupied doing them than in hunting for a helpmeet.

'I am sorry, Eleanor.'

'So you should be. Sitting up here idly while I slave for the family. How you would all get on without me, I cannot conceive.'

'What can I do now to assist you?'

'Oh!' Eleanor gave a contemptuous glance at the ceiling and flung wide her hands. 'It is all done. I have done it all.'

Caroline, on the edge of her patience, said, 'Then why must you interrupt me?'

Unable to say truthfully that she had come to complain and be self-righteous, Eleanor said firmly, 'It is time you were thinking of dressing.'

Caroline took out the watch that had been her mother's, and which she wore on a green ribbon at her waist.

'It does not take me two hours to dress, Eleanor.'

'I wish you to look well. It is most gracious and good of Lady Lennox to ask us, and I wish you to be a credit to Papa.'

'We are none of us ever a credit to Papa to look at. You know that as well as I. It is he who is a credit to us.'

'When you are in this frame of mind, Caroline,' Eleanor said furiously, 'conversation with you is quite impossible.'

'I am sorry,' Caroline said again.

'You are always sorry, eternally sorry, but I see no signs in you of any real desire to be other than you are. What is your life to become if you do not try to be more positive about it?'

Caroline shrugged helplessly. The question went far too deep for a quick answer. Eleanor was right, what was to become of her? Nothing, she supposed, as nothing always had. She expected nothing and there was after all nothing for a parson's daughter of limited means and no looks to expect in 1775. She would end up as companion to old Mrs Whitecross or Miss Lumleigh or Lady Fyfield and people would only remember her because she painted miniatures. She looked up at Eleanor with a face full of misery, and saw the severity in Eleanor's face and let her own gaze drop again.

'Please do not scold me,' she said in a low voice.

'If I do not scold you, Carrie, who shall? What use are you dreaming and idling your way through the days like this?'

The cottagers of Stoke Abbas might have had stout answers to this, but humble Caroline had none. Eleanor had abruptly opened such a black abyss before her through this sunny morning that she was horrified at the prospect. When she considered in her mind, she could not think in what direction her usefulness, if any, lay. Eleanor ran the house, controlled the accounts, and shaped their lives to suit their father. Caroline was not at all sure that she could do any of those things even if she were given the chance. She taught some of the cottage children to read, but it never occurred to her that that was useful since her affection for the children made the lessons a pleasure to be looked forward to. She sat with bent head and despised herself.

Eleanor sighed and rustled to the window.

'I beg you will not wear the blue.'

Caroline looked up bemusedly, her mind still drowning in the prospect of her empty life.

'Blue?'

'Your blue silk. It is a most – most unsuitable colour.'

'Unsuitable? Unsuitable for what? I wore it to church last Sunday. Surely what is suitable for church is also suitable for Stoke Park?'

'It was not suitable for church,' Eleanor said firmly. 'I am sure Papa thinks so.'

'Indeed he does not!' Caroline said indignantly. 'He said it reminded him of Mamma, who loved blue above all colours!'

Eleanor's own colour rose.

'Papa has too good a heart to hurt your feelings.'

She moved back to the door, and stood with her hand upon the knob.

'I beg you will wear your grey. Or the muslin.'

Caroline raised her chin.

'I will be ready in one hour and a half, Eleanor.'

'In the grey if you please, Carrie,' Eleanor said, and closed the door behind her with decision.

When she had gone, Caroline went quickly to the door and bolted it. Then she crossed the small room and cast herself upon her bed, where she lay, staring dry-eyed at the ceiling, her hands clenched tightly at her sides.

Parson Harding still kept his own carriage. Eleanor complained that it was a needless extravagance, but it reminded her father of those happy days of early marriage when it had seemed possible to be both spiritual and extremely comfortable, and he would not let it go. He climbed into it that afternoon, distinguished in his black, and glanced briefly at his children with the usual slight sinking of the heart that their appearance caused him. Why Robert seemed to feel that a clergyman had no sartorial obligation to both his Maker and his fellow man, Parson Harding could not conceive. He glanced from his own lean and elegant calves trimly clad in black silk, to Robert's which were approximately covered in black worsted. His coat wrinkled at the shoulders, and the sleeves were too short, and his wristbands had nothing of the dazzling whiteness of his father's. Eleanor looked neat and unremarkable in black, above which she wore an expression like a thundercloud. Opposite her Caroline sat wearing a dress of exceptionally pretty delphinium blue. It did not become her skin or her hair, both of which seemed deadened by the blue, but it was a pretty colour in itself.

'A charming dress, Carrie.'

Caroline looked up to give her father a delighted and delightful smile.

The journey to Stoke Park proceeded in silence. Eleanor was clearly in high dudgeon over something, and neither Caroline nor Robert were ever great volunteers of conversation. If it were not for the social burden they represented,

Parson Harding would have thoroughly enjoyed the prospect of dining at Stoke Park. He probably knew Lady Lennox more thoroughly than any man alive, even her husband, and this knowledge gave an irresistible edge to their relationship.

Lady Lennox and her family were all in the drawing room grouped artistically about the great light white and blue room with its shining floor of parquet. Caroline's pleasure in her father's compliment and temporary small confidence in her appearance faded instantly the moment she saw Georgiana Lennox.

Both Caroline and Eleanor wore dresses of simple cut, the fabric of bodice and skirt falling unbroken by any seam but the waist seam, to the floor. Their necklines were modest and square cut, their sleeves only slightly caught at the elbow. As both dresses had been made by the village seamstress, there was a certain irregularity and puckering here and there, and Caroline was painfully conscious that the neckline of her dress was far from true. Their hair was unpowdered and caught up behind their heads, severely in Eleanor's case, and with an unsuccessful attempt at ringlets in Caroline's. But Georgiana was gorgeous in striped silk, a dress whose overskirt was looped with ribbons over a matching petticoat ruffled and trimmed with narrow velvet. There were snowy ruffles at her throat and elbows ornamented with black velvet bows and roses, and her lightly powdered hair was piled into a ravishing cascade of curls and ringlets. Her plainly visible buckled shoes had scarlet heels, and the sticks of her fan were lacquered scarlet too. To Caroline, she was a wondrous and discouraging spectacle.

Eleanor was clearly unconscious of any sartorial discrepancy, but Caroline immediately felt the old sensation of utter dowdiness fall about her like a mantle. Her dress was too short behind, too low-waisted, too narrow in the sleeves and a crude colour. She bent her eyes upon the floor and was very miserable.

'Miss Harding! Miss Caroline! What a pleasure to see you on this beautiful day. Is it not a beautiful day?'

Lord Lennox stood affable and large before them. Eleanor made some suitable reply and Caroline managed to lift her eyes as far as her host's impeccably folded stock. Past him, she could see Jane and Robert in halting conversation, and her father and Georgiana laughing delightedly together. There seemed also to be an assembly of young men about, as usual, but Caroline dared not look. Lady Lennox did not allow her her solitude for long.

'Caroline! I have not seen you in a month. I suppose you have been much occupied with your charming painting and your little pupils. I wish to present Lord Lovell to you, Caroline.'

Caroline looked up briefly, and Frank Lovell caught a flash from those gleaming grey eyes that made him feel a little less apprehensive at the prospect of this dull and awkward creature in his charge for the next hour. Caroline managed a smile, but was inwardly much daunted by this fashionable young man in his exquisitely cut breeches and lavish linen.

'Delighted, Miss Harding.' He had a slight drawl, and when nervous, it became worse.

'You must tell her about India, Frank. I am sure you know nothing of India, do you, Caroline? Frank knows a good deal about India.'

Caroline, whose knowledge of India was confined to hazy notions of goats' milk in brass pots and thin brown men in huge jewels, said gratefully, 'I shall be glad to listen.'

'I hope you will help me a little more than that,' Frank Lovell said.

'I will try, Lord Lovell. I – I am not much use at conversation. But I should dearly like to hear of India.'

He offered her his arm, and they followed the older people into dinner. Behind them Georgiana was teasing Robert who sounded utterly bewildered and entirely bewitched in his stammering replies. Caroline smiled involuntarily, partly out of sympathy for Robert, and partly because she could see he was fair game for Georgiana. Frank Lovell saw her smile.

'Is she not fascinating?'

'Entirely,' Caroline said.

Frank Lovell beamed upon her with approval.

At the table, Caroline found that several feet of gleaming rosewood separated her from Lord Lovell on her left and John Lennox on her right. This isolation gave her some comfort. Across the table, Georgiana was showing Robert no mercy. His eyes were fixed upon her face and his expression was stunned. For a while it seemed possible for Caroline to eat in silence, since both her neighbours were engrossed in Georgiana and left her mercifully alone. She had not much appetite through shyness, but noticed that Georgiana ate almost nothing and thus felt it possible to leave her own plate half-finished.

As the lamb was borne in, Lady Lennox called down the table, 'Are you now much better informed about India, Caroline?'

To Caroline's horror, the table fell silent to listen.

'I – I am sure I soon shall be, ma'am.'

'Where have you been in India?' Parson Harding enquired.

'In Bengal, sir. My cousin is on the council of the East India Company at Calcutta.'

'Your cousin, Frank?'

'Yes, ma'am, my father's elder sister's only son, Sir Edward Ashton.'

'I knew an Ashton at Cambridge,' Parson Harding said irrelevantly, and the conversation flowed back again.

Caroline would have liked to ask whom Sir Edward Ashton counselled and on whose behalf, but she was afraid to venture a remark across four feet of space.

Lord Lovell helped her by saying, 'We had a wild time, Miss Harding, a wild time indeed. I think my cousin was thankful to see me leave.'

'Did – did you go with a companion, Lord Lovell?'

'No, no, I did not. But India is a most sociable place, you know. Calcutta is full of the best fellows imaginable and – ' He was about to say some of the best women as well, but remembered in time that most of the women he had met in Calcutta were neither of a colour nor a status to be suitable for conversation.

'I was never in bed before four in the morning, Miss Harding –'

'And neither shall you be when we are married,' declared Georgiana from across the table. 'I intend to amuse myself all of every night and sleep during the day. Will that not shock you, Mamma?'

'Immeasurably, my love.'

'Can you be so dissipated in such heat as we hear of in India?' Parson Harding asked.

'Indeed yes, sir. I believe almost more than in London. I met one man who said he did not need above four hours' sleep in India.'

'Who was this phenomenon?' enquired Lord Lennox, ready to prolong any topic that gave him respite from Eleanor.

'John Gates, sir.'

The effect was electrifying. Every face around the table registered amazement and there was a sudden, concerted indrawing of breath.

'Johnnie Gates!' Lady Lennox exclaimed.

'Our bad Johnnie?' Georgiana said hopefully.

'I thought he was in Madras,' Lord Lennox said.

'He was, sir. But the Company moved him to Calcutta. I did not make his acquaintance intimately – '

'Just as well,' Lord Lennox said.

'Johnnie Gates!'

'We have not heard of him in seven years!'

Eight, Caroline said to herself. Eight years since Johnnie had been sent to India, eight years of knowing she must die an old maid.

'Was he prospering?' Parson Harding asked. 'He was indeed a bad boy, but something in him makes me hope he prospers.'

He was not bad, Caroline cried silently, he was just young and wild and – forgetful.

'I think he does, sir,' Frank Lovell said doubtfully. He had only seen Gates in the evening when he was more or less drunk. He was said to have several native mistresses, but to have made just enough money to be comfortable – well, to be comfortable in India at least.

'He is some connection of ours,' Lady Lennox explained. 'His mother was my husband's sister, and upon her early

31

death and her husband's he became our ward. He grew up as one of our children.'

She did not add that she considered he had but poorly repaid that upbringing, nor did she mention, because she did not like to think of it, that a considerable part of the Lennox fortune left in trust for him by his parents would pass to John Gates on his uncle's death. He would get none of the property, and this she was most thankful for. However, a large sum of money that his mother had brought upon her marriage to his father, and that she would dearly like to see spread among her own six, was to be indisputably his.

'He was the best playmate in the world,' Georgiana said, 'and easily the most wicked. Do you remember, John – '

'Georgiana!' her mother said.

'Very well, Mamma, but if you will not let me tell tales of Johnnie's naughtiness in boyhood, will you please permit Frank to tell us of Johnnie's naughtiness in manhood, for I am sure he is no better behaved.'

'Is he, Frank?'

Frank Lovell looked doubtfully at his future mother-in-law, and seemed uncertain of speech.

'I see,' Lady Lennox said. 'We will discuss the matter no further. Now, Mr Harding, I hope you will confess that the strawberries at the Park are far superior to the strawberries at the Parsonage?'

Once more conversation spread gently along the table. Caroline longed to go home, to the seclusion of her bedroom and the privacy of her thoughts. When Johnnie Gates had been mentioned so suddenly she had abruptly felt, only for a fleeting moment, that she was eighteen again and that all those emotions which had slept so quietly for eight years were free and dancing once more. She stared down at her plate and hoped nothing showed in her face. There was no doubt everyone had forgotten her part in Johnnie Gates' last months in England, and for the greater part of the last eight years, so had she. But she had remembered now, and she longed for the luxury of going on remembering, alone in her own room at the Parsonage.

Lady Lennox rose at last, and led her own and Parson

Harding's daughters to the drawing room. To Caroline's dismay, card tables were set up.

'You were once very skilled at bezique,' Lady Lennox said to her.

'I am sadly out of practice now, ma'am.'

'Then you shall play with Lord Lennox who loves to win. Georgiana, do not yawn. Come and assist me with the cards.'

It seemed an age before the men came in, and another age before all the tables were seated to Lady Lennox's satisfaction.

After an hour of cards, tea was brought. None of the young Lennoxes made any attempt now to repress their yawns except Georgiana, who was seated by Parson Harding and thus kept very busy being fascinating. Parson Harding was delighted to be fascinated, and only with true reluctance, remembered the hour and rose to his feet. His children followed him obediently. He smiled and bowed and kissed Lady Lennox's hand and she thought for the thousandth time how unlucky it was that none of his poise and charm had descended to his children.

As soon as the Harding carriage had rolled away up towards the village, Lady Lennox went to her boudoir, and asked that Lord Lovell be sent to her. He entered looking extremely troubled.

'My dear Frank, pray do not look so anxious. I only wish to continue the conversation that it was clearly impossible to continue at dinner.'

'Johnnie Gates?'

'Precisely so. You say you saw him in Calcutta?'

'Yes, ma'am. Not above three or four times.'

'In his own house?'

'No, ma'am, always in the houses of others.'

Lady Lennox did not believe in beating about the bush. 'Was he drunk?'

Frank Lovell swallowed. 'Slightly, Lady Lennox. We all – it is customary – it seems in India that . . . '

'I understand you very well. Has he married, do you gather?'

'No – no, he is not married. There are not many married men in Calcutta. The Company tries to send possible wives out to Bengal, I believe, because the shortage of – of suitable women makes for – for men – '

'Taking native mistresses? Does Johnnie Gates have an Indian mistress?'

Although he would have delighted in imparting this information to his Georgie or her brothers, Frank Lovell was most uncomfortable at doing so to Lady Lennox. He avoided her eye and said indistinctly that he believed so.

'And has he children?'

'I have no idea about children, Lady Lennox.'

'Did you gain the impression, Frank, that he is extravagant?'

Being extravagant himself, Frank Lovell had no idea what extravagance was.

'I believe he has horses, ma'am, and an excellent cellar.'

Lady Lennox sat thoughtful for a while. Then she rose and walked to her bureau, and contemplated her children's portraits.

'Is it your opinion, Frank, that although we must take for granted that men live a somewhat more unconventional life in Calcutta than they do here, John Gates' way of life is debauched even by the standards of Bengal?'

Frank thought of his cousin's orderly, almost scholarly life, and compared it with the other lives he had seen, those of Company men, attorneys, soldiers. They all lived self-indulgently by comparison to Sir Edward Ashton, but perhaps he had never seen anyone sprawled unconscious among the debris of dinner quite so often as Johnnie Gates.

'Your answer is important to me, Frank.'

'Yes, ma'am. I believe his life is perhaps a little more – more – '

'Exactly so. More than most of his peers?'

'Yes, ma'am.'

'Thank you, Frank. Now go and find Georgiana.'

After the door had closed behind him, Lady Lennox sat thoughtfully by her desk. Johnnie Gates had been sent to India because it was thought that the rigours of the climate and the discipline of the East India Company would reform him, and it was both irritating and disturbing to find that this plan had failed. After Johnnie had been gone a year and a half, Lady Lennox had ceased to write, and had thankfully assumed that her difficult and wayward charge of nearly twenty years was now in other and sterner hands. Indeed, if Johnnie's soul was all she had to worry about, she would not be worrying now, but it was not simply a matter of his soul. It was a matter of Lennox money. Lady Lennox had no intention of letting Lennox money pass into hands which would drink and gamble and squander it when it might be used far more efficiently. She was powerless to stop Johnnie receiving the money, but she was determined to use all the influence in her power to dictate how he should spend it.

There was, after all, only one way that she could ensure the money would not be wasted. Johnnie must marry. What is more, he must marry a sensible, thrifty, plain-living woman who would not abet him in his extravagances. It would also be an advantage if she was either of an age or physical type unlikely to prove fertile; since then the money would revert to what she considered its rightful inheritors. Only such a marriage, as far as Lady Lennox could see, would avoid shame and scandal being breathed about the name of Lennox, and the senseless waste of a good deal of money that her six darlings would have been able to make such excellent use of. It was a matter for true thankfulness that Johnnie would get no property, but the money was bad enough. And if Johnnie was behaving as badly as Frank Lovell described, Lady Lennox must take action soon before he was too dissipated for any sensible woman to look at him twice.

Caroline Harding had supposed inaccurately at dinner that no one remembered her association with Johnnie Gates. Lady Lennox had glanced sharply at Caroline, and had recalled most accurately, when she saw Caroline's self-conscious downcast face, all that had taken place in the spring and summer of 1767. There, of course, thought Lady Lennox now in triumph, there is the perfect wife for Johnnie! She has a wretched position at the Parsonage, she has no occupations of importance, she was once deeply attached to him, and she is used to a most simple and inexpensive way of life. She is also, thought Lady Lennox, lucky to be offered a husband with those looks and manners, and the consideration of looks reminded Lady Lennox that Caroline's thin form looked splendidly unpromising for motherhood. Jubilant, Lady Lennox rose from her chair, and began slowly to pace the room. Letters must be written, to Johnnie himself, and perhaps to Frank Lovell's cousin to make it all seem as if every care for Caroline's happiness were being taken. Yes, she should enquire of Sir Edward Ashton if he thought the plan suitable, and as the Company had numerous employees in Calcutta it was to be hoped that he should not know enough of Johnnie Gates to disapprove.

The door opened and Lord Lennox came in.

'Well, my dear. And are you on your way to bed?'

'Not yet, Harry. Come and seat yourself.'

'I was rather thinking of bed, my love.'

'Not yet, Harry. I have a great deal to explain to you.'

3

Caroline Harding entered her bedroom at the Parsonage that evening in a very different frame of mind from that in which she had left it. She was agitated and slightly exalted, and very grateful that the day was done and that she had now time for her own thoughts. She undressed quickly in the darkness for the bright summer moonlight made nonsense of her candle, and in nightgown and cap, with her straight pale hair falling down her back, climbed into bed. She deliberately left both bed and window curtains open so that she might gaze at the pale square of June night sky as she gave herself up to the luxury of recollection.

She had known Johnnie Gates all her life, if you could call a furtive and frightened admiration from afar, knowing. When she was born, he had already been at Stoke Park for two years, and was a vigorous and destructive child, adored by nursemaids for his looks and deplored by Lady Lennox for his mischief. Contact between the nurseries at the Parsonage and the Park was slight, but the Parsonage children knew via the servants every breath and deed of those gilded little children in their palatial quarters down the hill. The Parsonage children knew what the Park children ate and played with, heard every lisping cleverness repeated, knew all likes and dislikes. They saw them in church ruffled and beribboned, the boys in taffeta-tied shoes and pointed lace collars. They heard much about Johnnie Gates for there was much to hear. He upset churns in the dairies, tied the cats' tails together, hobbled the dogs, threw apples accurately at stooping gardeners, left toads in the maids' bedrooms and was entirely irrepressible when corrected. Robert, Charles and Harry sat open-mouthed as the nursery maid regaled them with fresh outrages as they ate their suppers by the fire. Eleanor would shake her head and click her tongue disapprovingly, and Caroline would long to hear more.

The children met seldom, on walks perhaps, or rides when the Parsonage children, taking turn and turn about on the old pony, would meet a fully mounted and beautifully equipped cavalcade of little Lennoxes, with the groom in attendance. Sometimes there were parties, sometimes there were agonizing visits when pretty Mrs Harding took her awkward brood to the Park and left them to be miserable in the great nursery while she chattered to the Lennoxes in the drawing room below. When adolescence came and all the boys of both houses went away to school, contact became even more broken but the snippets of gossip and news went on, so that Caroline still knew, with awe and fascination, that growing up was not having a sobering effect on Johnnie Gates.

When Caroline was sixteen, the gossip flared up into something more solid and dramatic. Sophia Lennox, at eighteen ravishing to look at and entirely heedless and reckless in her behaviour, had always been Johnnie's chief goad to wilder and wilder exploits. As children they had never been left alone together for long because the havoc they could wreak and the mischief they could concoct between them was terrifying. Gradually as their adolescence wore on, this partnership in misbehaviour deepened, as it was bound to do between two young, healthy and handsome creatures, into something more compelling for both of them. The groom noticed that on rides they managed to get themselves separated from the main party and Lady Lennox observed endless glances of complicity across rooms, or tables at meals. While she was gathering her information in order to confront them both with her displeasure – for Sophia was intended for someone much more considerable than the family orphan – matters came to a head of their own accord.

Caroline heard – or rather overheard – a conversation between her parents. Parson Harding had been summoned to Stoke Park in a hurry, and had gone immediately despite a wild wet October evening and no moon. The Harding children waited about the stairs and landings, burning with curiosity but not daring to risk a snub from their mother or a later chastening from their father for asking impertinent questions. At length Parson Harding returned and went straight in to his wife in the drawing room. Caroline, in the study across the hall ostensibly hunting for her mislaid Shakespeare, heard their muffled voices through the closed door.

'What will Lady Lennox do, Henry?'

'He must go away, dearest, and immediately. The carriage will take him to Salisbury tomorrow.'

'But what then? What will become of him?'

'Lord Lennox is to make arrangements for him to go abroad, probably to the East.'

'It is very dreadful for them all.'

'It was almost the ruin of Sophia, dearest. If the stable boy had not – '

At this point Parson Harding, who was apparently pacing the room as he spoke, came dangerously near the door and Caroline, with a beating heart, slipped quickly across the hall and up the stairs to impart whatever she knew to her brothers and sister.

By next morning, they knew it all. The house, despite Parson Harding's edict that the subject should never be mentioned again, was buzzing. The previous day, bored by the confinement indoors dictated by the weather, Sophia had gone down to the stables, followed after a decent interval by Johnnie Gates. They had been seen by the head groom patting the new grey hunter, and had then vanished. Some time later, a stable boy, climbing into the loft to hurl down hay bales for the afternoon feed, found Johnnie and Sophia tumbling in a flurry of shirt tails and petticoats. As far as Sophia's marriageability was concerned, they were disturbed in the nick of time. Lady Lennox sent for Parson Harding at once with the sensation that the situation needed official moral authority as well as parental discipline and decisions.

So Johnnie was gone, not to the East as it turned out, but to a distant relation in Scotland which was felt to be remote enough to offer him no chance for wrongdoing. Before a year was up Sophia, who had shown nothing but resentment at being interrupted in the hayloft, had become a countess, and had been taken off to London. As the months wore on reports of her goings-on in London made the hayloft incident recede into insignificance. Gradually the whole affair dwindled, and with the two participants gone, there was nothing to prevent its vanishing into oblivion. General opinion blamed both Sophia and Johnnie equally for a few months, then they slowly ceased to be a topic of interest, and were talked of no more.

At the Parsonage it was quickly forgotten because other shadows were falling there. Eighteen months after Johnnie's dismissal, Mrs Harding was dead, and the lives at the Parsonage had to take a new and drearier shape. Of all the children, Harry and Caroline were the most desolated. Harry because he was only six, and Caroline because she had adored her mother and seen in her all the feminine charm that she knew she lacked herself. In that bleak spring of 1767, eighteen-year-old Caroline had been quite broken with grief and had felt that life would never have a light in it again.

One wet morning in April, Parson Harding was summoned to the Park. He returned for dinner punctually. His children waited silently for him to divulge any news he had, for he had unconsciously developed a habit, since his wife's death, of including his elder children in matters that before he would have reserved for Mrs Harding's confidence.

'Lady Lennox has received a letter from John Gates. He has written to beg her forgiveness, to assure her that he is a reformed character, and to ask permission to visit Stoke Park.'

Eleanor, in her new role as chatelaine, said, 'I trust you advised her to refuse him, Papa.'

Parson Harding looked up with a distinct amusement gleaming in his eye.

'Indeed I did not, Eleanor. John Gates did wrong, no doubt of it, but Sophia was no less blameworthy than he. He is not evil, Eleanor, merely self-indulgent and young.' He paused and looked out of the window at the wet garden. 'No, I advised her to forgive him and let him come.'

'For good?' Caroline asked, trying to suppress the eagerness in her tone.

'No. Only for a few months. The relation he has lived with in Scotland has obtained a post for him in Madras, with the East India Company. He sails for the East in the autumn.'

Caroline wondered if this move on the part of the Scottish relation meant that Johnnie was no better behaved than he had been. She said nothing because she was astonished at the flutterings of pleasure the news gave her. She looked up and smiled at her father, and he smiled in return, saying, 'I am glad you agree with me, Carrie.'

Three weeks later, it was known Johnnie Gates had come. Parson Harding and Eleanor went to dine at the Park, and the latter reported Johnnie wholly unchanged, adding that she felt Lady Lennox had made a grave error in accepting him back. Secretly, Caroline chafed to see him, though she knew she would have been tongue-tied if she had. She had not seen him since that episode in the hayloft and she burned with curiosity – and with something more.

One Friday a message came from Stoke Park begging that the Hardings might take advantage of the early peas, since there was such an abundance at the Park it was feared some might be wasted. Lady Lennox hated to see waste, but never thought of the cottagers when she had a superfluity of any delicacy. As Eleanor knew her father loved the first peas of the year, she found Caroline, absorbed in a book as usual, and despatched her, despite many protestations, down the hill with a basket and the old pony.

The only consolation of this alarming errand as far as Caroline could see was that she need only go to the kitchen door, and thus avoid the awesome terror of an official reception. She rode into the Park by the back gates, and trotted across the level grass in the direction of the orchard and kitchen quarters beyond. As she neared the orchard walls, she could hear voices, and the nearer she came the more obvious it was that the voices belonged to the young men of the house. Caroline thought of turning back, but then thought of Eleanor's displeasure, and decided that if she rode close under the orchard wall which was a good eight feet in height, she might get by unobserved.

The voices were shouting now, and there was a good deal of stamping and thudding. They must have a pony with them, she thought, pressing her own pony close to the wall, and bending low so that her hat was not visible.

'Johnnie, take care!' someone shouted. 'He will have you off under a tree. . . .'

There was a crack, a shout and a heavy thud, followed by the pounding of hooves. Then Caroline could hear cries of;

'Catch him! Catch him!'

'Are you hurt?'

'Not in the least. Catch him, I say!'

'Not again, Johnnie, it is not safe. . . .'

'Catch him, Henry, you fool, catch him!'

At this moment, to Caroline's horror, the wall stopped, and she found herself separated from the orchard only by a wooden gate and entirely exposed to the young men beyond. Henry Lennox and Johnnie Gates, dressed only in breeches and shirtsleeves, were standing panting and tousled by the nearest tree, Johnnie holding a plunging pony by its reins. They looked at Caroline in amazement, as astonished to see her materialize in the gateway as if she had dropped from heaven.

'It–it is Miss Harding, is it not?' Henry Lennox said at last.

Caroline nodded dumbly. Johnnie Gates' presence made it impossible to speak or to look up. His dark hair was rumpled, his colour was heightened by exercise and his ruffled shirt had come open at the neck. All this she took in at one swift and fascinated glance before fixing her eyes upon her pony's ears.

'May we assist you in any way?' Henry Lennox said. He had come up to the gate and was very near her. She could smell leather and sweat. She swallowed uncomfortably.

'I – I did not mean to disturb you. . . .'

'You did not disturb us in the least, Miss Harding. I am only sorry you were too late to see Johnnie tumble off. Is there something I can do for you?'

'I – I was going to the kitchen for – for some peas. Lady Lennox kindly said we – we might have some.'

'I am delighted to hear it. We are weary of peas for every meal here and I should be glad to give you a cart-load. Hand me your basket, Miss Harding, and I will fetch you peas from the kitchen.'

Caroline was horrified. And leave her here alone with Johnnie Gates?

'Oh, no – no, you are too kind – no, it is no trouble – I had rather . . . '

'Nonsense, Miss Harding. Get off your pony and seat yourself on my coat beneath the trees over there, and I will not be ten minutes.'

Johnnie Gates materialized at her side. He seemed much larger and brighter than she remembered.

'Allow me.'

She felt his hands on her waist, and she was standing before him on the grass. He tied her pony to the gatepost and opened the gate for her.

'Entertain Miss Harding well, Johnnie.'

'Indeed I will, trust me.'

He turned and smiled at Caroline, and she felt a sort of breathlessness seize her.

'Do you ride much, Miss Harding?'

'Oh no – not much at all. Papa has horses, but Eleanor and I do not ride them.'

Johnnie Gates crossed to the apple tree where the pony was tethered, its flanks flecked with foam, tossing its head impatiently. With one hand on its neck, Johnnie turned and said slowly and casually to Caroline, 'Will you try this pony?'

Caroline's head flew up.

'That pony! No indeed! I should not dare!'

He did not take his eyes from her face.

'I think you would.'

'No! No. Indeed I should not! I should fall immediately. . . .'

'I do not think so.'

Caroline was by now shaking with fright. All she could see before her was the pony straining on its tether, and Johnnie's half-shut eyes and small smile.

'Please, Mr Gates, I cannot, indeed I cannot! Do not ask me, I cannot, I cannot!'

Johnnie left the pony and came up to Caroline, standing so close that the open ruffles of his shirt nearly touched the sprigged muslin of her dress. His hand moved to brush her arm as lightly as a leaf.

'I think you can,' he said.

Something broke inside Caroline. The mounting panic and fright exploded in a crescendo and some strange unfamiliar strength, a sort of unnatural calmness, surged through her in its place. She waited a moment while this great wave of unaccustomed power spread itself through her body, then she walked towards the pony and put her hand on its neck.

'Will you help me up, Mr Gates?'

He said something she could not hear in an excited tone, and then she felt his hands on her knee and ankle, and she was astride the pony and the world was plunging and wheeling about her. She had no thought for what Eleanor would say to her, her skirts rucked up, her hat come off, her hair tumbled, being whirled about the orchard on a half-broken pony as the result of a dare. She had no thought of anything in fact, but that she must not fall, and with this consciousness lending steel to her muscles she clung like a limpet while the pony beneath her surged and spun in an attempt to be rid of its burden. She was dimly aware of Johnnie's white shirt here and there, of his shouts that seemed to come from far away, and of trees spinning about like grotesque creatures with a life of their own. Sky, grass, walls, trees all dipped and rocked in a crazy kaleidoscope, but still she clung. Johnnie's shouts came nearer, and suddenly the pony seemed to shudder to a halt and the world righted itself about her. Caroline looked down into blue eyes blazing with triumph below her. She crouched where she was while he led the pony to a tree, tied it, and then turned and lifted her down as effortlessly as if she had been a baby. He stood her on the grass before him, and he did not take his hands from her waist.

'You were afraid,' he said, and his tone was pure admiration.

'Yes,' she said, and raised her head and he caught his breath at the queer silvery gleam of her eyes in that thin tawny face.

'Why did you do it? Were you afraid I should laugh at you?'

'No. I was afraid of my own remorse later.'

He looked down at his hands and noticed how they almost met about the slenderness of her waist.

'I will never laugh at you again,' he said fervently.

'There is plenty to laugh at.' She looked up at him and smiled with this beautiful new confidence borne of her success.

He thought of Sophia, of Jane and Georgiana with their luxuriant hair and shapely limbs and air of healthy vigour, and looked at Caroline and her frailty and light straight hair.

'I know no one like you,' he said.

The intimacy of this remark made her realize that his hands were still holding her. She moved backwards to disengage herself and the moment she was free of his warm grasp began involuntarily to tremble.

'Come, you are shaken. Come here. Let me put my coat about you. I would not have frightened you for worlds.'

'I am not frightened,' she said truthfully, 'I am simply very surprised at myself.'

'I am surprised at you also. Surprised and delighted. Miss Harding, may I – '

At this moment, Henry Lennox called from the gateway.

'Your peas, Miss Harding! I hope you have been well amused. I see you have purloined Johnnie's coat which is very sensible of you as you will take much greater care of it than he.'

'Miss Harding was cold, Henry. You were such an age about those peas that she took cold.'

His arm was about her as they moved forward to the gate. Henry took that in, also the fact that Caroline's hair was loose on her shoulders, that she was hatless and looked much better than usual.

'May I fetch your hat, Miss Harding?'

Caroline was immediately confused and began to stammer. Johnnie said smoothly, 'Certainly you may, Henry, while I help Miss Harding to mount.'

Henry Lennox came back with the hat in his hand and his lips twitching. He bowed and handed it to Caroline who placed it on her head, and attempted with shaking hands to tie the ribbons. As she fumbled, two warm capable hands took over and tied the ribbons competently beneath her chin, lingering for a fraction of a second on her cheek.

'Now give me the basket, Henry, and tell Aunt I may be late for dinner. I am going to take Miss Harding home.'

Caroline spent the next three days in a trance of incredulous happiness. Luckily her return to the Parsonage was unobserved by her family so she was not molested by reprimands from Eleanor or teasing from her brothers. She felt the whole incident had been like some fairy tale, and found it difficult to recall any precise word or look, but simply dwelt in delighted astonishment upon the seductive atmosphere of dangerous excitement that had imbued it all. She remembered the sensation of feeling that she could do anything and, equally, that anything might happen, but she could not recall in any detail exactly what did happen. She felt intoxicated by the memory but, being Caroline, never expected any kind of sequel. It had been a small but thrilling adventure and she saw it as complete in itself.

But on the third day afterwards, crossing the Stoke River homewards after a visit to the Wells' first baby, she saw a lounging figure on a stile the far side of the bridge. Her heart beat a little quicker as it always did at the alarming prospect of a stranger, but she was too short-sighted to recognize Johnnie Gates. He watched her with amusement as she came, an amusement that now had no derision in it, realizing that she could hardly see him. She wore an old lilac print gown made over from one of her mother's and heavily frilled at the hem and elbows. Her wide straw hat was unadorned with any decoration but a wilting bunch of ladysmocks stuffed into the hat-band, and she carried a small covered basket of fresh butter as a present for her father from Mrs Wells. To Johnnie, used to the rustle of silks and white hands unencumbered by anything heavier than embroidery wools, she was an astonishing and enchanting sight. He rose slowly from the stile and came towards her.

Caroline stood stock still on the grassy cobbles of the bridge, clasping the butter basket, and gazed at him with a smile of sheer delight.

'I am glad you do not frown to see me, Miss Harding.'

'Oh, indeed no, why should I?'

'I have thought I behaved hardly gallantly the other day. I should not blame you if you reproached me for it.'

'Reproach you? Oh no, indeed not.'

He shook his head in wonderment.

'I can scarcely believe it. I have never met a woman before who could resist the chance of reproaching me. What kind of miracle are you?'

Caroline reddened slightly.

'You promised you would not laugh at me.'

He took the butter basket from her hands, placed it upon the parapet of the bridge and came back to stand close before her as he had done in the orchard.

'I am not laughing at you,' he said in a low voice.

Not raising her eyes from the double row of buttons on his waistcoat she said, 'Now I do reproach you. I reproach you for laughing at me. You are quite aware of what the – the Lennoxes think of me, indeed I expect you join in the teasing. And they are right, quite right in what they say. So you can see that to be called a miracle when I know all too well what I am, only humiliates me.'

Three days ago she would never have believed herself capable of making such a speech. Johnnie, entirely unused to perception or introspection in women, bent to take her hands.

'I am not laughing,' he said again, stooping to see beneath the brim of her hat, 'and every word you say induces me to believe more and more that indeed you are a miracle.'

Caroline tried to free her hands. The bridge not only led to the track that was a parallel and much-used alternative to the village street, but was also a most exposed and public place. Indeed, if Mrs Wells happened to glance from her parlour window at this moment, she would see them both quite clearly.

'I will let you go,' Johnnie said, 'if you will let me see you home again.'

The cart track led past the back of the Parsonage garden and was therefore as unobtrusive a way to go home as any. Caroline consented with a quick nod, and set off towards the comparative seclusion of the track, only to remember that she had forgotten the basket. She spun round quickly and was immediately caught in a firm embrace. Her hat, only balanced upon her head since she had long since lost the ribbons, slipped to the ground and her arms, wide flung in surprise, came to rest gingerly upon Johnnie's shoulders. Slowly her gaze travelled up the buttoned waistcoat inches from her nose, up the casually tied stock, and came to rest at Johnnie's chin. He took one hand from behind her back and tilted her chin further so that the sunlight struck full into her curious eyes and made them glimmer like moonlit water.

'I have thought of nothing else for three days,' he said, 'nothing. I am quite bewitched. You live up there like a princess in a tower and I could not think how to rescue you until I conceived a plan of discovering from your servants where you went and when. The Parsonage kitchen proved most fruitful.'

She did not dare to reply lest the wonderful dream should be broken. His hand moved from under her chin across her cheek to her hair and neck and came to rest across her shoulders, pulling her securely to him.

'When shall I see you again?'

She thought wildly. None of her little errands about the village seemed appropriate places for trysting.

'I – I do not know. . . .'

'Do you not want to see me again?'

She nodded, her eyes now fixed on his.

'You have so much to teach me, gentle Caroline. We shall meet often. I must see you every day. Somehow we must meet every day.'

'Yes,' she breathed.

He released her then, and took her hands and kissed her palms and folded her fingers over the kisses.

'I – I must go home.'

'If I may come with you.'

'I have said you might.'

He smiled at her.

'Caroline,' he said.

For three weeks they met daily with a secrecy that as- tounded Caroline to look back upon. She devised lengthy routes home from all her missions about the parish – Eleanor luckily detested visiting cottagers – and always found upon the return journey that beloved lounging figure in some hedgerow gap or gateway. Some days they would wander on while he taught her popular songs and she returned speeches from Shakespeare and pieces of favourite poetry. Johnnie Gates' knowledge of literature was minimal and he had never before encountered a human being who read entirely for pleasure. Some days, as May blossomed into June, and the summer grasses were lush and inviting, he would take off his coat and make a couch for her.

'There, my Caroline, a sofa fit for a queen. Lie there and chant to me.'

She would lie down, pillowing her head on an upflung arm, and gaze at the blue sky behind his head, and recite to him until he silenced her with kisses. She had never been kissed before, and the first time quite literally took her breath away. She had been coming home from some out-lying cottage when she had seen him racing and leaping towards her through the buttercup meadow that tilted away from her feet. She stood laughing as he came bounding and shouting on towards her, and then all of a sudden he was before her, his arms were about her and the summer day was quite blotted out. She pulled her mouth from his at last, quite gasping for excitement and lack of air.

'I am the first!' he shouted jubilantly, spinning her round him. 'The first! The first!'

Caroline cast herself into his arms to be kissed again.

It is impossible to keep any secret successfully in a small community like Stoke Abbas. At length the servants at the Parsonage, who were all too aware of Johnnie's reputation and Caroline's naïvety, deputed Patsy, who had served her master since his marriage, to inform Parson Harding of what was going on. The parson, with a secret leap of relief that Carrie was perhaps not wholly unattractive after all, received the news with due solemnity, and sent for his daughter.

'Well, my dear, and why have you not seen fit to inform me of this new acquaintance you have made?'

'I – I did not think to, Papa.'

'And why not? Is it of so little consequence to you that I need not know?'

'Oh no!' Caroline cried. 'It is of – of a great deal of consequence! To me,' she added in a lower tone.

'In that case, I must inform Lady Lennox. Unless, of course, Mr Gates has already done so.'

Caroline was sure he had not. She was, for the first time in a month, deeply apprehensive. What had seemed so free, so lovely, so possible, was about to be channelled by convention and authority into something dull and probably impossible.

'May I not see John – Mr Gates once more, before you speak to Lady Lennox?'

'My dear Carrie, I am aware that you are both young and inexperienced, but surely you see that your behaviour has been quite improper enough already without compounding it with a further indiscretion?'

Caroline looked unhappily out of the window. Johnnie would be waiting for her in that part of Stoke Wood which came right down to the river and was thus an excellent and romantic spot for lovers. Perhaps he would guess from her absence that there had been some mishap. She looked miserably at her father.

'He has promised me nothing, Papa, and I have offered nothing. There is nothing to tell Lady Lennox.'

'I must acquaint her with what has happened, Carrie. I am not chastising you, my dear. I am sure you have been no more than foolish. Now go and assist Eleanor and think of something else for the present.'

Caroline spent an anxious afternoon and night, made worse by the fact that Patsy had seen fit to inform Eleanor while the latter was in the dairy that morning.

'Indeed, Carrie, I am quite astonished at you. Such a little mouse of a thing as you to throw yourself at a man whom we all know – except Papa whose heart is truly of gold – to have the worst of reputations. Who has seen you, I wonder, Carrie, and what must the village think of you? No wonder your dresses are always in such a state and your hair so disordered. I hope you are deeply ashamed of yourself for your own weak folly, that has brought such shame upon the Parsonage.'

At last Caroline fled to her room and bolted the door. She

tossed herself on her bed and lay, without weeping, staring rigidly at the ceiling. She wished she could weep for tears must be such a release, but she was not a person to whom they came at all readily. So she lay, with clenched fists, and wide dry eyes, and listened to her hammering heart, and despaired.

The next day, to her terror, Parson Harding announced that she and he were to go down to Stoke Park.

'Oh, need I go, Papa? Can you not say to Lady Lennox how much I regret any distress I have caused her? Can you not beg her pardon for me? Oh, please, Papa, do not make me, do not compel me to go!'

'There is no question of staying behind, Carrie. You are central to this whole matter.'

She was too agitated to notice the smile that sat upon her father's lips. In the turmoil of her own thoughts, she did not even notice that he was humming as the carriage jolted its way downwards. She descended clumsily at the Park and entered the house behind her father with downcast eyes. She was conscious that there were three people in the drawing room and she waited wretchedly for Lady Lennox to speak in a tone of icy displeasure.

'My dear Harding,' Lord Lennox said with great heartiness, 'and Miss Caroline! Charming to see you both.'

'It is indeed,' Lady Lennox said warmly. 'Now come here, Caroline, and give me a kiss.' Utterly dumbfounded, Caroline laid her cheek against that of Lady Lennox. As she did so, she saw that the third person in the room was Johnnie Gates, and that he was smiling broadly. She drew away, quite mystified.

'Seat yourselves, my dear Parson, Miss Harding. Well now, this is all very pleasant. Ring for wine, Johnnie my boy, would you?'

When he had complied, Johnnie came back across the room and seated himself close to Caroline. She felt she should not look at him, but she could not help herself, and saw when she did so, that he was gazing at her quite openly with a mixture of understanding and encouragement.

'Will you speak to Caroline?'

'Certainly, Aunt. But I beg the privilege of doing it alone.

As she was the only one not present yesterday, it seems hardly fair to astonish her in public.'

'Astonish her!' Lord Lennox said, with hearty derision, 'I hardly think she will be astonished!'

Johnnie rose and held out his hand to Caroline.

'May I take Miss Harding to the rose garden, Aunt?'

'Indeed you may, but do not be long about it. Rose garden, forsooth! Would not the library be more comfortable?'

'Comfortable, yes, but hardly romantic. And after all,' he added, greatly daring, 'we are used to the open air.'

Outside, among the pink and creamy profusion of flowers, Caroline woke a little from her trance. The flowers were real enough, so was Johnnie's arm under her own, but she could scarcely credit what he was saying.

'I fear I have done this in a somewhat backhanded manner, Caroline, but I did it to make certain you would not refuse. I am to go to India in September as you know, and I had intended that my life there should be a bachelor one – '

He stopped, and took his arm from hers in order to place it round her waist.

'I do not want to be a bachelor any longer, Caroline. I never expected to feel what I have felt this summer, I never thought to meet a being who would bewitch me as you have done. I do not think I could live without you now, and I have some little hope that you would be unhappy without me.'

'I should, I should!' she cried fervently. 'I could not bear it!'

'We must bear it just a little while. I shall sail in early September, and find a house in Madras, and engage servants for – for us. And then, perhaps you will come to me and we may be married.' He paused and said in a low voice, 'If you will have me.'

She flung herself into his arms.

'Oh, yes, yes, Johnnie! Yes!'

He relaxed his serious air, and whooped exultantly, whirling her round him on the smooth green grass.

'Then I have nothing left to wish for!'

'Nor I,' she cried passionately.

He pulled her to him and kissed her roughly.

'Shall you not mind India? The heat? The snakes? The strangeness? Will you dare it all for me?'

'Yes, I will!'

'My Caroline.'

'I love you,' she said fervently, 'I love you.'

He walked her slowly back to the house and to a benign reception. The whole matter had been settled when Parson Harding called the previous day to inform Lady Lennox of the affair between his daughter and her nephew. Johnnie had been summoned and had professed with such open sincerity that his intentions were entirely honourable, that both Lady Lennox and Parson Harding had felt their indignation mellowing into approval. The only person who was not there to consult was Caroline, but Johnnie was accurately confident of her response. She drove back to the Parsonage that night the promised wife of Johnnie Gates.

He sailed at the beginning of September, with promises they should be together by the Christmas of the following year. Caroline saw him go with anguish, partly at the thought of at least sixteen months' separation, and partly out of fear at what might happen to him on that dreadful and dangerous voyage. It would be six slow months of tedium, discomfort, and frequent alarm. The prospect did not alarm Caroline for herself, as she expected to sail the following summer but she suffered vicariously for Johnnie.

He promised he would write from every port, and at first they came, letters from Lisbon, letters from Cape Town, gradually moving further east. As the ship sailed further away, the letters grew further apart, and their tone became less loving and more informative.

In March of 1768 Johnnie wrote to say he had reached Madras, but added nothing of his search for a house or entreaties for her to join him. This unsatisfactory epistle reached Caroline in September, and it was the last she was ever to receive. Lady Lennox immediately began to besiege the Directors of the East India Company in India House in Leadenhall Street and was, to her indignation, brushed aside. They knew nothing of such trivia concerning a mere clerk in the Company, and they cared less. Letters to Johnnie, from everyone except Caroline, throughout 1769 and 1770 brought no response at all, and eventually even the indefatigable Lady Lennox told Caroline what she already knew full well, that she must resign herself to remaining at Stoke Abbas, a spinster.

What Caroline endured alone in her small bedroom, no one knew, for she was stony in response to sympathy from anyone, even her father. The general assumption was, eventually, that she regarded the incident as over and done with, as everyone else was all too ready to do. And indeed it was true that after five years or so, although Caroline had not forgotten, the agonizing pain of heartbreak was over in its first raw savagery. She resigned herself to life as it must be for her, and never blamed Johnnie Gates for having shown her a brighter horizon for a while. He had been like a meteor across her heavens, had blazed a wonderful trail and had gone, leaving darkness. But the darkness was no blacker than before his coming, and Caroline was used to it. There was no doubt, however, that this evening, almost eight years after that parting, had brought a small glimmer back into the darkness. He was still alive, still in India, still, it seemed, a bachelor. She thought of the wild pony and the buttercup meadow, and with a little smile of remembered pleasure, she turned upon her side, and slept.

4

The month of December 1775 saw the arrival in Calcutta of two letters from Stoke Park, both addressed in the same firm hand and both asking for immediate response. The *Duchess of Grafton* was to sail again as speedily as she could be made ready and the writer begged she might not return without replies.

The letter addressed to Sir Edward Ashton found him soon after he had been respectfully awakened by a group of servants in his house near the Court House in Calcutta. It was not a fashionable house, being built of mud, not masonry as the new modern houses were, but the mud kept it cool, and its rooms were large with extensive views down to the Hooghly River. That December morning the Ashton servants were in a state of disarray and distress. Their equable, benevolent and ascetic master was in a mood so thunderous that they had leapt back from his bedside as quickly as if their politely folded brown hands had been scorched by touching him. In ten years of service, they had never known him to be so, and if he had chosen to confide in them, he would have informed them that in ten years he had never known himself so, and that was reason enough for bad temper. Sir Edward Ashton, scholar and statesman, one of the most respected members of the East India Company's Council in Calcutta, and a staunch supporter of the Governor General, had his first major hangover in a decade.

It was common enough for all his fellow Englishmen to get through seven different wines at dinner, followed by two or three bottles of claret apiece, quite apart from huge quantities of port, but Edward Ashton was the exception to the rule. He would drink but a glass or two throughout the length of those interminable and gargantuan meals, and was regarded with public amusement and private admiration by most of his contemporaries. He had no idea, searching his pounding brain, why he had indulged himself so insanely the night before, unless drink had seemed the only escape from the monumental boredom of the two pretty and witless girls either side of him at dinner. He was always given pretty girls at dinner, because his magnificent physique and air of distinction made mothers enormously optimistic about their daughters' chances of happiness with him. It was reasoned among the drawing rooms of Calcutta that a man of forty, prosperous, esteemed and solitary, must be sorely in want of a wife. Last night's hostess had exceeded herself in being able to produce two charming nieces who were under her protection for the winter and had watched in dismay while the decanter stopped constantly before Edward Ashton and he had regarded it alone with never a glance for poor Fanny or poor Sophia.

The truth was, in fact, that poor Fanny and poor Sophia were no more than the final straw in Sir Edward's burden of mounting contempt for Calcutta society in general. Indeed, if it had not been for his warm regard for, and much-needed support of, Warren Hastings, and his almost passionate fondness for India, he would have cut short his term of office years since and gone home to Herefordshire, however bleak an alternative that offered. As it was, he was only kept at a bare level of endurance in Calcutta because of an annual habit of setting forth to escape the European community in Bengal, and to find the alternative India. In this way there was hardly a Moghul palace or Hindu temple in Upper India, past or present, which had not had Sir Edward Ashton as guest or visitor. He had catalogued these edifices minutely, from the deserted red sandstone city of Fatehpur Sikri to the voluptuous carvings of the caves at Ajanta; the great forts of Agra and Delhi and Jaipur had all sheltered him at some point in the last decade. He had been one of the first European visitors invited to admire the new pink city of Jaipur, carved and fretted and painted the colour of peach sherbert. He had ridden elephants up the ancient rivers of the Jumna and the Ganges, camels across the desert wastes of Rajputana, and sailed at dawn across to the Lake Palace at Udaipur. After all these voyages, he had returned to Calcutta in elation with some measure of tolerance for the riotous and vulgar immorality of the city; but for two years now, pressure of work had kept him chained to a society which he could only endure with equanimity if allowed regular escape.

It was not that he was a priggish man, but rather that he felt that sin, like the classic definition of tragedy, only achieved greatness, and therefore any kind of distinction and interest, when committed by the great. Those people around him in Calcutta, those tawdry, scrambling little people, obsessed by their lust for gold and pleasure, seemed to him to fall as far short of greatness as was humanly possible. The stature of Warren Hastings as an administrator did, in some measure in Sir Edward's eyes, elevate his irregular cohabiting with a lady who was the estranged wife of Baron Imhoff, into sin of some consequence, but he was the sole example. For the rest, they aroused in Sir Edward nothing but scorn, and he retreated from them into the consolation of his studies in Persian and Arabic and his catalogues of Moghul architecture.

Persian and Arabic, however, could not shield him impregnably from the most determined of hostesses, nor from official obligation. Once or twice a week he must sally forth to witness just what he would have fled from and his ability to bear the onslaught of Calcutta society had been declining rapidly in the last year. He had sought refuge, first in silence, preferring his own thoughts to any conversation, but then, finding his muteness made him awkwardly conspicuous and a target for just the heavy rough-house he abhorred, he had discovered that to take a glass or two more than his customary small ration of wine gave him enough brief, false gaiety to participate sufficiently to escape notice. What had happened to that slenderly increased ration last night he could not recall, but clearly it had been no ration at all. The triviality and coarseness of the dinner party must have been in precise proportion to the quantity of wine he had recklessly swallowed.

Well, he thought savagely, surveying his bloodshot eyes and stubbled chin in the glass, he was paying dearly for his indulgence now. The headache and nausea and sense of utter dehydration were bad enough, but worse was his shame and humiliation. He could remember nothing after dinner, nothing at all. He was still in last night's shirt, a fact which repelled so fastidious a man, and which made him bellow furiously for the reason from the shaking clutch of servants in the corner.

They exchanged anxious glances, rolling their eyes, spreading their hands.

'Answer me!' Edward Ashton shouted. 'Why am I not in my nightshirt? Answer me, you dolts!'

Could this be the man on whom they relied so heavily for his steadiness and amiability, the man they had not thought of leaving for more glittering posts in the ten years they had served him? Could Sir sahib be sick? In the head, perhaps? Gocul, a little braver than the others, stepped out of the shivering band, shrugging his narrow shoulders apologetically.

'Sir sahib was so wild, we feared – '

'Wild?' Ashton said with incredulous emphasis.

Gocul waved his thin, muslin-clad arms and rolled his eyes.

'Wild, Sir Sahib, that we were fearing injury.'

Edward Ashton regarded him sombrely. Had he been brought home, then, shouting and singing and flailing his limbs like any green clerk or cadet? Had he been so violent that the servants had been unable to undress him? They had clearly tried, he noticed, since he was without breeches or stockings. He surveyed his bare feet gloomily.

'Sir sahib is sick?' Gocul ventured bravely.

The other servants crept nearer. They had known full well that Ashton had been drunk the night before, but they had expected, so great was their faith in him, to see him rise refreshed at seven according to his custom, like a phoenix from the ashes of his excess. He raised his head despite the lead weights that slithered about inside it and managed, painfully, the smallest and tightest of smiles.

'Only sick for a little while,' he said.

'We are rejoicing,' Gocul said fervently amid a breath of relief from the men around him.

Ashton ran a hand over his chin.

'Where is the barber?'

'He is waiting, Sir sahib. He is waiting since seven o'clock.'
'What time is it?'
'It is being ten, Sir sahib.'

'Ten!' Ashton bellowed, instantly wincing with the pain his own voice gave him. It was unthinkable. He was, despite the Calcutta custom of not being at one's desk until nine in the hot season or ten in the cool one, always at work by eight. And now it was ten, and he had, unthinkably, missed a breakfast to be given by the Governor General for two most distinguished French attorneys passing through Calcutta. His absence would be a source of astonishment since he was commonly so reliably punctilious. Well, there was nothing for it but to shave and dress and rescue as much of the day as it was in his power to do.

Shaving was soothing. Warned by Gocul, the barber attempted no conversation and wisely desisted from his usual morning practice of cleaning Ashton's ears. Ears, Gocul had pointed out, were not only sensitive but very close to what was, at the moment, an area of acute pain. Unable to refrain from all customary practices, however, the barber knelt reverently to clean and cut Ashton's nails and received a blow which sent him flying across the room.

'You did them but yesterday, you fool!'

'But they are growing,' the barber quavered from the corner where he had fallen, 'always, Sir sahib, they are growing!'

'Today, let them grow,' Ashton growled. A sweat of feverishness was beginning to mingle unpleasantly with the dampness of the skin that was customary in the wet heat of Calcutta. Noticing his master's beaded forehead, a servant with a fan came gingerly forward attempting to create a cool draught above that scowling brow.

'Go away!' Ashton shouted.

The man sprang back, caught the barber's table with his foot and overturned a silver bowl of soapy water and a clatter of razors upon the floor. Ashton put his head in his hands and groaned pitifully.

The door opened to admit Gocul bearing his master's dressing gown. Ashton was assisted into it and helped solicitously to a breakfast table in the adjoining room where tea and toast were laid out for him. He sat down weakly and surveyed the silver and china and white linen, but at the sight of the butter floating yellow and oily in a silver dish of water, he went greenish white and closed his eyes.

'Take it away.'

'All, Sir sahib?'

'All, everything, at once, far, far away.'

When he opened his eyes the table had gone, quite silently, and the hairdresser was standing anxiously across a space of carpet in the shadows. Sir Edward Ashton was a great disappointment to him always, because he refused to have his thick, strong hair powdered. The hairdresser had been trained by the most fashionable French coiffeur in Calcutta, and he felt it to be an insult to his professional skills that a man whom he could have coiffed so admirably would have no truck with powder, pomade or wigs. In vain he assured Sir Edward that in Versailles pomade was worn as thick as butter, and that if only he would wear three rows of side curls he would be able to sport one of those new and stylish French hats. On an ordinary morning, Sir Edward would merely laugh at these notions, and would then read absorbedly instead of indulging in the delightful gossip the hairdresser enjoyed so much. It was but the work of minutes to smooth that heavy chestnut hair back into its broad black bow, and it always left the hairdresser dissatisfied and unfulfilled. But this morning, he did not know if he even dared venture across the carpet. Sir Edward had no breakfast to distract him, no book even, and his expression made a typhoon seem a gentle thing by comparison. He looked about him desperately, licking his lips, and figdeting his brushes. To his unspeakable relief, the double doors beside him opened and Ralph Buxby, Ashton's secretary, entered with a lacquer tray of the morning's papers.

Ralph Buxby had enormous respect and affection for his superior and was genuinely distressed to see him in such discomfort of mind and body. He motioned to the hairdresser to proceed, as he knew that an immaculate appearance would be soothing at such a frayed moment. The hairdresser scuttled like a crab round the outer edges of the room and reached the haven of the back of Ashton's head with visible relief. Buxby crossed the stretch of carpet slowly, his face registering both sympathy and concern. In his self-disgust, Sir Edward Ashton wanted neither.

'I require no pity, Buxby. I deserve every twinge. What have we this morning?'

'Not a great deal, sir, apart from more trouble at the silk mills up at Kasimbazar, and a packet of letters from England.'

To many Englishmen in Calcutta, the second item of news would have been cause for great excitement. Every East Indiaman coming up the Hooghly brought with it the chance of news from England. Bur Sir Edward Ashton had few contacts left in England now beside his sister who was keeping Ashton Court ready for his retirement, and she was a dull correspondent. She wrote dutifully and regularly, but her letters were no more than long household accounts and details of ailments among the servants and the dairy herd that grazed the fat Herefordshire pastures. Her letters never made her brother homesick but rather made him forget the particular and enchanting atmosphere that was so much a part of Ashton Court. He looked dully at the lacquer tray.

'What trouble at Kasimbazar?'

'More inland trading, sir.'

It was well known that clerks of the Company supplemented their meagre salaries of a few hundred pounds a year by steady and profitable private trading on their own accounts. It was possible to make five-figure fortunes in five or ten years, and to go home a wealthy man. But occasionally the private trading inland got entirely out of hand, and began to conflict with the Company's own profits and then, of course, it had to be curbed. Ashton looked up painfully.

'What has gone missing, Buxby?'

'The *Sea Horse* put in a month ago with broadcloth and fire-arms enough to exchange for two shipments of silks. Both guns and woollens have unaccountably vanished, and the silks sent down to be loaded at Calcutta were diverted on the way and have been sold to the French. They are now two weeks on the way to Marseilles.'

'Why did I not hear of this before?'

Buxby hesitated.

'I told you of it yesterday, sir.'

There was an uncomfortable silence. During it, the hair-dresser finished a perfect job, and tiptoed away into the shadows. The hookah-burdar, waiting behind a screen, gestured to him to ask if he should go forward and slide the mouthpiece of the hookah's snake into Sir sahib's hand, as was the custom when his hair was dressed. The hairdresser, remembering the look on Sir sahib's face at the sight of breakfast, shook his head. The hookah-burdar nodded. He had spent the previous evening standing behind Sir Edward's chair, and understood better than any what ailed him this morning. He squatted down in the dimness behind the screen and resumed his endless, patient polishing of the hookah's silver chains and rosettes.

Ashton said, 'What letters from England?'

'Three, sir. Shall you read them?'

Ashton squinted at the covers and observed miserably that the writing on all three appeared to squirm nauseat-ingly across the paper.

'Read them to me, Buxby.'

With an ivory knife, Ralph carefully opened the first of the letters. It was from Ashton's London lawyer who, writing on behalf of the agent at Ashton Court, begged leave to restock the lake with carp and trout purchased with the profits from the sale of some veal calves. Ashton sighed irritably. It was precisely these minor decisions that he had hoped his sister and the agent would make between them without this tedious waste of time and money. It would mean a delay of a year in re-stocking the lake, and thus in fishing it again. His irritation mounted when the second letter proved to be from his sister with precisely the same question in it, in addition to the information that ten out of the thirty young oaks he had ordered planted had died and that her rheumatism was giving her no peace.

'Shall I open the third, sir?'

Ashton closed his eyes.

'Read it to yourself, Buxby, and repeat to me anything I might wish to hear.'

His head seemed almost worse with his eyes shut. He opened them again and noticed gratefully that the servants had placed the screens of dampened grass that usually stood across the doorways, across the windows, too. The glaring sunlight outside was reduced considerably by this means, and filtered faint and greenish into the cavernous room. He was sorry already to have shouted and bellowed at them this morning. He knew they were fond of him, and he knew too that they did not exploit him indecently. The servants' quarters contained far more human beings than the forty he employed – and forty was then a modest number – and he knew he provided for them all, but he was not prepared to complain without great provocation and that point had never been reached. He could see the hookah-burdar's foot protruding from behind the screen and guessed he had remained there out of diplomacy. Sir Edward smiled very faintly to himself, a smile that vanished abruptly, when Ralph Buxby cleared his throat loudly and sent an arrow of pain through Ashton's temple.

'I do not seem to understand this letter thoroughly, sir. It would appear it has some connection with Lord Lovell.'

'He is not coming back?' Ashton said in horror. He had never endured anything so stoically as those eternal months with Frank Lovell and his brainless, pleasure-loving energy.

'No, sir.' Buxby looked up and smiled at the relief on Ashton's face. 'No, far from it. It seems he is about to marry Miss Georgiana Lennox, daughter of Lord Lennox of Stoke Park in Dorset. This letter comes from her mother.'

'Her mother?'

'Yes, sir. Will you read the letter for yourself?'

'No – no, Buxby. Tell me what she says.'

'It appears that she has the incumbency of Stoke Abbas in her gift and it is presently held by a Parson Harding. He has a daughter, a Miss –' Ralph paused and searched the letter, while astonishment spread over Ashton's face, 'a Miss Caroline Harding, who was once promised to a certain John Gates –'

'What is this nonsense?' Ashton exploded. 'Who are these people? I have never heard of one of them in my life!'

'I am not quite done, sir.'

'Well, finish then, but quickly.'

'Sir, it seems that John Gates is in the Company's employ,

63

and is yet unmarried, and Lady Lennox wishes you to inform her if you think he would make a suitable husband for Miss Harding.'

His eyes blazing with incredulity, Sir Edward Ashton rose to his considerable height.

'Are you telling me, Buxby, that a perfectly strange woman in – in Dorset, is asking me as to the suitability of some trifling clerk for the hand of a – a parson's daughter of whom I have never heard?'

'It seems so, sir.'

'It is perfectly preposterous. She must be a madwoman. What is the world coming to if I must be subjected to lunatic requests about possible nuptials from complete strangers half a world away? I am speechless, quite, quite speechless.'

Ralph waited a moment and then said, 'What would you wish me to reply, sir?'

'Reply?' Ashton said, as if his secretary had suggested flying to the moon. 'You will reply nothing. You will put that paper to the only use fit for it, that of a taper.'

Ralph looked at the coat of arms at the head of the letter, and the strong purposeful handwriting, and felt that he must make one more effort.

'May I not merely acknowledge it, sir, and say you have no opinion on the subject?'

Ashton cast himself back into his chair. The lead weights were now quite untethered and were crashing about his skull most agonizingly. It was useless to contemplate constructive thought of any kind that day.

'Oh, do what you will, Buxby, do what you will. I do not care. Today, I do not care for anything.'

Ralph rose, and picked up the tray. Kasimbazar would obviously have to wait. He stood looking down at his superior, and saw that a thread or two of grey hair was appearing on that handsome head.

'Shall you rest until dinner, sir?'

'I want no dinner, Buxby. I want no supper. You will cancel whatever engagements I have, and no one is to come near me until seven tomorrow morning. If I am not recovered then, I shall throw myself into the river.'

Buxby thought of avowing that he would prevent that event at all costs, but decided this was no moment for protestations of loyalty.

'I shall see you are not disturbed, sir.'

He crossed the carpet again and turned in the doorway to look back. Sir Edward Ashton, in dressing gown and bare feet, looked for all the world like any other hungover Englishman in Calcutta, slumped in his chair, eyes closed, brows contracted. It was perhaps comforting, Ralph thought, to know such a paragon had some human failings, for there was normally precious little sign of any. He was charming to women, but appeared indifferent to almost all of them, he drank little, ate moderately, read interminably, and worked harder than almost any man in Calcutta. It was unprecedented that he should forget such a matter as Kasimbazar. Sighing, Ralph settled himself at his desk, and took out the letter from Lady Lennox. Unaccountable it might be, but it certainly provided light relief from the crushing load of official papers that littered his desk. He pulled out a sheet of paper, took up his quill, and sat for a moment gazing at the quiveringly hot prospect beyond his window.

Dear Lady Lennox,

Sir Edward Ashton begs me to thank you for your letter of June 16th, 1775. He instructs me to inform you that he knows of no objection to the proposed marriage between Miss Caroline Harding and Mr John Gates.

I remain your humble servant,
Ralph Buxby

He re-read it with satisfaction. It was a constructive letter, yet contained no absolute commitment. He folded it, addressed it, sealed it and then dropped it upon the brass tray whose contents were to be taken down to the *Duchess of Grafton* before she sailed.

Johnnie Gates was in high spirits. The profits from his share of the French deal were enough to cover all the gambling debts of the last six months which had amounted to the frightening total of twenty thousand pounds. It was a good thing the French appetite for silk was so insatiable. He had, for him, only a small headache that morning, he was to be permitted to stay in Calcutta for the remainder of the winter, and he had the prospect of an excellent dinner party ahead of him. Humming, he leant back in his chair while the dark curls that Caroline had admired so much were subdued beneath a wig that a friend had purchased for him at Boulogne when the *Sea Horse* had called there on her way east. Although he admired the effect of this splendid creation with its rows of side curls and high crest once it was on his head, there was no doubt it was confoundedly hot and his scalp frequently prickled maddeningly under its burden.

Tapping his teeth with the ivory mouthpiece of his hookah, Johnnie surveyed the room. It was a shocking mess, shocking, he must get the servants moving, indeed he must. He shouted arrogantly. The sircar appeared, wiping his hands on the greasy tatters of his gown. It was a mystery to Johnnie that a man who absorbed so much money could manage to be so down at heel and disreputable. They had endless sessions, the sircar and Johnnie, the one whining, the other shouting, and the sircar invariably winning. He was responsible for hiring all Johnnie's servants, claiming a necessity for fifty-one, and arranged all the daily household expenses of which Johnnie had no notion at all. Visits to the money-lender, who always seemed to be a cousin of the sircar's, were frequent and expensive. Things had been better when George Campbell had shared the house but George had gone home and Johnnie found it unaccountably difficult to find another bachelor willing to live with him.

He regarded the sircar with imperiousness. 'I want this room entirely cleaned and put in order by nightfall. Indeed, I want the whole house attended to and there will be no more slovenliness. There are enough of you to keep a palace in order, let alone one man and a house.'

The sircar, servile and ragged, shuffled his feet. Being merely a broker, he had no direct responsibility for running Sahib Gates' household, but on the other hand, as he had installed himself in Sahib Gates' servants' quarters without permission, he did not like to point out that he was no housekeeper. It might bring his parasite's position to Sahib

Gates' notice, and his profitable and comfortable way of life would be at an end.

'It is not being possible, sahib.'

'Not possible, damn you?' Johnnie roared. 'I do not care if it is impossible. It will be done, do you hear me, it will be done!'

The sircar shook his head.

'I cannot be doing it, sahib. You are not paying the servants, they are going away and there is nobody to be cleaning.'

Johnnie clutched the arms of his chair while his face reddened with fury.

'I have paid them, you odious, cringing toad! I gave you money for wages not a week ago! What have you done with it, what, tell me what or I'll wring your worthless neck!'

The sircar backed away a little.

'There were many, many needing the paying, sahib, that I could not be paying for the servants. I am paying for the dhobi, and I am paying for the money-lender and I am paying for – ' he stopped and gave a little yelp as a huge volume, its leather covers mouldy with damp, missed his head by inches.

'I would throttle you!' Johnnie yelled, 'but that it would foul my hands. Get out, get out or I will kick you out!'

The sircar, remembering a time when he had been quite literally booted from the verandah to fall ten feet to the shrubs below, hastily retired. The mornings were always the worst. By two, the sahib had gone to dine and thereafter the mellowing influence of wine caused him to forget household affairs. Most mornings, too, wracking headaches and nausea prevented the sahib from thinking of anything but his own misery and it was only the occasional morning, like this one, that he was in a fit state to be a trouble to the sircar. He went to his rattan bed in the servants' quarters and drew out a small metal trunk from beneath it. It was satisfyingly heavy. From around his neck, the sircar took a key and unlocked the box. The sight within was very gratifying, very gratifying indeed. That was a lot of gold for a man who had been born on a mud flat in the Ganges delta. In gratitude to the good Sahib Gates who had done this kind thing, he, the sircar, would see that his bedroom was put in order. Not cleaned, of course, as that would be most wasteful for such a generous but unobservant sahib, but things would be picked up from the floor, and perhaps, as a special gesture, the bed linen might be changed. That was indeed a special gesture, as a drunken man does not notice his bed linen, but this month had been an especially profitable month for the sircar, and Johnnie should have a clean pillowcase for his generosity. The sircar went to the door of his hut and shouted for his sons and nephews.

In the house, Johnnie sat and fumed. The man was no more than a robber, a daylight robber. He looked angrily about at the dust and the dirty linen and his disordered bed. Every chair was heaped with clothing, none of it clean, and a heavy, unsavoury smell filled the hot, damp air. It was monstrous, Johnnie declared to himself in a wave of self-pity, monstrous that a man brought up as he had been should be condemned to live like this, deceived at every turn, uncared for and miserable. His mood of optimism had quite gone, ruined by that cringing toad.

With a final tweak and pull, the wig-barber stepped back, and Johnnie could not help a wave of gratification at the sight of himself in the glass. It was a pity he had put on weight so, but then, he had the height to carry it and he saw no diminishing of the handsomeness of those features he had gazed on so fondly for thirty years. He slipped into the heavy brocade coat held out for him, woven with a brilliant and complicated pattern of flowers, and consoled himself that so dazzling was his coat that the imperfect whiteness of his breeches would not signify. He was handed his snuff box, handkerchief and cane. A heavy signet ring was offered to him on a tray. It never struck him that the same ring was offered every day because all the others he had brought with him in a heavy morocco box had mysteriously vanished. Thus arrayed, he left the squalor of his bedroom, and proceeded on horseback across Calcutta to his desk.

He arrived, behind the customary procession of servants, at eleven. His office had been busy for a good hour by then, and he took care not to swagger to his desk too ostentatiously. The twenty-minute ride in the blazing sun had done his head no good at all and he would have given a good deal for a bumper of claret. Breakfast had been inedible that morning as the bread was mouldy and the butter rancid, but at that hour he had been cheerful enough to overlook both. Now his stomach growled, and his head throbbed and his eyes felt gritty at the edges.

Nodding cheerfully to fellow clerks, for his main aim in life was the maintenance of appearances, he arrived at his desk and the disorder it bore. Other clerks around him discarded their gaudy coats for quill pushing, and worked in plain shirts and sleeved waistcoats, and starched white caps in place of their cumbrous wigs, but Johnnie disdained such practicality. When he had arrived in Madras almost eight years before, he had come with a magnificent wardrobe purchased at all the French ports his ship had put into. He had stepped from the masulah boat onto Indian soil resplendent in velvet and lace, strikingly handsome and debonair, and had been immediately christened 'Beau Gates'. It was the high spot of his popularity, and he was never aware that admiration for his wardrobe had dwindled as his taste and self-indulgences became more excessive. So he sat down at his desk in his stiffened and heavily cuffed coat, and prepared to attempt the task of writing, severely impeded by his ruffles and ring.

In the midst of all the thumbed and tattered papers that had lain gathering dust this last month, lay an unfamiliar item. It was a letter with an English stamp, addressed in a hand that was uncomfortably familiar. Johnnie stared down at the cream-coloured square, and from that bold black hand rose images of England, green pictures of horses and rain and hedged fields. He touched the letter nervously. He had thought and hoped she had given him up, but he should have known Lady Lennox better. What could she find to say to him now? Was Lord Lennox dying? Johnnie, already sweating profusely beneath his wig and brocade, broke out into a fresh cold sweat of anxiety. He looked about him. Everyone seemed deeply absorbed, the only sound the swish of fans held by servant boys, and the buzzing of flies. Johnnie ripped the letter open.

His eye ran quickly and nervously down the page. She

had crossed the letter, a sure sign she did not think him worthy of a second sheet of precious paper. He read it several times with slowly dawning comprehension and then replaced it with a shaking hand on his muddled desk. He felt sick, very sick indeed. The letter was a threat and a most unpleasant one. It amounted to the fact that if Johnnie did not marry, the money that he was entirely relying upon for his return to England, since he was too wasteful to make enough for his retirement in India, would go to his cousins. He was not at all sure that Lady Lennox could prevent his receiving the money, but presumably she had discovered some legal loophole and that was what had prompted her to write to him in this blackmailing manner after a silence of six years. After all, if she could not stop him receiving the money, why should she bother to write at all? He sat and shook, and concluded exactly what Lady Lennox had intended him to conclude.

After a long and sickening time, Johnnie picked the letter up again by the extreme edges as if it might bite him. One fact had now sunk in, the fact that he must either marry, or lose the money upon which his whole future depended. But there had been something else which his panicking brain had skimmed over at first reading. He looked at the letter again, and saw with renewed shock that Lady Lennox was not only dictating his marriage, she was dictating whom he should marry.

'I am sure you have not forgotten Caroline Harding,' wrote Lady Lennox, 'and as she still lives at the Parsonage it is evident that she has not forgotten you.'

Johnnie put the letter down again, and closed his eyes. How Lady Lennox could manage to affect him so powerfully and distressingly from thousands of miles away he did not know, but there was no doubt that she was successful. If she could have seen him as he sat at his desk, shaken and entirely unmanned, she would have been highly gratified at the strength of her own influence. Luckily, Johnnie thought grimly, she could not see him and thus he could give way to all the upset and resentment that he so strongly felt. The more he thought about it, the more injured he felt. He was trapped and he felt it deeply unjust that he should be trapped. He had to comply if he was to have any comfort to look forward to, and he could not conceive of a life without comfort. The whole situation was intolerable, quite intolerable, and yet he had no choice, given his tastes, but to tolerate it.

He stared unseeingly at the confusion of papers in front of him. He, Johnnie Gates, Beau Gates, renowned in Madras and Calcutta for his dash and courage and gallantry, was to be condemned to marry Caroline Harding. He felt no particular fury against Caroline herself, indeed she had provided the substance of a very delicate and pastoral interlude in his life all those years ago, and he thought of her, on the rare occasions he thought of his English past, with a sort of pleasant sentimentality. He had been mildly sorry to let her down, but then he had been so cornered by his aunt and uncle and old man Harding that he really had had no choice but to profess honourable intentions of marriage. And she had been so sweet, and so very besotted that the notion of marrying her had briefly seemed a pretty thing. But of course he had never meant it, and he was sure that she would never blame him. She was not that sort of girl. Those mild, gentle, shy girls never blamed a fellow, they always supposed the fault their own and that was an aspect that made them such endearing companions. Endearing for a little while, that is, for no full-blooded man could want such milk and water stuff for his permanent diet.

Unfortunately, milk and water seemed about to form a major part of his future nourishment. Lady Lennox was a scheming old witch and would have no trouble in bending Caroline to her will. Caroline would arrive in Calcutta and be too frightened to speak and Johnnie's social life would dwindle to nothing, and he would die, within months, of boredom. A lump of profound self-pity rose in Johnnie's throat for the second time that morning and tears of sheer compassion at the intense pathos of his own situation began to prickle at the edges of his eyes. He looked miserably about him, and surveyed his fellow factors with an envy so violent they must almost have felt it burning through the brocade of their waistcoats. They were free, free as birds to live their lives as they chose, and he, Johnnie, was to be

71

shackled as a convict upon a prison ship. There was no justice in the world, indeed there was not.

Across the room George Carew, a man who shared Johnnie's idea of pleasures to a large extent, had watched his companion with amused fascination for a good hour. He always enjoyed Johnnie's entrance in any case, with its peculiar mixture of swashbuckle and furtive anxiety about constant unpunctuality. But this morning had been a rare treat, beginning with the spectacle of that astounding wig (of which George Carew was a little envious) and then watching such a performance of writhing and blanching that the theatre at its most dramatic would seem tame by comparison. After an hour however, the entertainment seemed to become more static and George perceived that Johnnie had now sat slumped and glum without stirring for at least ten minutes. Adjusting his cap on his glossy dark head, George was about to stroll casually in Johnnie's direction well armed with witticisms, when Johnnie started up and cast such a glance of anguish round the room, that George was halted in the very act of rising from his chair. The poor old boy was clearly in a bad way. Subduing his facetiousness, George straightened, squared his shoulders, and began to pick his way among the servants crouched reverently about their masters' desks.

'Run out of luck, Johnnie boy?'

Johnnie raised a ravaged face.

'Clean out.'

George cast himself into the chair that had been instantly and silently provided.

'What's up?'

Self-pity had quite obliterated any discretion Johnnie might have had.

'I'm done for, George, quite done for.'

'No, you ain't. You won enough last night at whist to keep a king going for a week, not to mention the French fiddle.'

'It – it is something quite other.'

George Carew never beat about the bush.

'Poxed again, Johnnie boy?'

Johnnie shook his head miserably.

72

'No, no – I believe I'd almost welcome that. No, it is very much worse.'

George gave a yelp of laughter. If a man was clean and had a full pocket he could not imagine that anything else could ail him.

'There ain't nothing bad left!'

'Oh, you are wrong, George, so wrong. I am done for, quite finished.'

'Spit it out, then!'

Johnnie leant forward, his eyes fixed intently upon George Carew. In tones of the deepest melancholy he said, 'I am to be married.'

The grin left George's face abruptly. In quite an altered tone he said, 'Married?'

'Married. I'm not to come into my family money if I don't marry whom I'm told.'

'To hell with family money!' George shouted. 'You don't need it! You're making your fortune out here!'

Johnnie looked at him without speaking, and in the silence that followed they both reviewed Johnnie's way of life, and saw what a struggle a fortune would have, to emerge from that extravagant circus.

In a much quieter tone, George said, 'Who is the bride?'

'Oh, a dear little quiet, shy creature,' Johnnie said scornfully. 'Wouldn't say boo to a goose.'

'Well looking?'

'N-no,' Johnnie said reluctantly, 'but quite a – a something – some sort of – '

'Pity. Docile?'

'Oh, very.'

George stretched his legs out, using a conveniently kneeling Indian as a footstool.

'Then you'll have no trouble.'

'Trouble?'

'About Rani.'

Rani! In all the turmoil of the morning, Johnnie had quite forgotten her. Rani! Reputed to be the most accomplished and sophisticated courtesan in all Calcutta and for the past two enthralling months his faithful mistress. How could he have forgotten her? Indeed, she had started last night in his bed, and where the deuce she had got to, he did not know. She was always doing that, vanishing and then reappearing at just the precise moment he wanted her. The possibility he might have to give her up was a fresh blow to his battered mind.

'God, George, will I have to give her up?'

'No, Johnnie boy, no, no, don't be absurd. You'd be mad to give her up. What I meant was that if your wife is a biddable, meek sort of creature, you can still do what you like, just as you always have, Rani included.'

It was the first ray of hope that had pierced the dreadful gloom of the morning. Johnnie seized upon it with desperate fervour.

'Do you think so, George? Do you know any fellows who have wives and can still please themselves? Do you really think it possible, George?'

'Certainly I do! She'll be as scared as a rabbit to be in India anyway, and you must see that you are master from the moment she steps on shore. You must begin as you mean to go on.'

Johnnie sat back in his chair and pondered a little. Small memories of Caroline were filtering back, the chief among them being those examples of her enormous desire to please him, to do just what he wanted. In his mind's eye he saw her standing before him when he had lifted her off the pony and saw again the strange light of glory in her curious eyes because she had done as he told her and was overjoyed to have pleased him. Perhaps, if he had to have a wife at all, Caroline Harding might not make such a bad one. She would never squeal, she would just endure. He looked at George gratefully.

'I think I might set her up right.'

George rose and clapped Johnnie on the shoulder.

'That's my Johnnie boy. You'll be as free as a panther and you'll get that pigsty of a house put in order for you to boot.'

It was yet another ray of sunshine. No more squalid and exhausting bellowings at the servants, no more inedible food and unwashed clothes, but instead someone to care for him and hold his head and shield him from the sordid everyday matters of living. The whole project seemed to be taking on quite another aspect and it appeared that he, Johnnie Gates, *bon viveur* and seducer of other people's wives, was going to be able, as usual, to have his cake and eat it.

He stood up and stretched, feeling his unpleasantly damp clothes peeling away from his skin as he did so.

'Where are you dining, George?'

'General Russell.'

'Shall we go together? I'm in no mood to work, and in any case it's too late to start now. Come home with me and help me to write my death sentence to England and we'll go on together.'

'I've a shocking thirst, Johnnie boy,' George said, linking his arm through the other's.

'We'll celebrate!' Johnnie cried. 'Come home and drink a toast to Johnnie Gates, husband and bachelor!'

5

The autumn and winter of 1775 passed with customary quietness at Stoke Abbas. All the issues raised so enticingly at the dinner party at Stoke Park appeared to have died a quiet and natural death as anything of interest always seemed to do in that remote and uneventful society. Caroline spent several weeks reliving her past in moments of solitude, then saw there was as usual to be no sequel to that brief glimpse of adventure, and banished Johnnie Gates from her reveries. Lady Lennox naturally said nothing to her of any schemes, and very soon the arrangements for Georgiana's wedding took precedence over any other consideration in all the minds at Stoke Park.

Unable to bear Eleanor's scoldings and goadings, and ever more conscious of her own futility, Caroline took to spending as much time as she possibly could away from the Parsonage. She made herself a regular circuit among the cottages and the inhabitants of Stoke Abbas became used to seeing her steady appearance, and in many cases began actually to look forward to it. Out of her slender means she bought expensive oranges which she would take to the malnourished cottagers, as well as chickens and broths begged from the Parsonage kitchens where she was a favourite and had staunch supporters. As the winter wore on, and the villagers saw that no weather seemed to daunt her faithful visiting, she began to gain a reputation equal to that of the local doctor.

Then, in March of 1776, she had a triumph. The cottage children she visited suffered very commonly from rickets and grew up with a deformity of limb that distressed Caroline acutely although the sufferers seemed quite cheerful about it. Caroline, who read voraciously upon any topic she could find, came across a pamphlet containing the novel suggestion from a London surgeon that a diet rich in calcium, most easily found in milk, might prove beneficial in counteracting the effects of rickets. It was a theory that appealed to Caroline for it caused no pain to the patient as many medical treatments did in the eighteenth century, and the milk was cheap and plentiful and readily available to the poor.

Among Caroline's regular dependants was a family whose steady courage in the face of poverty had always gained them a special place in her heart. Samuel Hedges had lost a leg in a man trap while pursuing poachers on the Stoke Park estate, and thus could now only do a limited range of work for Lord Lennox. Lord Lennox paid him the small wage he earned, but failed to take account of his disability, the circumstances in which he had been disabled, or his growing family. The family increased and the small wage did not. The youngest child, now two, had rickets acutely. The local apothecary had visited the family out of pure charity because he liked Sam Hedges, and had prescribed the customary treatment for rickets, that the child should be daily anointed with a scalding hot ointment, then have his limbs strapped to splints and that he should never leave his crib until the treatment was done.

One wild morning in March soon after the apothecary's visit, Caroline came battling across the windswept park with a basket of soup and fruit for the Hedges. Even before she reached the cottage she could hear the most blood-curdling and terrible screams, the screams of some small thing in appalling pain. Alarmed that some evil had befallen the family, she picked up her skirts and ran as fast as she could against the buffets of wind to the cottage door. When she flung the door open, the sight that met her eyes horrified her more than the spectacle of any brutal attack might have done.

The littlest boy, dressed only in filthy rags, was being held forcibly by his brothers and sisters across his mother's knee. She appeared, with tears streaming down her face, to be smearing some greenish paste from a smoking pot onto his little crooked legs, already raw with the most terrible ragged blisters. The child was screaming with panic and pain, his

77

face distorted with suffering, and all the children round him were almost in the same state. On the floor lay four splints of wood and coils of filthy greenish-stained bandages.

Caroline sprang forward to the group.

'Mary, Mary, stop it at once, what are you doing? Stop it, Mary, you are crucifying him!'

Mary Hedges could scarcely speak for tears.

'I know it, miss, I know it. But Mr Pears says I mun do it. I mun do it to save 'is legs. It do kill me to do it, miss, but he says I mun.'

'Nonsense!' Caroline said briskly. 'Absolute nonsense. And why is he so filthy dirty? You should be ashamed, Mary, you are always so particular. Why is he so dirty?'

'Mr Pears says I'm not to change 'im till 'tis done. 'E's only allowed from 'is crib for the treatment. 'E mun lie in 'is filth, miss, Mr Pears said so.'

Caroline glanced at the crib, and looked hastily away.

'Will you trust me, Mary? I have a notion that will get him better quicker than Mr Pears' remedy and will give him no pain at all.'

'Oh yes, miss,' poor Mary said, thankfully. 'I'll do anythin', miss, anythin' so's not to 'urt 'im more.'

'Very well.' Caroline looked round the poor, bare room and knew that there was not a morsel there to spare of anything. Commanding the boys to turn their backs, she lifted her skirt and slipped off her white cotton petticoat.

'Take off those disgusting rags, Mary,' she said, 'and we'll wash him, and wrap him in this.'

The baby's howls had subsided now to a whimper. He lay clinging to his mother, great eyes full of fear beneath his dirty, tousled hair. Caroline could hardly bear to look at the devastation of his legs or to see the shudderings of his little body under the remains of his shirt. She beckoned to the biggest boy.

'Take all that bedding and his nightshirt, and those splints and that evil green mess, and make a bonfire of everything.'

'Yes'm.'

'Oh, no, Miss Car'line!' Mary cried, 'I've no more linen for 'im! I'll wash it best I can, but don't burn it, miss, please don't burn it!'

Caroline knelt down by her side and took one of the baby's filthy little hands in hers.

'I shall get you new linen,' she said gently. 'I shall send your Jane up to the Parsonage, and she shall ask in the kitchen for some old sheets we do not use, and for two little shirts I made for Tom Thwaites' boy, but he is not ill and so must do without. And I shall give your Meg money and she must go to the Park Farm and bring a quart of fresh milk.'

'Milk, Miss Car'line?'

Caroline smiled at the little boy.

'He must drink as much milk as he can. That will be his only medicine. And you must keep him clean and let him have plenty of air on those poor little legs.'

'I can wash 'im, miss, I'll wash 'im every minute if 'twill 'elp 'im, but we can't buy 'im milk, miss, you know we can't.'

'Don't worry about the milk, Mary. Just send one of the children to the farm and you will be given two quarts a day. Try and get him to drink all he can, and the others may finish what he cannot.'

Mere weeks later, the smallest Hedges was unrecognizably better. His legs were fast healing and though they would never be straight, their crookedness would never be worse. He had pink cheeks and clear eyes and Sam and Mary Hedges knew not how to thank Caroline.

She shook her head at them. 'I want no thanks. It is enough to see him so recovered.'

She wished she were brave enough to ask Lord Lennox to recompense Sam Hedges better for his long and steady hours of labour, but the confidence and ease she felt among the cottagers deserted her entirely among people of her own or a higher class. She knew she was cowardly, and she tried to still the voice of self-scorn within her by purchasing nourishing foods and making warm clothes for the needy. In some measure she succeeded and the recovery of little Abraham Hedges gave a distinct glow of achievement to her normally unconfident thoughts. She told nobody of her success, and meant no one to know, but she had not accounted for the Hedges's admiration and gratitude.

Six weeks after that first visit to their cottage, she met Pears the apothecary on the field path behind the Parsonage.

He had been attending a sick maid, and Caroline **was** returning for dinner. She saw him approach with some apprehension, fearing he would feel professionally insulted by her interference over little Abraham, and was astonished and relieved to notice the warmth of his expression as he came nearer.

'I am glad to see you, Miss Harding, very glad. I began to think you were eluding me deliberately.'

'Oh, no,' Caroline said untruthfully.

George Pears had not the social standing of Dr Thornton in the district, but he was an educated and perceptive man, and very little about Caroline Harding had escaped his notice.

'No, Miss Harding? Do you mean to tell me also that the rise in milk consumption among the cottagers in Stoke Abbas and the marked improvement in the ricketty children have no relation either to each other or to yourself?'

Caroline coloured slightly.

'I was afraid to offend you, Mr Pears.'

'Do you think I am so mean-spirited as to be offended by such sensible and effective help as you have offered? No, indeed, Miss Harding. You have been of more unobtrusive benefit to this village than it will ever realize. I have merely wished to see you to praise and thank you.'

Caroline's colour deepened.

'It—it was nothing—simply, only—only something I read—'

'And that I should have read and that I have indicated to Dr Thornton that he should read. He has been profoundly impressed by your actions, Miss Harding.'

Immense gratification and panic at the thought of such public notice battled visibly across Caroline's countenance.

'You are most kind – but Dr Thornton! He will think me unpardonably interfering!'

'He thinks nothing of the sort, my dear Miss Harding. You forget we are professional philanthropists, we medical men, and the improvement of human health is to be wished for at all costs and must override all petty personal considerations.'

Despite the splendour of this assertion, Caroline still looked doubtful.

'You have been more than kind, Mr Pears, more than generous. I meant no one to know because – ' she stopped, realizing that the chief enemy of her visits about the village was Eleanor, and that as a sister, even Eleanor deserved some loyalty.

'It is too late,' the apothecary said, triumphantly. 'Dr Thornton was appraised two nights ago and is full of eagerness to congratulate your father on his admirable daughter. I must bid you good day, Miss Harding, with the wish that your good endeavours may prosper.'

'Good day, Mr Pears.'

As she walked on homewards, even the fear of public attention subsided under the glowing realization of how sweet the apothecary's praise had been. He had not criticized her or patronized her but had spoken with frank admiration and gratitude to her, and had told her, actually told her in so many words, that there were people in the world who were the better for her existence. It was a dizzying thought. It meant not only that she had achieved something of her own, something attributable to nobody but herself, but also that she, as a person, mattered to some others. To the villagers, to George Pears, perhaps, oh shaking thought, even to Dr Thornton, she was a person of a little consequence. She was no longer simply Parson Harding's second plain unmarried daughter, but Caroline Harding who had helped a village's children most materially.

She leant on the garden gate and surveyed the vegetable plot, and observed that each little springing row of green seemed to have a new brightness, a new significance. The April sky seemed to be blue with a new delicacy, the air fresher than before, the day, the world, more full of promise. Caroline looked down at the grey stuff of her gown and felt its ugliness, for Eleanor had given it to her as a birthday present, to be immaterial. Her hands were shaking a little and she felt a sort of exhilaration that knows not hunger nor thirst nor weariness nor any bodily claim.

'I shall never forget this moment, never, never.'

'Miss Car'line?'

She spun round. Patsy was standing by her, twisting her apron in her hands.

'Beg pardon, Miss Car'line, but Miss El'nor says will you come in to dinner?'

Eleanor was sitting looking especially majestic and injured on her father's right. Parson Harding looked up and remarked inwardly how different Carrie looked, quite elated, almost approaching being a little handsome. Her eyes were gleaming like beacons and there was faint colour along her cheekbones.

'A good walk, Carrie?'

'Oh, wonderful!' Caroline said with more emphasis than any familiar walk could deserve. 'Quite wonderful.'

Eleanor sniffed.

'Which way did you go, my dear?'

It was always possible to be truthful about her routes, even if the omission of the visits to cottages almost constituted a lie.

'Down by the river, Papa. The air is like wine and everything is bursting out so new and bright and clean, it is quite a miracle to see.'

Eleanor sniffed again.

'Perhaps I should ride down there,' their father answered. 'I have not been near the river in months. Rivers are somehow most melancholy in winter.'

'Oh, Papa, today it was not melancholy! It was joyful, running over the stones in the sun, so clear and brilliant. It would do you such good to be away from the house!'

Eleanor spoke with awful emphasis. 'There are those whose duty and lot it is to stay within the house.'

'But that does not apply to Papa!' Caroline cried, thinking how appetizing the mutton looked and how unused she was to feeling so delightfully hungry.

'It is not Papa to whom I refer.'

A chill silence fell on the table. Caroline was astonished to find she felt none of the usual dread at the onset of one of Eleanor's outbursts. She said, as casually as she could, 'I imagine you refer to me.'

'I do.'

'Now, now, my dear Eleanor, let us have no unpleasantness. It is such a delightful day, and surely it is a harmless enough thing if Carrie has enjoyed her walk.'

'No, Papa, it is not harmless. It does a great deal of harm, and all to me: I must bear the whole burden of running the house and looking after you and Robert and the boys, because Carrie is too selfish and empty-headed to assist me in the smallest way.'

'That is wholly untrue,' said the new brave Caroline.

Eleanor's eyes flashed. 'It is absolute truth, Carrie. You use me as some manner of housekeeper, so that you may spend your days idling about the countryside and painting pictures. I work myself to exhaustion for you for not one word, or look even, of gratitude or – '

'Stop,' said Caroline. She put down her knife and fork, and stood up.

'I am very sorry to spoil dinner, but I am not sorry for what I am about to say. I am of no use in the house, Eleanor, because you absolutely will not allow me to be. I am permitted no duties, no responsibilities, I am not even allowed to arrange the flowers any longer. I am accused of being incompetent at everything, fit for nothing and best out of the way. So I have kept out of the way because I cannot bear the scolding and I cannot bear to be inactive. If you are short of assistance Eleanor, you have no one to blame on earth but yourself.'

She came quickly round to the head of the table, kissed her bewildered father, gave a brief but encouraging smile to Robert and left the room. When the door had closed, Eleanor began to cry. Parson Harding and Robert looked down at their half-eaten plates, decided the final half had lost its savour, and followed Caroline stealthily from the room. Under cover of Eleanor's outraged sobs, Parson Harding said quietly to his son, 'If anyone should want me, I shall be in my study until supper.'

From his study window, he witnessed the astonishing spectacle of seeing his daughter, Caroline, almost dancing down the steep road to the village. Her step was so light, so elastic that it could hardly be called walking, and her grey dress, whose solid fabric and outline her father deplored, swayed about her as if it were made of gossamer. What had come over Carrie? Was it possible that a pretty, though ordinary, April day could have this joyful effect on anyone, particularly one of Carrie's grave temperament?

Parson Harding shook his head in puzzlement and sat down before the fire. It had rejoiced his heart to see her come in for dinner looking so illuminated, and it had discouraged him very much to have Eleanor's inevitable outburst act like a snuffer upon a candle flame. He was too tired to battle with Eleanor, whose energy in matters of her own emotions was inexhaustible. It was a pity the girls could not love each other, a pity they could not live in harmony. He regretted that Caroline no longer did the flowers for she had arranged them so beautifully, always putting sweet scented ones in the study, and Eleanor arranged them as if dragooning soldiers. All the bowls of pot-pourri had gone too, he reflected sadly, and the lavender bags he liked among his linen. Caroline had seen to those little touches. It was a pity, indeed it was. His head fell, with gentle regretfulness, onto his chest, and he slept.

Caroline spent the afternoon tiring herself out. She walked as far and as high as she could in the spring wind, and felt always driven on by a strange and wonderful sense of ease and power. She felt keenly observant of everything she saw, and deeply appreciative of it, and when she approached the Parsonage in the beginnings of dusk, she found her feet were indeed weary, but her heart and mind felt as buoyant as ever.

There was a strange cloak in the hall. Evidently her father had a caller. She went into the parlour, still cloaked herself, to make her peace with Eleanor who always spent the early evening there doing her accounts or mending church vestments. She was sitting, as usual, some distance from the fire, as if she would not allow herself the pleasure of being really warm.

'Eleanor?'

There was no reply. By the light of a tallow candle which she insisted on using for reasons of economy despite an ample supply of wax, Eleanor was writing minutely in her account book. Caroline had read it secretly once and could not believe such details were worth recording.

'Eleanor. I am come to apologize for distressing you.'

There was a sniff, but no word. Caroline laid her cloak on a chair and went to kneel before the fire.

'It is never my intention to distress you, Eleanor. I am all too aware that my cast of character is a great irritation to you, and that is why I try not to be before you too often.'

A page was turned behind her. After another pause, Eleanor said, 'Will you retract those evil things you said at dinner?'

'No,' said Caroline calmly. 'But I will modify them. I said them in the heat of the moment, and I meant them, but I can rephrase them to sound less fierce, if you like.'

Eleanor began to weep again.

'No one understands the burden I bear. You least of all people, Carrie. You have no heart, no heart at all.'

Caroline rose from the hearth and came to kneel by her sister.

'Why will you not let me help you a little? Why should you suppose I like to see you so tired? May I not assist you in some things?'

Eleanor surveyed her over her handkerchief doubtfully.

'You are woefully undomesticated, Carrie.'

'No, I am not. Try me, why not try me – '

The door opened at the same moment as it was briefly knocked upon. Eleanor frowned at the servant.

'Th' parson wants Miss Car'line.'

'Are you sure?'

'Quite sure, Miss El'nor. Miss Car'line's wanted in the study.'

'I am coming directly, Patsy.'

The door closed and Caroline rose to her feet. Self-pity was beginning to suffuse Eleanor's features again.

'What can he want with you, Carrie?'

'I will go and see.'

Caroline put her hand on her sister's bony shoulder and pressed it, and wished she felt the smallest inclination to kiss her. Outside the door, Patsy was waiting with a candle, and escorted Caroline across the dusky hall. Caroline tapped on the study door. At her father's 'Come!' she opened it, and saw that on the hearth, his face illumined by six flames in a great candelabra, was the imposing figure of Dr Thornton.

'Come in, my dear, come in, don't hesitate so.'

'We only came in here for punishment as children.'

Caroline said, 'and obviously that thought still lingers with me.'

Dr Thornton laughed genially.

'I am delighted to see you, Miss Harding. Your father and I have had a most delightful half-hour in contemplation of your success, but I would not leave until I had been able to congratulate you in person.'

Caroline came forward and seated herself by her father.

'Papa, I am having a most astonishing day. I met Mr Pears on my way home this morning, who said wonderfully kind and pleasant things to me, and now . . .' She stopped and looked down.

Her father took her hand.

'I am both very proud and very delighted, my dear. It does relieve my mind a little to know that all your long absences from home were not spent merely strolling the countryside, but I am delighted that your time has been put to such constructive purpose.'

'Admirable,' Dr Thornton said. 'Wholly admirable.'

Caroline found she could not raise her head. This morning's praise had quite sufficed and Dr Thornton's large impressive presence was superfluous.

'I did not want – I did not mean it to be known,' she said in a low voice.

'But my dear lady, it is known,' Thornton cried. 'I called at Stoke Park this afternoon to ensure that Lord Lennox's gout had not reappeared, and had the pleasure of informing both Lord and Lady Lennox what a remarkable daughter our Parson has.'

Caroline felt quite confused. Dr Thornton meant only kindness, but his excellent linen and air of health and great watch and seals only made her feel all her usual awkwardness. She had felt none of that in front of George Pears in his shabby coat that morning.

'Will you thank Dr Thornton for his great kindness?' Parson Harding said gently to her as if chiding a child.

'I do,' said Caroline to her lap, 'I do thank him – very much, but I – I did not do it – do anything for – for . . .' She stopped and rose quickly from the sofa. 'Will you excuse me,' she said, and was gone.

Both men surveyed the door fondly when she had closed it, the parson because he was genuinely proud of her, Dr Thornton because he felt a large man's protective fondness for feminine modesty.

'She does not mean to be ungracious, my dear Thornton. She is a very humble girl, very humble. She has never found it easy to be praised.'

'She seemed quite composed when she entered.'

'Ah yes, but that was before you praised her.'

'Admirable,' Dr Thornton said again with emphasis.

An uneasy truce reigned for some weeks between Caroline and Eleanor. Eleanor was mortified at Caroline's public acclaim, but forced, if not to submit to a position of utter ignominy herself, to show at least a small pleasure in her sister's success. She suggested on several occasions that the milk remedy had been pure accident, thus implying Caroline's achievement was no more than a mere stroke of fortune, but met only with rebuffs on all sides. It transpired also that rickets was not only confined to the poor cottagers round about, but prevailed occasionally in the more prosperous houses, and Caroline's name was thus often in mouths whose owners would not have countenanced her at all under any other circumstances. Both George Pears and Dr Thornton gave her, most handsomely, all the credit she deserved, and she became well known by name at least in the small locality that was her world.

Eleanor, with admirable restraint, said no more to her of their quarrel, but contented herself with a single quite different admonishment.

'I hope you will be very careful, Carrie. I can have, obviously, no objection to your visiting the cottagers since everyone seems to want you to continue, but it makes me very anxious that you may bring back some infection and we shall all be done for.'

Caroline laughed.

'Of course I am careful, Eleanor. What good is help if you endanger others by giving it? You are a goose to worry so.'

'I am not a goose, Carrie. I am simply thinking of Papa. In all I do I think of Papa.'

Caroline ignored the implications of that remark.

'I am glad you will not try to stop me, Eleanor, as it means more to me than you can know. I promise I will not endanger any of us.'

Eleanor sniffed self-righteously.

'Think of Papa,' she said.

6

By the summer Caroline had become something of a small
celebrity around Stoke Abbas. She was even able to accept
praise without blushing, although it never delighted her as
her own sense of usefulness did. She attempted no more
cures, but continued to visit, to feed, to bandage and soothe
with an effectiveness borne entirely of her new-found
confidence. To her secret joy, her relationship with her
father blossomed out of this new security of hers, and they
would spend long evenings together talking and reading,
evenings of mutual satisfaction to both of them. Eleanor
disliked this new bond, but could do nothing; instead she
waited in injured silence for the time when she was sure her
father would realize, and repay, her years of unstinting
devotion.

In late June, Caroline had been very busy. There had
been an outbreak of fever in the village, and, though
mindful of Eleanor's fears for their own safety, Caroline was
most attentive to the convalescent. In the midst of an
extremely occupied week, a note came from Stoke Park
summoning Caroline to see Lady Lennox.

'It is most strange,' Caroline said, holding the letter out to
a resentful Eleanor. 'I have not seen her but once this whole
year and that once at Georgiana's wedding. What can she
want with me?'

Eleanor disdained to look at the proffered letter.

'Medical matters, I presume.'

'Most unlikely, I fear. Oh dear, I do not care for going to
Stoke Park at the best of times, but going without any of
you for support makes it very terrible.'

'How you do fuss, Carrie.'

'Should you like to go alone?'

'I should not make this undignified commotion about it.'

'Why do you not go instead of me and see what it is she wants?'

'It is not me she has asked for,' Eleanor said enviously.

Caroline sighed. She was dressed, as usual, for walking, and a visit to Stoke Park meant a change into the blue silk left from last year, about whose colour she now had her own doubts. She sighed again.

'Papa says you may take the carriage,' Eleanor said crossly.

Thus arrayed in the blue silk which looked even more antiquated this year than last, and full of trepidation, Caroline jogged down the hill behind her father's greys.

Lady Lennox was waiting for her in the south parlour, compiling an impressive list of the planting she was intending to do in the Park that autumn.

'Lord Lennox has such a fondness for beeches, Caroline, that I think we will make an avenue of them down towards the lake. Do you not think that would make a pleasant walk?'

'Very pleasant, Lady Lennox.'

'And then you may walk there whenever you have time from your duties about the village. Lord Lennox and I were most gratified to hear of your success.'

Caroline detected a coldness in her praise, and rightly deduced that she did not care to have her own lack of liberality thrown into contrast by Caroline's care. Perhaps that accounted also for the fact that no word of praise had reached the Parsonage from the Park except second or third hand. Caroline looked dutifully out of the window at the gentle sweep of valley soon to be cluttered with beech trees.

'Thank you, Lady Lennox.'

'However, Caroline, that was not the matter I wish to discuss with you. Will you be seated?'

Carefully, Caroline chose a small chair with its back to the light. Lady Lennox leaned forward a little, clasping her large ringed hands in a gesture of uncharacteristic eagerness.

'I have the most wonderful news for you, my dear Caroline.'

Caroline felt at once both astonished and suspicious.

'For me, Lady Lennox?'

'Certainly for you. For no one else but you. You will recall, I am sure, dining here a year ago before Georgiana was married, and meeting Lord Lovell?'

'Indeed I do.'

'Then I wonder,' Lady Lennox continued with a hint of roguishness dreadful in so commanding a woman, 'I wonder if you recall a certain name that came into our conversation?'

Caroline recalled very clearly, for that was the only reason the dinner party was of any significance to her, but she was not prepared to be helpful.

'No name in particular, Lady Lennox.'

'Come, come, Caroline. Do you mean to tell me you did not colour up and start at the name of Johnnie Gates?'

To Caroline's enormous relief, her cheeks remained cool and pale.

'Perhaps I did, Lady Lennox.'

'Pooh, pooh, perhaps you did. Indeed you did, Caroline, I saw you do it. You are not going to deny that the name meant something to you?'

'It did . . . it might have done, Lady Lennox. Last summer, it might have meant something.'

'And now?'

'Now?' said Caroline with slightly less indifference, 'I do not understand you, Lady Lennox. What has now to do with it?'

With the triumphant air of a conjurer, Lady Lennox produced a letter from beneath a cushion, and brandished it at Caroline.

'Now for the wonderful news, my dear Caroline! I have here a letter from Johnnie, who remains a bachelor, a lonely bachelor, in Calcutta. He has written to me confessing his loneliness and the fact that he has never been quite heart-whole since he left Stoke Park – that summer. This letter contains no less, my dear Caroline, than a renewed offer of marriage. You are to set sail for Calcutta as soon as can be arranged as the future Mrs Gates!'

Caroline sat quite stupefied. The whole interview had become some monstrous charade, some scheme of tricks, some game where she knew not the rules.

'What do you say then, Caroline?'

'I – I do not know what to say. It is all so – so very astounding that – '

'Of course, of course, I knew you would be knocked quite breathless by it. Is it not quite wonderful? Shall I help you with a letter of acceptance?'

At the last question, Caroline's diffused gaze suddenly seemed to clear and concentrate.

'No,' she said.

'No? You will do it yourself? Of course, I was merely trying to – '

'Forgive me, Lady Lennox, but no, there will be no acceptance. I do not know by what machinations Mr Gates has offered for me, but I shall decline him.'

'Machinations? Decline him? How dare you, Miss Harding, behave in so insolent a manner? How can you refuse so magnificent an offer? You, insignificant, poor – '

Caroline rose from her chair and went to the window. She stood looking out at the sunshine with her back to Lady Lennox.

'Lady Lennox, did you persuade Mr Gates to renew his offer?'

'Indeed I did not, I merely suggested to him that his lot would be much happier – '

'If he married. And it would suit you well if he married someone who could be no rival to your own daughters. I do not, however, suppose he has any inclination himself to marry at all.'

Lady Lennox was hunting frenziedly again among the cushions. Eventually she produced the folded paper which she held out to Caroline.

'There is his letter to you. You will see for yourself how genuine is his desire to marry you. Read it, read it!'

Caroline looked at the strange desperation in Lady Lennox's face and made no attempt to take the paper.

'Thank you, no, Lady Lennox. As I am to refuse him, there is no point in reading his letter.'

Lady Lennox rose unsteadily and advanced upon Caroline.

'Do you mean to tell me that you will refuse him out of

sheer obstinacy and pride simply because the marriage, though entirely at his will, was not completely at his suggestion?'

'Oh no, Lady Lennox, not at all. I am not at all too proud to accept a man who asks for me as he is bidden to do. Oh no, the reason is quite different. I have no wish to marry now. I am not as lonely and purposeless as I was and I have no desire to leave Stoke Abbas or my father.'

'Can you mean it?'

'I can.'

'That a handful of ragged cottagers and a few words of praise from a mere country doctor are sufficient to induce you to lead a life of obscurity for ever?'

'Quite sufficient.'

'I do not understand you.'

'Nor I you, Lady Lennox. I do not understand why you wish me to marry Mr Gates, and I do not understand why he is so anxious to do your bidding. But I will not do your bidding because I do not care to jeopardize the small happiness I have.'

Lady Lennox sat down abruptly in the chair Caroline had vacated. She appeared to be struggling forcibly with her temper, and eventually to be gaining control.

'I think I may have surprised you, Miss Harding.'

'You did, Lady Lennox, very considerably.'

'Knowing the secluded life that you lead, it was perhaps misguided of me not to prepare you more gently for the future. I see that I have alarmed you.'

'I am not alarmed,' Caroline said calmly.

Lady Lennox ignored her.

'I shall give you two months. I think that would be fair. I shall not raise the subject or allude to it again until the end of the summer. Then I shall ask you for your considered opinion. Caroline, I shall give you the summer to think it over most carefully.'

'I do not need to think it over, Lady Lennox.'

'Two months,' Lady Lennox said with finality. 'I shall not mention the matter to your father, but shall trust you to reflect upon your situation with all the good sense you can muster. I shall send for you in late August.'

She rose and rang for a servant.

'Miss Harding is ready for her carriage.'

'Good day, Lady Lennox.'

Lady Lennox nodded and looked at Caroline intently.

'I shall see you in August, Caroline.'

'There is no use, Lady Lennox, I shall not, cannot, change my mind. I have everything now to keep me here and nothing but memories to induce me to accept. Please do not expect anything from me but another refusal.'

'Two months,' Lady Lennox said relentlessly, and the doors closed upon her.

At the Parsonage, Eleanor was waiting with ill-concealed impatience.

'You are back very quick, Carrie. I did not look for you yet. I hope Lady Lennox was quite well and that you said nothing to displease her. You look quite queer, Carrie, indeed you do. Most strange and – excited. What did Lady Lennox want with you, Carrie? Why did she send for you so suddenly?'

Caroline, whose first sense of outrage had subsided in the carriage into feeling the matter was merely laughable, shook her head under this barrage of statements and questions.

'It was nothing of significance, Eleanor, nothing at all. She merely said a kind word upon my doings in the village.'

Eleanor eyed her narrowly.

'In that case, I cannot see why you are so flushed. You always assert, Carrie, that the notice of great people is of no consequence to you, and yet one word of praise from Lady Lennox appears to be sufficient to leave you quite breathless. I do not believe it is all that passed between you.'

'You may believe what you choose and you may suffer on the thorns of your own curiosity if you please. Lady Lennox clearly feels as you do about my visiting, and – '

'Ah!' said Eleanor with satisfaction, 'so Lady Lennox quite rightly tried to make you see sense about going into those vile hovels, and you had the effrontery to differ from her! You have no gratitude, Carrie, no sense of what is proper. Can you not see that a rebuke from such a quarter must and should be listened to? Indeed, Carrie – '

Caroline turned to leave the room, but paused long enough in the doorway to say furiously, 'Nobody shall preach to me any longer, not you, Eleanor, not Lady Lennox. I will do what Papa wishes because it delights me to please him, but I will not do the will of those who are merely attempting to exercise their petty power!'

After tea that night, Parson Harding drew Caroline into his study, declaring he had some work that must be copied before the morning, and that it pained his own eyes to do it himself.

With his eye sternly upon Eleanor, he said to Caroline, 'I will dictate to you, and you shall write, and in solitude thus we shall get along famously.'

In dudgeon Eleanor shut the parlour door with more emphasis than was necessary.

'Now we shall make ourselves comfortable,' Parson Harding said with some relief. 'If you will but put another candle by me and seat yourself where I may see your face.'

Caroline smiled.

'So the business of the evening is not to be copying, but Stoke Park instead?'

'Indeed it is. I have often thought curiosity to be sinful but then, were I not curious, how else should I know where to advise and where to console?'

'Which do you think I look in need of, Papa?'

Parson Harding studied her thoughtfully.

'I have been trying to decide throughout dinner, and have only concluded that you need neither, but that I, on the other hand, need the consolation of curiosity satisfied.'

Caroline laughed affectionately.

'I will satisfy it, Papa, but you must prepare yourself for a surprise – no, almost for a shock. And also to hear what may seem disloyalty to your patroness.'

'I must bear that, I think, Carrie.'

'Do you mock Lady Lennox, Papa? I am surprised at you.'

'I am ever surprised at myself, my dear, and I am very eager to be surprised at you.'

Seating herself on a stool at her father's feet, Caroline

leaned her arms on his chair so that she might study every expression on his handsome face as she spoke.

'Lady Lennox summoned me, Papa, because she had wonderful news for me. She had written, for some reason I am not aware of, to Johnnie Gates in Calcutta and informed, or rather commanded, him to renew his offer of marriage to me. She was in receipt of his reply and had sent for me to inform me I was to be despatched immediately to Calcutta like any bale of broadcloth as Mr Gates' bride. There you have it, Papa, and I am gratified to see you look as dumbfounded as I felt this morning.'

Parson Harding put his hand over Caroline's. The news may have struck her forcibly at Stoke Park, but it dealt a much greater blow to her father who knew so much more of the people concerned and the world in general.

'Did – did she give you any reason for the plan, Carrie?'

'None, Papa, beyond saying that I had no life here and might as well accept – '

'No – no, my dear. I meant, did she tell you why she had written to Gates in the first place?'

'No, except for saying he was lonely.'

Parson Harding winced slightly. He had listened intently to all revelations of Johnnie Gates' Indian life, and had picked up all the implications of Frank Lovell's reluctance to be explicit. Furthermore, in his role as Lady Lennox's confidant, he was well aware of how the family money was to be disposed, and of her powerful opposition to any but her own children receiving any of it. It came upon him as he sat with Caroline's hand in his that Lady Lennox had been prepared to export Caroline to a life of heaven knew what suffering in order to ensure that Lennox money might be kept from being entirely dissipated. He could not quite visualize how she had put the matter to Johnnie so that he had come to heel so swiftly and compliantly, but he reflected that she was the only person Johnnie had ever feared or obeyed. He drew his breath a little and patted Caroline's hand.

'So what answer did you give to this dazzling prospect, my dear?'

'I said I must refuse.'

'Did you give any reason?' Parson Harding said quickly, to hide the spasm of relief that seized him.

'Certainly I did. I said I wished to stay with you, and in Stoke Abbas. I feel I belong here, I am beginning to have a life here, and I do not wish to leave it.'

'I am deeply thankful to hear it.'

'Then I am glad.'

'Was – was there any part of you that wished to become Mrs Gates, Caroline?'

Caroline looked away from her father's face and into the dazzling glow of the candle flame.

'Once, Papa, once, all of me wished to become Mrs Gates, and I suppose some part will always remember that wish. But it is all so long ago, and I am changed and he must be changed so that it could never be as it once would have been.'

Parson Harding reflected gently that it could in fact never have been as she romantically imagined, for Johnnie had had too much of a fatal weakness about him to make a woman happy. It was by the greatest good fortune that Caroline had escaped marrying him, and Parson Harding felt a little mild guilt that he had once connived at such a marriage himself. But then, he consoled himself, safe in events as they had happened, how could he have known that Caroline would turn out to be too good a thing, for such a one as Johnnie Gates?

'So, my dear, you have handled Lady Lennox with great firmness and I see the victor in combat before me?'

'I believe you do, Papa.' She sounded surprised at herself still.

'And it shall be our secret, Carrie?'

'Oh, please, Papa. Except – except that Lady Lennox would not take no for an answer and insisted on allowing me two months to reconsider my decision.'

'As there is nothing to reconsider, my dear, we shall think no more of the two months. We shall instead plan a winter of reading the poets of the last century, and until that winter comes, you may occupy a little time with your favourite pursuit.'

'Painting, Papa?'

'No, indeed, you goose. Visiting the sick and needy. I saw Sam Wells today and he says the children have all had the fever, but are recovered, praise God, and are very low and dispirited and would like to play a few games with Miss Caroline.'

'I should love to go, Papa. They are such dear energetic children, usually so packed with health. I shall go tomorrow, and take some currants. We have never had such currants as this year before, black, white and red all together. They are like jewels.'

'You may take all the currants you wish, my dear. Now go and amuse your sister for a while.'

Caroline rose and kissed him.

'It does me good to know that you are happy, Carrie.'

'I am, Papa.'

The following day dawned grey and still with a heavy warmth. True to her word Caroline filled a basket with small bright fruit and set off down the field path to the river and the Wells' farm beyond. She was sorry she had not been before, but the Wells, isolated as they were from the huddled cottages of the village, were usually healthy and to be visited for pleasure rather than succour. The great kitchen of the farmhouse, almost untouched since its medieval building, had an uncharacteristic air of desolation about it. Commonly it was full of bustle and activity, a confusion of dogs and children, stray hens and baking. Today a few children hung dismally about the great table, and a little maid from one of the poorer cottages was anxiously stirring a pot over the fire. As she entered, several of the children came slowly forward to greet her.

'Sam, Charlie, Elizabeth, how are you? And little Robert. Are you better? I was so sorry to hear you were not well.'

The smallest Wells endeavoured to inform her that he had been hot, so hot that he had thought he was burning all up. Caroline smiled.

'And now you are well again, and I have brought you some currants to help you get strong more quickly.'

She looked about the quiet room again.

'Where is your mother, children?'

'She hot now,' Robert said helpfully.

Caroline looked across at the little maid.

'Is Mrs Wells ill?'

The girl nodded fearfully. She was so terrified of Farmer Wells, and the fever and of her new and dreadful responsibilities that she did not know what she feared most.

'Where is she?' Caroline demanded.

'In – in her bed, ma'am.'

Caroline set her basket on the table.

'We shall make pastry, children, and then you shall cut pictures out for me from it while I go to see if your mother is comfortable.'

Ten minutes later, leaving all seven heads bent in concentration over the white slabs on the table, Caroline took water and a piece of clean linen, and climbed the uneven stairs to Mary Wells' bedroom. She lay in the bed in which her husband had been born, sweating and wretched, her face and hands scarlet with the fever's rash. She looked at Caroline wildly.

'Go away, Miss Car'line! Tidn't fit for you t'come near me!'

'I don't mind it, Mary. I have been by sick beds all year and caught nothing. Come, I will sponge and cool you and perhaps that will help to bring down the fever.'

'No, Miss Car'line! Tidn't right! Think if you was to catch the fever!'

'You will only make yourself feel worse, Mary, and you will not drive me away.'

Reluctantly Mary submitted to the cool water and gentle hands.

''Tis the nights as is terrible, Miss Car'line. Sam says I do rave like a mad thing and 'e can 'ear me from t'next chamber. I sent 'im there to try and keep 'im from it. 'Tis the children I fear for, if both of us was to die.'

'You won't die, Mary. I've seen far worse rashes than this and felt far hotter foreheads. You won't die.'

Mary looked at her with fierce hope.

'You mean that, Miss Car'line?'

'Of course I do,' Caroline said comfortingly, smoothing the coarse linen sheet, 'and I shall come back often to make sure you don't.'

' 'Tis right what they do say of you,' Mary said with desperate gratitude. 'You'm an angel, Miss Car'line, there's no two ways about it.'

'Sh – sh, you are to sleep now. I shall make sure the children are fed and you are not to worry yourself about them.'

Mary closed her eyes.

'While you'm 'ere, I'll not worry.'

Caroline descended to the kitchen again to find the pastry sculpture had degenerated into a battle, helplessly watched by the little maid. She made them clear up the flung pieces, find their bowls and horn spoons, and did her best to make the mess in the pot appetizing. With the aid of chants and rhymes she induced them to finish each last spoonful, and then despatched them all to play peaceably in the orchard until their father's return from the first haymaking in distant meadows. She left instructions for the maid, made sure that Mary still slept, and then set off for home.

Her father met her in the Parsonage garden.

'Ah, the angel of mercy, I see!'

Caroline kissed him.

'Do not tease, Papa. I have been to see the Wells, and all the children are fed and, I hope, occupied. Poor Mary has the fever now but not badly. She will recover, but I must find her some more help from the village for she will be very weak for a while.'

'A good morning's work, my dear. You shall have your reward in the shape of some excellent pullets Lady Lennox has sent up. Perhaps you might care to regard them as some sort of feathered peace offering.'

Caroline laughed.

'I must wash, Papa, and then I shall be ready to do the peace offering more than justice.'

7

A week later, Mary Wells was able to leave her bed for a few hours at a time and sit by the kitchen fire, thin and weak, but mending, while the children leaned against her in relief. They all regarded Caroline as some being with super-human powers, and Sam Wells vowed that the Parsonage should be provided with the best at pig-killing, all the cream and butter they could wish for as long as he had breath.

'It makes me uncomfortable,' Caroline said to her father. 'I have come to dread being thanked. It sounds complacent to complain of gratitude, but I simply do not know what to do with it!'

'If it comes in the form of bacon and butter, my dear, we shall all know what to do with it!'

'But if I keep going back to make sure Mary can manage, does it not seem as if I should like even more provender?'

'Certainly not. You must inform your conscience that oversensitivity is as bad as insensitivity. Would you be so good as to draw that curtain across a little?'

'Does the sun bother you, Papa?'

'I seem to have a slight headache, nothing more.'

She crossed swiftly to his chair.

'Papa, you never have headaches, never. What is the matter?'

'Nothing, my dear. I rode in the sun too long this morning, I fear. Now do not fuss or I shall send you away. Find some soothing verse and read to me. George Herbert perhaps, I have a strong notion to hear a little George Herbert.'

With half an eye upon her father, Caroline began. As she read she saw that he had closed his eyes, but his brows were still faintly contracted as if pain were drawing them to-gether.

She put the book down.

'Should you like some water, Papa?'

He opened one eye.

'Do you fuss over your patients in the village like this?'

'No, Papa, I command them but I do not think I should have much success in commanding you.'

'Certainly not. Now get me some water and then leave me to muse upon eternity.'

Caroline found Eleanor in the kitchen sorting raspberries.

'Papa has a headache, Eleanor.'

'Papa never has a headache,' Eleanor said finally.

'He has one now. I am to take him water.'

Eleanor took her hands out of the great basket and wiped them vigorously on a cloth.

'I shall take it.'

'As you please. But I do not think he – I think he wishes to be left in peace.'

'You are not the only person capable of nursing the sick, Carrie. Indeed there are many more fitted for the task than you, I am sure. Of course I shall not disturb Papa, I shall merely take him water and reassure myself that he is quite comfortable. Perhaps you might continue with these raspberries – but no, I think not, on the whole. You would not sort them as carefully as I do and I should only have the task to do all over again.'

'If you were to tell me how – '

'No, Carrie, no. It is best that I do it. Heaven knows there is enough to be done, but it is best that I do it.'

Caroline went out of the room with tightened lips, and up to her bedroom to soothe her feelings by painting until dinner. Robert had managed to catch a swallowtail down by the river and had mounted it, its lovely wings outspread, upon a piece of wood for her to paint. She touched the fragile velvety thing gently, more sorry to see it thus than to be pleased to have it as a model. She had drawn the outline upon an oval of ivory, and now there was the pleasure of adding colour. She sat down at her table and took up her brush, looking carefully at the butterfly, and then a small nag of worry about her father came between and she laid her brush down again. He never had a headache. In fact he never seemed to suffer physically at all; Caroline could not remember a single occasion when he had complained of discomfort, let alone pain. And he was so precious to her now, their new companionableness was so wonderful to her, so unexpected. She looked at the butterfly again and forced herself to concentrate upon the tiny, tidy patterns upon its pointed wings.

At dinner, Parson Harding was cheerful, but his cheerfulness seemed to need an effort. Caroline did not like to pester him with anxious queries, but she doubted from the look on his face that his head was better. Eleanor, assiduous in the role of chief nurse and administrator, took over the task of carving, but when she placed a plate of chicken before her father, he pushed it away.

'Thank you, my dear, expertly carved, but I do not seem to have much appetite.'

'Papa!'

'Do not look so anxious, Carrie. I have simply exposed myself to the sun too long this morning.'

'The sun is not fierce today,' Robert pointed out unhelpfully.

'I expect at my age the sun does not need to be fierce to have a fierce effect upon my head. Would you forgive me, my dears, if I returned to the study? The sight and smell of food – '

He stopped and blanched suddenly. Caroline and Robert were on their feet in an instant, but were motioned to sit down.

'No – no, sit down and eat. I shall be perfectly well if left to rest, perfectly well. Thank you, Eleanor, but I think I can manage the distance to the study unaccompanied. Forgive me – '

He closed the door behind him. The three left looked at each other doubtfully. A small and awful foreboding was beginning in Caroline's brain which robbed her immediately of appetite, but she would not speak of it. She might in any case be wrong and the consequences of raising a false alarm would be terrible.

'You are quite wrong to suppose the sun not fierce today,

Robert,' Eleanor announced, 'and it was most thoughtless of you to allow Papa to ride so far this morning.'

'I could hardly prevent him,' Robert protested. 'He wished to go as far as Monk Hill for the view, and he was in such good spirits that it never occurred to me the sun might affect him thus.'

'Nothing ever occurs to either you or Carrie it seems. It is as well that one of us takes thought for the morrow. I hope you realize – where are you going, Carrie?'

From the doorway, Caroline said, 'To my room. I do not seem to feel hungry either.' She closed the door upon a tirade on wastefulness.

There was no one in the study. Caroline ran to the window hoping to see her father under his accustomed tree in the garden, but he was not there. Filled with a sudden fresh anxiety, she went back through the room, across the hall, and up the shallow staircase. Patsy was coming along the landing with a bowl of water.

'Oh, Miss Car'line, I were comin' for you. The Parson ain't well, Miss Car'line, not well at all.'

'Why, Patsy, what has happened, quickly – '

'He'm sick, Miss Car'line. He just vomited, miss, and he do look like a sheet, so white – '

Caroline slipped past her to her father's room. He was lying, still dressed, on his bedstead, the half tester brought from France for his bride in which all his five children had been born, and in which his wife had died. He was ashen and his face looked alarmingly sunken. Caroline tiptoed to his side.

'Papa?'

He opened his eyes a little and gave her a glazed, unseeing look. He raised a hand from the bedspread and let it fall again.

'I – I fear I am not well, Carrie.'

'Oh – oh, Papa, I am so sorry, so sorry. . . .'

She stopped quickly and bent to put a hand upon his brow. He was too hot to console her.

'Will you let Patsy and I make you more comfortable? May we put you in your shirt so that you may lie between the sheets?'

Parson Harding smiled faintly.

'I should be grateful, my dear. Perhaps you will be able to command me, after all.'

A lump rose in Caroline's throat, and she said with difficulty, 'I am so sorry there is occasion for it,' and could not trust herself to say more. Her father pressed her hand lightly and his touch was hot and dry. She went to the door and found Patsy waiting anxiously outside.

'Come and help me make the Parson comfortable.'

Patsy nodded. Gently they undressed the old man and slipped the folds of his nightshirt over his head. He lay unprotestingly at their mercy like a doll, his eyes closed, his limbs limp. As they pulled the fine linen down his body, Patsy suddenly gasped.

'Oh, Miss Car'line, see this!'

Caroline went quickly round to the other side of the bed and stooped to see what Patsy indicated. On the white skin of the rib-cage, spreading from armpit to hip bone, was the unmistakable flushed stain of scarlet fever. Caroline dropped, shaking, to her knees, staring wide-eyed at the rash as if her gaze could burn it out. It was her fault, that was the fact of it. She had gone to the Wells deliberately knowing there was fever there, because she could not resist the self-satisfying chance of doing good, and she had come home bearing the fatal contagion and given it to the person she loved most in all the world! She had been like Judas, kissing and betraying. She had come up the garden, with the fever all about her like a shroud, fresh from Mary's bedside, and had kissed her father and dealt him this blow.

'Forgive me,' she whispered fiercely. 'Oh, Papa, forgive me, forgive me!'

His hand strayed across the sheet in search of her.

'There is nothing to forgive, my dear. What did I say to you about oversensitivity but a few hours ago? There is nothing in the world to forgive.'

'But there is! There is! It is I who brought you – '

Parson Harding's hand came to rest with surprising firmness across Caroline's mouth.

'And I sent you to the Wells in the first place, Carrie, so

you will not speak of such nonsense again. You nursed Mary Wells back to health, and now you shall nurse me.'

Caroline kissed his hand and rose unsteadily to her feet.

'Bring water and a sponge, Patsy. We must at all costs keep the fever down. Hurry.'

She went to the window and looked out at the rising, falling landscape, green and flowery under the June sun with the church steeple like a grey arrow against the soft hills. Slowly she drew the curtains across the brightness, and then went to sit by her father's side in the sun-speckled gloom. She must think collectedly, as calmly as she could always think when among the cottagers. But although she liked the village people, they were clearly not one hundredth part as dear to her as her father, and it was the very love she bore him that made it so difficult to be calm. The fever itself, she knew, was the danger. The rash would spread, but it was no more than an irritation and was itself no threat. But the fever must be kept down at all costs, and day and night someone must be by to sponge with cool water, endlessly sponge, to try to reduce the fever. She would do it all of every night as a punishment for her crime. She would sit alone through those long, silent, alarming hours and she would watch as vigilantly as if the lives of the whole human race depended upon her watchfulness. She stooped over her father and saw that he had fallen abruptly into the sudden, troubled sleep of illness, breathing fast and lightly. Eleanor and Robert must be told quickly, she must not be possessive. As Patsy came back into the room, Caroline rose.

'I am going to inform Miss Eleanor. I will only be gone a few minutes, and while I am gone you are to sponge his face and hands lightly and constantly. Do you understand?'

'Yes'm,' Patsy said tremblingly.

Caroline touched her shoulder.

'Do not be afraid, Patsy. I will only be a few minutes.'

Eleanor and Robert were leaving the dining room as Caroline descended the stairs.

'May I speak to you both one moment?'

Eleanor was instantly suspicious.

'What has happened?'

Caroline led the way into the parlour.

'It is Papa, Eleanor. When I went upstairs he was in his room, lying down, and he had vomited. Patsy and I have undressed him and I very much fear – no, I know, that he has scarlet fever.'

Eleanor's eyes blazed.

'Scarlet fever?'

Caroline's chin went up.

'Yes, Eleanor, scarlet fever. And you are right to be angry, because it was I who brought it to the house just as you said I should. And now I mean to nurse Papa as I have nursed many others.'

Eleanor's face was terrifying in its anger.

'You shall not touch him, Carrie! I knew I should be vindicated, I knew it! Because you could not resist the praise of others, a little renown, you have deliberately brought this sorrow upon us. You . . .'

'Eleanor, Eleanor,' Robert remonstrated. 'Papa has seen sick villagers, too, as well as Carrie. There has been fever all over the village. Do not be so violent.'

'I deserve it, Robert,' Caroline said wretchedly, 'though nothing Eleanor could say could hurt me more than my own feelings. You shall nurse him by day, Eleanor, and I shall sit by him at night.'

'Indeed, you shall do no such – '

'Silence!' Robert cried with uncharacteristic firmness. 'Of course she must take a turn, Eleanor! You cannot sit by him twenty-four hours a day. Go to him now and Carrie shall relieve you at eight.'

Astonished, Eleanor did as she was ordered. When she had gone, Caroline looked gratefully at her brother.

'Thank you, Robert, but I do deserve her anger.'

Robert shrugged.

'That is debatable. It is surprising that no one in the household has succumbed to the fever before. Do you think he has it severely?'

'I cannot tell yet. His age is against him, his health for him. It is the fever we must keep at bay.'

'He is in good hands,' Robert said, and smiled at his sister.

The fever rose and rose. By night Parson Harding was

delirious, shouting and crying out, twisting and tossing in his bed so that Caroline needed help to prevent him injuring himself. By wavering candlelight she watched his desperate unconscious face as he wrestled with nightmarish images, soothing and sponging his burning skin and talking to him in a gentle monotone. By day he was a little calmer, and sometimes knew Eleanor. Once he made the mistake of asking for Caroline, and reduced his elder daughter to helpless angry tears.

A ceaseless procession of anxious well-wishers began to come to the Parsonage door. Although she desperately needed sleep by day, Caroline saw them all, and accepted their little offerings of flowers and fruit and eggs and gave them what crumbs of comfort she could. Lady Lennox sent daily to enquire, her notes accompanied by baskets of exotic fruits from the Stoke Park orangery. Daily Caroline wrote to thank her. She did the household tasks Eleanor had used to do, and the everyday business of life went on, Robert riding round the parish and taking services, but without his heart in it. The movements were made, but there seemed no point to them.

The scarlet rash spread its red stain all over Parson Harding's body, covering all his hands and face except for a small pale patch about his mouth. It became impossible to cool him, and he slipped even further into the grotesque inferno of delirium. For several days he knew nobody, and the house rang with his wild shouts, shouts that were terrifying from a man whom none had ever heard raise his voice. The servants huddled in the kitchen, and Caroline dozed fitfully between her duties. She became as pale and gaunt as a wooden peg doll, her eyes even larger and more extraordinary in her ravaged face. She took to pacing the landing during the day when not sleeping or working, straining her ears for any sound that might give hope.

On the tenth day, as she paced, the door of Parson Harding's room was opened, and Eleanor's weeping face appeared.

'Come, Carrie,' she said hoarsely.

But it was too late to come. As Caroline approached the bed, her father was slipping swiftly away from her. Her shaking hand found no heartbeat, nothing. The fever had won.

The time that followed was a kind of dreadful limbo, a no-time in which nothing seemed real or relevant. Sunk in her own agonizing dry-eyed grief, washed up alone again, Caroline moved through the business of laying out and burying her father as though her inner self had nothing to do with her body. Eleanor wept ceaselessly, sobbing and accusing, red-eyed with anger and grief, but her storm of abuse fell upon Caroline as if she were encased in armour. She had no feelings for anything because all her emotional energy was absorbed in her unbearable sense of loss. The village thought it strange that she did not weep at the funeral, as Miss Eleanor did so copiously, but concluded kindly that she must do her weeping in private. They were wrong. She lay awake night after night consumed with torturing sadness and could not cry.

A week after the funeral, Lady Lennox sent for Robert and informed him that he should be incumbent of Stoke Abbas in his father's place. She had confessed to Lord Lennox that she was deeply reluctant to do this since Robert was a mere travesty of his father, but she could see nothing but destitution ahead for the Hardings if she did not perform this magnanimous act. Lord Lennox pointed out that there were certain advantages in having a tame clergyman dancing as a puppet on the string of their pulling and that to set out to find a wholly new incumbent who did not know the place would be most fatiguing. So Lady Lennox was gracious, Robert was humbly and profoundly grateful, and his patroness sat back and waited for his younger sister to capitulate.

She had some months to wait. Caroline crawled back to life so slowly that she began to wonder if she would ever be able to feel again. It was a painful reawakening, seeing her father's possessions, recalling looks and words, and becoming gradually less deaf and more sensitive to Eleanor's accusations. The armour of numbness that had shielded her developed chinks, then great gaps, and gradually fell away altogether leaving Caroline as raw and twitching and vulnerable as she had ever been.

'You realize that you have ruined our lives, Carrie. You are aware, I am sure, that if you had listened to even a single word I said you would not have brought this tragedy upon us. I am sure you are well repaid for your selfishness, your greed for praise and your stupidity. I only hope you know the extent to which you have damaged us all.'

It went on and on. Caroline only had to make the smallest domestic error, to open a window a fraction too wide, to throw away a pea shuck in which a single pea remained, to set the process in motion. She had not the heart to escape any longer since the cottages only served to remind her of the tragic effects of her work among them, and she could not bear it. She felt guilty about her neglect of the villagers and began to take pains to avoid the very people whose company she had so eagerly sought before, because their reproachful faces caused her such added misery. Round and round the Parsonage and garden she went, fleeing before Eleanor's persistent recriminations, hopelessly trying to find some occupation that would fill her mind and give her some ease. She would spend hours standing at her bedroom window or pacing hidden corners of the garden, fruitlessly regretting and accusing herself until her mind was quite worn down.

There came a particularly bad day. Robert, out of sheer clumsiness, had preached a sermon the previous Sunday whose liberalism, meant only to be humane, had been taken as a direct affront to herself by Lady Lennox. Robert had not expected to see her in church – indeed she had not attended for weeks – and was far too inept to switch his planned sermon for some more diplomatic improvisation simply because his patroness had appeared unexpectedly. Lady Lennox had endured twenty minutes of diffident suggestion that all men were equal in God's eyes and only integrity and virtue made a true hierarchy, and then had risen outraged, in a flurry of rustling silks, and swept from the church. Robert was summoned the following morning and crept back to dinner at the Parsonage with an air of wishing himself totally invisible.

'What did she have to say to you, Robert?' Eleanor demanded at dinner.

'Everything you might imagine, Eleanor.'

Eleanor laid down the carving knife.

'Please answer me directly, Robert.'

'No, Eleanor!' Caroline said indignantly. 'No, he shall not! You may very well imagine what passed at Stoke Park this morning, and it is merely cruel to make poor Robert relive it.'

Robert gave his younger sister a covert but grateful glance. Eleanor swelled with anger.

'How dare you speak to me thus, Carrie! You of all people have the least right to call any fellow human being cruel! You have acted with more selfish cruelty than any being upon earth and yet you dare to accuse me!'

There was a choking cry from Caroline's end of the table as she sprang up and fled from the room. Robert, emboldened by her courage, said to Eleanor:

'You must cease to chastize her, Eleanor. Papa's death was no more her fault than any of ours, and you make her grief intolerable to bear with your accusations.'

Eleanor glared at him.

'So! I am to have no defenders! I may not speak the truth and I must comfort the sinners for the wrong they have done me! If that is your doctrine, Robert, you may feed upon it alone for dinner!'

With relief, Robert heard the door slam behind her. When the parlour door was banged shut in the same manner, he rose quietly and began to carve himself some ham. He gave himself a much larger helping than Eleanor would have allowed him, and began to eat it in a solitude that was far from unpleasant to him.

Caroline's solitude upstairs was a far wilder thing. She was pacing her small room with clenched fists, muttering and trembling, her face full of an anger that no one would have believed she possessed. It was beyond tolerance, Eleanor's attitude, beyond anything that the most enduring of people could be expected to bear. It was bad enough that her own faults, however small and irrelevant, should be the triggers for Eleanor's tirades, but it was insupportable that any crisis in the house, even one that had no bearing upon Caroline herself, should be used as an excuse for a fresh flood of bitter reproach. I cannot bear it, she thought, I cannot bear it. I cannot live here for all my life and never be allowed to forget, never be forgiven. Robert is kind and fond of me, but he is too weak for Eleanor, and Eleanor makes no bones of her feelings for me –

She stopped abruptly as a thought cut suddenly across her mind. There was an escape, there was! She had meant never to take it and it would mean some humiliation, but it was a chance for freedom. Lady Lennox had given her two months to change her mind about India, and twelve weeks, twelve long and dreadful weeks, had gone by. It was to be hoped that Lady Lennox had not written to Calcutta saying the match was not to be; indeed Caroline must make all haste. She did not relish the prospect of submitting to Lady Lennox after all her fine proud words, but that was a small act of humility by comparison with the utter shame she endured hourly here. She went quickly to her writing desk. Patsy should take a note to Stoke Park immediately, begging that Lady Lennox might spare the time to see Miss Caroline Harding briefly the following morning. She wrote swiftly, and folded the paper. She must not think too hard about the consequences of that note, there would be plenty of time for thought later. The note must go before she had time to realize her future to the full. With it in her hand, she opened the door and ran quickly down to the kitchen.

8

In early October 1776, Robert Harding took leave of his parish for a few days to escort his sister Caroline to Gravesend. It was a wild and windy October, and Caroline's last view of Stoke Abbas was through a whirling cloud of golden leaves, flung about by impetuous gusts of wind. The carriage came slowly out of the Parsonage gates, for the horses were prancing and shying at the rough weather, and thus the little group of villagers gathered to wave goodbye had a long last look as Caroline moved past them. Lady Lennox had sent a note to wish her bon voyage so full of unconcealed self-satisfaction that Caroline had tossed it straight into the fire, but this small cluster of poorly dressed cottagers affected her very deeply. She pulled down the carriage window, and leaned out and called her thanks and good wishes into the gale until she could no longer be heard.

Gravesend was to Caroline a most romantic sight. They arrived in the damp dusk, and through the darkening air could see the East Indiaman that was to be her home for six months. Straining her eyes in the dimness, she could make out its great masts and the guns along its bulwarks, and felt her heart leap with a mixture of excitement and apprehension. Robert only seemed to feel the latter emotion.

'Shall you really go, Carrie?' he said over supper at an inn. 'I know all your belongings are aboard by now, but I am sure we could get them taken off again.'

Caroline smiled and patted his hand.

'Indeed I am going, Robert!' she declared. 'Even if my passage were not booked and all I have in the world already on the ship, you must remember that my fate is already sealed in a letter halfway to India.'

She did not add that the prospect of returning to Eleanor's scorn and Lady Lennox's anger was far more terrifying to her than six months at sea and an almost blind marriage.

She looked at her brother's doubtful face above his clerical bands.

'Do not worry about me, Robert. I am sure there will be delightful company on board, and I will send letters home by every ship we pass.'

'I shall miss you sorely, Carrie,' he said painfully, suddenly envisaging what meals at the Parsonage would be like without an ally.

'Perhaps my absence will force you to find yourself a wife.'

Robert nodded without hope.

'I am going to bed now,' she said, 'for my last night on land until the spring.'

The momentousness of this fact struck them both into sudden silence, Caroline elated, Robert appalled.

'I shall never sleep for anxiety,' he said miserably.

'You must. I do not want to be waved goodbye by a long face, Robert. If it were not for leaving you, I should be entirely pleased to be going.'

If Gravesend had seemed a romantic sight at dusk, the dawn was almost better. Along the quay stood merchants muffled in cloaks, and sailors with gold rings in their ears were loading great quantities of cargo aboard the ship. Caroline stood on the wet cobbles, wrapped in her new boat cloak, and found it difficult to believe she was herself, or that before nightfall, she and that great ship would be slipping away from England together. She could see nobody who might be a fellow passenger, in fact nobody at all apart from the sailors, except for a most impressive person in a braided coat and buckled shoes whom Robert whispered he was sure must be the captain. Caroline regarded him with awe.

'I do not believe it is still too late to come home with me,' Robert pleaded.

Caroline shook her head.

'I do not want to go home, Robert. I could wish you were coming with me, but I do not want to go home.'

She remembered the brief dry brush of Eleanor's cheek which was all the farewell she had had and felt a sudden strong resolve to put all of such memories behind her. She turned to Robert.

'I think I shall go aboard now, and see to my cabin.'

'No, no, Carrie, there is no need before midday. I have express instructions that passengers are under no obligation to embark before noon.'

'Perhaps not, but I have an express need. I am not enjoying saying goodbye, and I should like to see you safely on your way.'

Robert looked deeply troubled. He hated hanging about in Gravesend, and he hated to see her go, but he was most relieved to be told what to do.

'Do not look so anxious, Robert. I promise you to board the right ship for the right destination, but I should do so with much more peace of mind if I knew you were homeward bound.'

Without further protestation, Robert allowed himself to be stowed comfortably in the carriage. He had meant to sell it on his father's death, but was, on this murky day, profoundly thankful his indecision had prevented it. He let Caroline tuck rugs about him and kiss him swiftly on the cheek.

'I shall say goodbye quickly, Robert, just as if we were to see each other in a few days. You must write, and so shall I, and give my dear love to Patsy.'

She watched the carriage rumble away, and then turned eagerly back towards the quayside. Burdened by no more than her small box of personal possessions, she went quickly among the bales and boxes that littered the greasy cobbles, nodding to any sailor who looked her way, and conscious of an exhilarating sense of freedom. As Robert jolted out of Gravesend westward, his sister Caroline mounted the gangplank of the East Indiaman, quite alone, on her way to Calcutta.

Lady Lennox, in a flush of gratification over Caroline's capitulation, had been generous. She had regretted the generosity almost instantly, but it was too late to recall it. She had booked Caroline one of the sought-after poop cabins, and had realized with annoyance too late that

Caroline would have been quite content with something humbler. The poop cabins, after all, were usually occupied by persons of consequence, and Lady Lennox was perfectly confident that all the passengers would soon discover that Caroline was of no consequence whatsoever and thus the extravagance of a poop cabin would be entirely waisted. It was very vexing, and it was extremely doubtful that the vexation would have been lessened if Lady Lennox could have seen Caroline's huge gratification as she surveyed her little domain. She would have considered that gratitude was no more than her due for such reckless generosity.

A sailor equipped with a wooden leg limped before Caroline below deck to show her to her quarters. They passed a row of small cabins, divided only by canvas partitions, and in each one Caroline readily expected to see the narrow bedstead, washstand and small chair which Eleanor had graciously allowed her to take from the Parsonage. Each cabin was already furnished, mostly overfurnished, and great trunks stood on every floor, as well as piles of writing cases, fishing equipment, parcels of books and cases of wine. There seemed to be a flurry of servants everywhere, deep in trunks or gossiping between the cabins, and Caroline was suddenly bitterly conscious that she had no one with her, no one at all. It had crossed her mind to take a village girl as maid, but upon reflection, she had decided that it was too alarming a proposition to put to any girl who regarded Dorchester as the other side of the world, and had decided to manage on her own. Lady Lennox had pointed out, in her eagerness to encourage Caroline for her future, that Johnnie would provide her with a wealth of servants in Calcutta, where a raw Dorset girl would be quite superfluous. For a brief moment, however, Caroline would have given everything for the companionship of such a girl.

The sailor stopped before a pair of narrow wooden doors. He flung open the left-hand one and indicated that Caroline should enter. She took one brief amazed look and withdrew to the deck again.

'That cannot be mine.'

'You Miz 'Arding?'

'Yes, I am, but – '

'Port poop cabin, then, Miz 'Arding.'

He held his hand out hopefully. Caroline fumbled in her reticule and found a coin with no notion of how relevant it was to his services. He spat upon it, polished it, grinned and ambled crookedly away, leaving her small box upon the floor. After the crowded cabins behind her, Caroline's few bits of furniture seemed rather lost in the splendid space she had been allotted. The walls and floor were bare certainly, but the walls were panelled, and the end one was entirely occupied by a large window. A swinging lamp and tray were suspended from the ceiling, and Caroline's bed and wash-stand had been tidily arranged against one wall. Her writing case lay across the chair, familiar from the Parsonage nursery with its stretchers kicked bare by the boots of Robert, Charles and Harry. And there was something else, too, a small and pretty bureau, clearly the possession of some other passenger since it was quite unfamiliar to Caroline. She ran a finger over its satiny surface and admired the shell inlaid on the sloping front. She turned the small key to open it in case there was some hint of ownership inside, and found there a card from Lord Lennox, wishing her bon voyage and hoping she would accept this small gift on the occasion of her marriage. It was all quite delightful, quite unbelievably delightful. She threw her cloak across her bed and hugged herself and smiled out of pure pleasure.

A knock came at the door, which was then pushed open as unceremoniously as Eleanor would have done. But instead of her sister's uncompromising black figure, Caroline saw to her consternation that a ravishingly pretty girl, with dark curls and a high colour, was standing in the doorway.

'Now, do not look so startled. I know exactly who you are because I have just asked a matelot, and I also know from the same source that you have no maid, and so I am come with the express purpose of offering you mine for she is an idle madam and needs to be occupied.'

Caroline was stammering with amazement.

'You – you are too k-kind, b-but really, I – '

'Do not be a goose, Miss Harding, and refuse me. No one wants to unpack their own trunks when someone could perfectly well do it for them. Why! Do you mean you only have one? It will take Fatima but a few moments, I assure you it will, and in the meantime, you and I shall get to know each other.'

'You are m-most kind,' Caroline said faintly.

'Nonsense, I am not kind at all. I am extremely selfish because I want a friend exceedingly for this tedious voyage, and I am sure you will be she. Now, where are your rugs and pictures?'

'I have none – '

'None!'

'I have left them all behind. I was trying to – to leave as much as possible behind.'

The pretty girl surveyed her keenly for a moment.

'I understand you perfectly. Well, there is nothing for it but to lend you some of mine. I have brought an absurd amount as I always do, and shall be thankful to dispense with half of it. Stay here one moment, and I shall summon Fatima.'

She paused in the doorway, and added,

'My name is Isobel Grant, Miss Harding, and I know that yours is Caroline.'

Caroline stood quite stunned in the middle of her cabin and gazed at the doorway through which Isobel Grant and her green gown had vanished. It was clear that she occupied the adjacent cabin, and equally clear that she was of the class by whom Caroline was most alarmed. Poor Miss Grant would be doomed to find Caroline as dull and unrewarding as Sophia and Jane and Georgiana Lennox had all done, and it seemed wicked to accept her loan of rugs and ornaments when theirs was a friendship which had, because of Caroline's inadequacies, no chance of blossoming. But as Caroline stepped forward to try to prevent the transference of articles from one side of the poop to the other, Isobel Grant was already returning, her arms full of objects, with a plump, dusky-skinned maid in her wake.

'Now, Miss Harding, come with me and we shall sit in my cabin while Fatima makes yours presentable. What an enviable little bureau that is, to be sure, quite twice as pretty as mine. Fatima, to work, please, and we wish to be very much surprised and impressed.'

118

Isobel Grant's cabin could have been any small and fashionably pretty drawing room in London. Caroline sat nervously upon the blue silk padded seat of a small gilded chair, and looked about her in awe at the water colours and miniatures, rugs and embroideries.

'Are we not lucky, Miss Harding, to be in a ship so thoroughly modern? This is only her second voyage, you know, and these are supposed to be the most comfortable cabins in all the East Indiamen. I, of course, refused to go unless I was comfortable, and I am very glad that Lady Lennox felt you needed cherishing too.'

Caroline started.

'Lady Lennox? You – you know of Lady Lennox, Miss Grant?'

'Call me Isobel, Miss Harding, and then I shall be able to call you Caroline which I should much prefer to do. Yes, I know Lady Lennox, and now I shall tease you by making you guess how.'

Caroline could not help smiling.

'That is too difficult. I know nobody *but* Lady Lennox, you see, so have no knowledge to make guesses with.'

'How pretty your eyes are when you smile. Very well, I shall not torture you. I know Lady Lennox because my cousin Frank married Georgiana, last spring.'

'Lord Lovell!'

'The same. His father and my mother are brother and sister. I knew from Frank that you would be upon this ship, and I very much hoped we should be neighbours. Now, shall you tell me about yourself, or shall I tell you about yourself, instead, and then you can tell me where I am wrong?'

Caroline was laughing openly.

'You tell me.'

'Very well. You are the daughter of the Stoke Abbas parson who is recently dead, which is very sad, and you are bound for India to marry a childhood beau, which is more than I can say for myself, and you are wonderfully kind to the poor. Now, Caroline, I can see I am quite right because you are as pink as a rose.'

'You are almost right. Now tell me about yourself.'

'Oh, delightedly, there is no subject I am fonder of. I am very spoiled and very bored, and I am being sent off to stay with another cousin in Calcutta before I am clapped into irons and marriage for the rest of my life. My cousin is very important in Calcutta and much older than I am, and I am told I used to dote upon him when I was a baby. I very much trust he is preparing to dote in return upon me now.'

Caroline regarded her with warmth.

'I doubt he can resist you. How long shall you stay?'

'Until he throws me out. His mother was a most severe woman, very cross and disagreeable, and so is his surviving sister, and I am very much afraid that he will be entirely like them. So you see how I need a friend, Caroline, for I am so easily bored and cannot bear to be chided.'

'I should dearly like to be that friend, but I am afraid you will find me very dull.'

Isobel Grant looked at her in silence very carefully for a moment or two. Then she said decisively, 'I do not think so.'

The first few days of the voyage were terrible, and Caroline discovered that she was an appalling sailor. The moment the ship was beyond the safety of the Channel, storms fell upon her with fury, and waves as high as houses tossed her about as if she were no more than a toy. Sick and shivering on her bed, Caroline could hear the goats and poultry tethered in the round house above her bleating and squawking their dismay. She longed for air, but when her window was opened, the sea poured in in great grey gulps and swamped her cabin. If it had not been for Isobel, she did not know that she could have borne her wretchedness, but Isobel proved an excellent sailor and indefatigable nurse.

'You cannot imagine how much good it does me to be of use. I have never been of so much use before in my life. And I am so grateful to be safely here with you because you cannot conceive of how disagreeable the rest of the ship is. Everyone but me is ill, and all the furniture is rolling about through the canvas curtains like bulls got loose from their chains.'

Fatima had wished to be ill too, but Isobel would not permit it.

'If I am to look after you, is it not entirely reasonable that she should look after me? When you are better, and this horrid sea is flat again, then she may dally with the sailors if she pleases, but not until then.'

As suddenly as they had pounced, the winds withdrew, and Caroline emerged from her cabin in the calm evening to find the air balmy and the rigging hung with coloured lanterns. Isobel was delighted with her progress.

'Caroline, I shall take all the credit for it, every scrap. I do believe if it were not for me you would have died.'

'You believe quite rightly. I cannot thank you enough, indeed I cannot.'

'You do not need to, for I shall exact my pound of flesh, I promise you. I shall start exacting it this moment too, for here comes General North, the heaviest gallant in the world, who has been plaguing me these last three days, and you shall take him off my hands.'

With an exclamation of distress, Caroline was about to protest, but the general was immediately upon them, smiling and genial.

'My dear Miss Grant, indeed my – may I say so? – very dear Miss Grant, I had hoped to find you here.'

'Good evening, General, and what pretty medals you are sporting, to be sure. Caroline, may I present General North to you? General, Miss Harding.'

The general bowed stiffly from his vanished waistline.

'*Enchanté*, Miss Harding. Any friend of Miss Grant's – '

'She is not any friend, General, she is my most particular friend whom I have snatched from the jaws of death.'

'Indeed?'

With a rush of courage Caroline said, 'It is true, General, quite true. I – I never thought it possible to feel so ill.'

'Aha! This must be your first sea voyage?'

'It is.'

'Then you must expect to feel the effects, my dear Miss Harding. When you have gone back and forth to India with the regularity that I have done, you will feel nothing, nothing at all.'

In the same breath, Caroline said, 'Then you know

Calcutta well?' as Isobel declared, 'She is not going back and forth, General, she is going to be married there.'

'Married, eh? Married! Yes, I know Calcutta, Miss Harding, and I often wish I were spared its acquaintance. Madras is the place, you know, nowhere like Madras.'

'Is Calcutta so very disagreeable?' Caroline ventured.

'Pretty much so, pretty much. But I daresay you will not notice too much in your newly wedded bliss, eh?'

A small chill was creeping into Caroline's spirits.

'In what way is Calcutta disagreeable, General?'

The general looked about for Isobel to rescue him from the earnest direction in which conversation was tending, but found that she had slipped away in the shadows. He sighed a little, but endeavoured to do his best.

''Tis pretty hot, you know, and humid. And society there is very raffish. No standards, no propriety. Not, you understand, Miss Harding, that I do not know how to enjoy myself – '

He broke off, and said abruptly, 'Are you acquainted with Sir Edward Ashton?'

Caroline, whose thoughts were far away on the now slightly troubling prospect of Calcutta, looked at him perplexedly.

'Sir Edward Ashton?'

The name was very dimly familiar, but why she could not at present recall.

'Yes. Are you acquainted with him?'

'No – no, not in the least.'

The general looked disappointed.

'Pity. Fine fellow. He is the cousin to whom Miss Grant is going. He is one of the half-dozen most distinguished men in Calcutta, a member of the Council and a close friend of the Governor General.'

'The Council, General?'

By the faint light of the lanterns above their heads, General North regarded her with some surprise. This odd, stiff, plain girl whom that pretty creature seemed so fond of, appeared to have no notion at all of the place she was bound for for the greater portion of the remainder of her life. She appeared not to be aware of climate or conditions, nor of the administration that governed Bengal.

'Do you know anything of India, Miss Harding? Have you any connections there at all?'

'None – no, none, and I know nothing of India. General – ' she said suddenly, 'will you instruct me a little? Will you tell me something of the place, and of the East India Company?'

The general looked at her again, and noticed her curious gleaming eyes for the first time, and the softening effect that eagerness had upon her features. He thought a moment upon the prospect of weeks of uninterrupted instruction, weeks with a humble and grateful pupil, and concluded that the prospect was entirely gratifying. He bowed again.

'It will be my pleasure, Miss Harding. A most delightful task. Now, may I escort you below where I gather we are to have some music before supper?'

Caroline was astonished at the spectacle of the second deck. Isobel had told her of the splendid dinners served there each day under the autocratic eye of the captain (of whom it was said that he had ordered a passenger to be clapped in irons for being so disrespectful as to whistle in his presence), but Caroline was not at all prepared for the gathering that confronted her. Several ladies, all dressed with considerable care, were grouped gracefully about one of their number who was playing upon an enormous harp. A respectful audience of men, mostly in uniform, but with one or two civilians, sat about at their ease, a bottle at every elbow. Except for the gentle motion of the ship, and the faint and not altogether pleasant odour that was to become an increasingly obtrusive feature of the voyage, it might have been a scene in any English drawing room.

General North escorted Caroline to a seat, then bowed and left her to join the serious drinkers in the round house. The ladies about the harpist looked her way briefly and slightly inclined their heads. The gentlemen, who had looked up hopefully as she entered, sought their liquid comfort once more. Caroline sat back thankfully in the shadows, and thought how strange it was to feel so solidly supported, so secure, in a little wooden vessel on the deep. She would never have believed whilst still on land that a ship could seem so stable and safe. She looked furtively round at the dozen or so faces in the lamplight, and thought how much she should know about them when they reached Calcutta, and how familiar they would become. The lamps swung gently from the low ceiling, the harp twanged in the silence broken only by the plash of the sea, and Caroline felt that Stoke Abbas was now a spot upon another planet.

9

A week later, the coastline of Africa was sighted amid exclamations from the ladies and the event was recorded at once in most of the industriously kept feminine journals. General North, by now delighted by his pupil's appetite and aptitude for learning, suggested to Caroline that as the equator approached, she might like to keep a map of the southern sky. Caroline agreed with enthusiasm, for she had already charted the ship's progress and course with an accuracy the captain had loudly admired, and liked to have some tasks to give shape to the by now sometimes tedious days. As the equator approached, the soft warm wind dropped and dropped until, after a week of no more than creeping through the water, it died away altogether, and they found themselves becalmed.

It was an eerie sensation, lying quietly there on the flat and glittering sea beneath the hard blue African sky. The ship, which had seemed so redoubtable a haven while slipping on resolutely through the sea, became a vulnerable little object, and a watch was set to keep lookout for pirates said to lie in wait for stranded vessels. Alarming tales were told of the savagery of these pirates, and the ladies' spirits dwindled a little in the hot silence of their predicament.

'Are you not afraid of this horrid situation?' Isobel demanded of Caroline.

'I do not like it, but I am not much afraid of it. It is not that I am brave, Isobel, but simply that the last weeks have been so novel that I do not seem able to feel that anything has much reality.'

'Oh, Caroline, you are exasperatingly patient, indeed you are! Does it not madden you to be so hot and so bored and fidgeted by so small a space?'

Three long days later, a little wind rose, and the passengers crowded excitedly on deck to watch the great sails begin to belly and fill. Slowly the ship moved forward and a cheer rose as the blessed breeze soothed their burned faces and tired eyes. Even while becalmed, most passengers had spent their days on deck because the smells below were becoming formidable, and their skins had inevitably become dried and scorched by the relentless sun. General North had told Caroline with pride that the East India Company insisted that its ships should be washed down twice a week – an unheard of standard of hygiene – but these salt-water swillings were no match for the cramped living conditions, the livestock tethered about the ship, and the unventilated areas of the lower decks. Caroline often had cause to thank Lady Lennox for her unwilling kindness, when she opened the window in her comfortable cabin and filled it with air and sunlight. Her little bureau was now strewn with maps and charts, meticulously kept, to the astonishment of Isobel.

'What can this mean, Caroline? What are all these little arrows and hieroglyphics? What are these strange names? Oh, Caroline, why will you not embroider with me like any civilized girl?'

Caroline had fallen in love with the southern night sky. Every evening, escorted by the captain, the ship's doctor and General North, she would repair to the poop deck, and watch the constellations rise in their astonishing and exquisite brilliancy. She had never imagined that a cloudless climate could make such a difference to the stars, and was amazed anew every night as these incredible diamonds wheeled across the velvety heavens. The ladies, however, were piqued at the attention shown her, for they considered her clothes and lack of grace and accomplishments still an insuperable stumbling block. If it had not been for the fact that the exquisite Miss Grant seemed to dote upon her, they would have ignored her altogether.

'Take no notice of them, Caroline!' Isobel declared. 'They are all disappointed spinsters save Mrs Mayhew, and she is a disappointed wife if you consider the insignificance of Mr Mayhew, and that must be worse. What is more, Caroline, they are jealous of you.'

Caroline looked up from her careful etching of the Southern Cross. 'Jealous! Jealous of me! Do not be absurd, Isobel. Nobody is ever jealous of me.'

'Indeed they are. Every night you are escorted to the poop deck by no less than three distinguished gentlemen, all of whom admire you profoundly. Shall I tell you something? Today the doctor caught a flying fish, and we begged him to dissect it for us, but he would not do so because you were occupied and he did not consider the rest of us a worthy audience.'

Caroline laid down her pen.

'You are teasing me, Isobel.'

'I would not dream of it. I never tease those I love best, never. I will tell you something else that makes these faded flowers green again with envy. They are all part of the fishing fleet, and you, the promised bride of Mr Gates, are not.'

'The fishing fleet?'

Isobel smiled delightedly.

'Guess what they are fishing for.'

Caroline considered a moment, gazing out at the shore of Africa that sometimes seemed to her as if it would never end.

'Come on, come on! You are so slow, Caroline, I do believe you are the slowest – '

'Husbands?' Caroline suggested doubtfully.

'Of course, you goose! What else! Husbands! The whole of Calcutta is full of eligible husbands!'

Caroline rose and went over to the window, standing for a long while looking out over the blue interminable sea.

'I wonder then,' she said at last, 'if they have even more to fear than I.'

Isobel came swiftly to stand beside her.

'Caroline! Caroline, are you afraid? Are you afraid of marrying Mr Gates?'

There was a pause, and then Caroline nodded.

'Yes, Isobel, I am.'

'But you have known him since childhood. He is the only man you have ever loved! Is it not the most romantic situation you can conceive of?'

'I – I think I hardly knew him. I can recall so little about him, although I can remember what I felt. But Isobel' – with a sudden rush of feeling – 'I have not seen him for nine years, nor he me. Suppose when I get there I – he – '

'Then you shall not marry him!' Isobel declared roundly. 'I shall see that you do not!'

Caroline took her hand and pressed it.

'I have never had a friend like you, Isobel, and I cannot express what your affection means. But I must marry, I must. I know myself well enough to know that I have to have a purpose, an occupation. I am only content that way.'

'Nonsense, Caroline! An unhappy marriage is not an occupation, it is a terrible affliction. I will not allow the martyr in you to have its way. Come now, there will be no more talk of Mr Gates until we get to Calcutta and decide whether he deserves you in the very least. The captain says we shall be at the Cape within a week unless the wind dies again and at the Cape there are the best grapes in the world and we may actually leave this floating prison for a while.'

Two days before the Cape was reached, with its promise of dry land and succulent fruit, the first sailors died of scurvy. Sewn into their hammocks, they were pitched into the sea during rough and ready funerals which afflicted the passengers deeply, but had very little effect upon the crew. In fact Caroline was much startled to notice that in the midst of reading a prayer, one of the ship's officers broke off to bawl an order to the helmsman, and then resumed his pious reading as if the interruption had never been. Isobel could not watch as the canvas bundles plummeted into the water.

'It seems so heartless, Caroline, they are vanished as if they had never been. Do you suppose anyone knows if they died, or cares?'

The Cape seemed like Paradise. It was decided by the captain to remain at anchor for some time since many timbers of his new ship had shrunk while becalmed in the blazing sun, and needed to be waterproofed. General North took firm charge of Caroline and Isobel and found them delightful lodgings with a stout Dutch widow in a house

surrounded by blossom-hung terraces. In the midst of he
flowers and ferns and trees, the sun no longer seemed
oppressive but rather the greatest benefit upon earth.
Caroline's room opened directly upon a terrace, its balus-
trade entwined with bougainvillaea, and beyond the roofs
and gardens below it rose the square-topped splendour of
Table Mountain.

She had initially been worried over money. Her fare had
been paid, but it had not included a pause at the Cape since
favourable winds often induced captains to press on past
that delightful place. But Isobel had discerned her difficulty
and acted with her usual impulsive generosity.

'Do not think more about it, Caroline. You shall be my
guest. I have the most dreadful tendency to waste money
and should love to put it to good purpose. I could not bear to
have you far from me after living but a wooden wall away
these three months, so I will brook no argument.'

Caroline accepted gratefully, but as she unpacked her
belongings in her sunlight-dappled room she reflected with a
certain resentment how wonderful it would be not always to
be the receiver, rather than the giver of charity. Briefly,
before her father died, she had known how blessed it was to
give, but now she was back in her old humble position of
taker. She loved Isobel warmly, and was truly and deeply
grateful for all her kindness, but some part of her felt herself
diminished by this constant acceptance of others' generosity.
She had nothing to give Isobel but love, and had she been
surer of herself, she would have known that that was all
Isobel wanted.

For three weeks, Caroline was entirely happy. The small
circle in which she now felt quite comfortable, composed of
herself, Isobel, General North and an increasing troupe of
Isobel's admirers, met daily for the most delightful ex-
cursions. They rode out into the countryside, the admirers
taking enormous trouble to instruct Caroline in the hope of
ingratiating themselves further with Isobel, and stayed at
little inns, where they breakfasted on vine-covered verandahs.
The bacon, eggs and cheese were of the highest quality, but
the fresh bread was a universal delight after the months
of ship's biscuit. The gentlemen complained bitterly of the

local wine, which they claimed was execrable to taste and appallingly expensive, but as Caroline observed, it did not seem to daunt them in drinking it.

One day they climbed Table Mountain itself, an arduous but satisfactory expedition, urging Isobel onwards with promises of the view to be had from the summit. Watching the general toiling upward in his full coat and heavy wig, it struck Caroline how inappropriately they were all dressed.

'Would it not be possible for you to walk in your shirt sleeves, General?'

General North stopped to mop at his streaming brow.

'Possible, my dear Miss Harding, but entirely improper. This heat is nothing in any case. Wait until you feel the steam bath that is Calcutta.'

Just below the summit, when Isobel was declaring that if she was to reach the top she should have to be carried, a surprise awaited them. General North, who knew the Cape well, had arranged refreshments and there, in a cool cave, stood a table spread with chickens and hams and great baskets of fruit. Sitting there in the shade with the exquisite bay spread out below her and a plate of peaches and grapes before her, Caroline felt a physical contentment she had never known before. The warmth, the colours, the comfortable companionship of people whom she would never have dared to feel easy with before, combined to make her feel both languorous and elated in a way she had not known she could feel. Great butterflies were drifting about a flowering shrub below her and a small bright bird chattered on a rock by her shoulder.

'I do not think I ever want to leave this place.'

'Nor I,' Isobel declared. 'Shall I send a message to my cousin Ashton and say I have changed my mind?'

The admirers looked horrified.

'You cannot be serious! You cannot mean it!'

'Of course I do not but I wish I did. I am anxious I shall not enjoy Calcutta.'

General North refilled his glass.

'My dear Miss Grant, you will move in the highest circles in Calcutta.'

'Perhaps she does not think that a recommendation,' Caroline said.

The general turned to her.

'Miss Harding, you disappoint me. After all these weeks of instruction, you should know better than to suggest that the highest circles in Calcutta are to be sniffed at. I beg you will inform Miss Grant of the circles I mean, and then I shall know if you have listened to a word I have said.'

Isobel clasped her hands.

'Recite it to me nicely, Caroline.'

'Then you must listen nicely.'

Isobel unclasped her hands and looked demure.

'Pray commence.'

'Calcutta is the chief port of the province of Bengal,' Caroline began, her eye upon General North, 'which is the most important of the Indian states to the East India Company – '

Here there were cries of 'To the John Company!' from a few young men lounging in the grass as close to Isobel's feet as they dared.

'Persevere, Miss Harding.'

'The Governor General of Bengal is Mr Warren Hastings – '

'I thought there was a man called Clive,' Isobel said. 'What happened to the man called Clive?'

'Warren Hastings is his successor,' General North said. 'Shall I continue for you, Miss Harding, since I shall be able to suppress interruptions by sheer volume?'

'I should be grateful,' Caroline said, sinking back into her chair.

'He is assisted in his administrative duties by the Council, a small group of men, selected in the main by my namesake, our Prime Minister, and of whom your cousin, Miss Grant, is one.'

'All I know of Warren Hastings', Isobel said, wholly unimpressed by her cousin's position, 'is that he stole someone else's wife which was most fascinating of him.'

'Warren Hastings is a man of the utmost rectitude,' the general said portentously. 'A man of excellent principle, abstemious habits and infinite industry.'

Isobel sighed.

'He sounds quite impossible, General. Will you please reassure me that my cousin Ashton does not resemble him in any way?'

'Your cousin Ashton, my dear Miss Grant, is a most remarkable man. I believe', he added, turning to Caroline dreaming in her chair, 'that you, Miss Harding, and Sir Edward Ashton will find you have much of mutual interest.'

Caroline coloured and looked down at her lap. She did not observe the sudden and keen expression that fluttered for a moment across Isobel's lively countenance.

It was sad to leave the Cape, and discouraging to find themselves once more in the narrow confines of their cabins. Everyone seemed refreshed by the spell ashore, however, and one or two of the fishing fleet, as Isobel openly called them, were sufficiently revived to be almost gracious to Caroline. Caroline was grateful for these attentions, not simply because of her new-found delight in finding herself accepted by people whom she had formerly found terrifying, but also because they diverted her from her thoughts. As the ship moved away from the Cape and began to creep across the Indian Ocean, Caroline's thoughts were not of a kind to afford her much ease. Before she had started out, she had been so desperate to leave, so frantic to put thousands of miles between herself and the reproaches and bullyings of Stoke Abbas, that she had not given much thought to her future, except for the occasional grateful reflection that she had a future to go to at all. Even as they sailed away from Gravesend, she had been too preoccupied with seasickness and adventure and the dazzling novelty of Isobel to look ahead. All those long weeks it took to sail down the African coast had been so happily filled with little occupations and her daily instructions from General North about India that her mind was kept from being too reflective. The one pang of fear she had had, Isobel had diverted away, and then she had been so beguiled by the Cape and her pleasant little society, that she had felt herself secure in a magic world where the word future had no significance.

But the spell of the Cape was broken now, and Caroline

felt the beginnings of a most alarming foreboding. She had little to divert her now, for General North, though he paid her steady and affectionate attention when they met, was now preoccupied with defence classes for the young men upon the ship, in order to be prepared for any sudden attack from French privateers. Isobel was with her a good deal of course, but she was herself chafing now at the tedium of the voyage and needed Caroline to amuse her, an occupation Caroline doubted she had much talent for. All her waking moments now had a dark shadow at the back of them, and while other passengers scanned the horizon anxiously for signs of pirate ships, Caroline watched, too, but with eagerness, for she now knew that she would have welcomed any event that prevented her arrival in Calcutta.

It was not the prospect of Calcutta itself that alarmed her. She felt well equipped with knowledge as to the habits, lifestyle, food, climate, pleasures and dangers of India and would under other circumstances have looked forward eagerly to the adventure of another continent. But her marriage filled her with mounting apprehension, and the more she thought of it, the more she became quite convinced that the whole enterprise was madness. If only, she thought fiercely, she were a person of independent means, she would not always have to be handed from one household to another like a piece of furniture. Isobel, for instance, with her private fortune and the connections that went with it, was going out to India under just those free and dignified circumstances that Caroline could never aspire to, while she, Caroline, must be handed, dowerless, from the support of her brother to that of a man she increasingly felt she hardly knew. She had read his letter to Lady Lennox, but it was not written in a style that she ever remembered his using before, and she had wondered fleetingly if it was all his own work.

What, in fact, could she really remember of Johnnie Gates, except a sort of buttercup-filled summer idyll that seemed more like a story that she had read than part of her own life? She remembered the pleasure the recollection of his courtship had given her, only eighteen months before, but that pleasure now shamed her by contrast with the emotions she had known since. She remembered Johnnie as tall, square-shouldered, with a handsome challenging face and disordered curls. She remembered his magnificent clothes, outstanding in the comfortable dowdiness of Stoke Abbas, she remembered his dare-devilry and teasing, she remembered being kissed by him but not how it had thrilled her. To the older Caroline, now seeking something far steadier and deeper, it seemed she could recall nothing of importance, nothing but the dashing trappings of romance any eighteen-year-old might harbour.

The night their ship made the mouth of the Hooghly River, Caroline was at her lowest ebb. She lay in her narrow bed, steady for the first time in months since the pilot had advised mooring away from the banks to avoid the very probable danger of tigers leaping silently aboard, and resolved to lie low in the ship and set sail again for England even if she had to work her passage. As if by some sixth sense, Isobel crept in to her before dawn and knelt in the blessedly cool air by her bedside.

'Have you closed your eyes at all, Caroline?'

'Not once.'

'I knew it! I have been on the point of tiptoeing in all night and now I wish I had. You have been wearing foreboding writ large all over your dear face these past weeks and I am very afraid you will do something foolish.'

Caroline said nothing but put out a hand in the misty light and felt it grasped.

'Confess, Caroline!'

'I – I was thinking of running home.'

Her hand was lightly slapped in the darkness.

'Shame on you! Back to demon Lady Lennox and dragon Eleanor? I know very well how apprehensive you are about the charms of Mr Gates, but do you really mean to run away again?'

'Again?'

'Again. Think, Caroline.'

Caroline thought. Pictures of Stoke Abbas, of her father's empty study, of Eleanor frowning in the pantries, of Lady Lennox in her drawing room, pictures she had not summoned for weeks on account of her acute apprehension about marriage, processed steadily across her imagination. Isobel was right in her inference that home was no longer there to go to, she had run away from it, renounced it, chosen an alternative.

'Why are you so pessimistic, Caroline? Why should Mr Gates not prove everything you wish him to be? And if he isn't why should you not refuse to marry him?'

Caroline sat up in bed.

'Because I do not really have a choice. That is what frightens me. You are young and lovely and independent and those things make your security. I am the reverse of all those assets, and am, in the eyes of the world, astonishingly lucky to be handed such a chance as I have. If I do not take it, if I do not marry, I might as well not exist. There is nothing else on earth for me to do.'

'Nonsense!' Isobel cried. 'You shall live with me! I have enough for ten extravagant companions, and a dear mouse like you would not so much as nibble at my money – '

'No – no! Isobel, please – '

'Should you not like to live with me?'

'I should love it above all things, but not – not as an object of charity. If I had my own fortune there is no other companion I should choose – '

'And if you are an object of charity to me, you goose, why are you not precisely the same to Mr Gates?'

'It is different as a wife! I have a conventional role to play, I can make his life comfortable, run his home, see to his wants, I can feel that in some way I am repaying being kept by him.'

Isobel got to her feet and shook out her bedgown.

'I fail to see the difference between doing all that for him and doing it for me, when he might not want you and I most certainly do. But at least I have made you talk yourself into marriage, and that I must conclude to be a good night's work.'

She bent and kissed Caroline's cheek.

'Bother your stiff-necked pride, you dear and tiresome thing.'

'Do you not – understand it a little, Isobel?'

'I might, but I do not want to. I want you to be happy and I long to be instrumental in your happiness.'

'You already are! More than you know. My courage is up again, thanks to you.'

Isobel opened the narrow door and moved onto the deck outside.

'You still shan't marry him if I don't think him good enough.'

When the door had closed, Caroline slipped from her bed and went to the window. The greyness of dawn was growing rosy now, and across the still pale water of the river she could see a low bank and the outlines of groups of alien-looking trees. Smoke was curling blue from some clumps, the smoke perhaps of early breakfasts, Indian breakfasts. Despite her wretched night, a leap of excitement warmed her as she stood there and looked at this foreign waking world. She, Caroline Harding, of the parish of Stoke Abbas in the county of Dorset, England, was about to set foot in India.

10

Johnnie Gates was ill-prepared for any bride that March morning. He had allowed George Carew to assist him in lamenting the end of freedom so lavishly the night before, that death would have seemed preferable as he opened stiff and sore eyelids upon the squalor of his bedroom the next day. No servants were hovering since they were disinclined to face Sahib Gates in such a condition one second before they were compelled to, and in any case, Johnnie had quite omitted to mention that the pressing matter of welcoming the future Mrs Gates to Calcutta meant that he must be woken promptly and made as presentable as the limited resources of his house would permit.

'Ahmed! Ranjit! You insolent dogs, where are you? Here, I say, here!'

He raised himself from his greasy sheets and stared into the hot gloom.

'Ahmed! Ahmed!'

A shuffle of bare feet and two or three dim figures slipped into the room. They stood patiently by the door while Johnnie went into his customary morning pantomime of bellows and curses, interspersed with shrieks of pain at the suffering caused to his head by the volume of his own voice. When he was hoarse, they padded silently to his bedside and stood with folded hands, watching his frowsy, panting, bent figure as he sat on the edge of his bed quite spent with his own temper. After a considerable pause, he slowly raised his head and gazed at them with small red eyes.

'Clean linen. All clean linen. White breeches and my blue flowered coat. My new wig. And cane. And a bottle of champagne.'

'But, sahib – '

'Now!' Johnnie roared.

They scattered. There was, as usual, no clean linen, but some was most certainly cleaner than others, and, if resourcefully folded and pressed with the flat of the hand, might pass. Sahib Gates' vision was none too good this morning. The blue flowered coat had suffered a muddy tumble in a brawl several nights before, and no one had troubled to clean it, but if it were carefully presented to Sahib Gates with the back prudently concealed, what would be the harm in it? As for the wig and wine – ah, there mercifully there was no trouble, since no mice had yet taken up residence in the former, and the latter was the only commodity Sahib Gates made sure he never lacked.

An hour later, momentarily fortified by the champagne, Johnnie set forth in his somewhat grubby splendour. Shaved, scented, adorned with his single remaining ring – the sircar had plans for substituting an infinitely inferior copy but his cousin the jeweller had been so busy lately – and swinging his cane, Johnnie mounted his horse and set off in his personal cavalcade of ramshackle servants to the house of Mrs Rathbone. She occupied a house just on the edge of the desirable area of Garden Reach, and thus Fort William lay between her and Johnnie's less distinguished abode.

Johnnie had reason to be grateful to Mrs Rathbone. Though her husband might be the most unobservant upon earth, and though she might rejoice in the nickname of 'the Officers' Comforter', she was a generous and affectionate woman and boasted many true and loyal friends among those she had comforted. Some weeks before, she had come upon Johnnie sprawled unconscious on a staircase after dinner, his ludicrous wig tumbled off, revealing a tousle of dark curls, and a temporary air of attractive boyishness. She had summoned her servants, had them load Johnnie into her carriage, and had driven him home with her. She had left her fond husband a note to say she had retired with a migraine, knowing full well that port would have rendered him incapable of reading in any case, and took Johnnie to bed. He awoke in a surprising and unfamiliar multiplicity of frills and pink pillows, warmly – too warmly – cushioned by the affectionate amplitude of Mrs Rathbone. Falling upon her hopeful bosom he burst into tears and told her the whole story of his boyhood flirtation and how it had led to the jaws of matrimony that were about to close inexorably upon him.

'Silly boy,' Mrs Rathbone said cosily. 'Silly boy. Marriage will make you ever so much more comfortable, for sure it will. And if she's a nice girl, a sweet girl, as I am sure she is, she will not mind your visiting old friends just once in a while, now will she?'

Johnnie tried looking gratefully at Mrs Rathbone, but found her too close for comfort at this hour of the day. He edged away across the bed, took Mrs Rathbone's plump hand in his and kissed it.

'That is what George Carew told me.'

'Then George Carew is a sensible boy. Now then, when does your sweetheart come?'

Johnnie winced and fell back among the little pillows.

'In three weeks. She arrives on the *Sea Horse*. What am I to do with her?'

Mrs Rathbone gave Johnnie a playful nudge.

'As if you needed telling, you naughty boy! If I were to tell Mr Rathbone what you did – '

Johnnie put his hand over her mouth.

'Please!'

'Of course, I won't, silly boy: I'm no simpleton, I promise you and I believe in offering help where I can. So help you I will, and Miss Harding shall stop with me until your wedding day, and I shall befriend her and show her round the city.'

Johnnie looked about at the mirrors and gilding and plump pink furniture of Mrs Rathbone's room and contrasted it with the austerity of Parson Harding's study which was the only room he had ever been into in the Parsonage. Caroline would be like a cob nut in a dish of Turkish delight here, but it was a brave offer, indeed it was, and it got him out of a devilish hole. What else was he to do with her? Old Rathbone was a reasonable sort after all, said to be of quite good family, and the Officers' Comforter had a heart of gold even if her antecedents were unmentionable. He turned his head towards her.

'I thank you for that, indeed I do. And I accept your offer with the deepest gratitude.'

Mrs Rathbone wriggled coyly and pouted.

'Aren't you going to thank me, Johnnie? Thank me properly?'

Johnnie raised himself on one elbow, and swallowed.

'You know how I like men to say thank you, Johnnie boy, don't you?'

With a sigh and closed eyes, Johnnie flung himself across her.

Now, a month later, he was riding to escort her down to the quay. The tide was just right this morning, and all the tenders onto which passengers from the *Sea Horse* had been unloaded in the Ganges delta were due in at noon. By the dinner hour he would have seen Caroline again, and know the worst. This ride down the Hooghly to Garden Reach was the last entirely free ride he would ever have, the last time when he was able to do as he chose, and he alone. He looked at the dishevelled servants about him in the rags and tags of livery they wore as a sort of token to him, and envied them bitterly for their freedom. He looked about at Calcutta, blue and green and white in the spring sunshine, and thought of the free happy men everywhere in it, free to enjoy this gayest and wickedest of cities and not have to account for their every move to a wife. Engulfed in self-pity, he rode gloomily on.

Mrs Rathbone was not ready for him. There was a flurry of little shrieks from upstairs, followed by the startling appearance of Mrs Rathbone with her hair girlishly about her shoulders, clad in a peignoir the dhobi had not seen for some while. She kissed Johnnie warmly, emanating little stale puffs of last night's powders and pomades, rang for wine for him, and promised she would be but a moment. Johnnie drank his madeira in solitude, gazing miserably at his overstuffed, overdecorated surroundings, musing on his lot until he reached the conclusion that he even envied Mr Rathbone for the luxury of having such an accommodating wife. Caroline would never be like that, never. She would be shocked and resentful and priggish, and she was going to make his life a straitjacket.

Mrs Rathbone tripped in after an hour in a heavily embroidered gown of baby blue, looped up to show ruffled scarlet petticoats. There seemed to be a good deal of gold lace and fringing about her person, and she held yellow gloves and a parasol encrusted with embroidery in seed pearls and silver thread. She kissed Johnnie on the cheek.

'Do you like me, Johnnie dear? On the quiet side, I know, but I do not wish to alarm Miss Harding that we are too dressy here in India.'

'Admirable,' Johnnie said faintly.

The drive to the waterfront was not comfortable. Mrs Rathbone, delighted to be escorted by Johnnie, and equally delighted to be of service, waved and blew kisses to the smallest acquaintances they passed. The road was busy, for the *Sea Horse* was the first East Indiaman to put in for some weeks, and Calcutta was eager for news and letters and new faces.

'Is it not delightful, Johnnie? Are you not elated? I do not know when I have been so well amused! Look – look, I am sure that is Mrs Russell waving from her carriage – but no, I fear it – oh, but Colonel Bridgeman is bowing to me so nicely, Johnnie, and dear Mr Hicks, and that naughty Miss Glazer, what a wicked girl she is!'

By the time they reached the waterfront Johnnie wished to plunge into the river and drown. Sick with apprehension and misery, his head pounding and his face scarlet from his embarrassing journey, he felt his life had reached its lowest ebb. Because of Mrs Rathbone's delay, the tenders had all been in some time, and the quayside was a teeming confusion of Indians, passengers, soldiers, baggage and cargo. She was here then. Somewhere in this mêlée his fate awaited him. He glanced at Mrs Rathbone's rainbow finery and made a small but firm decision.

'I pray you will wait here in the safety of the carriage. I should hate to risk you being injured after all your kindness to me. I will go and find Miss Harding and bring her to the carriage.'

Bridling with pleasure at what she took to be the intended inference of 'all your kindness to me', Mrs Rathbone agreed. She watched Johnnie climb awkwardly from the carriage, then settled herself back to wave and smile at the crowd jostling by her.

Caroline and General North had been waiting on the quayside a full half-hour. Isobel had pleaded to be allowed to remain, too, but a magnificent person by the name of Sir Edward Ashton, with a posse of immaculate servants and a chaperoning widow of impeccable appearance, had swept her off. Caroline was desolate to see her go, but somewhat comforted by feeling that she did not want Isobel's perspicacious eye upon Johnnie at the same moment as her own. General North, staunch to the end, had offered to escort her until her betrothed arrived, and if he failed to show up, to take her to his old friends, Colonel and Mrs Clifton, who would welcome her as a daughter. As she stood on the hot busy waterfront, Caroline would gladly have exchanged being Mrs Gates for being Miss Clifton. She was disappointed with herself for being too full of misgivings to appreciate fully that her feet were now firmly on Indian soil for the first time, and these hordes of dark-skinned people were her first sight of real Indians. Suffocating in her boat cloak and unsuitable bonnet, she stood by General North, and waited.

They waited for an hour, while Johnnie plunged up and down through the crowds, uncertain of what he was looking for, and terrified of finding it. At last he found the *Sea Horse*'s captain and enlisted his help. He was directed back the way he had now been a dozen times, and told to look for a tall woman in a grey cloak, accompanied by a stout distinguished-looking soldier of sixty or so years of age. Ten feet away, Johnnie saw the grey cloak and almost panicked. He could not see her face, only the heavily pleated side of her blue calash, but as he dithered behind the bales and boxes that separated them, she turned and saw him. In the long moment before those glimmering eyes registered recognition, Johnnie took in her thinnness and plainness and unfashionableness and felt his heart plummet with dismay. She looked twenty years older, not ten, and had a maiden-auntish air that dismayed him unutterably.

Caroline's own feelings were no better. She had turned her head in no particular inquiry a moment before, and had seen a stout, florid, overdressed man in a wig like a cauli-flower, and a coat of a colour that became summer skies but not his particular girth or complexion. Something in his eyes, his small and anxious smile, made her look a second longer and in that second, she saw the smile melt from his face, and that face resolve itself into a gross caricature of Johnnie Gates. She put out a shaking hand and grasped General North by the sleeve.

'Well, my dear?'

Awkwardness and confusion followed. Neither Caroline nor Johnnie knew what to say, and General North could ill-suppress his surprise and disapproval. In a series of inarticulate questions and half-finished remarks, the three of them fumbled their way back to the carriage, and the multicoloured glory of Mrs Rathbone. General North shot one horrified look at her and pulled Caroline abruptly away from the carriage.

'My dear Miss Harding, you cannot go with such people, indeed you cannot. I cannot allow it.'

Mrs Rathbone, delighted to recognize General North, was calling from the carriage.

'Have no fear, General, Miss Harding will come to no harm. I shall personally see that she don't, indeed I shall. She shall stop with me until her wedding day, and I shall be like a mother to her.'

Caroline looked at the carriage and its occupant and at large, wretched Johnnie, and then back at General North's anxious face. Resisting the strong temptation to cast herself upon his gallantry she whispered quickly, 'I am quite determined to go, General. I thank you from the bottom of my heart for all your kindness, but I shall be quite safe, I do assure you, and I must go.'

She pressed his arm and moved quickly towards the carriage, smiling up at Mrs Rathbone.

'It is truly kind of you to shelter me, madam, and I am very much obliged to you.'

'Nonsense, my dear, I shall enjoy it, and so, I hope, will you. Now up you get – no, no, let the servants help you – and we can get busy being friends, eh?'

General North appeared in the carriage doorway.

'Madam, do you still live in the Garden Reach?'

Mrs Rathbone dimpled and tapped his knuckles with her fan.

'Indeed I do, General, and I shall be ever so pleased to have you call.'

'I inquired,' General North said firmly, 'since I wished to have your permission to call upon Miss Harding. There are friends who will be very anxious for news of her.'

'Call when you like, General dear, and if Miss Harding and I are not dressed, then it will be your lucky day, will it not?'

The door closed, and the carriage jolted forward. If Johnnie had wished Mrs Rathbone a million miles away on the journey to the waterfront, he was, on the return journey, profoundly thankful for her chattering presence. With a plump bejewelled hand on Caroline's knee, she prattled away steadily, and Caroline, though startled by her appearance, could not but be grateful for her generosity and desire to please. She hardly dared glance at Johnnie, but sat with her eyes fixed upon Mrs Rathbone, thankful there was so much about the lady to look at. She was not listening to the endless stream of revelations about dress, and people's private lives and the latest wickedness of Mr Francis, another member of the Company's Council in Calcutta, but instead felt herself to be in a state of stupefaction, induced by the sheer improbability of what was happening. The ship had in the end become a reality, a small intense reality, peopled with a tight little group of friends, the first friends she had ever made on her own. Then, just as the ship had become a world in itself, a world to be relied upon, the Ganges delta had been reached, the mouth of the Hooghly, and that safe small world had been broken up abruptly and dumped anyhow in tender boats, and the sense of improbability had begun. All her anchors had been wrenched away, first Isobel's young men to serve in the Company's army, greeted by alarming uniformed officers, then, worst of all, Isobel herself in a whirl of officialdom and grandeur that was both terrifying and yet enviable in its purposefulness, and then General North, helpless in his gallantry in the face of her determination. But that was something to hold on to, was it not? She sat in the hot carriage hardly daring to look from the windows, and knew she had scored a small victory for herself, for Caroline. General North had offered to snatch her like an opportune eagle from a most bizarre fate, and she had said no, the fate was what she had come for and face it she would. She would rather not look at it again, slumped on the opposite seat of the carriage, but she would take it.

Johnnie sat and despaired quietly opposite her. He never had the energy these days to do any more with any emotion, than perform it quietly. Without the stimulus of drink or danger or sexuality, he was a dull dog, he knew it. He shot covert glances at Caroline from beneath frowning brows, and thought what a fool she was to tolerate old Madam Rathbone's chatter, and then worried as to how he should ever introduce such a yellow stick of a creature to George Carew and other cronies. He fought about resentfully in his memory for pictures of young Caroline by the river, on the field path, in the ten-acre meadow, and could only dredge up hazy images of print gowns and eagerness that did his sour present mood no good at all. Her grey dress was hideous, her calash a public disgrace – did they really wear such monstrous bonnets in England? – and her nose – enough to make the world pity him. He thought of Rani for a moment, her supple, caramel-coloured limbs, her shining eyes and hair, and could have wept for himself.

If Mrs Rathbone thought Johnnie hardly played the part of an eager bridegroom, she allowed no sign of it. Caroline's appearance had struck her immediately by its ungainliness, but those brilliant silver eyes and that sweet and anxiously smiling mouth had overcome immediately the effect of her drab and clumsy clothing. Mrs Rathbone had decided, with the same maternal warmth that made her collect unconscious young men after dinner parties, that Caroline needed to be looked after and that she, Bella Rathbone, would perform that role.

'Here we are, dear,' she said unnecessarily as the carriage jolted to a halt. 'Home sweet home, and I hope you will come to regard it as such.'

Caroline looked out upon a house like a small replica of Stoke Park, a perfect small English house, set in an incongruously green garden of wholly un-English planting. She stepped out of the carriage onto a street of red dust, and smelt, for the first time away from the powerful odours of the waterfront, the curious sour, sweet, spicy, dusty, human smell of India. There seemed to be trees all about her, exaggerated, brilliant, alien trees, and scarlet and purple and cream and pink blossoms spread and fell all about the garden walls. She would have liked to exclaim at it all, and have run to examine and touch, but the phalanx of liveried Indian servants that lined the beaten dust path to the perfect Palladian-copy door seemed to make that sort of eccentricity impossible.

'A most elegant house, my dear,' Mrs Rathbone was saying, 'so fortunate, you know, to acquire it from dear Colonel Gordon when he went back to England, but it needed to be made more cosy, dear, more like a home, you know.'

Caroline followed Mrs Rathbone within, uncomfortably conscious of the unhappy bulk of her future husband behind her. They moved into a drawing room made dim by the screens of damp grasses at all windows and doorways, and still breathlessly hot, and Caroline perceived in the gloom that it was unlike any room she had ever entered before. There seemed to be a wealth of colours, an extravagance of gold, a proliferation of looking glasses. Every surface was littered, painted, gilded, stuffed and padded. For one brief mad moment, Caroline would have given all she possessed to shriek with laughter, but she pressed a corner of her oppressive cloak to her mouth and stifled it narrowly.

'Johnnie loves this house, do you not, dear? He is always here, you know; I think he feels at home. I like my friends to feel at home. Now, Miss Harding, dear, I shall have you shown to your room, and then we shall all meet again for dinner, shall we not?'

In the dimness, Johnnie made a small inarticulate sound. Caroline, who had no more wish to see him again at dinner, until she had adjusted her thoughts, than he her, said quickly, 'I am sure Mr Gates has a prior arrangement. It seems from what you told me in the carriage that Calcutta is very sociable so I am sure – '

'Indeed, no! Johnnie boy, can you think of dining elsewhere on such a day as this? The day your sweetheart comes to you. Fie, sir – '

'I must beg you to excuse me, ma'am,' Johnnie said on a high note of desperation, 'but Miss – Miss Harding is in a sense right, and I – I have not been at the office all morning, and am sadly behind in my affairs.'

Mrs Rathbone was scarlet with true indignation.

'You are a monstrous, mannerless boy, Johnnie, and do not deserve this sweet creature, indeed you do not! Indeed I feel – '

'Mrs Rathbone,' Caroline pleaded softly, 'let him go. I – I think no ill of it myself, and am quite confused enough by my travels to be glad of dining in a very small company.'

Johnnie shot a grateful glance not quite in her direction since he was terrified of meeting her gaze.

'Tomorrow then!' Mrs Rathbone commanded.

'Tomorrow, ma'am.'

'You will have to be very sprightly to make up for your behaviour today. Now bid farewell nicely to Miss Harding.'

'Until – until tomorrow, Miss Harding.'

His lips did not touch her hand.

'Good-day, Mr Gates.'

By the time they met again in the overstuffed splendour of Mrs Rathbone's drawing room, Caroline had tried to spend twenty-four solemn hours with her thoughts. It had not been easy to do. Mrs Rathbone had wished to drive out and show her every inch of the glittering city, in the hopes also that members of its glittering populace might be in evidence, but Caroline had pleaded weariness, and had managed to secure an evening and morning to herself in her lavish blue silk bedroom. Mr and Mrs Rathbone had confined themselves to a very small dinner party the previous afternoon, a mere dozen or so of overdressed and voluble people, and Caroline had felt no compunction in slipping away to her room the moment port began to circulate and the favourite Calcutta game of bread-pellet throwing was at its height.

Her hosts she felt were warm-hearted and good-natured, but their guests left her bewildered and dumb.

The morning was little better. She succeeded in persuading Mrs Rathbone that she must be left alone, but nothing seemed to daunt a steady flow of servants – amazing to her – wishing to dress her, dress her hair, manicure her nails and generally give her the kind of service she had never had in her life. A few spoke some words of English, most spoke only their native tongue, all were unobtrusive, smiling and astonished at her reluctance to be decorated. After futile attempts to make them leave her alone, she submitted miserably, so that by the time the dinner hour came she felt quite unlike herself and in the most distracted of humours. To come downstairs to the drawing room and find it full of brocade coats and spangled gowns, elaborately powdered heads and towering wigs, was no consolation. She felt protective and slightly defiant of her old blue silk gown and unpowdered hair and quite dismayed at the prospect before her.

'Ah, Caroline, my dear,' Mrs Rathbone cried, 'come forward, dear, so they may all see my new little English friend. There now! And where is naughty Johnnie, who is to be the lucky man! – there you are, you bad boy, now come along that we may all see you together.'

Cowering and wretched they stood together in a ring of false applause. Most of the women could scarcely restrain their amusement at Caroline's appearance, nor the men their barely concealed relief that she was poor Gates' lot, not theirs. In that particularly shallow and gossiping circle, Caroline felt a small gratitude for Johnnie's presence, and Johnnie wished he was on the edge of the circle rather than at the centre of it.

'I – I hope you are comfortable here,' he said.

'Oh, quite. It is most good of Mrs Rathbone to shelter me. I do not know what else I should have done.'

Johnnie refrained from saying, 'Nor I' in heartfelt tones.

'General North called at my office this morning.'

He was dismayed to see Caroline's face light up with eagerness. He knew it was a blunder to let her stay here, but what more suitable houses could she have gone to? He knew no others – at least, none to whom he could apply for favours.

'Oh – how kind of him!'

'He gave me this for you.'

It was a note in Isobel's writing. Johnnie knew quite well who it was from, from whose house it had come, and what it contained, since he had read it. It did not improve his temper. Caroline took it eagerly and thanked him with real warmth. It was their first exchange alone, and it was terminated then by the announcement of dinner.

From the menu card held in an elaborate gilt fleur-de-lis before her, Caroline saw that seven courses were between her and escape. The array of glasses before her was prodigious, and the baskets of fruit that marched down the centre of the table would have supplied Stoke Abbas with such luxuries for months. Johnnie was on her left, and an empty chair was, to her relief, on her right.

'Do not feel neglected, my dear,' Mrs Rathbone said, laying a gloved hand upon her shoulder. 'A very special guest is coming to fill up that place of honour. Your Johnnie's greatest friend, George Carew.'

Johnnie blanched. It was insupportable. He had had no chance to warn George of his fate. What would George think of him, saddled with this prissy scarecrow for life? He took up his champagne glass and swallowed the contents at a single gulp. It was instantly refilled, and as instantly emptied. Red-headed Mrs Grundy on his left, who had often much enjoyed him as a dinner companion and whiler-away of midnight hours, regarded him with a slight and cynical smile. Johnnie observed it. Caroline sat silent and tongue-tied. She wanted to ask Johnnie if they might meet somehow quite alone, but found it an impossible subject to breach. She looked furtively at him now and then, and was distressed to see the anger and misery that chased each other over his reddening countenance, but mostly she merely looked down at her soup and decided that, given the temperature of the room, nothing had ever looked more inappropriate or unappetizing.

The chair on her right was pulled back.

'Miss Harding, I believe? No, no, pray do not rise. I am unforgivably late. M'name's George Carew.'

'I am delighted to meet you. I believe you are a great friend – '

'Of the abominable animal's? 'Deed I am. Confounded hot, ain't it?'

'Why do we eat hot soup in this heat?'

'Deuced if I know, Miss Harding. Johnnie! Johnnie! Good day to you, sir. You've picked yourself a sensible woman here.'

'I have?' Johnnie said in genuine surprise.

'Don't care to drink hot soup in hot weather. What else don't you care for, Miss Harding?'

'Being made mock of, Mr Carew,' Caroline said boldly.

George Carew laid down his spoon and raised his glass to her.

'Caught red-handed, Miss Harding. Humble apologies.'

'Are you a Company man, also, Mr Carew?'

'For my sins, ma'am. How d'you like Calcutta?'

'I've not seen it yet. I arrived but yesterday and have been asleep or surrounded by servants since.'

'Won't change, won't change. That's how Calcutta is. Servants, sleep and much of this.'

He raised his glass again.

'Drink with me, Miss Harding.'

She shook her head.

'Why won't you?'

Caroline said levelly, 'I'll keep a clear head until I know more about you all.'

'My turn to be mocked, Miss Harding?'

'You must please yourself about that,' Caroline said daringly.

By dessert, Caroline was grateful for George Carew. Johnnie had said nothing whatsoever throughout dinner, but had eaten and drunk with the relentlessness of a man seeking both occupation and oblivion. Through soup and fish, mutton chops and quails, syllabubs and pineapple and all their accompanying wines, Caroline had watched him steadily plough. If it had not been for George Carew, she would have had no alternative but to gaze at her plate.

'Do guzzle, eh?' George said at one point, indicating Johnnie and a mountain of mutton chops. Caroline, who felt about hot meat as she felt about hot soup, preferred not to look.

At the end of dinner, Mrs Rathbone, pink with cherry brandy and heavily supported by the gentlemen on either side of her, rose to her feet.

'I wish to propose a toast, my dear! I – I wish to propose a toast of long life and happiness to my young friends, Miss Caroline Harding, and naughty Johnnie Gates! Now charge your glasses and drink with me!'

There was a good deal of roaring and shouting and everyone round the table rose unsteadily to their feet. Caroline dared not look at Johnnie. After a while the roaring subsided and George Carew hissed in her ear.

'Stand and say thank'ee, Miss Harding! They expect it, 'deed they do!'

Caroline looked at him in horror.

'Must I?'

''Pon my word, you must. Stand up and raise your glass and thank 'em. You too, Johnnie. Up we go!'

With a sensation of being fifteen foot high, Caroline rose to resounding cheers, her glass shaking in her hand. She raised it and felt the contents splash onto her hand.

'I thank you all,' she said, and her voice sounded small and unfamiliar and far away.

More cheers and shouts of 'On your legs!' to Johnnie. George went to the back of his chair and put his hands under Johnnie's armpits.

'Up, boy!'

Slowly, very slowly, Johnnie wavered to his feet. He raised his glass to Mrs Rathbone, drank from it, then prompted by shouts from the crowd tried to raise it to Caroline, failed and crashed prone, like a falling tree across the table, scattering pineapples as if they were no more than billiard balls.

There was a dead and expectant silence, while all eyes slowly turned and came to rest enquiringly upon Caroline. They were used to drunkenness, but was she? They waited, hopefully.

Caroline looked up from Johnnie's unconscious back.

'Would two gentlemen be good enough to help Mr Gates to somewhere more comfortable?'

'Bravo!' George Carew said under his breath.

Mrs Rathbone was mopping her eyes. All the romping that usually seemed so acceptable and amusing appeared deeply, dreadfully wrong in front of Caroline.

'Oh, my dear Miss Harding, my poor Caroline. Oh, forgive me dear – '

'There is nothing to forgive, Mrs Rathbone. You are hardly to blame. Mr Carew, would you escort Mr Gates home, since he clearly cannot take himself?'

George Carew bowed, and followed Johnnie's dragging figure from the room. Caroline, feeling that she could no longer bear that ring of incredulous and scornful eyes, went quickly after him, Mrs Rathbone sniffing and apologizing in her wake.

'I should have seen it coming, Miss Harding dear, indeed I should. Lord knows I've seen a boy with a skinful often enough! But before you, Miss Caroline! Oh, I could die of shame!'

Caroline put her hand on Mrs Rathbone's arm.

'Please do not distress yourself, Mrs Rathbone, pray be calm! I may not be as experienced in these matters as you are, but I have seen a deal of illness, and in many ways there is not much to choose between them. Come now, dry your eyes! It is hardly your fault, now is it?'

'For you to see him in such a state, Miss Caroline! For him to behave in such a way the moment his sweetheart comes!'

Caroline looked up and met George Carew's amused gaze.

'I feel that that may have everything to do with it,' she said.

George bowed again.

'You've a clear head on your shoulders, Miss Harding.'

Caroline smiled a little nervously and said in a low voice, 'It seems that I shall need it.'

'Oh come, come, Miss Harding! A douche of cold water and a bit of rest and he will be right as a trivet!'

'Until the next time.'

George Carew cleared his throat and did not reply.

'Oh, Miss Harding, dear!' Mrs Rathbone cried suddenly. 'Mr Gates and yourself were bidden to sup with General Russell this evening! And now what shall we do?'

Caroline gazed at her incredulously, visions of mounds of mutton chops dancing before her eyes.

'Supper, Mrs Rathbone? Supper? After – all this?'

'Oh yes, Miss Harding dear, it is quite the custom. You will find Calcutta very gay, will she not, George? We always sup at a late hour and hardly a week goes by without some dance or even a ball. We are never dull here in India, I do assure you.'

'I think, Mrs Rathbone, that I shall have to be a little dull to begin with, at least until I feel a little less disorientated. I hope General Russell will forgive me if I do not attend but I – ' she looked across at Johnnie's bulk sprawled upon a sofa, 'I had rather not appear alone.'

'You'll not be alone!' George Carew cried. 'We'll swill the old chum out and he'll escort you, I swear it!'

Caroline shrank back a little.

'No – no, I thank you but no. Will you oblige me greatly, Mr Carew, by taking Mr Gates home, and – and would you tell him,' she added, gathering courage, 'that I shall call upon him at noon tomorrow – that is, ma'am, if I may borrow your carriage?'

'Certainly, my dear, with the greatest pleasure in the world.'

George Carew motioned to several of Johnnie's servants who had materialized by some sort of instinct in the doorway, that they were to bear away their master. He turned back to Caroline and said in a voice of undisguised admiration, 'You are a woman of spirit, Miss Harding, and I hand it to you, 'deed I do. He'll await you at noon, ma'am, if I have to lash him to his chair.'

He bowed to Caroline, kissed Mrs Rathbone's hand and went out.

'Will you not think me unpardonably rude, Mrs Rathbone, if I go to my room? I am so sorry to be such a poor-spirited guest, but I feel that I must – must think a while.'

Mrs Rathbone patted her hand with no small relief. An uproarious party was going on now behind the closed dining-room doors, and it seemed a shame that she, the hostess, should miss it all.

'Not at all, dear, very wise, very wise indeed. I'll have tea sent up to you later, dear. You'd like that, would you not? Remind you of home.'

'You are most kind,' Caroline said faintly, and escaped. Mrs Rathbone watched her fleeing through doors that were silently opened as she came, and then with the pleasure before her of making something of an entrance, turned back to the riotous remains of her dinner party.

Alone in the hot silence of her room, Caroline eagerly pulled out her note from Isobel. It seemed much crumpled, but that was probably the effect of spending two or three hours in her pocket. She took it to a window, where the afternoon sun might fall upon it, and felt a lump rise in her throat at the sight of that familiar handwriting.

My dearest Caroline,

I am quite desolate without you and my desolation is made much worse by anxiety. I am staying in a most stiff and proper house, and should suffocate instantly except that the maids are an excellent source of gossip and most speak good English. But I do not like the gossip, I do not at all like it. They say your John Gates is a depraved and licentious man, and they make fun of him for his style of dress. If you allow for the exaggeration of gossip, that still makes him a man grossly unworthy of you. Oh Caroline, do be careful! I beg you not to let your stiff and silly pride lead you into something rash! Both the General and Sir Edward forbid me to visit you where you are, but I shall find your address from the servants and come. I am in a ferment to see you. Why do you not come to me? I beg you to – Sir Edward would welcome you.

Yours in frenzy,
Isobel

Dear Isobel! Caroline looked up from the letter and out onto that strange brilliant green garden with its high mud walls and still tanks of water. She must not let herself see Isobel yet, much as she longed to. If she did, the whole beautiful allure of that confident world Isobel inhabited would sweep her away, undermine her resolve. The first person she must see, must be Johnnie. There was something at the bottom of all this, some explanation for his apparent ardour while she was safely far away, and his evident panic now she was close at hand. Perhaps his easy charm of ten years ago was all he had ever had and now it had gone for ever, its absence to be compensated for now with wine. Depending on the outcome of her visit to Johnnie, she would then decide about seeing Isobel. In the meantime she would write to her, reassuringly, very reassuringly. She crossed the room and rang for paper and ink.

I I

Caroline hardly slept that night. The dreamlike sense of unreality, that had possessed her since her arrival, and prevented her from feeling things too keenly, was slipping gradually away and leaving her to face facts unaided. The first fact she had to face during those long black rustling hours was that it was amazingly, incredibly hot. Mrs Rathbone had said it was still the cold season, if only by a matter of weeks, but Caroline had never experienced such laughable coldness in her life. As she lay and tried not to toss, her whole skin seemed damp, steaming damp, and the heavy black air about her bed seemed to have the density of hot velvet. Her hair was damp, her sensible cotton nightgown was damp, her pillow and sheet were damp. How on earth, she wondered, could those men at dinner today endure those layers of stiffened, gold-laced brocade, those great white wigs, cravats like perfect explosions of lace? And the women had been no freer, beneath towering wigs adorned with entire harvests of fruit and flowers and jewels, and although bare-bosomed, they still trailed prodigious quantities of heavy silk about with them. Caroline had been very grateful for her cotton gowns during the daytime, and felt that her one silk was too shabby to matter spoiling, as it was bound to become. She had not believed it possible to sweat so much. Suppose one simply dried right out, like a husk or leaf, and blew away over the Ganges delta, unnoticed and quickly forgotten?

The second fact, even worse in its way, was the noises. Every so often there came a terrible anguished squeal, as of a child in pain, and each time it came Caroline would leap from her pillow, her throat constricted in apprehension. She had never heard a jackal call before, for General North's education had not extended to the sounds these beasts made, and every scream filled her with new terror. She began to wait for each next one, stiff and wide-eyed, straining to hear through the comfortable whirr of the crickets that soul-tearing shriek of sorrow and pain. In the intervals between the jackals, she could hear too the thin high drone of mosquitoes, wheeling and whining about in the dead hot air, many of them finding a successful entry through the shrouds of white gauze that wrapped her bed, and leaving her crazed with itchings. Starting up, casting herself down, thrashing and scratching, she gazed at the blackness of the windows and longed for the first glimmer of day.

When at long last it came, the sunrise was marvellous. A rosy glow began to steal through the billowing muslin and blue silk with which Mrs Rathbone had draped the windows and Caroline rose thankfully from her crumpled and un-refreshing bed and went to see what was happening. The skyline was sharply etched to the east in indigo, a skyline of flat-roofed dwellings, of trees, tall coconut palms with waving fronds, and the occasional dome and tower against an exploding apricot sky. The dreadful screams and rustlings of the night were giving way to more distinct sounds as the Rathbones' servants began to stir in their quarters, and the day was started in the small mud huts and houses beyond the garden walls. Plumes of blue smoke began to rise here and there, and with them curious cooking smells, strongly redolent of charcoal. She had spoken to no Indian successfully yet, she thought, a lack that must be quickly remedied. The little maids that had been sent to attend her remained dumb and smiling as they deftly fastened her gowns and brushed her hair. She hoped her tone conveyed what her vocabulary could not when she thanked them.

She breakfasted alone in the stuffy dining room, still faintly and unattractively redolent of last afternoon's cigars and mutton. She was brought toast and tea and butter, and the incongruous Englishness of it, in this opulent English room, made her smile to herself. She wondered if the silent servants who brought it thought it a curious meal and what had they eaten for breakfast instead. Rice perhaps? Scraps left from yesterday's banquet?

'Thank you,' she said.

They bowed.

'Will there be anything else the memsahib is wanting?'

'Nothing at all, thank you, until the carriage just before noon.'

There were three hours to think about that carriage drive, but Caroline resolved to be firm with herself and not to dwell on it. She would begin by a thorough tour of the garden, unadventurous perhaps, but a beginning.

The maids already busy in her room were horrified to see her come upstairs herself for her hat. They fluttered about her with little exclamations of dismay, tying the ribbons under her chin with light little butterfly touches. One held up a creamy pink flower with curved spikes for petals that Caroline did not recognize for her to smell. It gave off a rich, exotic, powerful fragrance. Caroline felt it tucked into the ribbon of her hat, another into the sash of her gown. Then they held up a looking-glass for her to see, and she felt it was so wrong that these little girls, so brown and pretty and doe-eyed, should be concerned with the adornment of a stiff plain spinster like herself. But they were so pleased with her, and with their efforts, that she smiled at each, and thanked them warmly, and they ran to open the door for her.

She felt a little leap of pleasure as she went into the garden. It was not fresh and cool and full of promise as an English spring garden would be, but the luxuriant and brilliant greenness was a balm to the eye after the heavily decorated interior of Mrs Rathbone's house. The garden had been laid out with the sort of formality Caroline recognized from engravings she had seen of French gardens, symmetrical shapes of grass and gravel bordered with low box hedges, and brilliant unfamiliar flowers blooming in regimented patterns in formal beds of sifted red earth. Gardeners in loin cloths were crouched all over the garden on their haunches, neatly weeding with thin brown fingers, but when Caroline spoke to them in what she hoped was a gentle and congratulatory tone, they fell on their knees before her and made her feel abashed and uncomfortable. There were little water boys everywhere, with great earthenware crocks of water, to be sprinkled with reverence. It was all perfectly fascinating.

Beyond the stretch of formal garden, Caroline found a wilder part in which she felt much more comfortable, where there was no gravel, only a stretch of elephant grass unevenly bordered with wonderful blossoming shrubs and trees, the blossoms in brilliant colours of scarlet and pink, purple and orange. She found one great beautiful white camellia with a scent like wine, and sat herself down in its shade to look at the splendours about her.

Shortly before twelve, she retraced her steps to the house, and waited in the drawing room for the carriage. Her calm solitary morning had both revived and soothed her spirits, and she felt, if not exactly prepared for the coming interview, at least not panic-struck with fear at the thought of it. She would not go upstairs to look at herself in the glass since she knew full well there was little point in that, but sat and waited in the dimness and heat and thought how infinitely preferable the camellia tree had been.

The carriage was punctual and emblazoned with gorgeous and thoroughly spurious-looking arms. Four servants in matching livery waited while Caroline climbed in, and she observed with a private twinge of amusement that their clothing was infinitely more splendid than her plain cream muslin. There was a pair of magnificently matched chestnuts to draw her, and a perfect army of servants to escort her. For a brief moment, which she despised herself for, she wished Lady Lennox could see her. They trotted forward over the smooth red dust road, and Caroline, having no Mrs Rathbone to distract her, watched eagerly from the window, determined to miss nothing, no detail of her drive.

She had not realized, when Mrs Rathbone had said that she lived on the edge of Garden Reach, how literal her hostess was being; but almost the moment the carriage left the coconut-fronded avenue outside the house, it plunged into quite another world. The green and white impression was gone, and in its place came a yellow and red impression, dusty and raw and dry. Leaving the smooth road, they began to lurch down lanes that were no more than rutted tracks, hard dun ridges of baked mud, between dwellings that Caroline at first mistook for mere piles of building rubble, such disordered heaps of planks and mud and mouldy matting they were. They huddled and straggled along the edges of these jolting tracks, the only shade afforded to them being from grotesque bearded trees, whose matted brownish tassels hung down from the branches like sheaves of unkempt hair. In the shade of these banyans were groups of squatting people, thin dark people in ragged cotton, their heads bound in cloths against the sun.

Dogs sniffed at the rubbish strewn everywhere, thin, dreadful limping dogs, and bare-bottomed children in tattered shirts squatted in the dust among goats and flies and mooning white cows. The children waved and smiled to her, the crouching adults raised faces with no animosity in them to her elaborate equipage, and went on calmly peeling oranges, fastidiously tearing away shreds of pith, and leaving the earth scattered with bright peels. The smells of poverty that drifted in to Caroline were very different from the smells of those poor cottages at Stoke Abbas; those stank of earth and mould and damp human dirtiness, but this powerful smell in Calcutta reminded Caroline strongly of the ancient dog at the Parsonage, tolerated solely because of his age, but banished always to the kitchen regions because of his almost tangible smelliness.

Eventually, these alarming lanes dwindled away somewhat, and the carriage entered small streets, not identifiable as such by their roadways which were of dried yellow mud as before, but because the hovels had given place to box-like mud houses, almost windowless to defeat the sun. Some of the houses were evidently in European occupation, with bright patches of garden and curtains at the glassless windows and an air of gentle activity that the presence of several servants gives. Occasionally, a house had clearly been modelled upon European style also, with steps up to double-leaved doors, and windows arranged with careful symmetry above and either side of them.

With a sinking presentiment that they were almost at their destination, Caroline's gaze fixed itself with almost prophetic certainty upon one of these small mud copies of houses upon Richmond Hill. It was yellow, like all the others, with a shallow flight of steps to a door beneath a chipped and crumbling portico that owed nothing to Greek art but the inspiration. The twin-leaved door had once been painted a dull terra cotta, but this had almost all flaked off, leaving the gasping grey wood cracking beneath. Rows of dusty windows confronted a space of dun rubble that might once have been designated a garden, and among the piles of stones it contained, crouched several children, mostly naked except for bracelets.

When the carriage actually stopped before this spectacle, she saw with some dismay that she was evidently expected. A double row of servants lined the shallow flight of steps to the front door which itself was instantly opened to the dark interior. The livery this respectful double file wore was, she noticed, hardly fit to be exposed to the merciless brilliance of the sun, being both tattered and filthy, each garment only vaguely approximating to the size and shape of its wearer. She stepped out of Mrs Rathbone's gaudy but well-maintained carriage, and mounted the steps between these lines of calm-faced scarecrows, observing further as she went upwards that all the rubbish that had clearly littered the steps before her arrival, had been shuffled away by twenty pairs of bare feet in haste, and now lay in squalid profusion behind the rows of dark servants' legs. It was an inauspicious start to a daunting interview.

If George Carew had not arrived promptly at ten o'clock that morning and pummelled Johnnie mercilessly into consciousness, Caroline would probably have found him still deep in the slumber of the unjust. The night before he had indeed gone out again, a bucket of water being, as George had pointed out, all he needed to restore his wits to some semblance of order, and had proceeded to repeat the performance which had taken place at Mrs Rathbone's dinner party. He had not intended to specifically, but as all he sought at this moment was oblivion, however temporary, drunkenness was, for Johnnie, inevitable. George Carew had worked very hard on him for two hours, since the former had conceived a surprised, but undoubted admiration for Caroline the night before, and he now sat and shook in the drawing room, clad in the cleanest clothes George could find from a wholly dubious wardrobe. He was pouring with sweat, the cold sweat of apprehension mingling with the customary steam in which the occupants of Calcutta lived, and his every coherent thought, few though they were, concerned the desperate impasse to which his affairs had come. If George had not been lounging at the window, apparently relaxed but in reality ready to tackle Johnnie bodily should he so much as stir, he would have fled.

'Mis' Memsahib Harding, sahib.'

The drawing room was very dim, for the windows were screened with great blinds of dampened grasses, but despite being scarcely able to see, Caroline was conscious of a well-proportioned smallish room which exuded a smell of warm mouldiness and dust. There seemed to be little furniture in it, and only pale patches on the walls instead of the pictures that once hung there. The sircar had cousins who repaired furniture broken in brawls and reframed pictures smashed by flying bottles, but somehow the cousins never seemed to disgorge these repairs.

'Good – good day,' Johnnie said in a low voice, his face slightly averted.

George Carew uncoiled himself from his sofa.

'Miss Harding, good day to you! Here's the rogue, good as my word.'

'I am grateful to you,' Caroline said doubtfully.

'Hope you will be, 'deed I do. I shall leave you together, but I'll not be far off, should you want me.'

Caroline curtseyed briefly, George bowed, smiled at her, grinned at Johnnie and left the room, humming. When his footsteps had died away across the hall, a thick silence surged back again into the room and seemed to stifle them.

At last Caroline said with difficulty, 'I hope you will not think me very impertinent, but I do not think I can speak to you in this darkness. Might at least one of the screens be moved?'

'Deuced hot,' Johnnie muttered, for whom the dimness was a comfort.

'Please.'

He barked a command briefly, and a shadow in the corner uncurled itself, and pushed away the screen from a small window at the end of the room. Sunlight blazed in, abruptly illuminating the dust and disorder, the bottles under chairs, books in mouldy confusion here and there, and Johnnie's hungover countenance.

'I have one more request,' Caroline said, looking with distaste about her.

Johnnie inclined his head without speaking. Fixing her level grey gaze upon him, she said gravely, 'Would you do me the great favour of removing your wig? It changes your countenance so entirely that I feel as if I am speaking to a total stranger.'

'Indeed, ma'am – ' Johnnie exclaimed, backing away from her.

'Just for this interview, sir. Would you not be cooler without it in any case?'

With an oath, Johnnie tore his wig from his head and flung it into the chaos of a corner. He came closer to Caroline, glaring slightly.

'Do I please you better now, ma'am?'

She looked up at his disordered dark head and saw instantly the vanished and glorious Johnnie captured in this overweight and intemperate caricature.

'Infinitely so. I thank you.'

Grunting, he fetched a chair for her, and placed himself opposite, in the edge of the shadows. Where had that sweet and adoring docility gone, which was about all he could remember of her? She was looking at him, steadily now with those brilliant silvery eyes, and he was not at all sure that some tiny spark of mockery did not lie in them.

'We are in a fix, are we not, Mr Gates?'

He shrugged. She pulled a letter from her pocket and held it out to him.

'If I had believed what is written in that letter, I should have been broken-hearted at your reception of me.'

Unwillingly, Johnnie reached out and took the letter by its very edge. He turned it over and saw Caroline's name written upon it in his own hand, and remembered what George had assisted him to write within.

He said, 'It was written some time ago.'

'It was written after a silence between us of eight years. If

163

eight years had not changed your feelings, I do not see that the one or two since its writing should do so.'

He said nothing, but sat gazing at his nails and hated her. She was his gaoler, his warder, she had come to India to put him in irons, to ruin the remainder of his youth. She seemed to have no sensitivity at all, for she was speaking again, still in that level, calm voice as if she were discussing something of no more consequence than the menus for the day.

'I asked to see you today, because I must discover the truth. I might not have believed this letter, but I did not disbelieve that you still had some desire, however small, to – to marry me. But I arrive here and find that I arouse in you a complete revulsion. You shun me, you can hardly bear to look at or speak to me. So I must conclude that there was more to your offer of marriage than I thought – or perhaps less, since you seem to have none of the feelings I – I hoped for.'

Her voice faltered a little, but she went on.

'You must try to imagine my situation a little. I have no one, apart from my brothers, all of whom are busy, to turn to. I came to India because I had nowhere else to go and be – because I hoped I was a little wanted here. I see,' she hurried on self-consciously, 'that I was quite mistaken in that hope, but I am now in something of a predicament, as you must see. You may not – want me, but as I have come here at your instruction, I think you must help me in what I am to do next.'

The sourness of Johnnie's expression had melted a little during this speech with its increasing diffidence of tone. A small understanding of her loneliness flitted briefly, very briefly, across his own vista of self-pity.

'Have you any money, ma'am?'

'None,' she said almost in a whisper.

'Money!' he shouted, suddenly. 'Money! 'Tis true that it it is always the root of evil! The lack of it and the need for it drives us to wretchedness, to untold suffering!'

She was looking at him in some perplexity. He got up and went to the window, standing for a moment with his back to her. He said, without turning round, 'If you have no money, ma'am, you are in the same case as I.'

'I – I believed you were employed here by the East – '

'Oh, I am, I am! But I am paid such a trifling sum that a dog could not live upon it!'

She moistened her lips.

'Perhaps I might help you to live upon it?' she suggested anxiously.

Johnnie turned from the window and came to sit quite close to her. Leaning forward, he said heavily, 'You are almost upon the truth of it.'

'I am? I do not – '

'I have little enough now,' Johnnie said, 'but if I do not marry you, I have nothing, no expectations, no future. If I do not marry you, I live like a jackal upon two hundred pounds a year until I die.'

Caroline leaned forward, and with a quite involuntary movement, put her hand upon his. He did not take his away.

'I do not quite understand you, I do not see why this should be.'

'Consider,' he said with something of a sneer, 'consider whose relation I am, to whose tune I must dance.'

Caroline sat bolt upright and said with a sort of angry triumph,

'Lady Lennox!'

'The very same.'

He looked up and saw the bright glitter of fury in Caroline's eyes.

He shrugged.

'Explain to me,' Caroline said in a voice full of anger.

'If you wish. Lady Lennox has contrived it that the fortune that is to come to me from my parents' will shall not be mine unless I marry. It is Lennox money, you see, brought to my father by my mother.' His mouth twisted a little. 'She does not like the way I live, reported to her in all its detail by that lily-livered traitor Frank Lovell, and thus wishes me to be curbed by marriage and its responsibilities.'

'But why should I come into any of this?' Caroline burst out.

'Because – because we once had an understanding, and because you are sober-living and used to poverty – ' he looked pointedly at her meagre frame and stopped. Not even Johnnie could say that the other reasons were that no one else would want a wife so plain, and also because her thin figure seemed ill-suited to the production of children, and thus she would present little threat to the Lennoxes as a producer of heirs.

Caroline looked at his troubled face with her clear gaze, and read his thoughts with unhappy accuracy.

She rose and began to pace about the room, twisting her fingers that were slippery with sweat by now. The heat seemed to intensify the oppression of her thoughts, pressing down upon her brow with a weight as painful as her new knowledge. She was simply a pawn in a game, an ignorant pawn in a sordid little game played by Lady Lennox. No wonder she had been so angry when Caroline had first refused to come to India! No wonder she had been so elated when Caroline capitulated after Parson Harding's death, and had written that infinitely complacent letter of godspeed when Caroline left for Gravesend! All her plans had worked quite wonderfully, quite as she had wished. She had killed two birds, whom she disliked, with one stone, and had ensured thereby that precious Lennox money should revert to her family upon Johnnie's death. Caroline bit her lip and felt herself more angry than she had ever been in her life.

'She shall not win!' she cried. 'We will not marry and she shall not win!'

Johnnie sighed hugely.

'If we do not marry, I am destitute.'

Caroline stopped pacing.

'I had forgotten that.'

'I had not. I never do. It has oppressed me this last year, I am never free from it.'

Caroline had an impulse to cry out, 'And what about me?' but saw the appeal would fall on stony ground and kept her lips tight shut. Johnnie's head was bent, he was clearly, she could see it, immersed in the sad contemplation of his own lucklessness.

She went over to him and said softly, 'All those years ago, did you even mean to marry me then?'

Johnnie looked away from her.

'I cannot say. I do not remember. My aunt and your father were so – '

'Please say no more.'

'But you asked me!'

'And I regretted doing so instantly.'

He shrugged. She walked away again into the hot stale gloom of the room and tried to cudgel her thoughts into some sort of order.

'It would seem to me that there is one sense in which each of us needs the other. You need me to secure your fortune. I need you to keep me from utter destitution.'

'I thought you had great friends here,' he said, not entirely pleasantly. 'I thought you were bosom friends with Miss Grant, now staying with Sir Edward Ashton. Would they not help you?'

'I do not choose to ask them.'

'You are very stiff.'

'Maybe so. I am also very tired of being an object of charity. To be someone's wife would give me a kind of status and an occupation. If I was your wife I would cost you very little as I am sure you have calculated, and in return I would make sure that you were comfortable. I would tidy up those servants and clean up this – this pig-sty, and I would see that your linen and food were as you liked them.'

Johnnie was listening more intently than he seemed to be. George Carew had said this very thing to him once, he distinctly recalled it. Perhaps she was right, perhaps she did have something to offer him, perhaps he might not do so badly after all. He stood up and looked at her. She was as plain as a pikestaff, but her added years had given her some strength of mind, no doubt about that.

'Shall we strike a bargain then?'

Caroline looked at his complacent smile and felt a surge of loathing. The promise of clean linen and swept floors had been all he needed to bring him out of his mood of petty self-indulgence. He had not thought once to ask how she felt, or to reassure her in the smallest way. In a tight voice she said, 'It can only be a bargain. Not a true marriage, only a bargain.'

'Agreed,' he said, and held his hand out. She put hers into it reluctantly and felt it slightly squeezed. When he smiled like that, little stabs of romantic nostalgia went through her. Perhaps she might get to be a little fond of him after all, recover a tiny part of the feelings of ten years ago. She smiled back.

'Your part of the bargain is that you shall support me and give me your name. My part is that I shall run your domestic affairs for you and make your life comfortable.'

He bowed.

'What freedoms will you allow me?'

Caroline thought with revulsion of dinner the day before, but recollected that the bargain allowed for no controls by one party of the other. She at least would stick by that.

'Any you care for – but one.'

'And what is that one, may I ask?'

Caroline hesitated, then said with a burst of courage, 'My bed. I do not want you in my bed.'

Johnnie's brow darkened instantly. It was true that nothing tempted him less than the prospect of making love to Caroline, but no woman in all his philandering life had ever laid down such a ban before. It was an outrage to his virility.

Caroline observed his reaction, and said quickly, 'If you think about it, you will realize I am only denying you something you do not want anyway.'

She suspected Johnnie's sexual habits after two days' conversation with Mrs Rathbone, but she did not wish to dwell on them, nor to give Johnnie overt carte blanche to indulge himself freely elsewhere. Those bridges, she decided, she would cross as they came.

'Is it possible that we can be married purely by civil ceremony?'

'There is no church in Calcutta.'

'No church!'

'Morning prayer is, I believe, said in the Customs Office every Sunday.'

Caroline looked relieved.

'I have no fear of desecrating the Customs Office. When should we arrange for – for it?'

Johnnie felt a slight rush of panic.

'You see,' Caroline went on, 'every minute I am still Mrs Rathbone's guest, and as I have already told you, I am anxious not to be in that position any longer. Must banns be read or may we be married soon?'

'George will know,' Johnnie said nervously.

'Will you call him?'

George was summoned, and came in with a quick light step and a distinct gleam in his eye.

'Congratulations in order, you old renegade?'

Johnnie nodded.

'Then my heartiest commiserations to you, Miss Harding! When shall it be?'

'That is just why we wished for your advice, Mr Carew. It must be soon for I have nowhere to go and I wondered if it was necessary for banns to be read?'

'Banns? In Calcutta? Nonsense, Miss Harding, we dispensed with such fripperies long ago. Deuce take it, I'll have you married by Saturday, on my oath I will!'

Three days later, Caroline Harding and John Gates were married in the Customs Office of Calcutta by civil ceremony. The only witnesses were George Carew and Mrs Rathbone, who wore purple silk and gold lace and cried a good deal. Caroline was thankful no one who knew her was present at the small and shabby ceremony, in which the bride and groom made their promises in tones quite devoid of any conviction and the drone of flies all but obscured their voices in any case. Caroline did not permit herself the indulgence of reflecting upon what she was doing, but went through the motions of the day in as mindless a state as she could manage. A subdued dinner and an even quieter supper followed the wedding, and Caroline went to bed alone on her wedding night, placing a chair back beneath the door handle before she slept since she had observed the lock was broken.

12

For Caroline, the first few weeks of marriage resembled nothing so much as the month of April at Stoke Parsonage, when Eleanor made everyone's life insupportable by relentless spring cleaning. She rose the first morning of finding herself Mrs Gates with the firm intention of making the house immediately habitable, and providing Johnnie with an alternative to his luxurious but dingy linen. They breakfasted together in some embarrassment, both slightly stunned at the speed at which they had become bound as man and wife, and parted for their separate days with ill-concealed relief.

Caroline had no qualms at dealing with her new army of dark-skinned, silent-footed servants; indeed, she rather looked forward to it. She ascertained from Johnnie, after a few days of finding how difficult it was to make any headway domestically, that household affairs had been in the sircar's hands for the last few years, and that if she wanted anything done she must apply to him. General North's instructions had included the information that a sircar was a broker, responsible for the hiring of servants and domestic finances. Looking about her, it seemed to Caroline that the latter responsibility appeared to weigh very lightly on the sircar indeed. When Johnnie had departed for the office with his retinue, resplendent in glittering white linen washed by Caroline herself at the cracked washstand in her bedroom, the sircar was summoned.

The feelings of warmth Caroline had so spontaneously for all working people cooled considerably at the sight of the sircar. He stood in the doorway, cringing slightly, dressed in a greasy robe of grey cotton over various unattractive and dirty rags. He smiled hopefully, clasping his hands before him in a humble manner; his smile displayed broken teeth, and never reached his small brown eyes which watched Caroline with a steady beadiness. Caroline, her hair tied up in a kerchief in preparation for an assault upon the drawing room, surveyed him without compassion.

'The memsahib is wanting me?'

'I have a good deal to ask you.'

The sircar winced a little at the relentlessness in her tone. He attempted a little fawning, a technique that had proved highly successful with Sahib Gates in the early days.

'It is not being seemly for the memsahib to be dirtying her hands so. If she permits, I will be sending servants to do the work that she may rest as is proper.'

'I would rest if I thought any work would be done, but I do not. Why is every corner of the house so filthy? Why have I had to turn away breakfast every morning because the milk has soured and the butter was rancid oil? Why is no laundry done? Why is the house cluttered with servants who do nothing but loll in the shade picking their teeth all day? Where is the rest of the furniture and the pictures? Why is the garden no more than a wilderness?'

The sircar tucked his hands into the sleeves of his gown, and began a long wailing, whining explanation. His heart was in it too, for he had detected in Caroline's quiet and steady voice a distinct note of purpose. After enduring the sing-song for two minutes or so, Caroline motioned him to be silent.

'That will do. It comes to nothing but the grossest negligence. You have been entrusted with the money to run the household, and the household receives no benefit from it. I wonder where the money has gone?'

The sircar fell to his knees.

'Always, always there is so much to be paying for, memsahib! Sahib Gates is not giving me what is necessary – '

'I do not believe you. I think you are a rogue and a liar.'

The sircar's forehead touched the floor at her feet. He lay there, glumly awaiting dismissal.

'Get up,' she said.

He shuffled to his knees, but deemed it politic to remain on them.

'You are angry with me, memsahib. But if you are sending me away, what am I and my children to be doing? In all Calcutta, there is nowhere for I and my children – '

'I never spoke of dismissal.'

The sircar ventured a brief glance upwards. She was not smiling, but her eyes looked very promising.

'I shall not dismiss you. I shall simply make you answerable to me in everything you do. You will hire no one and dismiss no one without reference to me. Food will be ordered by my consent, and the money you use must be checked before and after any purchase. Everyone will be given duties and will be expected to perform them scrupulously. An inventory of everything in the house will be made and missing items will be instantly reported. Do I make myself clear?'

'I am without speeches,' said the sircar, groaning inwardly at this appalling prospect of discipline and accounts.

'In return,' Caroline went on, now smiling broadly at his discomfiture, 'I will do what I can for you. If any servant is in trouble, and it is a trouble I know something of, I will help. If any servant is sick, I will try to make them comfortable.'

The sircar shrugged. The mere idea of a white lady being of any use whatsoever in that comfortable rat-run that constituted the servants' quarters was perfectly laughable. However, if she chose to entertain such ludicrous notions, he could not stop her. He felt very gloomy about the future, and saw what a painful necessity for deviousness there would be. For the past few years he had not had to tax his wits at all; now he would have to cudgel them. He would also have to see Sahib Gates alone on little matters of money. He sighed deeply and shook his head.

'Get up,' Caroline said again.

He rose slowly, and stood dejectedly before her with his shoulders and head bowed.

Caroline looked at him levelly.

'Shall we begin?'

A few days later it became necessary to apply to Johnnie for money. Huge quantities of whitewash had appeared mysteriously at the sircar's reluctant command and the house resounded with the slapping of brushes. A dhobi, yet again a relation of the sircar's, had agreed to take away every remnant and rag of fabric in the household and return it pristine, on condition that he might be paid upon the spot. Caroline promised readily, entranced at the prospect of fresh curtains and sheets, and then found she had nothing to pay with. At dinner that day, she ventured to broach the matter. Johnnie seemed in quite a good humour, encouraged by the new order sweeping through his house, and by the excellent mutton he was eating. His benevolence was further increased by the comfortable self-satisfaction of being very good to his new bride by staying in with her during these first few weeks until she felt able to venture into society.

'I regret having to petition you,' Caroline began, 'but I fear it will not be possible to run the household without money.'

Johnnie waved a hand airily.

'Think nothing of it. 'Tis the sircar's affair. When we are in straits, he always has a cousin who is a money-lender, and at most reasonable rates. Leave it to him!'

'I'm afraid I cannot.'

'Cannot?'

'No. I cannot. I have every reason to believe he has been pocketing money entrusted to him.'

Johnnie's brow darkened. It would not only be deuced inconvenient if that were true, but also make him look a pretty fool before the world to be tricked that way these last few years.

'Rubbish!'

Caroline said nothing.

'How do you know?'

'Because no bills have been paid this last year, laundry has seldom been done, furniture sent to be repaired has not come back, and yet the sircar has had a steady supply of money from you or from the bazaar on your behalf.'

Johnnie put down his knife and fork.

'Damn you!' he shouted.

Caroline had an impulse to flee, and resisted it.

'I – I am trying to improve matters – '

'You are an interfering woman, that is all you are and no

more! What ailed this house until you came into it, may I ask you?'

'Everything,' Caroline said stoutly.

'Rubbish! It ran like clockwork and it suited me, thank you, it suited me very well!'

'Did it?' Caroline said maddeningly. 'The dirt suited you? And the filthy clothing and rotten food suited you?'

Johnnie glared at her.

'Damn you,' he said again.

Caroline waited a moment and then said as gently as she could, 'If you would tell me how much I might spend in running the house and paying the servants, I will make quite sure that sum is never exceeded.'

'I don't know how much,' Johnnie said crossly. 'It is the sircar's damned business. Anyway, I have no money to give you. You know that.'

'What are we to live upon, then?'

Johnnie shrugged.

'It comes and goes. I make a little here and there, I never know when.'

'How much is the house?'

'Two hundred pounds a year. It's robbery. Who would live in this part of town unless you were condemned to as I am? And I have just spent forty pounds upon you, for that is the price of matrimony in Calcutta. Forty pounds!'

Caroline felt a slight chill come over her. She knew nothing of the inland trading with which the Company clerks heavily supplemented their meagre incomes, and it seemed to her that destitution was as near to her in matrimony as it had been when single. She knew that Johnnie's salary was only two hundred and fifty pounds a year, therefore fifty pounds only remained for domestic expenditure when the rent was paid. Servants' wages, if the sircar spoke anything like the truth, were exorbitantly high by comparison with England, and the number of servants wickedly extravagant.

'If – if I were to dismiss some of the servants – ' she began.

'Dismiss them!' Johnnie shouted. 'Are you mad? The servants are wholly necessary for me to maintain my position. I cannot dispense with a single one.'

'I have nothing to sell, I fear. If I had, I would, to help us until matters are better, but I have nothing.'

A slight gleam came into Johnnie's eyes. George Carew had mentioned the whist club that morning, and Johnnie had made a laborious performance of refusing because he had been married only a matter of days. But he was good at whist and lucky, and it was a wonderful chance of escape. He'd not drunk above three bottles a day since their marriage and felt himself to be quite parched with abstinence. He leaned across the table and patted Caroline's thin hand.

'I'll have money for you by morning.'

'How? How can you?'

He laid his finger to the side of his nose.

'Ask no questions.'

Caroline looked profoundly troubled.

'Is it something wicked?'

'To a parson's daughter, very wicked. To a man of the world a mere nothing. I shall see you at breakfast.'

'Breakfast? Shall you not be in to supper?'

'I shall not. Back to your whitewashing, my girl, and see that I've clean linen for this evening. I'll see you at breakfast.'

Inadvertently she saw him some hours before that. A terrible commotion aroused her from the deep hot sleep she had fallen into, and she went out in her dressing-gown to the landing, sure the servants were fighting. Below her, on the now gleaming and polished marble floor of the hallway, her husband was struggling and bellowing in the hands of his servants. Nobody noticed her, and as she went forward to the banisters to call down to him, he suddenly pitched forward and was violently and copiously sick. She drew back in revulsion and shock, astonished at herself for her own squeamishness. She stood indecisively for a while, unable to look down again into the hallway, then retreated back to her bedroom and despised herself.

Johnnie was assisted to bed by well-practised hands, hands that had been astonished at how little of this sort of work they had had to do in the past week. In the midst of shovelling Johnnie unceremoniously onto his bed, fully clad and still shod, Caroline appeared in the doorway.

Amazement struck every servant into rigidity. She approached the bed and lifted her candle to look at Johnnie's face, but gave it no more than a glance.

'Undress him,' she said quietly, in a voice that was not quite steady, 'and wash his face and hands, and put him into a clean nightshirt. I will return shortly and see that he is comfortable.'

She waited on the landing, telling herself that to satisfy her own standards she should have washed him herself, with her own hands, but she did not think she could bear to touch him, not any longer, now that his flesh had become so gross and his temper so petulant. She went quietly back into the room and saw him lying there, decently clad in clean white lawn with his dark hair rumpled and his mouth open.

'Thank you,' she said to the servants.

The sircar, who had come to watch this astonishing entertainment, made an elaborate ritual of hanging up the gorgeous coat in which Johnnie had graced the whist club. As he did so, he removed the pouch of money carelessly thrust into an outer pocket and slipped it neatly among his rags. He felt much soothed. It was a small but sweet revenge for the misery his life had become.

'I am wishing you peaceful sleep, memsahib.'

She nodded, and went back to her room and her thoughts.

It soon became abundantly clear that she must manage on her own, both for money, and for amusement. The whist club had whetted Johnnie's appetite for pleasure, and almost no subsequent evening saw him at home. He still dined with Caroline, for he had a profound reluctance to exhibit her as his chosen bride, and interfering gossips such as Mrs Rathbone were told not to call upon her until she felt more settled. Mrs Rathbone was secretly relieved for though warm-hearted, and very sorry for Caroline, she had found her slightly forbidding company. Caroline was indeed quite happy on her own for the moment, while she was so much occupied, and although the cheering thought of Isobel came into her mind quite frequently, she would not let it dwell there since she knew she had put herself upon another planet to that happy one Miss Grant inhabited.

As for money, she saw that she must borrow it. It seemed Calcutta did borrow money as a matter of course, and she must steel herself to do it. Unaware that she would cause a stir in the bazaar, she summoned the sircar and instructed him to assist her in this matter. The sircar was incredulous and horrified at the suggestion that she should visit a money-changer in person and flung himself prostrate again in an attempt to prevent her.

'Do not be absurd,' Caroline said calmly, poking him with the toe of her shoe. 'If I do not come myself, how am I to understand what I am doing?'

The sircar wished to explain that her lack of comprehension was what his own profit depended upon, but found it difficult to do. Wretched, and feeling himself to be a laughing stock among his fellow countrymen, he trailed after her into the bazaar, noticing she created the most sensational disturbance as she rode down the narrow and stinking alleys bordered with ramshackle little open shops and resounding with the din of little hammers upon brass and copper and the shouts and whines of pedlars. Tailors sat sewing cross-legged on the raised platforms of their shop fronts, and spice sellers, their garments splashed with ochre and vermilion, weighed their wares in brass pans, handing over the purchases in twists of rag. There were pyramids of oranges and watermelons, appalling butchers' shops where flayed hunks of meat hung on iron spikes in a fog of flies, and sandal makers stitching in a raw stench of poorly cured leather. The alleys themselves were jammed with people, some almost naked, some in brilliant silks, some turbanned, some moustached and sporting long black pigtails, and all of them with one amazed accord looked up at this astonishing white-skinned apparition, riding through them, and then down, with equal disbelief, at the figure of the sircar, shuffling miserably behind her. His cousin, the money-changer, squatting on his mat by a mud wall with his scales and neat piles of coins before him, was equally staggered and dismayed. There was a rapid exchange Caroline could not follow between the two men, while the sircar explained how necessary it was that there should be two rates of interest to justify the rigours of his own life at the moment, the difference between the two rates amounting to his commission for such suffering. The cousin promised rapidly, his eyes darting in bewilderment from the sircar to the astonishing figure of Caroline in her lilac cotton gown and straw bonnet. Little naked children, their eyes swarming with flies, were gathering round her, also an interested white cow, who clearly felt its sacredness allowed it an extremely close inspection. The heat was intense down here in these swarming alleyways, crammed with people and thick with the smells of dung and cooking and dust.

'My cousin will be helping you,' the sircar said.

'I need to borrow a hundred pounds,' Caroline said directly, conscious she needed to borrow twice that amount but not daring to be so bold.

Using the sircar as an interpreter the cousin explained his terms and rates of interest. Caroline considered them for a moment, weighing what seemed an exorbitant rate of interest against her desperate need for the money.

'It is too much,' she said at last.

The cousin argued violently for some moments, then conveyed the information through the sircar that he would reduce the rate by one per cent. Caroline was adamant. The cousin struck his forehead and whined and adjusted his figures again. Still Caroline shook her head. The cousin waved his arms and shook his head in reply.

'He is going no lower, memsahib,' the sircar said, conscious that one more drop would eliminate all his own profit.

Caroline picked her skirts up and said calmly, 'Then you may tell him that I will do my business elsewhere.'

She turned to go, full of a sudden sweet elation. Both men leapt at her at once, kneeling by her in the dust among the press of children, and pulling at her skirts. If she did not deal here, the cousin would never oblige the sircar again so accommodatingly, the sircar knew that, and the cousin was conscious that the steady flow of demand from households like the Gates' provided the basis of his livelihood.

Ten minutes later, she had mounted again and was picking her way back to the thoroughfare with a hundred pounds in her pocket, and the sircar growling in her wake after making the smallest profit on a deal he had ever had to lower himself to. Half a per cent! It was monstrous, truly monstrous to be outwitted by someone who had nothing but ignorance and strength of mind to recommend her. As she emerged from the packed squalor of the bazaar and was blinking in the brightness of the sunlight, Caroline saw a familiar and gaudy carriage bowl past her in the dust. She had just time to see Mrs Rathbone's incredulous face, and smile and raise her hand to it, before it had whirled away. It never struck her that there was anything odd in being seen riding, with only one bedraggled servant in attendance, out of a native bazaar.

At home, she proceeded to exert the authority of her borrowed wealth. She summoned all the servants together, and found that over a hundred persons lived, somehow, in the servants' quarters of her house. She selected all those whom she recognized from household duties and found herself left with a motley assortment of women, children, old men and cripples, all of whom claimed the closest of relationships to one or other of the servants. She hated to send any away, but she could not afford to support them. She explained that she was forced to cut their wages considerably and that any servant and his dependants who were dissatisfied by the new rate were quite free to go and she would give them references.

The room erupted at once in a perfect babble of dismay, which Caroline thought slightly illogical since no servant had received any money at all for some months, whatever his rate of pay was supposed to be. When the shrieking and scrambling had died down a little, Caroline perceived that the room was now only half full, and that the sircar was not to be seen. She counted those in livery of sorts, and discovered she now possessed eighteen servants and their families, which seemed grossly extravagant still, but a definite advance upon the fifty or so the sircar had claimed. She explained that they were to work for a fortnight more, and she would then pay them for the month they had served her since her arrival. There was a little shuffling and muttering at this, but no direct protest. She then delivered her bombshell.

'I am now coming to inspect your quarters. I wish to see

how you live and see if there is any way in which it might be improved.'

Consternation broke out again. Caroline wondered uneasily if she sounded exactly like Eleanor preparing for her weekly inspection of the attics where the Parsonage servants slept in draughty discomfort. But she did want to see how they lived, and perhaps help them a little, especially those pathetic little children with their dull eyes and swollen bellies.

Accompanied by a nervous escort of servants, Caroline went out into her dusty and disordered garden and through a broken hedge of tired oleander to a strange and wholly Indian world. Curious huts of mud and dung were grouped about an irregular courtyard dotted with cooking fires, and bisected by a stinking ditch. There were a few goats, and a dusty hen or two, and the sound of someone singing a high monotonous song. The huts were windowless, and contained nothing but mats, except for one which had a low bed and the disturbed air of very recent occupancy. A tall and serious Sikh whom Caroline had already noticed with approval for his gentleness and industry, came forward and explained that this hut had belonged to the sircar.

Caroline looked more closely. There was a clean square in the dust under the bed, and blurred marks before it as if a heavy object had been pulled hastily out. A tin or a box, Caroline thought, and wondered how much of their possessions and money were now being hurried away into the depths of Calcutta. She straightened up and looked at her dependants waiting patiently outside in the sun. She smiled at them, and called the Sikh to her, since he spoke some English.

'Will you explain to them that it will make them ill to have that ditch so near to where they live? Tell them it must be dug behind the compound, far from the huts, and that the animals must not live with them. It brings the flies.'

She stopped, suddenly overcome by an enormous weariness, the weariness of considerable exertion in intense heat. Ranjit said, 'You must rest, memsahib.'

She nodded blindly. Gentle hands took her arms and she was led back to the drawing room and seated by the open window with its scarcely moving grassy screens. Ranjit stood before her.

'I will help you, memsahib, now that the sircar is going.'

Caroline shook her head. General North had told her that the Sikhs were proud and warlike, and regarded the call to arms as the highest calling a man could aspire to.

'No, Ranjit, no, not you. Not a Sikh. It would demean you.'

'I am a servant already, memsahib. One day I will be a soldier again, but now I am helping you.'

Caroline looked up at his serious thin face.

'I thank you,' she said with fervour.

He left the room silently, and she lay back and gazed at the blank whiteness of the newly painted walls. The triumph of the day's achievements was receding with her tiredness, and she began to be apprehensive of Johnnie's reaction when he discovered what she had done. It was his household after all, and perhaps she had no right, however practical she thought herself, to diminish it for him without permission. She passed a damp hand over her damp face and abruptly wished very much for Isobel to lighten her spirits. She had told Isobel that she would see her in a few weeks, but now, looking at this shabby, empty little house, and knowing herself to be in debt for the first time in her life, she did not think she could. Every day seemed to cut her off further from any chance of maintaining her friendship with Isobel. In her present mood, it seemed a bleak and hard prospect, and it was made worse by knowing that the people she would have to force herself to know very soon would be just those loud and jeering people who had frequented Mrs Rathbone's house. She could not keep to the house for much longer on her pretext of becoming used to India, in fact only the day before Johnnie had mentioned a dinner party he had no intention of missing and at which he advised her to make her debut as it would be a large crowd which would easily absorb her. The thought was alarming, but some day it had to be done. Her mouth drooped unconsciously. Caroline let her head fall back against her chair and dropped into a hot and troubled slumber.

13

Isobel would have been fiercely indignant at the suggestion that Caroline had in any way slipped her mind. It was true that she was exceedingly, delightfully busy, that all Calcutta seemed to have taken a great fancy to her, and subsequently the days seemed full of charming, flattering people, but in any moment of quiet, such as the dawn or her prayers at the end of the day, she thought very fondly of Caroline. The periodic presence of General North reminded her of Caroline, though he seemed slightly reticent now on the subject, and Isobel concluded that his natural taste for pretty girls had reasserted itself over his brief absorption with a girl who had everything to recommend her but her looks. Isobel had received one letter from Caroline which had sounded both calm and happy and she had deduced that Caroline was disproving all the gossips who said such evil things of Johnnie Gates. Initially Isobel had fretted dreadfully over these snatches of malice the servants brought her, but Caroline's letter had dispelled her distress. How could anyone write a letter of such serene contentment if they did not mean it, and Isobel prided herself on knowing Caroline so well that she might see through any attempt at false courage.

She kept Caroline's letter in her jewel box and thus had reason to see it several times a day. Unfortunately, this habit had the effect of all familiarity, and the folded square of cream paper became as comfortably invisible as all the other objects in daily use upon her dressing table. Never in all her twenty years had her dressing table been so busily in use. She sat before it in the charming, light, white gauzy bedroom in Sir Edward Ashton's comfortable house, at least three times a day for prolonged periods, dressing with enormous care for morning calls, for dinner and then finally for supper parties and dances. She wore through three pairs of satin slippers in the first weeks simply by dancing, for she never sat out a single dance. She was indeed the toast of Calcutta, for no one a quarter so pretty had stepped ashore for a good five years, and even if any rival had been as pretty they could never have matched her spirit and wit.

These last two qualities had proved themselves extremely useful in outwitting the amiable chaperone Sir Edward had provided in the shape of old Lady Renton, widowed five years after a skirmish on the North West Frontier. Bewitched earlier and bemused, Lady Renton quickly succumbed to Isobel's powerful will, and at dances retired thankfully to the card room, leaving her charge to flirt with whom she wished on the dance floor. Sir Edward seldom accompanied them since he did not care for dancing, but on the rare occasions Isobel teased him into coming – 'so that I may exhibit my splendid cousin, dear Sir Edward!' – he was helplessly gratified by Isobel's undoubted success. He had dreaded her coming as a disruption of the quiet pattern of his life, but now she was here, he could not but appreciate the colour and light she spread about her. What was even better was that she bothered him for very little. He was accustomed to think that young women pestered one ceaselessly for frocks and ribbons, parties and parasols, carriage rides and lap dogs, but Isobel asked him for almost nothing. There was indeed one topic she referred to every few days, but he remained, upon General North's advice, adamant.

She seemed to have made a close friend upon the ship, a very quiet ladylike person upon General North's account, of whom she had grown very fond. The ladylike person was clearly, however, not what she seemed, for upon arrival in Calcutta, General North had seen with his own astonished eyes that she was greeted by a known renegade, and handed into a carriage belonging to, and occupied by, one of Calcutta's most promiscuous women. While uttering this sanctimonious speech, the general forebore to add how many times he had had reason to be grateful for Mrs Rathbone's easy generosity. The ladylike person was now residing in Mrs Rathbone's house in the Garden Reach, and Isobel longed to call upon her there.

'I fear, my dear, that it is quite out of the question.'

'But why, Sir Edward, why may I not?'

'Because I am reliably informed that Mrs Rathbone is not the sort of person with whom you should have any sort of association.'

'But I do not want to associate with Mrs Rathbone, I do not care a pin for Mrs Rathbone! I want to see Caroline, who is one of the dearest people imaginable – '

'So you informed me yesterday, and several days before that, and yet several more days before that. I am sure in your eyes, my dear Isobel, she is a perfect paragon, but in society's eyes she is living with a woman whose company renders her quite the reverse.'

Isobel began to protest, but he held up a hand to silence her.

'Society may be an ass, Isobel, indeed I frequently think it is, but as I am in the position of your guardian here, I cannot pursue either my or your inclinations and flout society.'

'Then poor Caroline must suffer because you are so pompous?'

He smiled at her.

'I take it you infer that the lady is poor because she must be deprived of your company?'

'Do not tease me. I wish to see her because I love her very much, quite as well as because I know I do her good.'

'I do not doubt it, but I am afraid that as long as she remains where she is, you must remain where you are. And if you disobey me,' he added, 'I shall replace Lady Renton with a much keener-eyed companion. Now go and change. The hot season will take its toll of you and you will find you are too wearied by it to dance another step, so you must make the most of your energy.'

'It is limitless,' Isobel said airily.

She went lightly up the shallow staircase, and into her bedroom, to find her bed already strewn with pale clouds of silk and lawn for her to change into. She sat down at her dressing table and opened her jewel box to look for the lovely rose quartz earrings Mamma had given her that would look so well with that pink silk gauze. As she took out the top tray a square of paper slipped sideways and fell among her brushes.

With Caroline still fresh in her mind from her conversation, the paper had a new significance. She unfolded it and ran her eye down the fine, neat writing. Yes, it was certainly a happy and contented letter, there was no real need to worry. Idly Isobel glanced up at the date on the head of the letter and had a small and guilty shock. It was two months old, a whole two months and Caroline had lived all that time with that disreputable woman and never had a word from Isobel! Poor neglected Caroline, she would write this instant. But as she rose to find pen and paper, a new thought smote her, a thought that took away her complacency and left disquiet instead. It was one thing to say that Caroline had been neglected by herself, but was it not quite another, and more anxious, to realize that she had had no news from Caroline? What of that childhood sweetheart, of that planned marriage, surely some progress in that direction must have been made?

Isobel sat down again, frowning and uneasy, suddenly filled with new and unpleasant apprehensions. She glanced at herself in the mirror and said resolutely to the pretty reflection there, 'I shall have to break the rules, shall I not? While Sir Edward is working tomorrow morning, I shall have to give Lady Renton the slip and go down to Garden Reach myself. There is nothing else for it, is there?'

Then, because the prospect of action always pleased her, she rang the bell for assistance and went about the business of the pink silk gauze with a much lightened heart.

Mrs Rathbone was very alarmed to hear that Miss Grant awaited her below. She knew very well who she was, since the newspapers and the gossips were full of little else, and after all, had poor Mrs Gates not travelled with her and no doubt entertained high hopes of such an association? Mrs Rathbone could only suppose, scrambling out of her beribboned bedgown into a brilliant assortment of clothes, that it was on the subject of poor Mrs Gates that Miss Grant had come. But what was she to say? She was not at all sure that what she knew was all truth, although there was no doubt that she had with her own eyes seen Caroline coming brazenly out of the native bazaar with all the nonchalance of someone riding in Rotten Row. But whether the gossip that she had dismissed half the servants, and dosed the children of the remaining half for worms, and then been hit by her drunken husband for her pains, was true, Mrs Rathbone really did not like to say. She surveyed herself in the imitation French glass that a man in the bazaar had made so cleverly, and wondered unhappily if emerald green and brilliant yellow were really too striking a combination when set off with gold fringing and orange braid?

She entered her drawing room wearing an anxious and placatory smile above this dazzling combination. Isobel, faultless in white and pale blue, fought down an enormous desire to laugh, and simply held out her hand, saying gravely, 'How very good of you, Mrs Rathbone, to allow me to interrupt your morning.'

'Interrupt? Oh no, my dear, it is a pleasure, an – an honour, my dear, I am charmed, quite charmed.'

She stopped uneasily, and motioned Isobel towards a fat satin chair on gilded bow legs.

'Make yourself comfortable, my dear, please do. Will you take some lime juice, so cooling, I always say, in this dreadful climate?'

Isobel accepted both offers, and watched with pleasure while Mrs Rathbone clucked and bustled among her silent servants. When at last she seated herself, and had spread out her green and yellow skirts to their best advantage, Isobel saw no reason to waste time.

'Forgive me for being a little abrupt, Mrs Rathbone, but there is someone of whom I long to have news, and I believe you are the only person who can give it to me. In fact I believe the person I seek still resides here.'

Mrs Rathbone fidgeted miserably, making her glittering fringes quiver. Oh dear, it was as bad as she thought, and clearly this elegant young person had no notion of the truth. She opened her mouth to reply, but could find no words, and gazed speechlessly at Isobel, her little round eyes full of distress.

'I seek Miss Harding,' Isobel said gently.

Mrs Rathbone nodded.

'Is she still with you? I know this is where she came. Is she still here?'

Mrs Rathbone shook her head and a small chill crept over Isobel.

'Where is she, Mrs Rathbone?' Isobel said in an altered tone.

'She – she is gone, Miss Grant. She left about two months ago. She – she – ' she stopped, and then said in a sort of rush, 'She is married, Miss Grant.'

'Married?' Isobel sprang to her feet, knocking her glass of juice onto the carpet. 'Caroline is married?'

Mrs Rathbone was much alarmed at her manner and voice, and could only nod again, like a mechanical doll. Exasperated, Isobel seized her shoulders and shook her.

'Tell me!' she insisted. 'Tell me!'

'She married John Gates, Miss Grant. They were married in the Customs Office, only myself and George Carew to see them wed, Miss Grant.'

Isobel let go of her and straightened up. Caroline had promised, she was sure she had promised, not to take any step without consulting Isobel. She had been most apprehensive of the marriage, indeed dreadfully so, and Isobel had sworn to save her from it if she wished, and now she had plunged into it without a word to a soul, and who could tell with what misgivings. Idiotic General North, who might have been such a source of information, was evidently too frightened to jeopardize his social standing with Sir Edward, by being seen too frequently at Mrs Rathbone's. Isobel clenched her fists.

'Is she happy?' she demanded.

Mrs Rathbone spread her plump hands hopelessly.

'Who can say, my dear, who can say? You don't look for happiness in marriage, Miss Grant, and maybe Mrs Gates has found what she was looking for – '

'She was looking for happiness,' Isobel said.

'Oh – oh, well, then – '

'Is he as bad as the gossips say?'

Mrs Rathbone smiled indulgently.

'Oh no, dear, not a bad boy, not a bad boy at all. A bit

naughty now and then, but you know how boys are, Miss Grant. He's a heart of gold, my dear, would not hurt a fly.'

Doubtless the rumour of Johnnie striking Caroline had no more truth in it, than the one that she was teaching some of her servants to read. People hit each other endlessly in Calcutta, it was the heat, simply the heat, bad for your temper it was, but blows meant nothing, nothing at all.

'Where do they live?'

Mrs Rathbone gave the address with some doubt. It was not a good part of the city and she was sure Miss Grant's distinguished guardian would not like to see her driving there. Tentatively, she offered herself as chaperone.

'No, thank you, Mrs Rathbone. You have been most helpful, but the rest I intend to see for myself, and by myself.'

In a flurry of fuss and anxiety, Mrs Rathbone watched Isobel mount the elegant carriage she had purloined from Sir Edward's stables, and be driven off towards what could only be the upsetting fact of Caroline's marriage. It was no consolation to her, in the turmoil of her thoughts, to be patted absently on the shoulder by her husband, who had seen Isobel depart, and now remarked that, as callers went, the last one was a cut above the average.

Isobel could hardly have chosen a worse morning to make her call upon Caroline. She had bargained on finding Caroline alone, on the understandable assumption that Johnnie would be at his desk until dinner, and she was not to know that a wild night the evening before on Johnnie's part, and a most disagreeable breakfast with his wife on the following morning, meant that he was still pacing furiously about his drawing room at noon.

Caroline watched him from her seat by the window. She had learnt so much in the last weeks she felt as if she were quite another person to the ignorant and unsuspecting creature who had landed on that brilliant waterfront in March. She had learned, with the gentle help of her servants, that she must not expect her huge Pathan bearer to have anything to do with the sweeper who dealt so humbly with the household refuse because of caste. For the same reason, she had learned that she must not touch utensils belonging to her servants, for she had seen the same sweeper dash his drinking bowl to the ground after she had picked it up out of curiosity and therefore defiled it for him. She had learned that to insist upon doing her own shopping only exposed her to the grossest exploitation, but that if she allowed Ranjit or the cook their small 'dastur' or commission on everything they bought for her, she was treated with faultless honesty and loyalty. She had learned that the Mohammedan cook must never be asked to cook bacon and that the gai-wallah who brought his cow to the door each day must be prevented from watering the milk. She had learned to stand all the legs of furniture in bowls of water to protect it from marauding armies of white ants and she had learned that the only way to deal with the agonizing menace of prickly heat was to resist the powerful temptation to scratch. She learned that her servants had their own highly developed sense of demarcation in the tasks they were prepared to do, but that they were equally prepared, given this condition, to serve her impeccably. They were proving themselves as easy to respect and love as the circle into which Johnnie had unwillingly introduced her had proved itself despicable and dislikable. Caroline could find nothing sympathetic about them, but she had, in a hard lesson in self-schooling, learned to endure. She had also learned not to ask Johnnie for money.

This particular morning, however, she had been forced to ignore this lesson and petition as delicately as she could for money. Her hundred pounds, so dashingly captured, was dwindling fast now that the servants had all received their long overdue wages, and the drawing-room and dining-room furniture and pictures had been reclaimed, with difficulty, from the bazaar. All these expenses came on top of the normal running expenses of the household, and the cost of living in Calcutta seemed to Caroline exorbitantly high. Imported commodities from Europe such as ham and cheese, both of which Johnnie claimed he could not do without, cost twelve and thirteen shillings a pound, and Johnnie's twice-daily visits from the wig barber would have kept the whole household in ham and cheese for months. But if

Johnnie was the prime incurrer of such expenses, he did not seem to see that he should pay for them. He appeared, Caroline thought, to regard her part of the bargain they had made as the ability to wave a magic wand over all domestic troubles and expenses, and make them vanish.

'What can you want money for?' he shouted ill-temperedly, his head thudding with pain.

'Merely to pay for what we eat, what we drink and for – for your expenses.'

'My expenses?' he said in outrage.

'Your tailor, your barbers, your wig, your horses – '

'Leave it to the sircar!' Johnnie bellowed. 'Don't meddle, woman! Leave it to the sircar!'

It was the Parthian shot he had intended it to be and Caroline fell silent. He knew as well as she that the sircar had gone a month since, and he only wished to remind her of the rage he had been in when he arrived home to find his household arbitrarily sliced in half. He had been incoherent with anger, and she had had a black eye for two weeks to bear witness to it. He had not meant to hit her or at least not to hit her so hard, but her prim parsonage ways, her mealy-mouthed competence and prudence, her exasperating predilection for being right had driven him to it. And now she was whining on about money again, having chosen precisely the morning when he was hard-pressed himself to meet debts incurred the night before. He glared at her, and thought that it would become a woman in her supplicating position to weep just a little, but she was looking back at him, evidently distressed but maddeningly dry-eyed.

'How are we to live?' she said faintly.

'I shall live as I have always done,' he said, 'and you will keep your side of the bargain and see that I am comfortable.'

She wanted to scream that his side of the bargain had been that he would save her from destitution, and how was she to make even a dog comfortable without a single penny, but pride forbade her. She would not beg or appeal any more, not to such a man – or monster – as this. Indeed she would not. She had made her spiritual independence before, and now, though God alone knew how, she must make her material independence too. There was a hundred pounds to be restored at interest at the end of three months, and some-how she would achieve it. If Johnnie would give her no money, she would sell some of his pictures to raise it. He had not noticed their absence for repair, so it was strongly probable that their final disappearance would be equally invisible to him. She lifted her chin and stared levelly at him.

'Bargain!' Johnnie said with furious despair. 'Bargain! A man-trap maybe, but a bargain!'

He moved heavily towards the door, which swung open silently at the hands of servants and revealed the immaculate white figure of Isobel without. Caroline sprang up with a cry of heartfelt delight and pushed unceremoniously past the bulky figure of her husband to fling her arms about her friend. Johnnie, whose instincts for gallantry were highly roused by this ravishing apparition, masked his fury and headache with just those smiles and impudent glances that had been so fatally attractive when he was twenty. Isobel, her arms tight about Caroline, despite the temperature, regarded him coolly over Caroline's shoulder.

'Mr Gates, I imagine?'

Johnnie bowed with a flourish.

'The same, Miss Grant.'

Her likeness had been in all the papers, there was no mistaking her. His eyes travelled lingeringly over her face. What a jewel!

Caroline released Isobel, and lifted a face quite trans-formed with delight. Isobel looked at her critically for some moments and then, without taking her eyes from Caroline, she said to Johnnie,

'What have you done, Mr Gates, to deserve this angel in the smallest degree?'

Johnnie floundered. The harsh words of the morning were still thick in the air about them, the effect of his temper still written on Caroline's countenance.

'Nothing,' he said weakly.

'I am glad you admit it,' Isobel said, and turned her blue gaze upon him, scrutinizing him as carefully as if she were assessing every particle of him, every stitch he wore, for its possible purchase value. Under her unfriendly eyes, his flirtatious poise began to diminish into just the nervous awkwardness only Lady Lennox could reduce him to. In his reddened eyes and extravagant clothes, Isobel saw everything she had feared to see. Caroline's old cotton gown, drearily familiar from those daily appearances at sea, and extreme thinness spoke equally eloquently. And what was that faint smudge along her cheekbone? Isobel's heart was twisted with pity at the spectacle of Caroline's evident suffering and equally evident gallantry in the face of it.

'May I speak to Mrs Gates alone?'

Johnnie bowed.

'I should not wish to intrude, Miss Grant.'

When he had gone, Isobel turned and took Caroline's hands in hers.

'I had hoped you would weep in relief at seeing me,' she said teasingly.

'I wish I could, dearest Isobel. I feel the relief, but I cannot weep, I never could. Even when Papa died I – but how blooming you look! Everywhere I hear of your charms and how the beaux fight to quaff from your slippers!'

'I have not come to speak of that.'

'I was afraid not,' Caroline said sadly.

Isobel seated herself on the newly restored sofa, and pulled Caroline down beside her.

'Now then. What is the meaning of all this?'

Caroline looked away. 'Please – '

'No, you shall not get away with it. I want to know what you mean by throwing yourself away in this dismal manner.'

'Please do not let us speak of it, I beg you, please.'

Isobel dropped her bantering tone and spoke with un-accustomed earnestness.

'You promised me you would do nothing without telling me. You promised you would not throw yourself away. You promised.' She felt a sudden thrust of self-reproach and said in a low tone, 'I know I have neglected you dreadfully, and been giddy and silly and all the things Sir Edward says I am, but why did you not tell me?'

Caroline had a sudden mental picture of the shabby incongruous figure she would have cut in Sir Edward's splendid apartments, for splendid they must be, and could not restrain a small smile at the thought of it. 'Do not be absurd,' she said gently, her hand on Isobel's. 'What sort of reception would I have had, dusty and down at heel, asking you among all these glittering people whether you thought I should marry or not?'

Isobel looked at her solemnly.

'Are you very unhappy?'

'Not very.'

'Oh, Caroline, Caroline! Not very. You deserve, oh how you deserve to be intensely happy. And that brute – '

Firm fingers were laid across her mouth.

'No, Isobel. We will not speak of him. I married because I should have begged otherwise and he married because he does not know how to keep house. That is all.'

'I do not believe you. Why must you insist on your stiff-necked pride always? Why could you not let me help you? I should love to help you! There is no one I'd rather help!'

Caroline kissed her cheek.

'And I love you for that. But if you will not think me ungrateful, I must tell you that I am tired of gratitude, tired of being obliged to people. I must have been born with the wrong spirit for my position, a spirit that only likes to receive when it feels perfectly sure that it is fully entitled to receive. I felt that briefly once just before Papa died, and I feel it now. As far as Mr Gates is concerned, I will truly fulfil my part of the bargain.'

She did not add that as far as being kept by him went, it very much looked as if she would have to keep herself from now on. Isobel still gazed at her with eyes full of troubled incomprehension.

'I know you think me mad. How could it be otherwise? You, with your gentle upbringing, how could you bear to live in this sad little house with no one to amuse you? But it is different for me, indeed it is. I love my household! I do not care very much for the house itself to be sure, but at least it is my domain and I have it mostly to myself. The garden may look to you like a dreary little desert, but the malis and I have great plans for it next cool season and it will blossom like the Garden of Eden. I intend to learn all about Indian flowers. Come now, dearest Isobel, none of it is so very tragic and really there never was anything else to be done.'

'Given your character, there never was, and that is what I cannot bear.'

Caroline stood up.

'Then you must have a diversion, and think no more of it. Look, it is nearly one. Does Sir Edward know where you are?'

'No,' Isobel said absently, her mind still bowed down with anxiety over Caroline's lot, 'I stole his carriage and ran away. I was so desperate to see you.'

Caroline looked horrified.

'I could not bear him to be angry with you on my account.'

'He will not be. He is a kind of angel too, though not of the arch variety that you are. Promise I may see you again soon?'

'If – if Sir Edward thinks you may.'

'He must,' Isobel said decidedly. 'I shall insist you are invited.'

'No.'

'What can you mean, no? Do you not want to see me?'

Caroline's gaze dropped.

'Above everything. But we – we are not fit for the kind of society you move in now.'

'Nonsense!' Isobel said furiously. 'Unspeakable nonsense! Wait but a day or two and you shall see whether it is not the most ridiculous nonsense!'

'Please think no more of us,' Caroline cried apprehensively. 'It would only be awkward. Use your excellent sense and you will see how awkward it might be for all of us.'

'No,' said Isobel decidedly. 'The time has come to please myself, and as what pleases me in a feminine capacity is your company, I shall have it if I can. Every other woman in Calcutta is a dolt compared to you. Do you want to make me miserable?'

Caroline smiled affectionately and shook her head.

'Then leave everything to me. I must go now, but we shall be together again shortly.' She kissed Caroline warmly. 'I have plans for you,' she said.

14

If the invitation consequent upon Isobel's visit had come during the long hours of Caroline's solitude there is no doubt what its fate would have been. Caroline would simply have torn it up, and said nothing of the matter to Johnnie, while steeling herself for Isobel's indignation. But fate did not decree it thus. A packet was delivered by a bearer in unmistakably splendid uniform at just the moment that the Gates – on Caroline's part most reluctantly – were setting forth to dine with George Carew. The packet was addressed to Caroline, and Johnnie commandeered it on its way across the room to her. She said nothing with difficulty, feeling that if he came across some indiscreet opinions of Isobel's about himself, it was no more than he deserved for his mannerless interference. He ripped the paper open and gave an exclamation of delight.

'Ah, madam! I see you are to be some use to me after all! We may yet shoehorn ourselves into higher circles, indeed we may. I imagine we owe this honour to your imperious little friend – ah, a note from her, let me see – '

'You shall not,' Caroline declared, springing from her seat and whipping the paper from his hand.

Sneering faintly, but too satisfied with the splendid social prospect before him to be bothered to retaliate further, Johnnie withdrew, saying she had better be in the carriage in two minutes or he should leave without her.

Isobel's note was highly self-satisfied. She had secured an invitation for the Gates for an evening party to be given by the Nawab of Fultar, and all high Calcutta was to be there. 'I promised I would try to rescue you from your dismal little situation,' she wrote, 'and this is only the beginning. Sir Edward is persuaded and I am delighted.' She did not add how difficult Sir Edward had been to persuade, nor how he had only consented because he said that the Nawab always gave enormous parties, thus dubious guests such as Isobel suggested would, with luck, be lost in the crowd.

He was, in fact, irritated by Isobel's persistence in a matter that seemed to him tasteless and trivial, for his mind was much more occupied with professional matters at the moment. Not only did the Governor General need every ounce of support Sir Edward could give him against the opposition he faced in almost all matters from the other members of the Council, none of whom knew Bengal as Hastings did, but there was a new and thorny problem for the East India Company. The outbreak of war between England and her American colonies had diverted British eyes westwards, and the French seemed to be seizing the chance offered by this averted gaze to recover the losses made in the seven years of war. A French agent had arrived in western India, and was doing all he could, and successfully so far, to make French interests a formidable opponent to British interests. The best way to thwart these designs occupied most of Sir Edward's waking hours at present, and to be constantly diverted by a matter which seemed to him wholly worthless made him irritable and irrationally dictatorial. He had given way at last out of sheer exasperation and immediately thought no more about it.

Caroline would have been grateful to be able to think no more of it either, but she could not. Isobel followed up her initial assault by a series of flying visits, all made when she was officially on the way elsewhere, to bully Caroline into accepting the loan of her hairdresser, the gift of a dress.

'No,' said Caroline to the latter.

Isobel stamped.

'I despair of you and I begin to think you are growing horns where once I thought you had wings. I insist you have a dress, I absolutely insist. I have given you no wedding present since I am so disgusted with your wedding generally, but you will simply have to regard a dress as such if you will take it no other way. You are hardly gracious, Caroline, indeed you are not.'

Caroline was instantly contrite.

'I never meant to offend you, Isobel, and I cannot tell you what a welcome change a new gown would be. I am only – only sorry that I need to be assisted thus, if you understand me. I had hoped by marrying that – but no matter. You are good and generous and a new gown will be a joy to me, I promise you. The ones I have are worn threadbare by the vigorous attentions of the dhobi, I have nothing fit for a party.'

Isobel was delighted.

'It shall be cream-coloured, Caroline, to set off your skin, silk gauze, I rather think, over underskirts of satin – '

'Simple,' Caroline begged.

'Be quiet, Caroline, you have no taste whatsoever and must heed mine until you know better. In any case it is my present and I shall therefore dictate my terms.'

Like an eager Pygmalion, Isobel set to work on Caroline. The latter, who had no notion that Isobel had concocted a far more complicated plan than the mere attendance at a party, submitted with surprised pleasure, surprised because it had never struck her before that personal adornment could be pleasurable. To a pretty person certainly, such as her mother had been, or Isobel was, but not to her plain, awkward self. Her aim had always been to look inconspicuous at best, and inoffensive at worst. Isobel, it seemed, took quite another view.

On the day of the party, an elegant French coiffeur arrived, despatched by Isobel. Despite the disdain he clearly felt for this humble little household, and Caroline's panic at having him there at all, he managed to effect a complete transformation. She clung tenaciously to her refusal to be powdered at all, and watched in the mirror as he grimaced with despair at her lack of sophistication. After an interminable space of time, he stepped back, and declared he could do no more. Caroline surveyed herself and thought that the whole effect was very artless and milkmaidish for so many hours of effort, with its tumble of loose curls at the back of her head and the smooth rise above her forehead. But there was no doubt it was extraordinarily becoming and presumably it was fashionable; at least she trusted so. It looked like no head she ever saw in Calcutta, but perhaps that was no guide. He had managed to create an effect of having far more hair somehow, it really was most flattering, most – Caroline hardly dared admit it as she sat in unaffected delight before the glass – most encouraging.

The exquisite gauzy dress which had seemed such an incongruous garment for her but that very morning, did not seem quite so inappropriate now. She had never possessed a dress remotely like it, and it filled her with a kind of awe. She stepped into the underskirts of cream satin, lightly quilted in swirling patterns of shells and ferns, and felt the overdress of cream-silk gauze, satin-striped and edged with fragile embroidery in seed pearls and silk thread, lifted over her head and arms like a cloud of petals. It might be absurd, but she could not help smiling. Despite the desperate wet heat of the June night, despite the terrors of the party ahead and the known pitfalls of going anywhere with Johnnie in public, she could not at this moment feel anything but the most piercing, elating delight.

The servants were enchanted with her. Chinking with jewellery themselves, it seemed most strange that the memsahib should possess no adornment at all except the little watch she always wore at her waist. Nothing daunted, however, they darted into the rapidly darkening garden and came in with handfuls of creamy jasmine blooms, the last brave flowers to survive the onslaught of the summer heat. Choosing the freshest, they pinned them into the curls behind her head and crowed with delight at the effect.

Even Johnnie, Caroline was gratified to notice, looked considerably startled when she entered the drawing room. He was fortifying himself with a little champagne against the dangers of the journey ahead – dangers that only existed because the drunker he was, the more insistent he became about driving the carriage himself. He had twice upset them both, and the last party had ended with Mrs Rathbone bringing Caroline home since Johnnie, bellowing furiously from the box of the carriage, seemed in a mood to break their necks.

'You look very fine, ma'am.' A thought crossed his mind that he might be called upon to pay for the finery, a thought so painful to him that his face contracted abruptly.

'It was a gift,' Caroline said smoothly, reading his expression as if it had been a book. 'It was my wedding gift from Miss Grant.'

'Wedding gift? Wedding gift to us? What use is a dress to me, may I ask?'

'It was a gift to me.'

He snorted.

'May you get good use from it, for you'll not have another in a hurry.'

They drove in silence, the coachman for once being permitted to perform the duty for which he was hired. Night had fallen with the Indian suddenness Caroline still found surprising, and only the red glow of cooking fires and the dull yellow of oil lamps here and there along the way enlivened their rolling passage. The Nawab of Fultar, although he possessed an admirable palace in his dominions down in the Ganges delta, preferred to entertain in a magnificent new pleasure dome he had built himself among the parks and gardens of fashionable Calcutta. Caroline wished she could see more. She knew, from Isobel's chatter, that there was a part of Calcutta that in no way resembled the mud-built sprawl of her own area, indeed, she had had brief glimpses of green splendours when she sheltered with Mrs Rathbone. It was clearly this area of trees and luxuriant gardens and great houses that they were bound for now, and it was most frustrating to be able to see nothing in the velvety blackness but the occasional pinprick of light.

As they drove onward, they were joined by other carriages, and the streets began to boast, albeit ineffectually, some sort of lighting. The phaetons dashing past them were all full of groups of uproarious people, it seemed to Caroline, and the passing of their carriage lamps gave her brief but unmistakable glimpses of the envious dissatisfaction on her husband's face. If it were not for her, she thought, he might have been in one of those noisy carriages of bachelors, but then cheered herself by recollecting that if it were not for her, he would probably not be going at all.

The Nawab of Fultar did not wish his palace to be mistaken for any other. Enormous forethought went into these huge receptions he gave; forethought that began by illuminating his house with such myriads of lights and permanent explosions of fireworks that the glow surrounding it was visible a mile off. The sky all round the building was rippling with waves of brilliant light, green and rose and white, and as they drew nearer, in a now jostling throng of carriages, the thin high wail of an oriental band came floating down to them.

Johnnie groaned. 'God help us, not that, not their music. I've not come out simply to hear Indians caterwaul. It's nothing but the most horrid screeching.'

Caroline, leaning from the window, hardly heard him. They had swept through a gateway like a triumphal arch, and were now bowling up a great sweep of drive, bordered by the tallest palms, beyond which stretched lawns and huge tanks of water strewn with perfect floating blossoms. Every tree was hung with lights, every tank edged with them, and servants in gold and scarlet turbans stood at the edge of the drive, shoulder to shoulder, bearing flaming torches. The carriage suddenly swept round in a circle, and came to rest at the foot of a great flight of white marble steps, leading up to the most incredible and magnificent building Caroline had ever seen. Huge white domes seemed to float like giant pearls above her, supported on columns and fretted pillars with screens of pierced marble between. The whole seemed illuminated from within by a shimmering glow which made the entire building look as if it was as insubstantial as gossamer.

'Oh, do look!' she cried to Johnnie, but he was looking the other way, to see if he saw familiar faces among the carriages around them.

They climbed the steps several feet apart, seeming to onlookers that they had no wish to be regarded as arriving together. A ribbon of crimson carpet ran down the steps, and muffled their tread. At the top they passed between huge doors of latticed marble, set with panels of jade and coral, and before them lay a breathtaking vista of white space, and light and height and size. Caroline gasped, and heedless of the people pressing behind her, stood stock still on the threshold of this gleaming spectacle to stare and stare. The ceiling vanished away into the vaulted domes that roofed it, domes inlaid with a mosaic as intricate as embroidery, and seemingly as high above Caroline's head as the heavens. Delicate fluted pillars, like the slender trunks of young trees, soared upwards in support, their surfaces inlaid as the entrance doors had been, with semi-precious stones fashioned into flowers and birds and fruit. The floor was white, the walls were white, all made of marble and thus gleaming like the inside of an oyster shell. The window spaces were screened with marble, too, marble worked as if it had been as malleable and fragile as lace, carved into twisting patterns of amazing intricacy. Perhaps there were five hundred people there, perhaps more, but they seemed diminished to far fewer by this glowing white cave of a room.

Caroline looked round to express her feelings to Johnnie, and found him gone. She peered anxiously about her in that throng of brocade and powder but could see no sign of his cornflower blue coat or considerable stature. He had clearly spied some acquaintances, and used her absorption in her surroundings to make good his escape to their comfortable company. It was too bad of him, too bad indeed. She had no notion of how to proceed at an occasion such as this, she could only stand by a pillar, grateful for its smooth coolness, and hope that she did not look as miserably awkward as she felt. Should she slip down those steps again and see if their carriage still lingered, so that she might flee home unnoticed? Should she patrol the room to find an ungracious and unwelcoming Johnnie? Should she wait and hope for a glimpse of Isobel? She laid her cheek against the coldness of the marble and surveyed the crowd of Indians and Europeans surging brilliantly before her, and prayed that a familiar face might come.

'Are you admiring my house?'

Caroline took her cheek away abruptly from the pillar and looked round. A small, old Indian, in a turban encrusted with jewels and a tunic of purple brocade, was smiling at her with enormous kindness.

'Oh! I beg your pardon, indeed I was only – '

'There is no pardon to beg. I observed you in the doorway and I was much gratified by what I saw. Do you like my house?'

Caroline said with fervour, 'I do not believe I ever saw anything more astonishing. Or beautiful.'

He bowed.

'I am most pleased. Are you not amazed that my English is so excellent?'

Caroline smiled.

'It is indeed excellent.'

'My father was a most modern man, a most modern man. He did much business with English merchants and instructed all his sons in English. I am most pleased you like my house.'

Light suddenly dawned on Caroline.

'*Your* house?'

'Indeed so.'

'Then – then you are the Nawab of Fultar?'

'That is so.'

Stammering a little, with a faint colour along her cheeks, Caroline said, 'You must forgive me if I did not react properly when you addressed me. I fear I am but newly come to India and most ignorant. Should – should I have curtseyed to you?'

The Nawab laughed delightedly, clasping his little brown hands before him, and shaking his turbaned head.

'I do not wish it, no, no, I do not wish it! You smile for me and that is enough.'

'You are most kind.'

'No, no, I am not kind, I am pleasing myself. Always I am pleasing myself. It pleases me to give parties, it pleases me to hear music and drink wine, it pleases me to have in my house ladies like flowers who admire my house.'

Caroline's answering smile was radiantly grateful. Ladies like flowers indeed! Never, never could she remember anyone saying anything so delightfully poetic, so wonderfully romantic to her. Her eyes were as brilliant as moonlit water as she looked down at the gallant little Indian.

'Will you tell me about your house?'

'Most gladly. I have the inspiration from the Taj Mahal. You know, of course, of the Taj Mahal?'

Caroline shook her head.

'The Emperor Shah Jehan built it in the last century as a tomb for his wife whom he loved dearly. He built it in the plains of India, and he built it all of inlaid white marble, in domes with screens and pillars. It is most beautiful and I wished very much to have one too. But mine is not a tomb! Mine is a place for life!'

Across the room Isobel was flirting competently with two young officers steaming in the splendour of full dress uniform. Beside her, immaculate in dark blue with white linen, stood Sir Edward Ashton, fighting with boredom and a mounting desire to go home. He had not wanted to come in the first place, but Isobel had been most insistent and in the end he had agreed to stay for supper only, but to drag her home before the nautch began. He used to enjoy a nautch once, but Europeans were so sneering about them now, so supercilious, that the comments of his fellow guests ruined his pleasure and made him ashamed to be one of them.

He looked round for the Nawab, to congratulate him on his architectural skills. He was nowhere to be seen, which was hardly surprising since he was, like most native princes, an impeccable host, endlessly circulating at these huge receptions to make sure each guest had what he wanted. Shifting his shoulders uncomfortably, conscious of the linen peeling away from the damp skin of his back, Sir Edward put his eyeglass to his right eye and looked irritably about. The usual faces, of course, the usual unremarkable faces saying the usual unremarkable things to each other. Across the nodding sea of powdered and turbaned heads, Sir Edward found the unmistakable figure of the Nawab at last, solid with jewels, and talking animatedly to a most remarkable-looking young woman. Sir Edward took out his eyeglass, and polished it vigorously on his handkerchief, then replaced it for closer scrutiny. She was a most fascinating-looking creature, all the colour of honey, hair, skin, dress, and although no beauty in the accepted sense, she had a face of considerable distinction. Her hair was unpowdered, too, and woven with flowers. She was unlike anything Sir Edward had ever seen before, and she was conversing with the Nawab with an air of concentration that represented a challenge to the watcher across the room. He turned quickly and gestured to Lady Renton, seated peacefully gossiping by the wall.

'There is someone I must speak to, Lady Renton. Would you be so good as to look after Miss Grant for me?'

He threaded his way rapidly through the crowd, unaware of Isobel's satisfied gaze watching his passage. Caroline, deep in her first lesson of Moghul history, was unaware that anyone had joined herself and the Nawab, until a voice beside her said, 'Would it be unforgivable to interrupt, Nawab?'

She looked up and found herself immediately dismayed. This tall, impressive man, with his splendid presence and air of dignity, was none other than the alarming person who had whisked Isobel away on the waterfront three months ago. He was the man who had forbidden Isobel to see her and who openly disapproved of her and her husband. Muttering stammered excuses, she endeavoured to curtsey and move away, for it was evident that it was the Nawab Sir Edward sought.

'I beg you will not go,' he said in a low voice.

'No, indeed, you shall not go. You have listened to me so charmingly and now you shall listen to Sir Edward for a change. This delightful lady much admires my house, Sir Edward.'

'I am not surprised, Nawab.'

'I must present her to you, Sir Edward, but I have been so charmed by her conversation I have quite forgotten to ask her name.'

'It is of no consequence!' Caroline cried hastily. 'Please, it does not matter. I am sure I am intruding and that you wish to speak without me. I will withdraw, indeed I – '

A firm hand held her elbow.

'I hope you will do nothing of the sort, and I hope the Nawab will forgive me if I tell him that I did not cross the room to speak to him, but to speak to you.'

Startled out of her shyness, Caroline looked straight up at him and saw that his eyes did not belie his words. He did not take his hand from her elbow but went on holding her with his firm grasp.

The Nawab, observing this, was chuckling delightedly again, rocking back and forth on the toes of his golden slippers.

'I see I have two guests who will be happy! It pleases me

to have guests who are happy! May I persuade you to stay after supper for the nautch?'

Caroline removed her bemused gaze from Sir Edward and said dazedly, 'The nautch?'

'Aha!' the Nawab cried delightedly. 'You have never seen a nautch! You have not lived, you have not lived! I have the most beautiful, the most witty, the most graceful girls in all India. I have girls from Lucknow, girls from Delhi. I have the best of all girls to perform for you! Is not that true, Sir Edward?'

Sir Edward said to Caroline, 'Will you stay? If you will stay, the Nawab may at least count upon an audience of two.'

'I should like to if – ' Caroline began doubtfully, still anxious as to the effect of the revelation of her name. But the Nawab waited for no more.

'Splendid! I am delighted! Now, Sir Edward, you will look after this charming lady for me at supper?'

'If she will allow me.'

The Nawab bowed, smiled and vanished into the throng to seek out any other lonely guest.

'Will you take my arm?'

Caroline hesitated.

'I – I feel I should tell you who I am. I know who you are, I am sure most of this room knows that, but I fear you – will be displeased when you hear my name.'

'I refute that entirely. Will you trust my equanimity and reveal this dreadful truth?'

'I am Caroline Gates. I came out on the *Sea Horse* with your cousin, Isobel Grant, to marry a man I have known since childhood.' She stopped, and then with a burst of honesty said, 'You do not countenance the man I have married and you have forbidden Isobel to visit me.'

'I must be mad,' Sir Edward said.

Caroline looked up at him earnestly.

'Please do not make light of it. You have been very angry with Isobel for visiting me, and I do not want to embarrass you by being seen with you!'

For answer Sir Edward picked up her hand and placed it within his arm.

Supper was laid in a room whose floor space almost equalled that of the great reception hall. The ceiling was painted with jungle beasts and men in turbans and girls in veils and jewels, and from it hung hundreds of lamps suspended on brass chains threaded with flowers. Sir Edward took Caroline to a table by a screened window and introduced her to the dozen or so men and woman already seated there. She was greeted most kindly and sat down with the feeling that she was in a most happy dream which was certain to be broken by the coming of morning.

'Tell me again why you are in Calcutta,' Sir Edward said, pulling his chair close to hers.

'I came to marry.'

'And did you?'

'Yes – yes, I did.'

'I do not give a fig for that,' Sir Edward said.

'But it is – how things are.'

'Maybe. And how were things before that?'

'I come from a village in Dorset, a very small village called Stoke Abbas.' She stopped. It was so long since she had tried to recall it that the wheels of her memory seemed stiff. 'It is supposed to be a model village, of grey stone cottages running down a steep green hill to a river and a park. I think it is perhaps more a model to look at than to live in.'

Sir Edward looked at her keenly.

'Do you miss it?'

'I – I do not know. My feelings are so bound up with the people there. I did think today, however, that I would give a good deal for a wild autumn English day, with wet gusts and keen air. I was in the garden with the mali this morning trying to learn what I can expect to grow in the cool season, and I suddenly longed so passionately for a windy October day of driving clouds and yellow leaves!'

'You are as remarkable as you look,' Sir Edward said. 'I know no woman in India who bothers with her garden herself, who will take trouble to learn from, rather than instruct, the mali. I know no woman who sensibly attempts to grow Indian fruit and flowers instead of trying in vain to rear frail English ones. And I know nobody, man or woman, who has been able to induce in me the smallest pang of homesickness in ten years in India before now. But you have, and like you I would give anything at this moment for a stormy autumn morning in England.'

'I would not willingly induce homesickness in anyone.'

'Do you suffer yourself? I asked you before and you evaded me. Do you want to go home?'

Caroline looked down at her plate.

'Since my father died, I have not really got one to go to. The house is there still – but not what is necessary.'

'I understand you.'

She looked directly at him.

'Do you?'

'Certainly I do. I have a house in Herefordshire I have not missed in ten years for there is no one there to return to, and I have no one to take back to it. It is simply a house.'

Caroline felt her arm touched. The man on her left, a distinguished servant of the Company who had known Bengal for twenty years, wished to compliment her upon her hair.

'I hate this powdered fashion, hate it. Your curls are a pleasure to look at, my dear, a feast for the eye.'

Sir Edward could not hear her reply. He looked at those light twists and loops of hair, and their burden of flowers, and had to restrain in himself the desire to thread a finger through a loose curl lying on her shoulder. Her shoulder itself caught his attention, and the skin of her arm, so smooth and tawny, quite flawless, quite even. So strong was his inclination to touch this time, that he found his hand had involuntarily curved itself in the air above her arm that lay on the table, and he had to clench his fist to stop himself. He waited impatiently for her attention once more.

'You have no jewellery,' he said to her abruptly, forcing her to turn to him.

'I possess none.'

'Your flowers are perfect. Will you eat nothing?'

'I am not hungry. There seems to me too much food in India, too many meals.'

'You are too thin,' he said. 'You must not be too thin, you must look after your health.'

The nautch passed for Caroline in a dream. She was dimly aware of shrill oriental music, and of astonishingly supple girls in scarves and jewels dancing endlessly and tirelessly on a shining space of floor. They sang occasionally, answered repartee from the Indians left among the guests, and passed before Caroline's eyes in a blurred haze of gleaming skin and gems. She sat in the shadows at the edge of the room, conscious of very little beyond the fact that Sir Edward Ashton was behind her chair and that she only had to tilt her head back a matter of inches for her hair to brush his waistcoat front. She did not do so. She sat and stared before her and never noticed that Johnnie had gone or that Isobel, from her circle of beaux across the room, was regarding her with an expression of delighted achievement. When the nautch ended finally in the dawn, and the lamps were re-lit to show only a small and yawning group of Europeans remaining, Caroline woke from her trance and asked for her carriage. Sir Edward endeavoured to prevent her, to escort her home himself, but she was adamant. Day had come and ordinary life must be resumed. She stepped into her carriage just as the first glorious glow of a Calcutta sunrise was spreading over the sky, and turned to say goodbye with no idea of how she should do so. But he was before her.

'*Au revoir*,' he said as he kissed her hand, and stepped back for the carriage to roll by.

Half an hour later, at six in the morning, Ralph Buxby was woken by a bearer. He was initially extremely angry, assuming the bearer had mistaken the hour and woken him early in error. However, a paper was thrust into his hand, and a lamp was brought so that he might read. The message came from his superior, Sir Edward Ashton, and contained express instructions that Buxby was to discover everything he could about a man named John Gates, and to have that information on Ashton's desk by noon.

15

Ashton was at his desk by ten. His servants had watched his homecoming with some trepidation, for only once before did they recall his returning at dawn and the consequences of that had been terrible for all of them. This time, however, though elated, he was clearly entirely sober and wore an expression of private joy that made them put him to bed with more than their usual reverence. They were summoned three hours later since he appeared to wish to rise, and found him still and most uncharacteristically remote and calm in his manner. He seemed not to notice as he was shaved and dressed, appeared unconscious that breakfast had been put before him and when the hookah-burdar slipped the mouthpiece of his pipe into his hand, he let it slip to the floor as if he could not feel it. Only when seated at his desk did he seem to recollect himself, and summoned Buxby with almost more than his usual vigour.

'Well, Ralph, and what news have you for me?'

'You indicated noon, sir,' Buxby said anxiously. 'It wants still two hours to noon.'

'It does?' Sir Edward said vaguely, looking about him as if evidence of the correct hour hung about him in the damp hot air.

'I am doing all I can, sir, I do assure you.'

Buxby licked his lips. He remembered very clearly the tiny episode eighteen months before in which John Gates had figured, and in which he, Ralph Buxby, had taken it upon himself to play an unauthorized part. He knew, for half Calcutta knew by now, exactly whom Sir Edward had spent the previous evening with, and now feared some consequence of his presumption.

'I am sure you are, Buxby. Do not look so perturbed.' He

gazed into the spaces of the room in an abstracted way for a while before pulling himself together with a visible effort. 'Any news from the Governor General?'

There was plenty, Buxby was relieved to be able to say. The French were digging themselves comfortably into Poona, and were doing all they could to undermine the Company's presidency in Bombay, a presidency that had none of the strength or wealth of that in Calcutta. They were employing a divisive policy among the Marathas, the ruling people of that part of western India, and it seemed that assistance from Calcutta in the form of money and men was imminently necessary. Hastings had, as usual, his own decided ideas on the best course of action, and was, also as usual, opposed by all other members of the Council in what he wished to do, and therefore desired to hear Sir Edward's views as soon as possible.

When Buxby had gone, Sir Edward sat with pen and paper in a kind of benign abstraction. His views on dealing with any challenge to British dominion in India were usually as adamant as Hastings' own, but somehow this morning it was curiously difficult to bring his mind to bear on the probable necessity of raising several more regiments of sepoys, and the difficult task of selecting a man to lead them. He drew patterns idly on the margin of his paper, watching with interest the dimples of dampness his hand left upon it in the heat. After a while he gave up the task of even attempting to marshal his thoughts on paper, and flung his pen down, his hand then reaching out instinctively for the soothing influence of his hookah. The smooth coldness of the mouthpiece was briefly pleasant to the touch, and the comfortable bubbling sounds and draughts of spiced Persian tobacco contributed to his instinct for reverie.

Ten minutes before noon, Buxby was back, visibly damp with effort. He came into the room cautiously, not in the least sure of his reception, and found to his astonishment that instead of the furiously scribbling figure Sir Edward usually presented, he was lounging back in his chair with an expression of indescribable pleasure.

'Sir Edward?'

'Ah! Buxby!' The lounging figure swung abruptly up-right. 'What news have you now?'

'I have information, sir – and a confession.'

'Which will you give me first?' Sir Edward inquired serenely.

'The information, sir.'

Sir Edward nodded and fixed his eyes upon Buxby's sweating countenance.

'John Gates is the nephew of Lord Lennox, sir, Lord Lennox of Stoke Park in Dorsetshire. He was apparently something of a reprobate as a boy and, after a skirmish with Lord Lennox's eldest daughter, was sent out to Madras. I gather a relation in Scotland had some influence with the Company and obtained him a post as a clerk. It seems that his ways are unchanged from his boyhood.'

Ralph paused. He knew George Carew reasonably well, and therefore had a great deal more detail about Johnnie's life to hand than he had given. He decided that in view of his superior's present mood, sordid revelations of Johnnie's habits were unnecessary.

'Lennox,' Sir Edward said thoughtfully. 'Lennox. Why do I have a small recollection of a Lennox?'

'We are coming more nearly to my confession, sir. May I say in advance that I deeply regret my presumption and never, since that time, have I exceeded my duty in such a manner.'

'I expect you to exceed your duty, you dolt,' Sir Edward said with a smile. 'What use to me is a secretary with no head on his shoulders?'

'Two years ago, a man came to Calcutta who forms a link between yourself and – John Gates. Your cousin, Lord Lovell – '

'I do not wish to recall him, Buxby.'

'I must, sir, in order to remind you that he married Lord Lennox's youngest daughter, and it was through his information that it came to be known to the Lennoxes that you were in Calcutta. They might not have needed this knowledge except that it seemed Lady Lennox wished for your opinion on a matter relating to John Gates over a year ago and I – I gave it to her.'

'What?'

For the first time that morning, Sir Edward's eyes seemed to be focusing clearly upon his secretary. Buxby quailed a little, but persevered.

'I gave her an answer, sir. She wrote to ask you if you knew any reason why the daughter of the incumbent of the living in her gift should not marry John Gates. The daughter was a Miss Caroline Harding. I replied by saying I knew of no impediment.'

He watched while his information was translated into understanding in Sir Edward's eyes.

'You said, Buxby,' Sir Edward said slowly, 'you said you knew no reason why this innocent girl should not marry a known blackguard! You said that?' His voice suddenly exploded into a bellow. 'How dare you presume to decide such matters? How dare you act in such a manner without consulting me?'

'I did consult you, sir,' Ralph said staunchly.

'You did?'

'Yes, sir, I did. But I do not think', he added bravely, 'that the matter concerned you as nearly as it does now.'

'When was this?' Sir Edward's tone was still dangerous.

'The winter before last, sir. During the troubles over excessive inland trading. Lady Lennox's letter came on an – unfortunate morning, sir.'

'Unfortunate? Why was it unfortunate?'

Buxby shifted uncomfortably. Most men had hangovers as their houses had mice, but if a man only has one monumental hangover in ten years it becomes both legendary and unmentionable.

'It – it is difficult to remind you, sir.'

There was a pause.

'I need no reminding,' Sir Edward said shortly. He sat bent over his clasped hands for a while and contemplated the consequences of the past. He could remember very little of that painful day except the suffering of his spirit as it wrestled with humiliation and self-disgust. He could recall that Ralph had presented him with a whole series of matters he could not begin to deal with in such a state, and he had no reason to doubt that in such condition, blind to everything but his wretchedness, he had allowed Caroline Harding to be sent as a lamb to the slaughter.

It was no good reasoning to himself that he could not possibly have known what she might mean to him, nor in arguing that if he had prevented the marriage she would never have come to Calcutta in the first place, and thus he would never have known her. The facts of the matter bore down all such reasonableness and left him full of remorseful anguish. Her look of happy gratitude last night, her thin and fascinating face dominated by those exquisite eyes and crowned with a halo of pale hair and flowers, flashed suddenly upon his inward eye and gave him resolution. She should not be squandered upon a reprobate, especially not when he was so entirely sure that he would want her for himself. If convention had to be flouted, well, so be it. He had trapped her in this marriage, and he would now open the cage and release her. It was as simple as that. He rose and smiled at Buxby.

'Find Miss Grant for me, would you, Buxby? I have a small task for her.'

Caroline's morning had given her no chance for happy reverie. She had been woken after a few hours only of deep unnatural slumber, because Ranjit's anxiety that Sahib Gates was still not home could be contained no longer. None of the servants who had accompanied them to the reception had seen him leave, all assuming that while the memsahib was still present, the carriage must stay and them with it. They stood before Caroline with clasped hands and bent heads and awaited reprimand. Her Hindustani was far from good, but she had enough now to speak simply to them.

'Did you see him go? Did any one of you see Sahib Gates go?'

They shook their heads. One had in fact noticed him climbing into a carriage with George Carew and a party of ladies, but he did not feel he wished to mention the matter. Johnnie had not summoned anyone to attend him and therefore wished to be left alone. He stared at his feet and said nothing.

'Then, Ranjit, you will take a letter to Sahib Carew for me.'

The note despatched, she sat down to a breakfast she did not want and tried to put her thoughts into some kind of order. She had scarcely even allowed herself a glimpse of the recollection of Sir Edward Ashton before there was a knock on the door and the great Pathan who had his eye upon Ranjit's position announced that a money-changer from the bazaar wished an audience with the memsahib.

Caroline felt a clutch of panic. In the last few days of fairy tale, when she had been so absorbed in sartorial delights and the joy of Isobel's enlivening company once more, she had quite forgotten that the repayment of her loan must begin. What was worse, was that the household was in want of money again, if she was to pay the servants as promptly as she had promised, and keep the kitchen stocked with the expensive European commodities Johnnie demanded. She rose with as much calm as she could muster and asked for the man to be shown in.

He entered with a smile that bore a disagreeable family resemblance to the sircar's.

'You are very prompt,' she said in a faintly accusing tone.

'And the memsahib is being most honourable, I am sure.'

She thought rapidly. Her one desire was to get him out of the house in case Johnnie should return and her secret be revealed. A few rupees still remained out of the hundred pounds, a few rupees destined for that week's food, but it would have to be sacrificed.

'I shall pay you a little today, and more next week when – when I can lay my hands on a larger sum.'

'The terms, oh gracious memsahib, were repayment in full after three months – '

'It cannot be,' Caroline said, surprised at the decisiveness of her tone. 'You shall have your money, and the interest, but I do not have it by me today.'

The money-lender shrugged. He was not unduly concerned, and knew very well how to make himself a nuisance, so much a nuisance in fact that no sum of money seemed too much to pay to get rid of him.

'I will return, memsahib.'

'I do not doubt it,' Caroline said faintly, and turned away as he left the room.

No use now to let her thoughts dwell luxuriously on forbidden pleasures. If she were to survive at all, she must put her thoughts to work and cudgel out of them some solution, however temporary. There were Johnnie's pictures still, of course, but the notion of taking those, however justified she might be, had grown distasteful to her. She must calm herself, she must. Nobody could think constructively while their minds were so distracted with anxiety. She cast about the room for some occupation with which to settle her wits and her eye lit upon the only painting of her own she had presumed to hang up, a miniature of the Parsonage painted from memory on that long and happy voyage. She would paint again! That was it. She would force herself to tackle some intricate and detailed subject, something so absorbing that it would allow her mind no escape until it was calmed and would once again work for her.

There was something heartachingly familiar about her materials, the ovals of ivory, the paints and brushes, the rags of torn-up petticoats still smeared with the paint and memories of the past. She looked out of the window on to the baked yellow earth of her garden with its struggling shrubs dusty in the merciless sunshine and saw no inspiration there. She glanced back at her miniature on the wall, and a sudden idea came to her. She would not paint India at all, India was all around her, she would paint something English, some cool, wet, green evocation of England. She closed her eyes for a moment and saw a tuft of young bracken, the brilliant green fronds uncurling soft and moist from damp dark earth, and snails among them, tiny snails with iridescent shells and questing horns. The idea was so captivating, so far removed from the oppression of her present situation, that she was suddenly in a ferment of eagerness to begin. She sat down at the table and sought her pencil and a suitable piece of ivory. There could be a spider's web, spangled with drops, and a ladybird for a single note of scarlet, and a mossy cushion at the base.

She was so deeply absorbed that the announcement that

she had a caller startled her. She was dismayed to find her mood abruptly shattered, so dismayed that she could not move for a moment but sat bemused on her chair until Mrs Rathbone grew tired of examining the shabbiness of the drawing room and sought her out unheralded. She was bursting to see Caroline, to talk over the night before, and to see whether this odd self-contained girl was in the least affected by the great attentions paid to her.

'My dear Mrs Gates, Caroline, dearie! And how are we this morning? We are the talk of Calcutta, I do declare! Sir Edward Ashton has never been known to pay the smallest attention to any woman before, and it is said he did not take his eyes from you once! What a conquest, my dear, what a triumph!'

Caroline was silent. The mere thought of being the talk of Calcutta was repugnant to her, even though she knew the city thrived on gossip and grew quickly tired of any item of it.

'I am sorry to be the subject of any talk, Mrs Rathbone.'

'Sorry? Sorry? My dear, you are a foolish girl, my word you are. Sir Edward never stays anywhere beyond midnight, and there he was still dancing attendance at dawn. You should be pleased as Punch, my dear, I vow you should.'

Caroline shook her head helplessly. She knew Mrs Rathbone meant to congratulate her, and she knew that one of the motives, albeit a small one, of her visit was kindness, but she could not bear that the previous evening was the plaything of vulgar gossip. She had hardly had time to reflect upon it at all, but she sensed that it was probably one of the most precious occasions of her life and for that reason she bitterly resented that it should, even briefly, be public property. Mrs Rathbone watched her brightly and deduced that she had either been hopelessly overawed or entirely infatuated by her distinguished admirer.

'And what are you doing in here at this hour, my dear? I thought you were our early bird, always breakfasting with the dawn, putting us all to shame – '

'I was painting.'

Mrs Rathbone glanced at the table, and her casual air immediately became bright with interest. She peered intently down upon the little painting.

'My dear! I had no notion, no notion at all, that you had such a talent! It is charming, quite charming. It reminds me so of England, my dear, I could quite weep, I declare I could.'

She looked up at Caroline with the slightly challenging air of one who cannot resist acquisitions.

'Would you paint one for a friend, my dear, as a very great favour?'

'No,' said Caroline suddenly, seized by an inspiration. 'I wish I could afford to do that but I cannot. I only paint for purchase.'

'Hard-headed creature, Caroline!' Mrs Rathbone laughed and tapped her with a tasselled fan.

'Not by nature, Mrs Rathbone, but out of necessity.'

Mrs Rathbone looked about her at the run-down air of the room, the whitewash already streaking, the patched curtains and absence of silver and an inkling of the nature of Caroline's life came to her.

'Are you short of money, dear?'

'Yes,' Caroline said briefly.

'Does – does Johnnie keep you short, dear?'

Caroline said nothing, but fidgeted the pieces of ivory on the table. Mrs Rathbone clicked her tongue sympathetically.

'What shall you do, my dear?'

'I will sell miniatures, Mrs Rathbone, if you will help me. I wonder I never thought of it before, but Calcutta is so full of idleness and money that I feel I must have some small success.'

Mrs Rathbone's eyes lit up with pleasure at the thought of such a project.

'Caroline, what a wise head you have upon your shoulders! I think we may well start a new fashion for mementoes of England, indeed I do.'

'Will you help me? Will you be very kind and show my work to your friends?'

Mrs Rathbone thought of the happy diversion that the examination of miniatures would provide from the endless, though pleasureable, topics of dress and scandal. Quite apart from that she could see clearly that help was necessary, and help was something she liked to give. Within a quarter of an hour her carriage was bowling homewards, and she carried with her Caroline's promise that within two weeks some half-dozen of these tiny paintings would be at her house ready for sale. For every ten she managed to sell, Caroline would paint an eleventh of a subject of her own choice as a gift. Mrs Rathbone smiled contentedly to herself. Would people pay four guineas apiece, or dare she ask five? She thought of Caroline's neatly mended gown and the dining-room furniture placed discreetly so as almost to cover, but not quite, the worn patches in the carpet and decided she would stick out for five. Five guineas was, after all, no more than an average hairdresser's bill and Caroline was quite evidently in desperate need. Naughty Johnnie, Mrs Rathbone reflected with cosy disapproval; what a reckless, extravagant boy to keep his poor wife in such awkward penury, and what a providential thing that she, Bella Rathbone, had chanced to call. Suddenly Mrs Rathbone sat upright. It was too bad, indeed it was! In all the happy little arrangements about the pictures she had entirely forgotten to squeeze from Caroline every drop of fascinating information about Sir Edward Ashton!

Still in the dining room after Mrs Rathbone's departure, and elated at the prospect of some small release from her difficulties, Caroline went back to her painting with renewed vigour. If she rose each morning early, she calculated, and instructed the servants as to their tasks while she breakfasted in order to save time, she could see that five or six hours were at her disposal until the dinner hour, five or six hours for her meticulous work. Her father had once said it was hardly good for her weak eyesight to strain for too long over the tiny details, but he had never contemplated that she would be in such straits as she now found herself. She had always worked fast, it was in her nature, and now she imagined that with practice she would become faster, indeed she had to. Over twenty miniatures had to be sold before she could regard herself as out of debt and beginning to make a profit. Twenty miniatures were well over two months' relentless work, given that she had no interruptions. She shook herself resolutely and settled sternly to the completion of the first.

She had not been working above a further hour when a letter was brought to her, a letter in Isobel's dear and familiar hand. It was an invitation to dine on the morrow for both herself and Johnnie, and Isobel indicated that Sir Edward was in no frame of mind to brook refusal or a prior arrangement.

'We dine at two, and will be eagerly looking out for you. You shall not refuse, dearest Caroline, without causing the wrath and dejection of your host, at whose command I gladly write. Tell Mr Gates I shall be sure to give him amusing companions at dinner, since I feel he may need some lure to be got up here at all to a house where his wife will be made so rapturously welcome.'

Caroline sat and gazed at the letter with a mixture of apprehension and joy. Within twenty-four hours or so, then, she was to see him again, he had remembered her, he had asked for her! Her face was illuminated by a quite involuntary smile, a smile of absolute happiness that was abruptly extinguished as she remembered guiltily for the first time in hours that not only could she not at this moment accept for Johnnie, but she also had not the smallest notion where he was. She rang immediately.

'Have you any news of Sahib Gates?'

'He will be returning after dinner, memsahib,' Ranjit said. 'He is detained but he is returning then.'

'Why have you not told me this before? Where is he? Is he hurt or ill?'

Ranjit could not look at her. He had not come to her immediately with the news of his master's whereabouts because he had been busy in the servants' quarters with a fierce dispute over whether he should tell her at all. The great Pathan had declared that the memsahib had the heart of a lion and could bear all truths, but Ranjit's own gallantry had made him wish to temper the truth and not put that lion's heart to the test. The truth was that Johnnie had indeed been at George Carew's house, and the servants there had informed Ranjit that Rani, Sahib Gates's old mistress, had come there in the dawn and that Sahib Gates had wept when he saw her, and pressed gold into her hands, and they were still together. Sahib Carew had told Ranjit that he would see Sahib Gates was home before nightfall, and that the memsahib was not to worry. This part, at least, of the message, Ranjit felt he could give.

'Then I will dine alone, Ranjit,' she said quietly. 'I will dine at four since I wish to continue painting. And I thank you, Ranjit,' she added, discerning from his manner that his news was edited, 'for what you have left unsaid.'

Johnnie came home in a lowering temper and last night's sweat-soaked linen. Only when he wrenched himself from Rani's entwining arms to seek the rival attraction of George's cellar at the dinner hour, did he hear of Caroline's triumph the night before. His reaction was initially to be furious, to feel himself cuckolded and diminished, and to declare roundly to the table of red-eyed, stale-mouthed gentlemen in George's dining room that Sir Edward Ashton must be an ass to waste his attention on a woman with no more charms than a broom handle. He muttered and complained his way through a prodigious quantity of claret, swore that some rogue had thieved what he had won at whist the night before, and was packed into George's carriage to go home, still demanding the company's pity for the fool he had been made to seem. He arrived back to find Caroline still wearing the traces of the previous night's elation, and in possession of an invitation to dine at a house where Johnnie had fruitlessly sought entry for six years or more. He cursed and swore at her for a little while to soothe his feelings and to disguise his eagerness to accept, and then, shouting for fresh linen, he declared his intention of passing the evening at the whist club. Out of an unspoken mutual desire not to know the truth, he did not ask her about the previous evening, and she made no enquiries as to where he had been.

16

At two the following day, Johnnie was nowhere to be seen. He had breakfasted with Caroline in silence, casting her resentful glances and heaving sighs of self-pity, and had only broken his silence to say he would return at noon and she was to order the carriage for a quarter to two. She had tried to paint that morning, but was in such a state of happy trepidation that she knew the results were not her best work. She was slightly ashamed of how frequently her thoughts ran on the vexing problem of how she should dress. Isobel's present was clearly out of the question, being a dress only for after dark, but the choices it left were in truth extremely dreary, and would inspire none of that sartorial excitement she had felt when dressing for the great reception. At long length she selected a dress of pale blue muslin, for although the fabric would be conspicuously humble amid the splendours of Sir Edward's dining room, it was the dress that fitted her best and contained the Stoke Abbas dressmaker's fewest errors. She only possessed one silk dress in any case, and she had come to detest it for it had been the last new dress before her father's death and was inextricably mixed up in her mind with her guilt and suffering over that event.

She sat in the sweating gloom of the drawing room and waited for Johnnie. Her servants had made an excellent imitation of her French hairstyle of two nights before, and one had, in a last moment of inspiration, wound a blue ribbon high about Caroline's throat for ornament. It chafed her when she swallowed, but the effect was almost elegant. It was difficult to sit still, difficult not to glance eternally at her watch, difficult to subdue her mounting excitement. At a quarter past two, she made a sudden resolve and rose to her feet. She would go, she could not bear not to, and Johnnie must follow as best he could.

Her consciousness of being late filled her mind with far more alarm than the decision whether or not to wait for Johnnie. As her carriage halted before the great square white house by Calcutta's Court House, with gardens about it and the river glittering below, she felt it would in fact be impossible to mount those steps alone and enter a room full of self-possessed strangers knowing that she was late and with the added embarrassment of being unaccompanied.

As she stepped reluctantly from the carriage, a young Englishman appeared at the top of the steps, called to a servant and then, before Caroline was even halfway up that daunting flight, Sir Edward Ashton himself was in the doorway and leaping down the steps towards her. He was beside her in a moment, seizing both her hands in his, all without giving a single glance towards the carriage which he must have presumed still held the unwanted Mr Gates.

'I thought you had failed me.'

She looked up at him with difficulty in the blinding sunlight.

'Oh, no, no, I would not – I am so sorry to be so late, I do apologize, but my husband is not home, he has sent no word, I – '

'Think nothing of it.'

Still holding the hand closest to him, he began to lead her up the steps.

In the stripes of sun and shadow of the doorway, he turned her to face him, and in the shadows behind them, Buxby waited in interested amusement, watching their black profiles against the sunlight turned earnestly to each other.

At last Sir Edward raised the hand he still held and kissed it.

'I fear I must share you with some dozen others. It is all arranged by Isobel for I have the social instincts of a hermit. Buxby, do not slink in the shadows like a servant. Come and be presented to Mrs Gates.'

Ralph bowed before her with a hint of self-consciousness. She smiled and he saw her eyes and the warmth and happiness in them, and a pang of shame made his own returning smile difficult to achieve.

Isobel was waiting in the drawing room in ill-concealed excitement.

'Oh, thank heaven you are come, Caroline! I thought you had played the coward at last, I truly did, and Sir Edward has been pacing like a caged tiger since noon – '

'Hush, Isobel!' Caroline said in a shocked whisper, keenly aware of the sudden attention of everyone else in the room and of her left hand still firmly and conspicuously imprisoned.

'Caroline, you are a goose,' Isobel declared. 'I do assure you', she went on to a man beside her, 'that Mrs Gates has more to congratulate herself upon than the rest of us women put together, but she has not the first notion how to do it.'

The man came forward, took Caroline's free hand and kissed it.

'We can only admire such modesty, Mrs Gates, and school ourselves to the impossible task of ignoring your enchanting friend. Your servant, John Eyre, ma'am.'

They all seemed about her then, smiling and presenting themselves, eager to see, in all her detail, this phenomenon who had so obviously captivated Calcutta's most eligible and obstinate bachelor. There was to be much discussion later, of course, discussion on the provincial drabness of her dress, the remarkable fact of her unpowdered head, her astonishing quicksilver eyes and her quietly independent behaviour. She was pronounced hopelessly plain, unfashionably thin and awkwardly shy, but there were also opinions that declared her face to be one of considerable distinction, her manners appealing in their gentle diffidence, and her figure elegant among some of the more solid flesh about her. Whatever the world, in the shape of twelve English people in Calcutta in the summer of 1777, thought of her appearance, their views were all coloured by respectful astonishment before dinner was over.

Caroline found herself on Sir Edward's right, her own right flanked by the comfortable stocky figure of John Eyre. The room bore many resemblances to the dining room at Stoke Park, except that the painted wood that panelled it was laid against mud, and the floor was of marble. She looked about her with pleasure, at the pictures on the walls that spoke so powerfully of England, at the pierced brass hanging lamps one saw everywhere in Calcutta, at the polished wood and silver, the Indian rugs and embroideries.

The talk ranged easily about her, talk of the French, talk of the decaying Moghul princes living out lives of voluptuous splendour, talk of England and Lord North's government that sought to direct the East India Company with a more official hand than it had ever felt before. Caroline listened with absorption, ate a little of everything that was put before her, and raised her glance every so often to reassure herself that everything was real, and to find Sir Edward gazing at her often with a kind of delighted triumph.

When the fruit was laid upon the table in great woven baskets, a man who sat several places down the table from Caroline, and who had introduced himself as Piers Lawrence, called to attract her attention.

'We have given you enough time, Mrs Gates, to establish your composure, and I now propose to test it.'

'You will do no such thing,' Sir Edward asserted.

Caroline had detected a gleam of challenge in Piers Lawrence's eye, and felt herself serene enough to meet it. He was a handsome man, a black-haired handsome man with a sardonic air and mocking eyes.

'Oh, please, Sir Edward, let him speak.'

'Do you wish it?'

Caroline nodded.

'You are a fortunate man, Piers, but I will brook no insolence, not the smallest suggestion of it.'

'Insolence could not be further from my thoughts, Sir Edward. I merely wish to know from Mrs Gates if certain rumours are true.'

At the mention of rumours, Caroline froze, but it was too late to retract now.

'Rumours, Mr Lawrence?'

'I gather, Mrs Gates,' he said slowly, 'that you are perhaps the most intrepid in our number. I gather you have been seen in the native bazaar, attended by no more than one servant, I might add – ' he paused, and a little ripple ran round the table.

'Pray go on,' Caroline said.

'Perhaps you are unaware that it is hardly customary for an Englishwoman to enter the bazaar? Perhaps you are equally unaware that it is not expected that an Englishwoman shall meddle with her servants' lives, dose their children, teach them English, interfere with their living habits, and be on terms with them that I can only describe as familiar?'

Sir Edward was on his feet.

'Get out! I said there was to be no insolence and you have exceeded yourself! Get out, I say!'

'No – no, please, Sir Edward!'

He looked down. Caroline had her hand upon his sleeve and was looking up at him with irresistible earnestness.

'No, you must not dismiss him, Sir Edward, you must not. Everything he says is true. It is only that the interpretation I put upon my actions is wholly different to his.'

The table, which had erupted into excitement, was instantly stilled. Unwillingly, Sir Edward lowered himself into his chair again.

'I have every faith in your interpretation,' he said.

Caroline looked down at her lap for a moment, aware that while she could defend her affection for her servants, she could not explain the emotional desert and threat of destitution that had driven her to them and to visit the bazaar. She raised her eyes at last and stared unwaveringly down the table at Piers Lawrence.

'This country is not ours, Mr Lawrence, we may plunder it and use it to our advantage, and many Indians may profit from our being here, but it is not ours. It seemed to me, arriving as a complete novice, that I would only understand India through the Indians. It seemed to me that the society which involves most of Calcutta could be better found in Bath or London. We English live a parasite's life here, and I did not wish to do that. How do I know if Indians resent my presence here, your presences, all our presence? It would seem that the humblest way to live here for me – I do not speak of men of affairs – is to let India teach me. How do I do that if I do not know my servants, the people who are closest to me? How do I learn not to offend them if I do not know how they live, how they market, how they pray? And if I come to the conclusion that I like them, that I admire them and that there are ways in which I can help their children to be less sickly, make their problems of speaking to their employers less difficult, why should I deliberately hold back that help because I am English and they are Indian? They help me immeasurably. May I not return some of that help? If you disapprove of such opinions, Mr Lawrence, I cannot help it, but I could wish, for India's sake, that your mind were not so narrow.'

She was trembling when she stopped. She realized that all these thoughts had been mere instincts before, that she had never rationalized them until now, and that in doing so she had sounded as dangerously priggish as Eleanor. She dropped her eyes.

'Forgive me,' she said in a low voice to the table at large. 'I fear I have presumed a superiority I do not feel. I have no right to judge Mr Lawrence, no right at all, forgive me – '

There was a burst of cheering. She could not look up, but sat and wished very much that she had held her tongue. In the babble, she was conscious of Isobel kneeling at her side, smiling, and talking rapidly, but she could make no reply. Someone broke through the circle and stood by Isobel, someone whose exquisitely cut breeches and silk stockings, which was all Caroline dared glance at, betokened a man of fashion.

'I surrender completely, Mrs Gates.'

'It is Piers!' Isobel whispered. 'Be gracious, Caroline!'

Caroline looked up and saw that his eyes were no longer mocking.

'It – it is very handsome of you, Mr Lawrence, I feel that I – '

'You were magnificent, Mrs Gates, and I have nothing but admiration for your spirit. Will you accept my humblest apologies?'

'Gladly.'

226

He drew back a little, and the press of people, still murmuring in undertones of excitement, drifted back to their places. Caroline ventured to steal a glance in her host's direction, terrified to find, because of his silence, the blackest disapproval written there. But he was regarding her with a look of admiration so unmistakable that she was held motionless by it, as a rabbit in a snare.

'You are matchless,' he said at last. 'Matchless!'

At home in the gathering dusk a most peevish Johnnie awaited her. He had deliberately delayed himself that morning out of a small resentment that Caroline should be the instrument by which he entered great houses, and also because he was perfectly certain her social timidity would force her to wait for him, however late he was. He arrived but minutes after her departure, and burst instantly into the flaming and violent temper the servants had known daily in his bachelorhood; now he vented it upon Caroline instead, and they were out of training for such an onslaught. By the time he had been changed and had consumed a bottle of champagne to console himself for his wife's callousness and shameless social climbing, Ranjit was forced to point out gently that it was almost three o'clock.

'What of it, you dolt?' Johnnie shouted.

He strode out on to the landing and bellowed for the carriage.

'Memsahib is taking it, sahib.'

It dawned slowly upon Johnnie that if he wished to get there at all he must ride and furthermore the distance would take him twenty minutes or more, at which point he would be an hour and a half late, not to mention dusty, exhausted and drenched in sweat. Swearing and cursing, Johnnie kicked his way downstairs, banged into the dining room and bellowed for mutton and wine. All Calcutta would be dining by now, all his friends deep in happy conversation and quaffing wine they had not had to pay for, and all because of Caroline's inordinate selfishness he was forced to sit here alone with a solitary chop and only a bottle for company. She had promised always to look after him, she had sworn to make him comfortable, but clearly her idea of comfort only concerned herself. Oblivious of the days and nights Caroline had spent alone in their gloomy rooms while he was out pleasuring, forgetful of the fact that she had made his life more comfortable than it had been in ten years in India, Johnnie sat in the dim room and chewed and muttered and vowed he would be even with her.

When she did return at last, and he marched out into the hallway to vent his furious resentment on her, he found that he might as well have addressed a brick wall. She gazed at him with a kind of calm remoteness, her eyes fixed upon some inward picture, not absorbing the spectacle of his temper at all, and then, without so much as a word, she shook her head slightly as if to get rid of some disagreeable sensation about her ears, and climbed the staircase to her room. He shouted still as she went, but his words and insults bounced off her like hailstones, and then, as he paused for breath, he heard the door of her room shut softly. He started up the stairs after her still bellowing, then halted abruptly halfway up.

'Damnation take you, you bitch!'

The key would be turned by now. She had had the lock of her door mended.

17

By the time the monsoons came, Calcutta was weary of the subject of Mrs Gates and Sir Edward Ashton. Affairs, after all, only retained their fascination if one or both of the participants was prepared to be flamboyant and thus sustain public appetite for sensation. By September, Calcutta was used to them and bored by them, and now had a new target in any case. Warren Hastings, having lived with the Baroness Imhoff openly in Calcutta awaiting her divorce, at last received that eagerly awaited news in the summer of 1777, and instantly married his lady. With a new Mrs Hastings to flatter and toady to, who could be bothered any longer with plain Mrs Gates, however impressive her admirer?

For her part, Caroline was thankful when the glare of public interest was diverted. July and early August had passed for her in an enchantment so powerful she had quite forgotten to observe the reactions of those around her. If she had looked, she would have seen that the gossips were still astounded that Johnnie could not quite bring himself to behave heavy-handedly, because he was very doubtful he was a match for Sir Edward, and that Isobel, Mrs Rathbone and George Carew saw in Caroline what could only be called a flowering. There was a distinct bloom about her, an aura of freshness and vitality despite the appalling heat. Her hair seemed thicker, her cheeks to have more colour and her body seemed less the awkward collection of angles it usually presented.

'My dear, it is no more nor less than a fairy tale,' Mrs Rathbone said to a friend. 'She'll never be a beauty, poor dear, but you never saw such a change in anyone, I swear it.'

Isobel, free now to see Caroline as often as she chose, observed the same to her friend's face.

'Dearest Caroline, you are hardly the same person. Indeed, if it were not for these dreadful old muslins you will wear of a morning, I doubt I should recognize you.'

Caroline knew she was indeed not the same person. The combination of the difficulties of her everyday life in Calcutta and the splendour of being loved by such a man as Sir Edward Ashton, had caused her to emerge at last from the chrysalis of her diffidence. Mrs Rathbone had proved, for all her garrulity, a faithful ally in the matter of the miniatures, and the little paintings, diplomatically unsigned, were now springing up in drawing rooms all over Calcutta. It was in truth becoming quite the fashion to have a whole collection of these nostalgically English miniatures hung tastefully to one side of the chimneypiece; so much the fashion, Mrs Rathbone reported, that she had even seen two dormice and a bunch of primroses hanging incongruously among the jewelled splendours of an Indian harem. Prices in Calcutta were so outrageous that Caroline found she could ask ten guineas quite brazenly, almost all of that sum being pure profit since Ranjit brought her all the ivory she could want from the bazaar at a price she could hardly credit was so small. She was, as a result of this secret and successful traffic, out of debt and well on the road to running the household without having to apply to Johnnie for anything, a fact he never seemed to notice, but rather took for granted.

It was, indeed, all deeply satisfactory, except for the fact that to comply with what seemed an insatiable demand she was having to force herself to paint eight or ten hours a day, and her eyes were sore and strained as a result. She rose at dawn, painted until the dinner hour, and then, if she were not dining out, painted again until the light failed. The results were not as meticulous as those first few she had done in the weeks of oppressive need to pay her debt, but they seemed to suffice. Calcutta's taste, she concluded, was for show and, fortunately for her, not for exquisite workmanship.

But all this paled into insignificance beside her other achievement. Supporting herself and, in some measure, her household was indeed a matter for congratulation, but it was a small thing, a trivial, material thing, beside the fact that she was in love for the first time in her lonely adult life, and that that love was returned an hundredfold.

Sir Edward did not seem to find her dull or gauche or plain, he did not appear to think her existence pointless or her ideas trivial. No opinion seemed too small to excite his notice, no gesture or comment too slight to excite a reaction from him. She saw a good deal of him all that summer for between them, he and Isobel saw that she was invited to anything they might attend themselves. At every meeting he would bear down upon her like a knight who has at last found the Holy Grail, and carry her off to some secluded corner and the miracle of his undivided attention. He never, in all those glittering weeks, said in so many words that he loved her, but Caroline, timid, pessimistic Caroline, who had doubted almost every pleasant occurrence in her life, never doubted for one moment that he did. She only had to look up to him and find his steady gaze bent upon her to reassure herself that it was true, it was real, it was her he wanted.

In any other city, the consequences of such an entanglement would have pressed upon Caroline and Sir Edward Ashton quite quickly; but not in eighteenth-century Calcutta, a city so rife with reckless immorality that high-principled behaviour was conspicuous rather than the opposite. It was also assumed that any affair that did take place was doomed to a short life, since the climate, the short terms of office of most Europeans, and the presence of plenty of other and more tempting fish to fry, conspired against emotional steadfastness. Caroline had horrified herself initially, but then even she saw how calmly her own behaviour was taken, and abandoned herself to the happiest weeks she had known. She tried not to think ahead, discouraged Isobel from speculating, and presumed Sir Edward was in the same thoughtless limbo of bliss as herself.

She was wrong. Sir Edward had never been a soldier, but his mind had the same aptitude for successful forethought and planning as an able commander's. Wrenched, albeit willingly, from the Persian and Arabic studies with which he used to beguile his solitary hours, to dote upon Caroline, he did not allow his wits idleness. The very morning after he had met her, he had resolved what he would do for her, and he was simply, with a fierce and possessive tenderness, waiting for such a time as she might feel she could trust him without reservation. It was not a plan he could have proposed in London, perhaps not anywhere save Calcutta, but luckily society here, much as he might disapprove of it, made it possible.

'I beg you,' he said to her once in his own drawing room, while the monsoon rain fell from the sky in solid masses, 'that you will gradually, as you feel comfortable, tell me everything of your history. You must know by now that I am greedy for every crumb that you can give me as soon as you feel it is possible.'

Caroline had never believed it would be possible to speak of such matters as her father's death, or to recall her relationship with Eleanor impartially. They were all so bound up with her own sense of inadequacy that she had believed they would be too painful to voice, but not, it proved, to Sir Edward.

'My dear Caroline, I would give a good deal to love my own sister, and the fact that I do not is quite as much her responsibility as it is mine. Eleanor must come to meet you halfway.'

It was a novel idea. When she eventually told him of her father's death and the lurking fear of responsibility that shadowed her memory of him, Sir Edward reacted just as her father himself had done.

'Why your fault? Why any more your fault than any servant's?'

Caroline remembered the Judas kiss.

'Did your sister never kiss him? Did the servants not handle the food he ate? Come, look at me and do not turn away. Don't indulge yourself with these morbid fancies. I could wish selfishly that he were not dead so that I might indulge myself in talking to him of you, but if he were not dead you would not be here and – '

He stopped abruptly, and reached out to take her hands.

'There is one more avenue we must explore if you will not think me an intruder. Not today,' he added, observing the effects of recalling Parson Harding's death still evident on her face, 'but when you are ready. Will you tell me how you came to agree to be Mrs Gates?'

Caroline nodded.

'Another day.'

He raised her hands and kissed the fingers bent over his own.

'When you wish it.'

In all these weeks of happy confidence, Caroline saw little of Johnnie. He had, at the beginning, intended to demand honourable satisfaction for being cuckolded, and to challenge Sir Edward to a duel. George Carew, lazing beside him at his desk, pointed out the absurdity of the notion.

'You'll look a damned fool, my boy, indeed you will. You're no cuckold for a start, for I'll wager all Calcutta will tell you he's done no more than kiss her hand. Deuced if I know what they're up to, but it ain't what you're up to seven nights a week.'

'I look a fool,' Johnnie complained. 'She's never with me, and all the world knows where she is.'

'You don't want her with you,' George pointed out reasonably. 'You do nothing but shout at her when she is. Added to which, you're a damned poor shot these days and I'm told Ashton has the eye of a hawk. Pity to die for a woman you don't want.'

'I do – ' Johnnie began petulantly.

'Do you, my boy?'

Johnnie shifted in his chair and muttered inaudibly.

'I will say', George said idly, 'that you are a prettier sight since she came, and you wouldn't know the house from the hovel it was. But you don't lust for her, boy, do you?'

'Certainly not!' Johnnie said indignantly.

George got up slowly.

'Then leave her be. Why shouldn't she have her bit of fun, then? Deuced sight more harmless than yours. It'll all be over by Christmas in any case, and then you'll thank me for not getting yourself winged for nothing.'

The monsoon vanished as abruptly as it had come, and the blanket of wet heat that had accounted for the large number of funerals in the past weeks lifted, and air with a delightfully crisp edge to it came as a reward for endurance. Caroline, temporarily secure in her financial affairs, spent hours with the mali in the garden, kneeling beside him to press seedlings into the damp red earth. Things grew with gratifying speed, she observed, as she watched this veil of brilliant green, the result of the recent rains, bringing the dry yellow bones of her garden to life.

Not only winter was stirring in Calcutta. With quite a new source of information in Sir Edward Ashton, Caroline was beginning to be conscious of an India far and away beyond her small house and even the furthest reaches of Calcutta. The French, working on in western India, were now posing themselves as a considerable threat in reality, and it was Warren Hastings's opinion, an opinion shared by Sir Edward, that war between the English and French in India was a strong probability.

'War!'

'Do not look so alarmed,' Sir Edward said. 'Calcutta is quite secure. In any case, we have a lot to do in western India before the French spread here. But it does have some unhappy consequences, one of which is that I must send Isobel home.'

Caroline was aghast.

'You cannot, truly you cannot! She was to stay for a year, till the end of the cold season! She will miss all the things she loves most! You said yourself the French are no immediate threat, so why send her so soon?'

He came to sit close by her.

'It must be soon. If war breaks out between us, the seas home will not be safe and in half a year Calcutta may not be safe either, and I shall have failed in my guardianship lamentably. If I send her now, she will reach England in the spring, and it is unlikely that there will have been much direct conflict here by that time which means that English ships will not be molested on the high seas.'

Caroline thought of life without Isobel, without that delightful companionship, that spirit-lifting gaiety. As if he read her thoughts, Sir Edward touched her hand lightly and said, 'I shall see that you are not too desolate.'

'Oh – oh, forgive me, I did not wish to seem – it is just that she has opened up such a life for me, she has meant so much to me – '

He nodded. They looked at each other gravely for a moment, aware of what each owed to Isobel.

'Send her,' Caroline said at last. 'I could not bear harm to come to her. Send her at once.'

In the slightly reflective and vulnerable mood that fell upon Caroline after Isobel's departure, Sir Edward saw his chance. He was aware he must take it quickly, for his opportunities to meet Caroline were fewer now that Isobel no longer offered a ready and eager excuse. In any case, he had subdued his natural impatience long enough, and although he knew, from a boldly outright question, that she did not leave his company at night to share her husband's bed, his desire to have her for himself was increasing daily.

They were invited to supper one clear November night by John Eyre and his pretty, indolent wife. Johnnie was, as usual, about business of his own, and Caroline, since it was perhaps the twentieth occasion she had done so, felt no compunction in setting off to sup in this new and happy circle of friends, without informing him. It was an occasion late enough, she felt, to warrant Isobel's dress, but slipping into it this time, she had a sensation of melancholy rather than excitement, for the donor was no longer there.

She arrived alone at the Eyres' house, quite accustomed now to doing so, and was ushered into their most elegant drawing room, ablaze with candelabra. In an alcove, she noticed with pleasure that there was a familiar miniature of cowslips.

'Is it not charming?' Mrs Eyre was saying of it in her comfortable drawl. 'I cannot discover where they come from, but I dare say that does not much matter.'

'Finely done,' a gentleman said, screwing in his eyeglass. 'Must be English in execution. Exquisitely observed. Wonder who does them?'

'Do you buy them in Calcutta, Mrs Eyre?' Caroline asked innocently.

'Yes, yes, I do. Should you like me to obtain one for you? It is no trouble. I do it through friends.'

'Thank you,' Caroline said with an irrepressible smile. 'I do thank you, but I must not indulge myself just now.'

Sir Edward Ashton was at her elbow.

'Then let me indulge you. You will not allow me to indulge you in anything, and I long to shower you with treasures. Even the books I would gladly give you, you only borrow. Let me buy you one of these enchanting pictures. Please me this once.'

Caroline, her face alight with laughter, shook her head.

'You cannot,' she said with difficulty. 'I fear you cannot.'

He eyed her suspiciously.

'There is more to this than it would seem. What is the reason for all this mirth, Caroline?'

'I cannot tell you just now,' she said looking up at him with eyes still shining with laughter. 'One day I will tell you, I promise it, but not now. And when I tell you, you will understand my laughter.'

'I don't care for riddles.'

She shrugged delightedly and walked with him to supper. Whatever her secret was, it had illumined her face like a lamp within and given her a gladness and a confidence that encouraged him to feel that tonight was the time he should speak. Even the sight of George Carew, an unexpected guest at such a gathering, did not diminish her gaiety, and the moment supper was over, and card tables were being set up, Sir Edward drew Caroline away to a secluded corner by open windows where the sweet cool air could blow in upon them.

Whatever Sir Edward had decided for that evening, Caroline seemed to have made resolutions of her own. It was in just such a mood, it occurred to her at supper, that she could tell Sir Edward of how she had agreed to be Mrs Gates without becoming oppressed at the memory of Lady Lennox's successful trap. She felt buoyant enough to treat the matter quite lightly, and thus, when Sir Edward seated himself opposite to her, as he loved to do, she gave him no chance with the matter on his mind.

It sounded a curious story as she told it. She hoped her portrait of Lady Lennox was a reasonably fair one, but felt very much as she drew to a close that the person who emerged most feebly from the whole pattern was herself.

'You will think me very weak, I fear, to comply so obediently with what were strange commands but I was so – so desolated by Papa's death, and the future looked so empty, that I made the only decision I felt I could.'

'It is an outrageous story.'

'Do not be angry, Sir Edward! Please do not. I know it seems to you that my behaviour was feeble-witted – '

'It is not that in the least,' Sir Edward said, leaning forward to take her hands. His eyes were blazing. 'It is nothing to do with you. You, as usual, made precisely the choice I find understandable. But that – that woman! Lady Lennox. What proof have you – no, look at me, do not turn away for an instant – that Lady Lennox had any legal right to withhold an inheritance from John Gates?'

'Proof?' Caroline said stupidly.

'Yes, proof. By what information did you learn that she had such power over the inheritance?'

Colour was beginning to rise in Caroline's face.

'Johnnie – told me. He had a letter. A letter from Lady Lennox. He said that she told him if he did not marry me he – '

Her voice tailed away. Sir Edward continued to look steadily at her.

'Do – do you mean we – we have been duped?'

'I have no proof of that any more than you have proof Lady Lennox had a right to direct you both as she has done. Have you seen no legal document, no lawyer's letter, even?'

'Nothing,' Caroline whispered.

They sat in silence for a minute or two, Sir Edward contemplating with inward fury, some of it directed at himself, what an innocent pawn Caroline had been in the lives of people to whom she was only useful for a brief interruption; Caroline was only appalled at her own naïvety, at the raw gullibility which had led both her and Johnnie to accept Lady Lennox's word as law. After a while she raised a confused countenance to Sir Edward and said in a low voice, 'You must think me – unforgivably incompetent and unworldly.'

He was on his knees by her chair in a moment.

'If I did think so, I can promise you I would think it no fault. If being unworldly results in a nature so deeply sympathetic and gentle as yours, then it is something we should all strive for.'

She bent her head, struggling with her own humiliation after these months of independence that were so sweet to her.

'Listen to me – Caroline, dearest Caroline, for so you are.'

He put a hand beneath her chin and turned her face forcibly to his.

'There is nothing about you that I would change, nothing, except your married state. I see in you all I have unconsciously sought all my life, unconsciously because I did not know such a creature existed, a woman of strength and sympathy, a woman of pride and compassion, the only woman I have ever met who had every cause on earth to be self-satisfied, and who is humble through it all.'

'Please – '

'Does it displease you to be spoken to thus? I have waited all these months because I feared to alarm you, but I cannot wait any longer. Is what I say unwelcome?'

'Nothing – nothing, no speech was ever more welcome.'

His hand still firmly beneath her chin, he leaned forward and kissed her.

'If you knew how I longed to do that! Every night I have seen you I have hardly known how to restrain myself. What are you thinking, my Caroline?'

'You – you are sure?'

He smiled at her incredulously.

'Sure? I was never more sure of anything in my entire life!'

'But – ' she hesitated, it seemed so foolish a thing to say, but then, it was something that had haunted her all her life, 'but – I am considered – I mean, I – am so very plain.'

'Plain!' he shouted. 'Plain? How can you possibly be plain when I love so to look at you?'

At the sheer arrogance of this remark, Caroline burst out laughing.

'You are anything but plain. You are fragile and delicate and lovely, and I shall never tire of gazing at you. Indeed,' he said ruefully, 'I find it very difficult indeed to keep my hands from you.'

'I wish – I wish – '

'And I shall grant it.'

'You can't,' she said.

'Can't?'

She did not speak, but simply held out her left hand which was adorned with nothing but a narrow wedding ring.

'So?' he said dismissively.

'It – it is all too late. You know it is. I am not free to – to – '

'Nonsense,' he said.

He stood up and pulled her to her feet. His face was alive with excitement.

'There need be no obstacle. You shall come to live with me as my cherished wife, mine in everything but the eyes of the law and somehow we shall obtain a divorce for you and then the world will be satisfied. I do not give one anna for the world's opinion personally, but I want the world to treat you as you deserve. You see, dearest love, how simple it is and how happy we shall be. Your past life is over, over for ever, and no woman on earth shall be prized as you shall be.'

There was a fractional pause, and then Caroline raised her eyes to meet his elated gaze.

'No,' she said.

'No?' He was shouting again.

She freed herself from his embrace and stood a little apart, her eyes glittering with quite a new expression.

'No, Sir Edward. No, it must be no.'

He came a step nearer.

'Is it convention that troubles you? Do you think anyone in Calcutta cares for it? If it disturbs you, I will build you a palace outside the city and you may live there in perfect seclusion. May I remind you that Mr and Mrs Hastings are but lately wed themselves? I do not think you need fret yourself over convention.'

'I do not. I do not care for it any more than you do. It is not that.'

He was close to her again, his hands on her shoulders, and through them she could feel that he was shaking.

It was so difficult to articulate, so painful to explain. Her brain surged with powerful feelings of obligation and duty, and among these emotions shot bolts of panic, at the thought of losing the independence she had struggled so hard to gain.

'I – cannot leave him, he is so weak and – and helpless. And I cannot be – your possession, your object, I cannot – '

'You would be my treasure, can you not see that? If only you will live with me I will allow you any freedom you require. I no more want to cage you than a songbird. You owe that blackguard nothing, nothing at all. I will not hear such pointless loyalty. Come to me, Caroline, I beg you – '

'No,' she said.

He took his hands from her shoulders.

'You do not care for me, then. Were you flattered, was that it? It is unlike you to take and not give. I must assume you do not care!'

'I care – ' she said desperately, almost in a whisper.

'You do not,' he declared furiously. 'Look at you! You are stony-hearted and dry-eyed, the sight of my despair squeezes not one tear from you, not one! You are in love with your own achievements, Caroline, that is what it is, nothing but that! You want no human love for you have nothing to repay it with now, nothing! If that is the price of freedom, madam, you are welcome to your liberty!'

Hardly conscious of what she did, Caroline turned and stumbled from the room. His voice followed her, still accusing, as she hurried through the drawing room while people and surroundings passed in a blur around her. In the hall, George Carew, bored by the sheer respectability of the evening, was pulling on his gloves while waiting for his carriage. He saw Caroline come flying through the double doors of the drawing room as if pursued by some spectre, and purely instinctively held out his arms and caught her in flight. She was not weeping, but looked as if she longed to.

'Mrs Gates, ma'am!'

'George – Mr Carew – George, I beg you, take – take me home.'

She was shuddering violently. George took off his cloak and wrapped it round her.

'Directly, ma'am,' he said.

18

The atmosphere in Calcutta throughout that winter was a disturbed one for the Council of the East India Company. Sir Edward Ashton had not exaggerated the threat of French invasion. Although it was unlikely that they would attack Calcutta and Bengal by sea, it seemed increasingly probable, given their growing success in western India, that they might attempt an attack by land, their own army reinforced by native troops as they crossed and subdued the princedoms on their journey across India. Sir Edward was of the opinion that the French needed less than a thousand men, trained in European military discipline, to educate huge numbers of sepoys into fighting most effectively. As this French army crossed the vast states of upper India the numbers of natives whom they could quell and enlist as allies was truly terrifying, and, should this happen, all the areas of India upon which British dominion depended would, as Warren Hastings said, 'lie at their mercy'.

This threat to the entire stability of the Company was something Sir Edward might deplore, and resist to the last breath in his body, but this winter he was grateful for such an absorbing problem to divert his mind. Although he was a man of energetically held principles, he was not someone subject to cravings in life – until he had met Caroline. He had wanted her above all else, with a single-minded passion, and when she had so obstinately withheld herself, he was desolated.

He tried to throw all the energy of his anguish into the thorny problem of subduing the French where they were, in western India, before they began to seep eastwards, and in some measure he succeeded. His household found him so changed that a kind of anxious reverence hung about the rooms, the sort of respect for grief so evident at funerals.

Buxby found that his working hours, delightfully diminished during Sir Edward's absorption in Caroline, were infinitely extendable these days, but the sight of his superior's countenance caught occasionally off his guard was a deterrent to even the gentlest of complaints. He naturally dared not utter on this most delicate of subjects, and as for Sir Edward, the matter lay sealed in silence within him, and only from the abruptness of his manner and the tirelessness of his industry could it be deduced how much he suffered.

If he had some release, Caroline found she had none. She painted, of course – she had to paint – and she gardened, and she shunned company with all the panic she used to feel long ago in Dorset. Day in, week out, all those long months of winter, the months that should be the most pleasurable in northern India, she hardly left her little compound. As George Carew had said so casually to Johnnie, it was all over by Christmas.

All over. It was indeed. She would stand in her garden, now a cascading and brilliant tangle of bougainvillaea and jasmine, orchids and oleander spilling onto a green carpet of some close-leaved herb the mali had persuaded to grow like an English lawn, and consider that she was everything her garden was not. It was burgeoning and rioting, full of promise, and she was now no more than the dried-up yellow shell of dust and thirst it had been all summer.

During those long days, and longer nights, Caroline had come to realize, with a bitterness she could hardly bear, that she had made a mistake which would cost her her happiness for the rest of her life. For two days after the quarrel, she had been upheld by a kind of righteous elation, a feeling that she had stood up for what she felt to be true and vital, and that she had done a noble thing in paying such an agonizing price for it. Was it not the greatest thing in life to be able to hold up your head with the self-respect you had built yourself, painful brick upon painful brick, all yourself, from no beginnings? Indeed it was, and she had been right, very right, not to throw it away simply because she had found the companion of a lifetime.

Was it not also equally laudable to cling to your obligations, all the tighter simply because those obligations were so burdensome and unpleasant? Did she not owe Johnnie the fulfilment of her promise to him? Merely because he seemed not to feel any reciprocal debt to her was no reason, she felt in this high-minded vein, for shirking her side of the bargain. No, indeed, she, Caroline Gates, would be an example to all of endurance and courage, a pattern of honourableness.

After forty-eight hours of this exalted condition, reality and Caroline's true nature began to tarnish the splendour of her attitudes. To realize that what she took for a noble gesture was in reality a hideous and self-gratifying mistake was a dreadful experience, and one that stripped her, in a few short days, of all the confidence and contentment she had taken more than a year to acquire. There was plenty of time and solitude – indeed too much of both – to see the damage she had done.

Slowly but surely her own honesty asserted itself and she began to see that her freedom was nothing in itself. She had sought it because it gave her courage and because it was the only way she could endure to be married to a man for whom she had no feelings at all save disgust and contempt. She had thought, in her folly, flushed with her own success, that this independence was a prize in itself, but now, too late, she knew better. Her independence should have made her free to choose what she pleased, released her from her bondage to be unconventional and happy and oblivious to the world's finger pointing at her. She had made herself able to be Sir Edward's mistress, free enough to make that choice, and she had out of obstinate pride refused him and lost him, and lost herself in the process.

Mrs Rathbone was a steady visitor. She not only called to collect new batches of pictures, but also because her cosy and maternal heart could not resist Caroline's wretchedness.

'Come now, dearie, we mustn't give way like this. There are plenty of fish in the sea, and whatever we have done once we can do again.'

'It is myself I despair over,' Caroline said, 'I am so ashamed of myself, so weary of my lack of judgement – '

Mrs Rathbone patted her hand.

'There, there, my dear, we all make mistakes, do we not. To be sure, I've made many, my dear, so many – ' she paused and reflected with pleasure on a number of them, 'but you must not brood, indeed you must not. Tomorrow is another day and you must put it all behind you.'

Caroline managed a small and rueful smile.

'You are most kind to me.'

'Nonsense, my dear, it is no more than common charity. Besides, now that Miss Grant is gone, who are you to confide in, if not in me?'

'I feel that – that I deserve to bear the pain alone.'

Mrs Rathbone clucked disapprovingly.

'What a silly notion, my dear. Anyone would think you enjoyed being unhappy, I vow they would. Now then, what are we going to do to cheer you up?'

'I should dearly love to stop painting. It must seem ungrateful to you after all the months of help you have given me, but I am becoming unoriginal and the pictures are no longer fresh, I do too many.'

Mrs Rathbone eyed her for a moment, and saw the smudges of weariness under her eyes, and the tired droop of her shoulders.

'You need more company, my dear.'

Caroline looked startled.

'Oh – oh no, indeed no. I mean, I thank you for your concern, but I am grown so awkward in company, just as I used to be.'

'Not dinner parties, my dear!' Mrs Rathbone said, recalling what a difficult guest Caroline had been, sitting remote and shy among the flying bread pellets. 'Some companion. Some friend other than myself.'

Caroline was seized with contrition.

'Oh, Mrs Rathbone, I should hate to be a burden to you! Please do not feel you must come here if you have other calls – '

'I like to come, my dear. And you need a friend, but it's my belief you need more than just myself. I have an idea.'

She leaned forward confidentially, and spoke in the whisper she had perfected for passing on gossip in crowded rooms.

'Listen, my dear, I've a friend, a nice boy, a soldier, and he's being sent across to Poona under Colonel Leslie to fight the French. Six battalions are going, I'm told, to show the French they can't do as they please in India, for it's not theirs to have. Now, my friend, a Lieutenant Wheeler, has a little wife here in Calcutta, a pretty little thing she is, and a baby, and they have nowhere to go while he's away. Now, of course, I offered to have them just as I offered Johnnie – ' she hesitated for a moment then hurried on. 'But why do you not have them here? Frank Wheeler will pay their board, I am sure, and would it not amuse you a little? Think of a baby to play with, Caroline!'

'Would – would not Mrs Wheeler find it very dull?'

'Why should she? She's quite a timid soul herself, for all her looks, and has only been here a few months. The baby was born at sea, would you believe it, and Frank is as proud of him as if he'd borne him himself. Now, what do you say?'

Caroline still looked doubtful.

'I do not feel I am fit company for a pretty girl, Mrs Rathbone. I should dearly love to have a baby here, and I should be more than glad to help, but – '

'No more buts. I shall bring her to meet you. Now, then, what pictures can I take away with me this week?'

Anne Wheeler turned out to be a slight dark girl, quietly pretty but with an expression of gravity that did not lighten her features. She seemed quite undismayed at the prospect of living in the Gates' silent house, and her serious appearance stilled all Caroline's fears about her vulnerability to Johnnie should he feel moved to exercise his gallantry once more.

She had engineered that Mrs Rathbone should tell Johnnie of the arrangement, so that he might feel he was the first to know.

'Johnnie boy, I want you to do me a great favour. I think you'll feel I deserve one every so often, do you not?'

Johnnie, amply supplied with Mr Rathbone's port, grunted his permission for her to continue.

'There's a girl needs caring for, Johnnie boy.'

'A pretty girl, Bella?'

'You don't change, do you, you naughty boy? Pretty she is, but not for you. It's Frank Wheeler's wife. She'll be left all alone when the army moves west, and I wondered if you would offer her lodging.'

'Will she pay?'

'Naturally, she will! Though I hardly think that is the question of a gentleman.'

'I'm pressed for money, Bella.'

Mrs Rathbone thought of Caroline's lonely struggle with money and eyed Johnnie with less than her usual fondness.

'Don't tell me such stories, Johnnie. All you boys line your pockets with gold here in Calcutta, you know you do. There's not a man among you not amassing a private fortune enough to buy half Mayfair when he goes home – '

'Not me, Bella,' Johnnie said glumly. 'I'm beset with ill-luck.'

He gazed glumly down into his glass. He didn't even seem able to win much at whist these days and his facility for private deals which had paid for his lifestyle so comfortably a few years back seemed to have crumbled to dust.

George Carew had simple reasons for it. 'If you soak and whore as you do, my boy, you can't expect miracles. Damned if I know how you're still alive.'

Mrs Rathbone, once a faithful ally, seemed no more sympathetic.

'If Lady Fortune frowns on you, Johnnie, it's because she's tired of your selfish ways. You've a wife you don't deserve, indeed you don't, and if you knew what she did for you without a word – '

'Don't speak to me of her,' Johnnie interrupted savagely. 'No man was ever cursed with such a wife, never. When her great friends noticed her she was never there to do her duty by me, and now that they have tired of her, as I knew they would, she mopes about the house all day. Mark what I say, Bella, mark it well. The moment that woman stepped on shore, here in Calcutta, my life went from bad to worse. There was never a man as beset in his marriage as I am.'

Mrs Rathbone had risen.

'I'll hear no more, Johnnie, in truth I'll not. You'll not

have a soul left who will speak to you if you go on in that way. Now pull yourself together and do not always be so sorry for yourself. I shall send Frank Wheeler to you and you may make what arrangements you will.'

The arrangements that resulted were not wholly to Caroline's advantage. After an unseemly wrangle, which Mrs Rathbone insisted on watching to see fair play, it was grudgingly decided that half the money Frank Wheeler would contribute should go to the housekeeping costs of maintaining Anne and little Francis. The rest, Johnnie insisted he needed.

'I must have it, I must. It will go towards the cost of the additional servants we shall have to have with two extra people in the house.'

Tight-lipped, Caroline said, 'We have more servants than we need already, and in any case it is I who pay them, not you. I know full well the extra will go to the whist table and your other – pleasures, but I would rather not touch a penny than that we should squabble for it.'

Mrs Rathbone came to her rescue. A lump sum should be paid to Johnnie on Lieutenant Wheeler's departure and his wife would then give a weekly amount to Caroline.

Caroline was deeply distressed at the squalor of the arrangement.

'Forgive me, Mrs Wheeler, for this shameful penny-pinching. I would give anything to be able to offer you our house as our guests, however long your husband is away, and perhaps in time that will come to be.'

Ann Wheeler, in full knowledge of all of Caroline's history regaled in every detail in a whisper by Mrs Rathbone, merely inclined her head, and said gravely, 'It would embarrass me, Mrs Gates, to be dependent upon your charity for what might be months. I am easier in my mind that things are as they are.'

Within weeks, Caroline actually ventured to return one of Mrs Rathbone's endless calls. She found her friend in a flurry of excitement over a box of hats from Rheims come by the last ship, and sitting in her bedroom in a perfect ocean of plumes and ribbons.

'My dear, did ever you see such pretty things? I feel I

shall go mad with delight, indeed I shall. Come now, try the blue. Do, my dear, try the blue!'

Caroline resisted, laughing.

'No, no, thank you. They are charming, much too charming for me. I am come anyway to thank you, not to accept more favours.'

'Thank me, my dear?'

'Yes, indeed, most warmly. I am come to thank you for the introduction to Ann Wheeler. I am in your debt, once again, and most grateful.'

Mrs Rathbone turned from the mirror under a palm tree effect of nodding pink plumes.

'Do you suit one another, my dear?'

'Oh, so well! She is such a sweet, serious person, we have much in common, and she is so unobtrusive that I often do not know whether or not she is in the house. And the baby is a delight. I do not know what I should do without the baby.'

Mrs Rathbone removed the pink palm tree and came across to Caroline.

'Are you quieter in your mind now, my dear?'

Caroline nodded speechlessly. It seemed ungrateful to tell a lie and say her heart was quite healed when in fact it was as sore as ever, but on the other hand, what kind of reward for Mrs Rathbone's kindness was the truth?

Mrs Rathbone considered her for a moment, accurately interpreting her silence. Mrs Rathbone had had a most strange encounter two nights before, and the memory of it tempted her to ignore her small reserve of discretion. She had been asked to dine with Mrs Eyre, as a favour, she supposed with her no-nonsense awareness of social differences, after supplying the latter with four or five of Caroline's paintings. At the table had been, to her consternation, several of the great persons of Calcutta, including Sir Edward Ashton. He looked as impressive as ever, but the new hard lines about his eyes and mouth suggested to Mrs Rathbone that he had schooled himself rigorously in the last months. The idea of this made his presence less awe-inspiring to her and emboldened her considerably after dinner when the miniatures were again being admired.

She edged her plump person through the group of people in the drawing room until she was at Sir Edward's elbow, and could share with him a view of the picture of wild strawberries he held in his hand.

'Forgive my being so bold as to address you in this way, Sir Edward, but I can tell you something you might like to hear about these paintings.'

From his considerable height, Sir Edward looked down in some surprise at this highly coloured little person below him. She appeared to wish to emulate a rainbow in her style of dress, and was gazing up at him with a sort of roguishness women never dared employ with him usually. Mrs Eyre came to his rescue.

'Mrs Rathbone, Sir Edward. It is through Mrs Rathbone that I have acquired these charming miniatures.'

The light dawned.

'And so, madam, I presume you wish to inveigle me into a purchase too?'

'Will you step a little apart, sir? I feel we can talk more comfortably then, do not you, sir?'

Sir Edward gave Mrs Eyre a resigned smile and followed Mrs Rathbone to a sofa.

'Now, sir, you quite misunderstand me. I do not wish to sell you a picture, no indeed, for I have more orders than I can deal with as it is. No, it is not about the paintings I wish to talk, but the painter.'

Sir Edward looked at her with mild interest.

'The painter? I thought one of the charms of these miniatures, one of the elements that gave them such cachet, was that the painter was anonymous.'

Mrs Rathbone leant very close to him, and in the cloud of violet-scented powder she exuded, said, 'Anonymous to all Calcutta, but not to me!'

Sir Edward endeavoured to sound interested.

'Indeed, madam.'

Mrs Rathbone edged her brilliant skirts closer to him.

'And not to you, either, Sir Edward.'

'Really, madam?' The interest was less feigned this time.

'No, indeed. In fact, I believe the painter was at one time most – most – ' here Mrs Rathbone temporarily lost courage, but rallied to deliver her triumphal shot. 'It is Caroline Gates, Sir Edward, none other than Caroline Gates!'

If she had hoped for a reaction, she was not disappointed. He blanched completely, and the gaze directed at her grew so intense that she was suddenly frightened. Moving away a little, she began to apologize hurriedly for her intrusion, she would leave him in peace, he must forgive her, she only meant for the best, indeed she did. His hand shot out and held her like a vice.

'You – you know Mrs Gates?'

'I do, sir,' Mrs Rathbone said apprehensively. 'She – she is a dear friend of mine,' she added staunchly.

At that his hand relaxed a little on her arm.

'You see her then?'

'Oh, yes, often, often, several times a week.'

'How is she?'

Not entirely sure yet of Sir Edward's reaction, Mrs Rathbone determined to be loyal to Caroline.

'Doing very well, sir, to be sure. She has a sweet friend living there, with a baby, and they suit each other excellently.'

'She is quite content, then?'

Mrs Rathbone did not understand his tone. It was an alarming sort of tone, and she did not want to be alarmed again.

'Dear me, yes, I believe she is.'

There was a silence. Mrs Rathbone would have moved away, but she was still held captive by Sir Edward's hand. He sat gazing at the floor, and she could see from his hardened profile that every muscle in his face was tensed.

'What about these paintings, then, Mrs Rathbone?' he said at last, in an altered voice. 'Why does she not sign them?'

'She cannot, sir! No one must know! Can – can I trust you with a confidence, sir?'

Sir Edward looked at her pityingly.

'You may, madam.'

'The truth is, Sir Edward, that she is so shamefully used by her husband – a good boy at heart, I do believe, but weak with it – that if she did not paint she would starve.'

The hand on her arm tightened uncomfortably again.
'What?'

'It's as I say, sir. He never gives her money, and he never pays the servants, and she's that fond of her servants I believe she'd sell the clothes off her back to give them what she owed them. They'd die for her, Sir Edward, I truly believe they would. But we're getting good money for the miniatures now, you know – why, Mrs Eyre said she'd give me fifteen guineas for another if I could have it ready by the end of February! Think of that, Sir Edward!'

He said thickly, 'How long has this been going on?'

'Oh, all summer, sir, all autumn, seven months or more. Mind you, she is tiring a bit now, she's worked so hard.'

'All summer, all the time I – '

'Oh yes, sir.'

Sir Edward muttered something savagely to himself.

'Sir – Sir Edward? Would – would you like me to obtain one for you?'

Thoughts of a reconciliation were fluttering hopefully round Mrs Rathbone's head, but really he was a most difficult and daunting man to deal with, not at all like her boys. He looked at her now suddenly, and then almost as if he had forgotten it was there, removed his hand from her arm.

'Yes, I – no, thank you, but no, I could not bear – '

He rose and stood looming over her.

'Why did you tell me all this?'

Mrs Rathbone summoned all her courage with difficulty. 'I thought you should know, sir. I thought you should know what she has had to bear.'

'You are right. Quite right. But you do not think she has so much to bear now?'

Mrs Rathbone did not know what the reply was that he wanted, or indeed what the truth was. Caroline seemed content enough now but then, she never was one for opening her heart. She would consider Mrs Rathbone a gossip for meddling with Sir Edward, and suddenly Mrs Rathbone felt that indeed that was what she was. She gave Sir Edward the smallest shake of her head, and watched him stride away in silence. She left soon after, and at supper that night, drank too much cherry brandy to distract herself, and could not sleep a wink as a result.

Now, regarding Caroline rather gravely, she was considering whether to report this conversation. It struck her that she had not given the right answers to Sir Edward, for it was patently obvious now that Caroline was as far from contentment as she had ever been. She picked up a straw bonnet woven with lattices of ribbons, and played with it a little.

'I've something to tell you, dear.'

'Oh?' Caroline looked startled.

'Oh, never fear, my dear, nothing nasty. Quite the reverse. Guess who I met but two nights ago?'

Caroline looked at her steadily.

'None other than – Sir Edward Ashton!'

Caroline went pale.

'No – no, please, dear friend, do not, do not speak of him, I beg you, do not – '

Mrs Rathbone dropped the bonnet and seized Caroline by the elbows.

'You must listen to me, dear, you must! It is pleasant things I have to tell you!'

Caroline freed herself.

'No,' she insisted, 'please say no more, please. I have cut myself off quite from any – any possibilities – I have angered him beyond any redemption, it is no use. Nothing is any use,' she put her hand up to silence Mrs Rathbone. 'If you are truly kind as I know you are, you will not – not mention him again. I beg you will not. I will never – never heal again if you do. His – his name opens up everything, all the wounds. Forgive me, but I must go, truly I must. Ann is dining out, and I have promised to look after little Francis. Thank you for everything, thank you again and again.'

Mrs Rathbone felt a light kiss on her cheek, then the door flew open and instantly closed behind Caroline. For a few minutes the wind of her going still eddied among the finery on the floor.

19

Caroline had not exaggerated when she said she did not know what she would have done without the baby. He was a charming baby in any case, an open-faced laughing blond baby, with his father's merry blue eyes and a wealth of endearing dimples and creases, and his happy innocence, coupled with the inevitable demandingness of all babies, rescued Caroline in the nick of time from the blackest despair. The ayah whom Frank Wheeler had engaged found that she had to watch like a hawk for the scant hours when Mrs Gates was painting in order to get any share in her charge at all, and often was reduced to sitting dumbly by the baby's cradle watching his hot, damp, rosy daytime naps. Ann Wheeler was a mother whose children would grow in value to her as they grew in years, and she was entirely happy to surrender the repetitive amusement of a year-old baby to another, especially when that other seemed so passionate to be involved.

In the relative cool of the mornings or glowing early evenings, Caroline would take little Francis out into the garden and play with him on a blanket under the old banyan tree that grew close to the house and spread its hideous shaggy branches beneath her bedroom window. He would crawl and crow and examine minute objects in the dust about him with solemn absorption, before cramming them into his mouth. Caroline would sing to him and read poetry to him, out of volumes which she had failed to return to Sir Edward Ashton prior to their quarrel, and which she now could not bring herself to give back. Both the baby and Caroline were watched by a circle of malis affecting to garden, and by the under-occupied ayah. Ann Wheeler, free to play in the music groups she loved and to dine and sup out as much as she pleased, came to regard Caroline as one of the most benevolent accidents of her life.

'I fear that I exploit you, and I would wish you to know that I feel the deepest gratitude for the freedom your love and care for Francis gives me. I have missed my music sadly since coming here, indeed I did not know how sadly until I took it up again. Frank said I was silly not to trust the ayah with little Francis, but I think he is wrong. If he could see you with his precious son, he would acknowledge that he was wrong.'

Caroline looked up at her from the rug where she knelt by the rolling baby.

'You must not thank me, indeed you must not. It is I must thank you. I was in a very sorry plight before you came, and you cannot fail to have observed how solitary I am, thus your two presences here have meant more to me than I can express.'

She might have expresssed much more, but she did not care to. The truth was that the baby, with his golden blitheness, and his promise of future life and his demands for attention, was providing her with just the oblivion she sought. Not only did occupying herself ceaselessly with him prevent her dwelling on her own deep, private misery: it also partially obliterated the fact that her painting was becoming an intolerable burden to her; but the necessity of doing it, with the added strain of the Wheelers on the household, was no less pressing. If she painted five or six hours a day now, she could just run the household, provided that Mrs Rathbone could obtain a minimum of ten guineas for each one, but it was becoming uncomfortably evident to both Mrs Rathbone and Caroline, that as the early summer drew on, Calcutta was beginning, with its usual fickleness, to tire of the enigma of these nostalgic and anonymous miniatures. Caroline painted on, doggedly and increasingly mechanically, and pushed her realization of the dwindling numbers Mrs Rathbone took each month to the back of her mind by absorbing herself, in all free moments, with the baby.

What she would do when she could no longer earn a living, she could not imagine and dared not even try to contemplate. The spectre of destitution, of being forced to beg for some kind of help again, drove her to bury her face and her thoughts in the baby's neck and seek forgetfulness in the seductiveness of that contact. She had contemplated either telling Ann Wheeler or admitting to Mrs Rathbone that she knew her market was declining, but she had shrunk from both, preferring to go blindly on, too tired by the strains of the last year in an exhausting climate to confront the awful possibilities with her usual courage. The baby was her buffer against the future, her talisman, her touchstone. She carried him about with her and talked to him and gave him flowers, and reassured herself constantly that while he was with her, fate could strike no blow.

The Wheelers' coming had estranged Johnnie even further from the house. Within a few days he had recognized in Ann Wheeler's steady dark glance a girl who would be flinty in response to his decayed charms, and had come to see also that her allegiance lay increasingly with Caroline. With this new grievance of being driven out of his own house by a pack of malicious women and a squalling baby, he was only at home to sleep the last few hours of each night, and seldom even that. His sense of intense injustice was heightened by realizing that Caroline, either bent myopically over her damned daubing, or cooing over the brat, simply did not care whether he was there or not. His linen was immaculate still, he supposed his food was still provided though he never troubled now to come home to eat it, and it never crossed his mind as he departed in the third clean shirt of the day, to wonder how she managed to do it on no money whatsoever. She seldom even looked up now when he passed her, and if shouted at, replied with a vague remoteness that seemed to indicate she had no recollection at all of who he was.

George Carew could not understand why he was not satisfied. 'It's what you wanted, eh? Ain't it? All the comfort and none of the commitments?'

'It's my house, George, my house, and I'm a stranger in it! Those she-cats don't care if I live or die, all they care for is that drivelling brat.'

'Jealous of a baby now, Johnnie?'

'Confound it, I'm not!' Johnnie yelled. 'I'm not jealous of a soul on earth except the man who isn't cursed with a wife!'

In the hot dreadful weeks before the monsoons in the summer of 1778, Ann Wheeler became increasingly involved in a quartet who were to play a selection of Italian composers at a much-publicized musical soirée to be given by Mrs Hastings.

'I fear I shall be from home a good deal, Caroline, and I am anxious that Francis, as he becomes more active, is distracting you from painting. Would you allow the ayah, or any person you think fit to engage, to take the burden of his care from you?'

Caroline held the baby tightly to her and shook her head vehemently.

'Indeed no. I do assure you that the care of him is only a pleasure to me, never anything else. I beg you will go and practise your music with the freest conscience possible, knowing that you leave me doing what I love to do.'

Her tone was so eager that Ann Wheeler thankfully acquiesced, and took to spending the occasional night away at the house of the friend who had organized the quartet in the first instance. In these absences, Caroline, on the pretext that the baby was teething and restless, took little Francis into her own room at night and beguiled the black and awful hours in watching him and defending his small sleeping form from mosquitoes. During these vigils she would sometimes hear, in the dawn, the crashes and oaths of Johnnie's unsteady return, but more often than not, only crickets and jackals broke the hot and heavy silence and she would see the dawn come up brilliantly over a city in which her husband lay oblivious of her and her lover lost to her.

Three days before the soirée, Caroline had an unintentional caller in the person of George Carew, unintentional since he had not meant a formal call, but merely to offer Johnnie a seat in his carriage on the way out to dine. George had not seen Caroline since that fateful evening when he had escorted her home, and was struck by her dispirited and withered appearance, after the temporary bloom that Sir Edward's attentions had given her. She stood before George in a dress of faded lilac print, the rosy cheek of a plump baby pressed in painful contrast to her own thin one.

'You ain't unwell I hope, ma'am?'

'No, indeed, Mr Carew, I am not unwell at all. Like everyone I shall find the rains a great relief. Is there anything I can do for you?'

'You might produce your husband, in a trice if you would. We're deuced late as it is.'

Caroline's gaze dropped hastily.

'I would if I could, Mr Carew,' she said in a low voice, 'but I have no notion where he might be. He has not been home these two nights.'

'Not home? Have you not sent the servants for news of him?'

Her head still bent, she said in an even lower voice:

'No, no, I have not. It is hardly the first time. He comes home merely to change his linen.'

George Carew's drawl did not alter in speed as he said, 'And you think that no reason for concern, ma'am? Is a wife to show no more care than the orders she gives to a dhobi? Might he not be home more if he had more to come home to?'

Caroline's head jerked up abruptly and she glared savagely at George Carew over the round blond head of the baby. Tiredness and a sense of hopelessness were winning over her natural reticence and humility. To think that George Carew, rogue as he might be, saw any cause at all to pity Johnnie for a fate which was entirely of his own making, was more than her wearied mind and heart could bear.

'If this house is empty for him, Mr Carew, it is because he has made it so! Everything about it, even the fact that I am here at all, has been arranged to suite his monstrous selfishness. He pays for nothing and takes everything. I have, in every mechanical sense, kept the promise I made him and, if I have withheld my heart, it is because I would not squander it on a creature so worthless!'

The baby, sensing the upheaval in the bosom to which he was pressed, began to whimper. George Carew took a step backwards, grasping his hat more firmly in his hand.

'Beg – beg pardon, ma'am, I'd no notion – '

'Oh no, you have not, but you will have.' She was horrified at herself but unable to stop. 'I have a small talent which is luckily sufficient to pay for all household expenses. I have not received one penny from Johnnie since I married him, not one penny, not to mention a single flower or ribbon. The only money he has ever expended upon me was the forty pounds for the marriage licence, and I am sure that, indiscreet and greedy for pity as he always is, he has confided in you the reason for the marriage in the first place. He scorns me and insults me, so why should I care what sordid ends he comes to. If you care what has happened to him, you may find him.' She stopped for a moment and then said in a lowered voice, 'I will not lift a finger.'

George Carew was not a man who cared for apologies. He stood, turning his hat slowly for a while, wishing very much he had not been so foolhardy as to involve himself, and reluctantly coming to the conclusion that he had put himself into a position where he was committed to seeking Johnnie. It was damned awkward, for in truth he would not give any more to know where Johnnie was than his wronged wife did, but he saw no alternative.

'I'll fetch him home for you, ma'am.'

Caroline inclined her head, seeing no reason for gratitude, and hid her face in the baby's neck. George moved to the door and stood there for a moment, wrestling with vague feelings he did not recognize as familiar. After a long pause, he looked back at the still figure in the lilac print holding the baby, and said, 'Damned bad business.'

Watching him cross the hall, Caroline realized that she had just received both apology and commiseration.

It was after dark when George brought his prize home. Ann had gone, and would not be back until after the soirée; she had managed to obtain an invitation for Caroline, to the hopeful delight of Mrs Rathbone who knew Sir Edward Ashton was bound to attend, but Caroline had been adamant in her refusal. Ann had been quite open in revealing that a fellow musician in the quartet was a young man named Ralph Buxby, although she did not add that he was also a most open and ardent admirer of hers, and the combination of this link and the house in which the soirée was to be held made Caroline quite convinced that the presence she most wished to elude would have to be unavoidably confronted. So Ann had hired a carriage alone and gone off with her maid, genuinely grieved that Caroline would not come but profoundly relieved to abandon her child to such tender care. Thus, when George's carriage halted outside the small mud house where the only candle visible was burning in one of the upper rooms, Caroline was alone with Francis, and singing to him as he lay and tossed wakefully in the steaming heat of his cradle. Reluctantly she summoned the ayah, crouched hopefully as always outside the door, and went downstairs full of apprehension.

Johnnie was being carried across the hallway as she descended, on a sort of makeshift stretcher to which he had been tightly bound with a number of shawls. The reason for this became quickly evident; he was delirious and would have twisted himself to the floor in seconds if not strongly confined. His face was scarlet and running with sweat, and the shirt he wore – his coat being respectfully carried by a servant – was as wet as if he had swum in it. George Carew had found him in a bawdy house down on the waterfront just as he was, delirious, with a high fever, abandoned on a heap of sacks in a welter of empty bottles. It seemed he had succumbed to unconsciousness and fever twenty-four hours before after a night and day of relentless drinking, at which point the bawdy house lost interest in him as a potential customer and had tossed him into a corner to recover.

Caroline pressed herself to the wall as this grotesque little procession of servants, lit by flickering torches held by those below, bore its muttering and rebellious burden past her to Johnnie's bedroom. George Carew waited below in the hall, his face illuminated by the leaping flames about him, and looked upward to the jumping shadows where Caroline stood.

'What ails him, Mr Carew?'

George cleared his throat.

'The usual, ma'am, and a touch of fever. Will you have me fetch a physician?'

Caroline hesitated. She knew what she expected of herself, and she could not do it. She willed herself to want to nurse him back to health and sense, and could make nothing of it.

A doctor would give instructions the servants might carry out.

'If you would be so good, Mr Carew.'

He bowed and left. With mounting repugnance, Caroline moved slowly towards her husband's bedroom. Johnnie had been rolled upon the bed, and the servants were now standing back in some disarray, unsure what next to do with his flailing and slippery bulk. Two candles burned at the bedside, and the heavy bed hangings had been tossed up on the canopy to allow air and easier access. Caroline advanced to the bedhead and stooped to look closely at Johnnie's face, bloated and distorted with excesses and fever, and recoiled sharply at the stale stench he emitted.

'He must be sponged with warm water. Warm water, not cold. And he must be put in fresh linen, and left covered lightly.'

A wave of nausea rose in her throat and she stepped back quickly. A chair was instantly brought, and she sank into it thankfully, accepting the offered cup of water, and leaning her forehead against the smooth wood of the bedpost. She seemed to feel quite shaken, giddy and helpless and sick, so she did not move away from the sordid spectacle on the bed, but regarded what was going on there with the remoteness of an uninvolved spectator. When the physician came, to pronouce Johnnie thoroughly over-indulged and to prohibit all alcohol for a month at least, he found a touching picture of a devoted wife sitting at her sick husband's bedside to ensure the servants treated him as they should.

'You must be very firm with your husband, Mrs Gates. He is endangering his liver mightily with the work he gives it to do. Continue warm sponging as you have been doing, and administer this medicine four-hourly. It will clear the system and thus help to reduce the fever. He is to be on light foods, plenty of oranges, and no wine whatsoever until I pronounce him fit to take it.'

Caroline stood up, swaying a little, unintentionally giving every impression of a wife worn with loving anxiety.

'I fear that will be very difficult to achieve, Dr Campbell.'

He laid a hand upon her arm and said confidentially, 'But

you women know how to gain your ends, do you not? He'll not refuse you if you plead your case prettily enough. I'll call again in a few days or so and expect to find him supping broth. I'll bid you good night.'

When he had gone, Caroline turned back to the bed, aware that she should now sit by and watch the unattractive processes of Johnnie's system endeavouring to rid itself of all he abused it with.

As if he read her thoughts, Ranjit stepped from the shadows and said softly, 'There is no need for memsahib to be watching. We are watching and will call if we fear anything.'

With a look and smile at him of the purest gratitude, Caroline thankfully escaped to the sanctuary of her bedroom. Though still stiflingly hot, the air smelt only of flowers and dust, and above the gentle sounds of the baby's breathing and the old banyan tapping against her wall, she could hear nothing but the comforting crickets in the garden below.

Twenty-four hours later, Johnnie's fever had abated remarkably, and he was peevishly conscious enough to complain bitterly that he was denied any wine. Caroline could hear him ranting as she moved about the house, and knew full well that the curses he was hurling were all directed at her. She had told him that she was only repeating the physician's orders, but he chose to ignore her.

'You'll kill me, won't you! You'll murder me slowly and painfully, by depriving me of anything I need! No man has ever had wine withheld for medical reasons, not ever! It's a witchlike scheme of yours, you shrew, to make me suffer so that you may gloat over my pain! Well, I'll tell you something, you milksop daughter of sanctimony, you may starve me to death, you may dry me to death, but when I'm in my coffin, I'll have my revenge on you! I will, I will! When I'm gone, you mealy-mouthed prig, you'll not see a penny of Gates money nor Lennox money, not one penny. It will all go back to those who know how to spend it, and you'll beg for your bread and live to regret the shameless manner in which you treated me!'

To prevent his getting anywhere near the tempting bottles in the dining room, Caroline instructed the servants to keep his room locked. The insult of the imprisonment, added to the injury of being denied the wine he craved, caused his bellowings to rise to a crescendo, and the second night was rent with moans and cries and yells of rage as the craving and fever took their toll of him. Caroline spent the night apart, shuddering and sickened, kneeling by the baby's cradle with her fingers pressed to her terrified ears. What she would have done without that stoical and loyal band of servants, she could not imagine, for they pursued their duties about their master as if the sole aim of each one was to save the memsahib any knowledge, let alone hardship.

The second day was no calmer than the first. Ranjit intimated reluctantly to Caroline that his master was very violent when she pressed him for information, and when she went out into the hall after pushing away her untasted dinner, she could hear above the thuds and crashes of some unseemly struggle. Alarmed anew, she summoned Dr Campbell back.

'There's nothing I can do beyond give you an opiate for the nights, Mrs Gates. He's suffering badly from needing his wine and that's souring his temper in addition to the fever. But he'll have to sweat it out if he's to regain his health. You've no call to worry, with that fine bearer of yours, and in a week or so he'll be calmer.'

He did not stay above fifteen minutes, brisk, professional and entirely unaware of the engulfing undercurrents of the situation, of this man and woman bound by nothing but law, and existing in a state of siege between each other in the stifling little yellow house. As the evening wore on, Caroline's sleepless two nights began to tell on her with blessedly welcome heaviness of head and eyelids, and before ten o'clock struck she had closed her door firmly upon the ravings down the landing and climbed thankfully into bed.

Almost as she did so, Johnnie was dashing his sleeping draught to the floor. The bed linen was already splashed with the juices and medicines he had roughly spurned during the day, and the servants, without Caroline to make them fastidious, saw no reason to change the dirty sheeting. Tousled, sweating and foul-mouthed, Johnnie swore and ranted at them, falling back on his pillow in weakness every so often and groaning with pain.

Patiently, Ranjit prepared another draught and approached the bed again, only to see the glass swept from his hand a second time to splinter against the wall. He said nothing, but his mouth tightened beneath his carefully plumed black moustache, and he resolved that if the sahib was bent upon suffering, suffer he might. With a few swift, decisive gestures, he moved about the room extinguishing candles and drawing down the blinds, so that within a few moments, Johnnie found himself alone in the absolute blackness, not a servant within call, a prisoner of his own wretchedness. He bellowed and shouted until he was hoarse, and tears of self-pity were coursing down his streaming face. No one came. No one cared. Along the landing Caroline and little Francis slept in oblivion; outside his door, the servant left squatting as sentry stuffed rags into his ears and buried his head in his folded arms. Johnnie sobbed and swore and punched his pillows.

At long last, as Ranjit had surmised, he wore himself out and slept a hot, troubled, unnatural slumber among the squalid tangle of his bedding. The sentry servant unlocked the door, and tiptoed with a candle to the bedside to make sure that sleep held his master mercifully silent, and then, reassured, crept out and closed the door behind him. He then lay down himself across the doorway and pulled up his dhoti to wind about his head preparatory to the luxury of his own rest. Silence at last, silence after two days and nights of maniacal roarings, fell upon the house.

A few hours later, Johnnie woke in the thick blackness of his solitude with only one desperate thought in his mind – wine. He fumbled about for a moment or two in a vain search for either tinder or candlestick, and was about to shout for assistance when the extreme silence of the house struck him forcibly. He sat up in bed to listen more intently, and could hear nothing, no sound, no indication of humanity anywhere near. He tried to stand but found that his head whirled wretchedly, so dropped to his knees and began to crawl, ignominiously impeded by his nightshirt, towards the door. In the eagerness of the dawning of a new idea, he quite forgot that the door would be locked and thus felt no surprise when he reached up to the handle and felt it turn smoothly in his grasp as the door swung inward. By inches he missed stumbling over a prostrate figure across the threshhold, dimly outlined in the greyish light on the landing, and, with a supreme effort, he managed to pass the obstacle and continue his lumbering progress along the landing.

All around him, silence reigned. Caroline, Francis and the ayah slept on, the servants, far away in their quarters, secure in the knowledge their master was a prisoner, enjoyed the sleep of the just. Step by step, Johnnie lowered himself shakily down the staircase, his head spinning and his limbs weak and unreliable, but driven on by a blinding desire for his goal. His eyes became gradually used to the dimness, and as he dragged himself, trembling violently, across the hall, he could make out the three-branched candelabra that stood on the chest by the dining-room door, a tinder box beside it.

Painfully, he lifted it to the floor, and pushed it and the tinder box before him into the haven of the dining room. Once inside, with the door securely closed, he gave himself up to a moment of triumph and relief, stretched sweating and shaking upon the carpet. It took him an age to light even one candle, but at last, by dint of holding one jerking hand in the other, he managed a blaze of two lights and the room – and his goal – were clearly illuminated.

The wine, several bottles of claret, stood on the sideboard by the window, the curtains drawn as they had been since the dinner hour to keep off the afternoon sun. His heart bursting within his chest, Johnnie heaved himself to his feet with the help of the table and hauled himself around to the wine, pushing the candelabra across the table as he did so. He was sobbing with relief as he reached the first bottle, tearing the cork out with his teeth, and pouring the wine down his open throat while it splashed his face and hair and nightshirt with dark stains. It was gone almost in a moment, leaving him gasping and almost insensible, but possessed solely with the desire for more. He reached unsteadily for a second bottle, swayed as he lifted it to his mouth, and then, as the impact of more than a pint of alcohol hit his weakened system, a blackness blotted out his wits and he fell backwards against the lit candles, rolling with them into the folds of the curtains.

Caroline came down a long tunnel of nightmare to consciousness, a tunnel lit by a red glare and echoing with a faint but sonorous roaring. She fought her eyes open at last upon the spectacle of her bedroom door edged with a quivering line of scarlet and the sensation that the air about her had dried to a stifling cindery dust. She took a gasping and appalled breath, and her lungs filled immediately with acrid smoke, causing her to double up violently, choking out the fumes into the sheets of her bed. At last, holding her breath painfully, she stumbled to her washstand and the jug of tepid water that waited for her morning toilette; the movement seemed to bring her to full consciousness, to the sharp and frightful knowledge that a blaze roared beyond her door and would soon burst in upon her – and that little Francis was coughing desperately in his crib across the room.

Within moments she had dashed to the baby's bedside, and snatched him to her, pressing a soaked linen towel to his small, choking mouth. Then, with her free hand, she wrenched open a drawer in her chest and pulled out as large a handful of stockings as she could seize, and ran with both them and the baby to her bed. Perched upon its side, half her attention upon the strengthening flicker of flame around her door, and half upon what she was doing, she knotted the stockings hastily into a long bandage, and then, manoeuvring the baby so that his body lay against her bosom, lashed him as firmly as she could manage, twisting frenziedly to pass her makeshift rope across her shoulders and round her back for safety. The ends were firmly tied across the baby's back, and then, gasping and with streaming eyes, Caroline stumbled to the window and her only chance of escape – the banyan tree.

For a moment she sat upon the sill to breath the blessed air outside, but for no longer. Behind her, tiny, evil tongues of fire were flickering into the very room, and, in addition, the naked branch that stretched itself perilously below her was at least thirty feet from the ground, and did not invite contemplation of its possible dangers. It *was* dangerous, especially imbalanced by a now protesting and writhing baby, but it was not a danger to compare with the one behind her. As she lowered herself on to the scaly bark, and observed that she must inch her way astride for at least eight feet with no support whatsoever except that of desperation, she felt a sudden blast of heat and a dull roar as the fire sprang like a dragon into the room she had left but seconds before.

Below her now, the garden was full of little scurrying figures, the servants presumably, running hither and thither distracted by their own helplessness. Swaying and sick with dizzy fear above them, Caroline could hear their cries of alarm faintly above the fire, and although nothing on earth would have induced her to look down, she was aware of a leaping light below her as the fire fought at the windows of the drawing room, shuttered at night against thieves.

For several desperate moments, Caroline thought she must fall. She crouched over the branch, the baby kicking and screaming perilously in his frail harness and threatening to tip them both on to the baked earth far below. She could hold with nothing but her hands before her, and her thighs were clamped tight to the branch on which she sat. Then the baby struggled suddenly and violently, and in a frantic effort to save them both, Caroline dug her feet inwards and found them held in the comforting growth that bearded the branch below. Very gradually, using these wiry tassels for purchase, Caroline inched her way forward, her feet and hands gripping and pushing, her hair tangled and damp about her face and her breath coming in little gasps of strain. About halfway to her goal, there was a sudden explosion below her, and a yellow sheet of flame sprang out of one of the drawing-room windows, illuminating Caroline's struggling figure high in the shaggy tree, and blinding her with abrupt light.

She stopped, and cried out in shock and bewilderment. There were shouts from the servants and then a surge forward as, headed by Ranjit, they plunged towards the tree. Trembling violently, Caroline could move no further, but crouched, bowed and clinging, while her teeth chattered and her toes and fingers clenched themselves on the tree and its growth for support.

'Memsahib! Memsahib! This way! Look this way! The baba!'

In the jumping light, Caroline peered through her tangled hair. Ranjit was braced against the main trunk of the tree, his arms out towards her, his hands but eighteen inches from the baby. She must go on, she must. Staunchly refusing to look down but keeping her smarting eyes fixed upon that narrow dark face under its white turban, she began to creep on again along the branch, inch by inch, her skin grazed and sore beneath her nightgown, the baby loosening all the time against her heaving chest.

Then Ranjit was there, deftly cutting the baby free and handing him downwards, and his thin strong hands were on her shoulders, her waist, balancing her respectfully against the trunk so that she might recover breath a moment. Then she felt more hands on her ankles, guiding her downwards, and always Ranjit's on her hands and shoulders, downwards, shakily but blessedly downwards, until her feet felt the miracle of the dusty earth beneath her.

She turned dazedly.

'Francis? The baby? Where is – ?'

'Baba is safe, memsahib. Quite safe. All is being safe.'

She stretched out her hands blindly for him, and said something but her voice was faint and strange and far away and the baby did not come. She tried to step forward, but her knees were now shaking so convulsively that she could not seem to order them to obey her in the smallest way. Everything seemed to be throbbing and receding, black and yellow and jumping red. She saw Ranjit's face wheel past her, as big as the sun, before she crumpled soundlessly to the earth.

20

Mrs Rathbone was in her element. Her spare bedrooms were both occupied, there was a baby in the house, and the stream of callers to inquire after the consequences of the fire gave her a feeling of limitless popularity. She had been woken at dawn almost a week before, by Caroline's bearer, in a state of the greatest agitation and bringing news which, Mrs Rathbone uncomfortably suspected, would have caused a person of more gentle birth to faint outright.

But being merely Bella Rathbone, she did not faint. Instead she summoned her carriage and drove at once to the smouldering ruins of the Gates' house. Even she, with all her good sense, could not look at it, nor contemplate whose tomb it had become, but as an antidote to such ghoulishness, she had become extremely brisk and had collected Caroline and the baby from the corner of the garden where they had lain, and brought them home with her. Caroline had not spoken a word, but had lain back in the corner of the carriage with her eyes huge and vacant, seemingly unconscious of anything about her. Mrs Rathbone had thought it most improper to see Ranjit lift his mistress' body into the carriage with the most proprietary tenderness, but Caroline had seemed as oblivious of him as she was of Mrs Rathbone, her own safety or her grimed and half-naked condition. Mrs Rathbone watched her all the way home, examining her bare and dirty feet, her broken fingernails, her snarled hair and her great smudged empty eyes and could hardly see anything in her that was recognizable as Caroline. Only once that whole morning, when she went up to see Caroline, now washed and dressed in one of her own extravagantly ruffled nightgowns and lying in bed, was there the smallest sign of any kind of life.

'There, dearie, that's better, is it not? Bella will care for you, that she will, so you are to sleep till you are better.'

Caroline lay with no sign of seeing her, her eyes still open and as dark as thunderclouds. Mrs Rathbone took her limp hand and bent to kiss her forehead.

'I should have a good cry, my dear, I should indeed. Many's the time I've calmed my feelings with a hearty cry. It does you no good at all to keep it pent up inside, my dear, no good at all.'

She pressed Caroline's hand and smiled kindly, and saw her head on the pillow give a tiny, but unmistakably negative shake.

Ann Wheeler got no better response. She had been brought news of the events of the night while she breakfasted, basking in the success of the evening before and contemplating, not without pleasure, the basket of orchids which had awaited her wakening. They were from Ralph Buxby, and expressed a far more profound admiration than that felt by one musician for another. Into this mood of happy languor Ranjit had broken, bringing with him a tale that drove all thoughts of fiddles and orchids and compliments from her head. The house which had sheltered her for three months was a smoking ruin, Johnnie Gates and all her possessions were ashes, but her baby was safe, and it was Caroline who had saved him. She fled to the Garden Reach at once, delirious with terror and gratitude, and pausing only to give her surprised son an uncharacteristically passionate embrace, rushed to Caroline's bedside to pour out her blessings and thanks.

Caroline lay as if she could not hear her, her thin hands lost in the elaborate ruffles of her cuffs, as limp upon the sheet as if she could not feel them.

'I owe you everything, everything! I am desperately ashamed of my frivolity and cannot in any way express to you the gratitude I feel! I shall never be able to repay you, never, never! My life would have been a ruin if – if – '

One of the thin hands came up and brushed against Ann's mouth as if to silence her. Then it dropped and Caroline turned her head away, seeming to indicate that it tired her to hear more. Ann was weeping, hot thankful tears dropping onto the bed, Caroline, her own hands, but Caroline lay as if she were deaf and blind. At last, choking with emotion, Ann bent to kiss the hand nearest to her, and then crept reverently from the room.

Caroline lay entombed in silence for four days, accepting only the merest nourishment, and giving no sign to anyone what she thought or felt, if indeed she thought or felt anything at all. Mrs Rathbone sent for the physician, to whose examination she submitted as limply as if she were a rag doll.

'There is nothing to warrant anxiety, Mrs Rathbone. I would say that Mrs Gates is suffering no more than the effects of shock and strain upon a highly sensitive and over-wrought system. Give her light nourishment and let her rise when she will. Rest will be the best medicine.'

Clothes – the most subdued gown Mrs Rathbone could find in her extensive wardrobe, a dress of burgundy silk trimmed with cream lace – were laid ready in Caroline's room in case she should wish to rise from her bed for any other purpose than necessity. Trays of broths and custards were brought to her constantly, but mostly they were carried away again quite untouched. Her thinness began to acquire a fragile transparency and when the fifth day dawned, Mrs Rathbone confided to Ann that she was deeply concerned.

'If only she'd speak, my dear, I'd be so much easier in my mind. But nothing seems to rouse her, nothing at all. I sometimes wonder if she even knows I am in the room at all. If her eyes weren't open, I wouldn't believe her alive, I swear I wouldn't. I even offered her Baby to play with yesterday, but she didn't flicker an eyelash.'

Ann Wheeler reflected a moment.

'It can hardly be grief for – for – can it?'

'For Johnnie, dear? I hardly think so. I spoke to her of the funeral arrangements only yesterday, just to tell her how good George Carew is being to take it all off our shoulders, and there wasn't a sign she'd heard me.'

'He – he was not a man one would be likely to miss. He was a brute,' Ann added with some vehemence.

'He was a foolish and self-indulgent boy,' Mrs Rathbone

said firmly, 'but I'll admit she was too good for him by many a mile. Now, my dear, do you go up and have one more peep at her before I summon the physician again.'

Ann went up the staircase with some trepidation. There was something alarming in the consistency of Caroline's immobility, especially as Ann could not believe that those wide dark grey eyes hid a sleeping brain. She tapped at the door, but as usual heard nothing and slipped quietly in, to find Caroline fully dressed and seated in the speckled shadows by the screened window.

'Caroline! My dearest – should you be up? Why did you not call for help?'

Caroline turned a little, her neck startlingly narrow in its collar of extravagant ruffles. The dress hung hopelessly from her shoulders, designed for a body with many more amplitudes than hers, its swags and ruffles drooping dispiritedly towards the floor. Her face looked calmer, less empty of expression than it had, but her eyes were still as dark as if she had been contemplating nightmares.

'Caroline?' Ann said again, more softly.

Caroline nodded.

'Can you hear me?'

'I have heard – everything.'

'Then why – '

Caroline made an abrupt gesture, and Ann stopped. She came across the room and knelt by Caroline's side. Caroline put out a hand and touched Ann's dress, a green figured silk also from Mrs Rathbone's wardrobe while Ann's own surviving dress was hastily copied. She smiled faintly.

'We hardly look our best, do we?'

Tears were rising fast in Ann's eyes.

'It matters not a whit, dearest Caroline. All that matters is that you have spoken at last.'

'How is little Francis?'

Ann could not reply. The tears spilled over and she seized Caroline's hand and pressed it fervently.

'He is well?'

Ann nodded vigorously.

'Then all is well.'

There was a silence for a moment, while Ann fumbled for a

handkerchief with her free hand, and Caroline sat quite still, gazing into the shadows of the room. Then she began to speak, in a low, quiet tone, never looking at Ann, never moving.

'I have come full circle, you see. For years, it seems, I have struggled to make something of my life, of myself, I have built up my courage, tried to make myself free of my inadequacies. Once or twice I thought to be happy, but I see that was not a very possible hope. But I've had moments of contentment, moments of feeling I have done what I could. I am so limited by my own self, but I have tried. I fled from the things that bound me, and tried to do what was best in what was new. I made many mistakes, many, oh yes, one that cost me – but that is history. And now everything is history, too. All my life up to now has become history. I have travelled all this weary way in my life and I am only back where I began. No, it is worse, for I am less than I was. I am older, tireder, sadder, and quite destitute. I have nowhere to go but back to what I left – and which rejected me. You must forgive me for being so melancholy and self-pitying, I dislike myself so much for being so.'

She stopped quite suddenly and gave Ann's hand a little shake.

'Were you – did – did you ponder all this all this time? All these days, is that what your poor brain was about?'

'Yes.'

'But why do you think so sadly? Are there not countless people who would value your companionship in their households? Myself, Mrs Rathbone, Miss Grant – '

'No – no, please. Forgive me for sounding so ungrateful, but you see – you see, the unkindest cut of all is that I have always wanted to work out my own salvation. I have a tiresome nature that wishes to earn what it gets. Isobel said I had a stiff-necked pride, and she was right. I have. It is not so stiff as it was, and it has a great deal of fear in it also, but I suppose it is still a kind of pride. It – it is really all that is left, you know. All – all I have. I shall find myself a position as some old lady's companion, never fear. I thought when I was eighteen that that was what I must come to, so I am not quite unprepared.'

Ann said gently, 'You are very difficult to help.'

Caroline smiled and leaned forward to kiss her.

'I know it. It is a dreadful fault but I don't think I can root it out without destroying my will to live completely.'

'Is there nothing, nothing I can do?'

'You do it already. You do the only thing I have really ever wanted from anyone, I suppose. You show me affection. No – no, Ann, you must not weep again. There is nothing now to weep for. Your baby is safe, thank God and I – I am free.'

Ann wished to question her, but could think of no way to frame the words. After a while, Caroline added in a whisper, 'I cannot speak of that. I cannot. All I can tell you is that I shudder to think that the merest living creature should die that way.'

Later that morning the stream of callers included Ralph Buxby. He had been every day since the fire, finding it all too easy to obtain permission from Sir Edward Ashton to leave his desk earlier than was customary, and had brought profusions of flowers with him each time until Mrs Rathbone's drawing room was richly scented and quite obscured beneath blooms. Ann, sensible and sincerely attached to her husband, received him with frank pleasure but never permitted him to speak to her alone. This morning, however, he found her by herself, lost in subdued reverie in the drawing room with none of the open gladness in her face that he was accustomed to see.

'Mrs Wheeler – Ann – I do trust that nothing ails you, troubles you?'

She looked absently at the crimson roses he held, but not at his face.

'I am preoccupied with Mrs Gates.'

'Is she still not well? I am sorry to hear that she still has not rallied.'

'Oh, she has rallied. This morning I found her up and dressed, but so sadly depressed in spirits, so brave still, so –' She stopped hurriedly and bit her lip.

Ralph Buxby put his roses on the nearest chair, and assisted Ann to seat herself.

'If it would not be indiscreet, could you not tell me more?'

'How much do you know?'

'You forget whose secretary I am. I know a good deal.'

'And of Johnnie Gates? And her family in England?'

Ralph shrugged.

'Of the late Mr Gates I know what all Caluctta knows. Of her family, I know nothing. I believe she scarcely has one.'

'That is part of the trouble.'

'You mean that she has nowhere to go?'

'I mean that she will not go there. She has one sister whom – whom she does not care for. She came to India in part to escape her. Oh, Mr Buxby, it broke my heart to hear her talk so today! She will let no one help her, she is resigned to throwing herself away as companion to some old lady, she – she said she never wanted anything from anyone but love – ' here a sob broke from her, enabling Ralph Buxby to take her hands in sympathy. 'She has worked so hard, and been so good and she has nothing now, nothing at all. She deserves such love, oh, how she deserves it! Do you know that her bearer will not go? Mr Rathbone has been most good about arranging for other employment for her servants, and most of them wailed bitterly at leaving her, but we cannot make Ranjit go! He says he wants no wages, only to serve her. He has waited for her to see him ever since the fire, and he will not move from the house. That, you see, Mr Buxby, is the kind of creature she is, and that is why the awful emptiness of her fate is so hard to bear!'

Ralph was silent for a moment, part of his brain concerned with how enchanting Ann looked in her grave eagerness, and the other part involved with a dawning notion that he might in some way repay Caroline for the injury he had unwittingly done her three years before. He had told Sir Edward Ashton the outline of the story of the fire, in order to gain as much of his superior's sympathy and thus time away from his desk as possible, but as all mention of Caroline was painfully impossible between them he had not elaborated on her resourcefulness and courage.

'You say she will not be helped?'

'Oh, no. She admits it is a fault but says it is all she has to stiffen her.'

'Suppose we were to help her without her knowledge?'

Ann's dark eyes glowed.

'You have some plan?'

'Only a vague one. And given the chief participants, it may be doomed from the outset. You say that she wants nothing but love, and that her future is quite barren. I am in no doubt whatsoever that Sir Edward cares for her as deeply as he ever did, but that he, like her, is afraid to expose himself to hurt again. As they both so evidently need each other, may we not contrive to throw them together again?'

'She would never agree!'

Ralph Buxby smiled conspiratorially.

'Then she had better not be told.'

The following day, Caroline was persuaded to come down to the drawing room when she was sure that no more callers would come.

'Such a shy thing you are!' Mrs Rathbone exclaimed, 'when all that anyone wishes to do is to admire you for your courage, and praise you and make much of you!'

Caroline blushed and said nothing, but Ann spoke for her.

'That is precisely what she does not want.'

Caroline looked up at Mrs Rathbone from her seat on a low chair, the baby on the rug at her feet.

'I do not know what I should have done without you. You have been the most staunch of friends and your kindness has been unbounded. I do hope I will not have to trouble you much longer – '

'Trouble? Trouble, my dear Caroline? It has been the greatest delight to me to have you here and I will not hear any nonsense about leaving, I most certainly will not. Your head is full of the most absurd notions of independence, and until you are fully well, I will not even permit you to speak on the subject. Now come, my dear, and tickle Baby, for see how he longs for it!'

Before dinner was announced, Caroline insisted on returning to her room, despite the fact that Mrs Rathbone said that there was to be almost no company that day, a mere handful, not above three or four extra people. On the following day, Caroline again came downstairs, this time for a little longer, but again retreated to her own room before the house began to resound with Mrs Rathbone's hospitality. That evening, however, she came downstairs for supper, during the course of which she mentioned that she would like to see George Carew.

'Ann tells me he has been so good to me. He has – dealt with everything. I would like to thank him.'

'I shall tell him to call tomorrow, my dear. I shall send a note directly, and he may call on his way home from his office.'

Caroline nodded gratefully and bent her head over some fruit, while Ann and Mrs Rathbone exchanged a glance of some significance. When supper was over, and Caroline had gone slowly up the staircase, Mrs Rathbone drew Ann aside.

'Well, my dear, and is not her asking for George Carew an excellent sign? She is waking to the world at last! I think in a day or so, for we must capture her before she is strong enough to think of leaving, she may be ready to see quite another caller, do you not think?'

'I will write to Mr Buxby.'

'Do, my dear, this very evening. Now I must go, for I am bound for the tables again. I confess I am having such a run of luck at present that I can scarcely bear to be away from them!'

George Carew came as bidden, as languid and elegant in appearance as ever, but with an uneasy air as if he had recently been floundering in waters of sincerity hitherto quite unknown to him. Caroline received him still clad in the capacious and unbecoming wine-coloured gown, and with an unaffected warmth she had never felt for him before.

'"Twas nothing, ma'am, nothing.'

'It was a great deal, Mr Carew, and no one else was about to do it. I – I do not quite know how to express my gratitude –'

'I'd rather you don't try, ma'am.'

An awkward silence fell between them which George occupied by rubbing his thumb round and round on the silver top of his stick, and Caroline in wondering how she could ask what she felt she owed it to Johnnie to know.

'Mr Carew?'

'Ma'am.'

'Was – did, did anyone attend the funeral? I did not know myself that it was to take place, you see, so that I – '

'I never meant you to know, Mrs Gates. Had to shove the old rogue off quickly in this climate. No point in you knowing.'

Caroline was startled at his perception.

'But – but was there no one there? Besides yourself?'

'No, ma'am.'

'No one from the Company? No one at all?'

'Just myself, ma'am.'

She could not ask the next question, but as if he read her thoughts, George said simply, 'There was nothing left, you know. Nothing.' He stood up, and looked down at her for a moment as she sat contemplating the desolation of Johnnie's going. She roused herself abruptly and rose to bid him farewell.

'You have spared me so much, Mr Carew, and I do thank you for it from the bottom of my heart.'

George Carew bent briefly over her hand.

'Better I than you, ma'am,' he said.

'Yes, Mr Carew. Yes, you are right. Better in every way.'

Two days after this visit, Caroline was just preparing for her daily descent to an empty drawing room when Mrs Rathbone intercepted her.

'Caroline, my dear! Just in time! Look what I have brought you! Now, is that not pretty? I said to myself that you must be sick to death of that old red of mine, and I had the tailor take in this blue which is a prettier colour for you by far. Now come, dear, and we shall try it.'

Caroline demurred.

'You are so kind, but may I try it later? I would so much rather not change now. It does not signify to me how I look, I do assure you, and I am dressed for the day now. It is very pretty but I am quite used to this, and who is there to see me?'

Mrs Rathbone seemed strangely anxious, barring Caroline's way with her arms full of blue silk, but Caroline was adamant. She would not change, she saw no reason for it, and eventually escaped downstairs in the despised burgundy gown to the empty drawing room. She looked about her in some surprise. Usually, at this hour between callers and dinner, Ann would be seated there waiting for her, with little Francis on his rug, allowed as a special privilege to roll about in the drawing room for the delight of Mrs Gates. But today there was no one there. Presumably, Ann was on her way, perhaps she was still practising her music. Caroline listened, but could hear nothing. Well, she would wait. She would choose a chair near the roses that Ann's admirers, unspecified to Caroline, seemed to bring so abundantly, and sit quietly and inhale the scent and wait.

After some moments, she heard footsteps in the hall, male footsteps. Clearly Mr Rathbone was home, for there had been no sounds of a stranger being let into the house. The footsteps approached the drawing-room door and Caroline sprang up, ready to greet her host with the gratitude she felt he richly deserved for his hospitality, and found herself confronting Sir Edward Ashton.

She groped blindly about her for a chairback for support. He closed the door behind him, without taking his eyes from her face, and then began to move steadily across the room towards her. His face, oh his face! As remarkable as ever, as powerful, but so sad, so weary! Had she done that? Had she carved those long lines beside his mouth and across the forehead? And her dress! Her dreadful hideous dress, no wonder Mrs Rathbone had wanted her to change! It was all a plot, that was what it was, a plot to get her here alone –

'I fear you are the victim of a scheme,' Sir Edward said. His voice shook.

'Yes.'

'I hope you are not angry.'

'I – I am very much surprised.'

'But not angry?'

She shook her head slightly.

'I hear – heroic things of you.'

'Please, do not speak of it. It was – what anyone might have done – '

'That', Sir Edward said with more of his characteristic firmness, 'is nonsense.'

Caroline felt giddy. There was no time to collect her spinning thoughts, and precious little reassurance in Sir Edward's manner. He had addressed her by no name as yet, and it was impossible to tell what he intended from what he had uttered so far. He was speaking with the concern shown to a recovering invalid, and his hesitancy could be accounted for by the fact that their last exchange had been acrimonious.

She raised her head and said formally, 'I am most obliged to you for calling.'

He looked startled, began an incoherent sentence which he soon abandoned, and said, 'I wished to offer my – my sympathy and my admiration.'

She inclined her head but did not speak.

'You have suffered a great deal, I wished you to have my sympathy.'

'I thank you.'

Silence again.

'I wonder, Mrs Gates, what your plans are? May I assist you in any way? Do you need a sea passage to England?'

'I am most obliged, but I have all the assistance I need. I – I shall be returning to England certainly.'

'I should be delighted to help you get a passage should there be any difficulty.'

'There will be none.'

There was a pause. Caroline felt unfamiliar sensations of tension in her breast and throat, and her eyes were burning so that she could not raise them from the carpet.

'Would you think me impertinent, Mrs Gates, if I were to ask what you intend to do upon reaching England? If you will not let me help you here, perhaps my influence might be of some help to you there?'

'You are very good but – but I shall manage quite well. I can return to my sister in Dorset for some – for a short time, and then I shall – I shall – '

She stopped in unutterable confusion, aware only that some extraordinary exploding loosening was taking place within her, some strange wave of relief, set free it seemed by the desperate contemplation of her future. Clinging to the chairback with both hands she felt her face helplessly flooded with a wash of tears, hot, painful tears which coursed down her cheeks, while her throat tightened uncontrollably on sob after sob. It was terrible, appalling, unutterably humiliating to shed these violent tears, the first tears since childhood, in front of Sir Edward Ashton, of all people. Struggling blindly with the physical difficulty of weeping in itself, and the seeming impossibility of checking it, Caroline stretched out a hand in her helplessness, as if to make a gesture to indicate that she would recover herself in a moment, and felt it warmly clasped. She tried to pull away, but not only was one hand firmly imprisoned, but the other was then captured from the chairback and both were pressed to Sir Edward's shirt front while he spoke to her through her sobbing confusion. She strove to hear him but could make out no words; it seemed she hardly needed to, for his voice was full of all the old urgent tenderness, whatever he was saying. Then he separated her hands from his own, so that he might put his arms about her and hold her strongly to him.

'Caroline, my Caroline.'

She could only cry.

'You shall never leave me again, never. Do you hear me? If I have to chain you to me to keep you, chained you shall be.'

She said something brokenly.

'Forgive you? of course I forgive you! I have nothing to forgive, nothing, all is past, finished, forgotten, everything is but beginning. Look up at me, look up.'

She sniffed. She could not.

'I – I am ashamed of how I must seem – '

'You are absurd,' he said with the utmost indulgence. 'Also uniquely courageous, sympathetic, remarkable – and mine.'

The tears would not stop; it seemed as if twenty years of weeping must be accomplished in a few minutes.

'Yours,' she said with difficulty.

'Ah! Always?'

His voice rang with triumph. She nodded, wishing to heaven she might speak her promises, not be confined merely to indicating them. Sir Edward ran a finger gently along her cheek and contemplated the tears he had collected.

'I should preserve these, should I not, my dearest? Like you they are unique, for I shall see to it that they are the first and last of your time – '

The door opened; there, framed in the opening, stood Mrs Rathbone, Ann with her baby in her arms, and Ralph Buxby. The faces of all four wore the expressions of unconfined delight that follows a plan of perfect accomplishment.

21

It was a fresh November morning in 1778, one of those clear, bright days of the upper Indian winter that is a just reward for the heats and rains of summer. Mrs Rathbone, clad in a new boudoir gown of yellow Chinese silk, embroidered heavily with oriental hieroglyphics in emerald and scarlet, was seated at her new escritoire. It was new for she had never had occasion for one before, writing letters being an anathema to her and her family in England being without sufficient education to read any epistles in the first place. But she now had a new correspondent, and her life had blossomed so strangely and wonderfully in the last few months that she found herself eager to relate all that was happening to a sympathetic ear.

Ann Wheeler was now with her husband, having most properly decided that Calcutta was no place to be left without official protection. She had set off across India intrepidly in the rains of late summer, to be greeted with rapture by Frank Wheeler, whose regiment had been encamped some distance short of Bombay for many weary months while its commander endeavoured to coerce his natural dilatoriness into some sort of decision. Before she left Calcutta, she had extracted from Mrs Rathbone a promise that she would write with faithful regularity. Hence the new escritoire – beautifully copied from a French one by a clever man in the bazaar at one quarter the European price – and hence also an impressive quantity of thick new writing paper, emblazoned with arms which owed most of their flourishes to Mrs Rathbone's imagination. Mr Rathbone had pointed out that the most he was entitled to was a mailed fist, but Mrs Rathbone had added a laurel wreath, a rose of England and a portcullis, quartered on a gilded shield. She sat down before a sheet so glorified now, and selected a quill; it seemed that there was some pleasure to be gained in writing after all, when the results of one's labours were so eagerly awaited.

My dear Ann,

I hardly know how to begin, I have so much to report. It is quite difficult to think how changed everything is and in so short a time. I was looking at my green silk – the green with silver lace that you wore after that dreadful fire – only the other day and reflecting how long ago that seems already. I hope Baby is well and bouncing and that you are nicely settled.

My dear, you cannot imagine the circles I move in these days! Mr Rathbone says he hardly knows me, I am grown so grand. Only yesterday, Lady Ashton invited me to dine – that will be six times, my dear, in as many weeks – and I was put upon Sir Edward's right hand at table, would you believe! The place of honour! I said to myself, Bella Rathbone, you have little left to wish for, indeed you have not. I shook in my shoes for fear at the thought, you know, but he was quite delightful and not at all fierce, and only wished to dote upon Lady Ashton in conversation, which I was glad to assist him in. And during dessert, Lady Ashton said she wished the party to drink a toast to me as one of her most valued friends! My dear, I did not know where to look. I was quite ravished with delight and fear, but I managed to stand and thank them all, though my face was fiery, and then Sir Edward said he did not know how to thank me for the support I had been to his wife. And then, my dear, the Governor General came up to me himself and spoke so civilly that I could not utter a word, but stood like a dumb thing. I was much pleased I wore my new cerise, it is really very pretty and a perfect background to my peacock feathers. They are said to be unlucky, but what could be more lucky than such compliments? I declare, my head is quite turned.

You will want to hear more of Lady Ashton – she is so changed, except, of course, in her manner which is as sweet as ever, that I find it hard to think of her as our dear Caroline – and indeed she is the rage of Calcutta, would you believe it? I declare that wigs and powder are quite going out of fashion, and we all strive for curls like hers and hair on our shoulders. She has filled out a little, and her looks are so much improved, she has that bloom about her as she did when Sir Edward first loved her. She wore a gown of cream figured silk over an underskirt embroidered in pink and green and gold thread, and though it was all a little quiet to my taste, I must say she looked very well in it, and I expect to see copies all over Calcutta before the week is out. Sir Edward has given her a collar of pearls so lustrous that I could not keep my eyes from them, but she only wore flowers in her hair which seemed strangely countryfied.

My dear, I never saw a man dote as does Sir Edward! I do declare he is not happy if she is not by him, and his eyes follow her as if he could not see enough of her. It warms my heart, my dear, it does indeed. There's not a woman more deserving than she in all the world, nor is there one who knows her luck better. I am to sup with them tomorrow before a ball, and Lady Ashton insists I join them for a great picnic to celebrate her husband's birthday. I am in quite a flurry of choosing dresses, as you may imagine, and await the next ship with impatience as I have had to order a quantity of new things to befit the company I now move in. You would stare to see how grand I am become!

I must make the most of it, my dear, for Lady Ashton has whispered to me – in the strictest confidence, you understand – that they will go home at the end of the cold season. Sir Edward has done enough in India, and now is impatient to take his bride home to Ashton Court, which I hear is very fine and set in extensive grounds. It will be very dreadful without them, but I hope I can persuade Mr Rathbone to follow shortly.

Lady Ashton says she is about to write to you, but it's my belief Sir Edward scarcely allows her a moment to herself. She says she prizes the letter your husband sent her about little Francis above all others she has ever received, but says that all the thanks she ever wants are letters with news of Baby. Is not that like her?

I also hear news that Miss Grant is to be married next spring, an excellent match it is said to be, but Miss Grant has declared she will not allow any man to put a ring upon her finger until Lady Ashton has approved him. So you see, my dear, there are many reasons for her going back to England, and in any case, she has not the constitution for this climate. She thinks she may have to allow Ranjit to come with her as he will not leave her, but she is anxious he will find England unpleasantly cold and damp.

My dear Ann, how I have run on! I must close now as it is time to dress and the hairdresser has been clearing his throat this half hour. Send me news of how you do, and a kiss to Baby.

Ever yours Affectionately,
Bella Rathbone

ELIZA STANHOPE

Joanna Trollope

Wilful and unconventional, Eliza Stanhope despises the marriage of her cousin and childhood companion, Julia, to rich, self-satisfied Richard Beaumont. Richard is certainly the dullest man in Hampshire, and even Julia mocked him before she calculated the advantages his fortune would bring.

But when Richard's charming, younger brother, Francis, returns home from war, bringing with him his delightful fellow officer, Pelham Howell, Eliza sees some potential in the marriage. Soon she finds herself facing the bewildering and challenging demands of first love . . .

Joanna Trollope – a descendant of one of the great masters of the English novel – has written a brilliantly creative story that puts her among the front rank of historical novelists.

'Joanna Trollope writes dazzlingly . . . a highly accomplished novel' *Newsagent and Bookshop*

85p

BESTSELLERS FROM ARROW

All these books are available from your bookshop or newsagent or you can order them direct. Just tick the titles you want and complete the form below.

THE GRAVE OF TRUTH	Evelyn Anthony	£1.25
BRUACH BLEND	Lillian Beckwith	95p
THE HISTORY MAN	Malcolm Bradbury	£1.25
A LITTLE ZIT ON THE SIDE	Jasper Carrott	£1.00
SOUTHERN CROSS	Terry Coleman	£1.75
DEATH OF A POLITICIAN	Richard Condon	£1.50
HERO	Leslie Deane	£1.75
TRAVELS WITH FORTUNE	Christine Dodwell	£1.50
INSCRUTABLE CHARLIE MUFFIN	Brian Freemantle	£1.25
9th ARROW BOOK OF CROSSWORDS	Frank Henchard	75p
THE LOW CALORIE MENU BOOK	Joyce Hughes	90p
THE PALMISTRY OF LOVE	David Brandon-Jones	£1.50
DEATH DREAMS	William Katz	£1.25
PASSAGE TO MUTINY	Alexander Kent	£1.25
HEARTSOUNDS	Martha Weinman Lear	£1.50
SAVAGE SURRENDER	Natasha Peters	£1.60
STRIKE FROM THE SEA	Douglas Reeman	90p
INCIDENT ON ATH	E. C. Tubb	£1.15
STAND BY YOUR MAN	Tammy Wynette	£1.75
DEATH ON ACCOUNT	Margaret Yorke	£1.00

Postage

Total

ARROW BOOKS, BOOKSERVICE BY POST, PO BOX 29, DOUGLAS, ISLE OF MAN, BRITISH ISLES

Please enclose a cheque or postal order made out to Arrow Books Limited for the amount due including 10p per book for postage and packing for orders within the UK and 12p for overseas orders.

Please print clearly

NAME ....

ADDRESS..

....

Whilst every effort is made to keep prices down and to keep popular books in print, Arrow Books cannot guarantee that prices will be the same as those advertised here or that the books will be available.